# "WE CANNOT MARRY."

"We can. Now. Today."

"You cannot just up and get married."

"I'm the duke of Belmore. I will do as I see fit."

Joy couldn't counter that argument. A duke did as he pleased.

His finger ran down her jawline so softly. His lips feathered over hers and he whispered, "Marry me, Scottish."

Her eyes drifted closed. She'd do almost anything to hear him call her that again. He kissed her again. A few long, tender moments later he pulled back. "As I said, you have no arguments."

"Marriages are always planned."

He stiffened suddenly, as if something she said had angered him. "Not this one." An instant later his mouth hit hers, demanding, as if he could assuage some angry emotion by kissing the doddering wits out of her. His lips bit at hers. His hands held her head and he mastered her mouth, her senses, and gave her a taste of what passion was all about.

She sighed. "I'm a witch."

"And I can be a real bastard. We'll get used to one another. I don't care what you think you are. I just want you to marry me."

**Books by Jill Barnett**

Wonderful
Carried Away
Imagine
Bewitching
Dreaming
The Heart's Haven
Just a Kiss Away
Surrender a Dream

Published by POCKET BOOKS

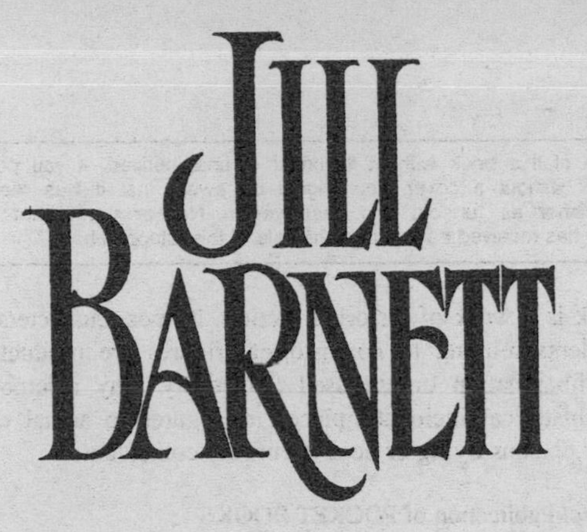


# Bewitching

POCKET BOOKS
New York London Toronto Sydney Tokyo Singapore

This book is a work of historical fiction. Names, characters, places, and incidents relating to nonhistorical figures are products of the author's imagination or are used fictitiously. Any resemblance of such nonhistorical incidents, places, or figures to actual events or locales or persons living or dead is entirely coincidental.

An *Original* Publication of POCKET BOOKS

POCKET BOOKS, a division of Simon & Schuster Inc.
1230 Avenue of the Americas, New York, NY 10020



ISBN: 0-671-77863-3

First Pocket Books printing October 1993

10 9 8 7 6 5



Cover art by Lisa Falkenstern

Printed in the U.S.A.

*For Kasey, the Joy in our lives*

Dear Reader,

I believed in Santa Claus until the ripe old age of nine. At ten, I spent my allowance on every new issue of Classic Comics Illustrated Fairy Tales, then, dreamy-eyed, I hung my long hair out of my bedroom window and waited to snare a passing prince . . . until the day it caught in the guava tree. A rosebush would have been much more romantic, but we lived in Southern California. I played with dolls until I was thirteen and exchanged my Pitiful Pearl for the wonderful world of Victoria Holt. My very first job was at Disneyland. And I married my first love. That should tell you something about me and about the stories I tell.

Experiencing an imaginary world is a wonderful thing, whether you're riding through It's a Small World or turning the pages of a book. This is a time when reality can be so hard on the spirit. We need love and laughter, to believe in wishes on stars and dreams that come true—and in a little magic. I hope that after reading *Bewitching,* perhaps you may think about those things again, even if it's only for a brief moment.

Keep believing,

Jill Barnett

P.O. Box 785
Pleasanton, CA 94566

# Once upon a Time . . .

**Do more bewitch me than when art**
**Is too precise in every part.**

"Delight in Disorder," Robert Herrick

# Chapter 1

There was magic in the air, yet few could see it.

To the mortal eye there was nothing but a brash, bullying Scottish storm that blew like the Devil's breath from the gray swirling waters of the Sound of Mull. Lightning splintered the midnight sky, and thunder bellowed. Rain poured down from the heavens, and the sea crashed against the huge granite rocks of the coast, splattering white sea-foam up the sharp cliff on which Duart Castle stood.

For five hundred of its six hundred years, the castle had been the stronghold of the clan MacLean and host to their cousins, the clan MacQuarrie. But the Battle of Culloden Moor had changed all that. On that dark, dank moor some sixty-seven years earlier, Scot stubbornness had caused many a clan to lose its holdings. The MacLeans had lost their stronghold to the Sassenach—Englishmen who cared not a wit for the braw, bold power of the place. The castle stood empty now, dark and abandoned.

Or so it appeared.

The skies bellowed and crackled, and the seas roared. To mere mortals it was only another storm, but to those who knew, to those of the ancient faith, it was more than just the heavens and the earth battling.

The witches were awake.

Now, there were witches, and there were *witches.* And then there were the MacQuarries.

'Tis a sad tale, that of the MacQuarries, a tale that had

begun hundreds of years before this night. An ancient forefather of the current MacQuarrie had been summoned to the fete of the spring equinox in what is now the south of England. There, on a wide plain, stood a massive stone temple where the witches and warlocks met to demonstrate their powers. On that special spring it had been decreed that the MacQuarrie warlock would have the cherished honor of making those most precious springtime flowers—the roses—bloom. Other witches and warlocks had already walked into the center of the temple and used their magic to bring life back to a winter-dead earth.

'Twas a sight to see that day when, in a matter of moments, green grass broke through the sodden ground. Wallflower bushes, buttercups, and dandelions spread a frosting of bright yellow across the fresh green that had magically sprouted. Soon the barren branches of birch trees were dripping with silvery spring leaves and tall elegant alders burst anew. Oak, ash, and elm came back to life with little more than the casting of a spell, the flick of a hand, or the flashing snap of a witch's magic. The scent of jasmine, primrose, marigold, and lavender filled the cool morning air, and suddenly it was spring. Birds and insects swarmed through the air and perched in the trees, and the melody of the lark, the hum of the bees and call of doves brought music to the land that had for too many cold, dreary months been silent.

Then it was the MacQuarrie's turn. The crowd parted as he made his way to the center of the stone temple. The room was silent, so silent one could have heard a blink, as each and every witch and warlock waited for that special moment. The MacQuarrie stood there for a long moment of quiet concentration. Then slowly he raised his hands toward the massive ceiling and with a snap of his fingers, let loose his magic.

No roses bloomed that day.

Instead an enormous explosion, the like of which no one had ever seen, blew the temple walls and roof into the sky. When the dust settled and the air cleared and the witches and warlocks picked themselves up off the ground, the temple was no more. Nothing stood except a few circles of stone arches.

Modern mortals look in awe at the ruins they call Stonehenge, but mention the name Stonehenge to the witches of the world and to this very day they shake their heads in dismay and mutter about the shame of the MacQuarries.

And it came to pass that in the year of our Lord 1813 there were only two witches left in all of Scotland—a MacLean and, of all things, a MacQuarrie. So on this brash night as the storm battered the shore of the isle of Mull, as it rained on the crumbling ruins of a once-proud castle perched upon that jagged stone headland, as the mortals on that tiny island cowered by their fires and listened to the heavens wail, the MacLean and the MacQuarrie made magic.

Joyous Fiona MacQuarrie bent down to pick up the scattering of books on the tower room floor. Ten golden bracelets jangled like sleigh bells down her wrists and echoed in the tense silence of the room. She was thankful for the noise; it gave her a blessed moment's respite from the impatient, penetrating glare of her aunt, the MacLean. With her face turned away from her aunt, Joy grabbed another book, tucking it under her arm as she muttered, "'Twas only one wee tad of a word." She picked up another book, to the accompaniment of those same tinkling bracelets, but as they settled on her wrists she could hear a new sound—a distinct, agitated tapping.

Her aunt's foot.

Joy peeked under her outstretched arm and winced. Her aunt's arms were crossed, and she shook her golden head in disgust. But worst of all, Joy could see the MacLean's lips move: her aunt was counting again.

Joy's heart sank; she'd failed again. With a defeated sigh she quietly returned the books to their ancient oak shelf and plopped onto a wobbly wooden stool after pulling it closer to the trestle table that stood in the center of the tower room. She rested a small chin in her hand and waited for her aunt to reach a hundred—at least she hoped it would be only a hundred.

A slick cat with fur as white as fresh Highland snow leapt onto the table and wound itself around and through the three time-tarnished brass candlesticks whose tapers bathed the battered oak table in flickering golden light. As the cat meandered along the table its tail cast strange shadows across the nicked tabletop. Entranced by the patterns, Joy tried to make imaginary letters out of those cat's-tail figures, her mind wandering off on one of its frequent journeys of fancy. That was her problem. She was a witch with a wandering mind.

The cat, Gabriel, was her aunt's familiar—an embodied spirit in animal form whose duty was to serve, attend, and in some cases, guard a witch. She glanced at her own familiar, Beelzebub, an ermine weasel whose coat was currently winter white except for wee spots of black on his tail and paws. The snowy fur covered a massive potbelly that made him look more like a plump rabbit than a sleek, almost feline weasel. He was at that moment, as at most moments, sound asleep.

She sighed. Beezle was the only animal who was willing to be her familiar.

Cats like Gabriel were proud, arrogant animals; they absolutely refused to be associated with a witch who couldn't control her magic. Owls were too wise to ally themselves with someone as inept as Joy. And toads, well, they took one look at her, croaked, and hopped away.

Plump old Beezle wheezed in his sleep. Joy watched his black-tipped paws twitch and reminded herself that at least she had a familiar, even if he was only a weasel. As if sensing her thoughts, he cracked open one lazy brown eye and peered at her as if calmly waiting for the next disaster. She reached out to scratch his plush belly and promptly knocked over a pot of cold rose hip tea.

Gabriel hissed and sprang out of the path of the spilled tea. Beezle didn't move that fast. Beezle seldom moved at all. The tea pooled like the tide around him. He blinked twice, looked at the tea seeping onto his white fur, and gave her a look not unlike the MacLean's before he shook himself, sending a sprinkling of tea in every direction. He waddled over to a dry spot and plopped back down with a soft thud, then rolled over, paws in the air, plump white and pink belly up, and stared at the ceiling. Joy wondered if animals could count. Beezle opened his mouth and let out a loud wheeze, then a snore.

Count in their sleep, she amended, drumming her fingers on the table.

"Whatever am I to do with you?" the MacLean finally spoke, having taken enough time to count to a hundred twice. Her aunt's stance was stern, but her voice held the patience that arose from what was almost a mother's love.

That love made the situation even worse for Joy. She truly wanted to hone her magic skills for her patient aunt as well as for her own pride's sake, and she was miserable because she couldn't get it right. She absently drew one finger through the dust on the table, then looked at her aunt and mentor. "Can one word truly make such a difference?"

"Every single word is of the utmost importance. An incantation must be exact. Part of the power comes from the voice." The MacLean took a deep breath and clasped her hands behind her. "The rest takes practice. Concentration!" She paced around the circular room, her strong voice echoing off the stone walls like bagpipes in the Highlands. With the suddenness of a wink, she stopped and looked down at Joy. "Now pay attention. Watch me."

Standing to Joy's left, she raised her elegant hands high in the air, allowing the fine gold threads in her embroidered silk robe to catch the candlelight and glimmer like the twinkling of fairy dust. Joy caught her breath. Standing as she was, tall and golden with the midnight sky as a backdrop through the tower window, her aunt looked like a goddess. Her long straight hair, which hung in a gleaming satin drape past her hips to the backs of her knees, was the color of hammered gold. Her skin was as flawless as pure cream and appeared ageless in the muted glow of the candlelight. The MacLean's robe was white—not the stark white of cotton or the ivory white of lamb's wool but the same shimmering white that the stars shone, that lightning sparked, that diamonds glittered and the sun glowed.

A breath of cold Scottish wind whistled through the tower room, making the candle flames flicker. The sharp smell of hot tallow mingled with the scent of midnight rain and the brine of the roiling seas that rode the whisper of wind through the room. Shadows danced a jagged jig up the granite walls, and the sound of waves crashing against the sharp coastal rocks below echoed upward, blending with the mournful call of gulls that roosted in the tower eaves. Then, with the suddenness of a lightning flash, all was still . . . silent.

The MacLean's deep voice called out, "Come!"

Magic quaked through the air—a live, animated thing, powerful, controlled, swarming toward the wall where heavy old leather-bound books stood on an oaken shelf. A huge brown book, cracked and tattered, slowly, inch by smooth inch, slid off the shelf, turned in midair, then floated to the MacLean. It hovered near her, waiting, until she slowly lowered one arm. The book followed her movement, lighting on the table as if it were a feather instead of a three-thousand-page volume.

Joy plopped her chin into her hand and sighed. "You make it look so easy."

"'Tis easy. One must simply concentrate." Her aunt replaced the book on its shelf and turned to Joy. "Now you try it."

With pure Scots stubbornness in her dark green eyes, Joy took a deep breath, closed those eyes, and with all the drama a twenty-one-year-old witch could muster, she flung her hands up into the air. Her bracelets flew across the tower room like soaring gulls. At the first clatter of metal hitting stone, she winced, then eased open one green eye.

"Forget the bracelets! Concentrate . . . concentrate."

She tried to concentrate, but nothing happened. She squeezed her eyes shut even tighter.

"Picture the book moving, Joyous. Use your mind's eye."

She remembered the way her aunt had made the magic

only minutes before. She threw her shoulders back and raised her determined chin, sending a thick cascade of wild and wavy mink-brown hair tumbling down to sway near the backs of her thighs. She opened her eyes and reached up higher. Taking one deep, cleansing breath for luck, she commanded, "Come!"

The book quivered, moved about two inches, then stopped.

"Concentrate!"

"Come!" Joy spread her fingers wide, bit her lip, and slowly pulled her hands back toward her, mentally picturing the book drifting toward her, then hovering in the air.

The book slid forward on the shelf, just reaching the edge.

"Come!" Joy shouted in a voice as deep as Fingal's Cave. She opened her eyes, determined to move that book, then snapped her fingers for good measure.

Luckily she saw it coming and ducked. "Oh, my goodness!"

The book flew past her as if carried on a whirlwind; then the next book and the next book, then another and another, sucked from the shelf with the pulling strength of the sea tide. With a horrendous crack the bookshelf ripped from the stone walls. It flew around the room, spinning and arcing, turning and turning, faster and faster. A dented tin pail spun off to Joy's left, then clanged against the floor. A broom sped to the right; three stools twirled like dancers, then tumbled end over end to bang against a pitcher, shattering it into a thousand pieces.

Furniture crashed against the walls, splintering, cracking. Candles levitated up . . . up . . . up. . . . The wind howled through the room, huffing and puffing and whirling. Instinctively Joy wrapped her arms around her head and hunched over. The teapot just missed her. From somewhere she heard a cat shriek, the patter of paws running. A coal bucket sent lumps of black coal flying through the room like rocks at a stoning. Then she heard a regal-sounding grunt—the MacLean.

"Oh, rats!" Joy clamped her hand over her mouth as a hundred gray rats scurried into the tower room, slithering down the walls, leaping from broken furniture, running amok.

Slowly the wind died down, growing softer until it was but a whisper, and after a long moment the air was still. The only sound in the room was that of the rats' scurrying feet.

Joy heard a choked cough behind her. She straightened up and turned around.

Waving away the coal dust, a black-faced MacLean extricated herself from beneath what had once been a two-hundred-year-old throne chair. She cast a malevolent look at the rats running willy-nilly through the disaster-struck room and snapped her elegant black-smudged fingers, sending up a small cloud of coal dust. The rats disappeared.

The once-white Gabriel, outnumbered by the rats, let loose another screech and scurried in a black ball across the room and under the MacLean's filthy gown where the hemline quivered for a long moment and a little dusting of soot sprinkled onto the wood-plank floor. The only sound in the room was Beezle's wheezing. Sprawled on his back, he lay on the table, paws up, belly slowly rising with each wheeze. He'd slept through the whole thing.

One tense but despairing stare from her aunt and Joy felt the weight of the world.

"I'm sorry," She whispered, turning her guilty green eyes toward her aunt.

"I cannot let you loose on the world, Joyous. I cannot." The MacLean dusted off her hands and surveyed the destruction. "I cannot in good conscience let you live in England all alone for two years."

Her aunt looked thoughtful for a brief moment while she tapped a coal-blackened finger against her lips. "Of course, letting you live there might be just what the English deserve after Culloden Moor . . ."

She glanced around the cluttered room with a scowl of disgust, then shook her head. "No, no. The English are already burdened by a lunatic king and a regent who would rather play than rule."

"But—"

"No." The MacLean raised her hand to silence Joy. "I

know you mean well, but all the good intentions in the world cannot control . . . this." She waved a hand at the mess in the room, shook her head, and went on, "You need protection, my dear. Someone to watch over you."

With that she raised her sooty hands in the air, snapped her fingers, and *zap!* the room was back in perfect order—chairs upright and in position, stools and table and teapot all in their proper places; the pitcher in one piece, the broom and pail standing against the north wall, and all of the books lined up on the shelves like stiff English soldiers. The MacLean, suddenly spotless, was once again a vision of pure white and glimmering gold perfection.

Joy knew what her aunt was really saying: that Joyous Fiona MacQuarrie needed someone around to clean up after her, someone to undo the havoc her cockeyed magic wreaked. But Joy had lived with her aunt for fifteen years, and now she wanted a chance to live alone, to answer to no one but herself.

When she was alone, maybe she could learn to control her powers. Maybe she wouldn't feel so tense and nervous because there'd be no one to let down but herself. She was deeply hurt by her uncanny ability to always disappoint the people she most wanted to please. She stood there, defeated, guilty, unhappy, feeling despair spread through her. She hurt; she had failed, and now none of her hopes would be fulfilled.

With her aunt leaving for a council position in North America, Joy was to be alone at last, a prospect she had anticipated eagerly. Duart Castle had been leased to a group of Glasgow doctors who planned to use it to house the battered and mind-shattered soldiers returning from war with Napoleon's France.

Joy was to go to her maternal grandmother's cottage in Surrey and live in relative obscurity for two years. She was sure she could learn her skills by then. She was positive. She just needed to convince the MacLean. Besides, her aunt would be gone and never know if she made a mistake or two. And there was one other argument in her favor: "If protection is what I need, how about a familiar?"

A loud feline scream cut through the air. Gabriel whipped out from under the MacLean's hem and scurried underneath a chest. He cowered in the dark, a pair of darting, wary blue eyes the only clue to his hiding place.

"*My* familiar," she corrected, just as Beezle twitched and snorted in his sleep. "Isn't a familiar supposed to protect a witch?"

"Joyous, the only thing that sluggish weasel will protect is his bedtime. You just cannot seem to concentrate—"

"Wait!" Joy stood, suddenly hopeful. "I have an idea!" She rushed over to a small battered Larkin desk, opened it, and rummaged through until she found what she sought. "Here!" She spun around holding a piece of paper, a pen with a small black box of pen points, and a squat jar of India ink. "I'll write the incantation down first. Then I can see it, on the paper in black and white. You'll see, I know I'll be able to concentrate then, I know it. Please . . . just give me one more chance."

Her aunt watched her for a long, decisive moment.

"Please," Joy whispered, lowering her eyes and holding her breath while her mind chanted a litany: *Give me one last chance, please . . . please . . . please. . . .*

The MacLean raised her chin. "One more time."

A smile bright enough to outshine the candle flame filled Joy's pale face. Her green eyes flashed with eagerness, and she hastened to the table, sat down on a stool, and dipped the pen tip into the ink. Smiling, she looked up.

Joyous Fiona MacQuarrie was ready.

But England wasn't.

**Fair is foul, and foul is fair:**
**Hover through the fog and filthy air.**

*Macbeth*, William Shakespeare

# Chapter

## London, December 1813

An elegant black carriage clattered over the damp, cobbled streets, its driver seemingly oblivious to the thick fog that hovered over the city. Past a ragman's cart in front of Green Park, past a watchman with a gin-sotted whore clutched in one hammy fist, past the plodding sedan chairs and rickety hackneys that filled the streets, the driver sped as heedless of the crowded streets as he was of the inclement weather. The vehicle whipped in a flash of raven black around a corner where a lamplighter was raising his hooked flambeau and lighting the last of the iron street lamps on St. James'. Quicker than a pig's whisker the carriage stopped, and a green-liveried footman had the gold and green crested door open before the frothing four-horse team had settled to a standstill.

Alec Castlemaine, duke of Belmore, had arrived at his club.

As his champagne polished boot hit the curb, a nearby shop clock struck five. It was Wednesday and, when in town, the duke of Belmore could be seen in front of White's at exactly five o'clock every Monday, Wednesday, and Friday.

It was ritual. It was routine. It was the way of the duke of Belmore. In fact only last season Lord Alvaney had quipped that he knew his watch had stopped when it read three o'clock as Belmore entered the club. The Haston Bakery turned its sign and locked its door when the black carriage rattled past, and many a wager had been recorded in

Boodle's betting book on Belmore's town schedule. It was as predictable as English tea.

And today the earl of Downe and Viscount Seymour accompanied Belmore. Richard Lennox, earl of Downe, was a tall, handsome man with blond hair and dark eyes, a biting wit, and of late, a sharp acid view of the world; Neil Herndon, Viscount Seymour was shorter and leaner with hair as bright as a new copper ha'penny. Downe had once said that Seymour was so nervous and fidgety he could make a dead man twitch.

The three men had been boon companions for nearly twenty of their twenty-eight years, and yet neither Downe nor Seymour really understood what made Alec Castlemaine tick. It was one of the few things on which the two agreed.

They knew Alec could throw a deadly right cross with what looked like no more effort than it took to swat a fly. They knew that there wasn't a horse alive that Alec could not control with the casual skill of the Devil himself. And they knew that whenever Alec desired something, he went after it and won it with what seemed to be determined ease. The duke of Belmore had but to snap his fingers and the world jumped.

Many women had tried and failed to win the heart of Alec Castlemaine. All they had received for their efforts, no matter how valiant, was the ducal glare. Richard and Neil were the two people closest to Belmore, and even they could not elicit from him anything more than a cool friendship.

Shortly after they met at Eton, the earl of Downe had taken up the challenge of goading some emotional reaction out of Belmore, and over the years Downe had done his best to crack his friend's icy facade.

This evening was no different.

Alec spoke to the carriage driver and then turned, only to find his path blocked by a rather remarkable-looking old woman no bigger than a ten-year-old boy. Her huge dilapidated red straw bonnet looked twice as big as her gray head, and her ragged gray velvet dress and a blue shawl hung loose from her narrow shoulders. She carried a wicker basket filled with fresh flowers, and in one gnarled hand she held up a small but perfect nosegay of English ivy and fresh violets. "'Ave a lovely posy fer yer lady, yer lordship."

"Your Grace," he corrected in an icy tone that had been known to freeze many an unfortunate man in his boots.

The old woman, however, did not move. She just peered up at him out of crinkled gray eyes.

He moved to step around her, but the sweet, fresh scent of the flowers stopped him. He paused for a silent, thoughtful moment, then took the posy and tossed the crone a coin, figuring he'd give the flowers to Juliet tonight at the Linleys' ball. He started to move toward the door when he felt a bony hand clutch his arm.

"Fer 'nother shilling, Yer Grace, I'll tell ye yer fortune."

Uninterested in such foolishness, Alec shook her off, but Viscount Seymour—who was known to be the most superstitious young man on English soil—stopped him.

"It's bad luck to pass her by, Belmore."

Effectively blocking the entrance, the earl of Downe leaned casually back against the door of the club, resting his good arm on his injured one, which he wore in a sling. After eyeing Alec he reached into his pocket and tossed the hag a half crown. "Best to listen to her," Downe said with a cynical smile. "Don't want to bring any bad luck down on the esteemed Belmore name."

Alec gave his friend a cool look, crossed his arms, and stood there as if he did not give a brass farthing about all the idiotic things the woman said. But even he had trouble looking bored when the woman started prattling on about his love life. Downe, however, was doing a poor job of repressing his mirth, and Neil appeared to be hanging on the hag's every word.

"Ye won't be marryin' the girl ye think ye will, Yer Grace."

Foolish woman, Alec thought. The announcement was to hit the papers the next morning. Lady Juliet Elizabeth Spencer, daughter of the earl and countess of Worth, would wed Alec Gerald Castlemaine, duke of Belmore. He had made his marriage proposal. Lady Juliet had accepted it, and the business details of their marriage were being negotiated at that very moment. After that, Alec's courtship ordeal would end.

"Who will he marry?" Seymour asked, glancing back and forth between Alec and the old woman with a worried expression.

"The next girl ye meet," she said with an odd glint in her eyes. She held up one finger and added, "She'll 'ave some surprises fer ye, that she will."

"I am not going to listen to any more of this." Alec pushed past Richard, who was laughing, and jerked open the door. Yet over his shoulder he heard the woman's parting words.

"Ye'll ne'er be bored again, Yer Grace! Ne'er again."

Striding across the parquet floor of the foyer, his boots making a series of sharp clicks, Alec pulled off his calfskin gloves with a distinct snap and handed them and his hat to Burke, the majordomo of the club, who in turn handed them to one of the ten footmen waiting to take the patrons' coats to the valet room where it would be dried and cleaned.

"Good evening, Your Grace," Burke said, helping Alec out of his greatcoat and handing it to the next footman. "And how are you?"

"He's annoyed," quipped Downe, who shrugged his coat off his injured arm and allowed Burke to remove the other.

"I see." Burke replied in a tone that said he never saw anything, but said the proper thing anyway because that was his job. He took the other men's garments, according them the same fastidious treatment all the club's aristocratic members received.

"Somehow I don't think you do," Downe said quietly, trying to follow Alec as he strode with athletic ease up the Florentine marble staircase to the main salon.

Seymour caught up with Downe. Eyeing Alec's broad back he whispered, "What do you think he's going to do about Lady Juliet?"

Downe stopped and looked at Seymour as if he had left his mind along with his coat at the club's entrance. "What the devil are you talking about?"

"The announcement. You know as well as I what a stickler he is for propriety. What's he going to do when the wedding does not take place, especially after his plans have been plastered all over the newspapers?"

"Don't be more of an ass than you already are."

"You heard the old woman. She said Belmore wasn't going to marry Juliet. I tell you I've had a bad feeling about that match ever since yesterday when Alec told us the arrangements had been made. Something is not right. I can feel it." Seymour paused and tapped his fist against his lean chest. "Right here." He gave Downe a look of pure conviction.

"You need to stop eating that pickled eel."

Grumbling, the viscount continued up the stairs, stopping when they reached the rose marble columns at the top. He turned and faced his friend. "I don't give a fig if you believe me or not. You wait and see. Whenever I have this feeling something odd happens."

"No girl, let alone one as intelligent as Juliet Spencer, is going to let the duke of Belmore slip through her fingers. Trust me, Seymour, what that old woman said was folly," Downe said as the two men entered the grand salon, where Alec sat at his usual table, a steward at his side watching while he tasted a vintage wine.

One quick but subtle nod of approval by the duke of Belmore and the steward discreetly disappeared.

To those who chanced a look at him, Alec epitomized the English aristocracy. His coat was cut of gray superfine, and the breadth of his shoulders had nothing to do with padding. His stark white cravat was tied with casual elegance that bespoke the precise hand of the best valet on English soil, and his buff breeches clung to the hard thighs of an expert horseman and the long legs of a man whose stature matched the quality of his breeding.

As usual, his square jaw was set, which hinted at a stubborn English nature. His face was handsome, his cheekbones Norman-high, and his nose hawkish. His lips quirked into a hard sensual line that said this man had no softness in his life; his was a heart untouched. His hair, though it had once been black, was now generously streaked with silver gray, a fact that had nothing to do with age but instead with the strength of the Castlemaine blood.

For the last seven generations, the dukes of Belmore had gray hair before they were thirty. Also, all of them had married in their twenty-eighth year, a Belmore tradition, and sired their first child—always male and the heir—with great dispatch. It had been said that fate seemed to cater to the Belmore dukes. And Alec, it seemed, was no different.

The earl of Downe slumped into his own seat. Seymour sat too, fidgeting with an empty wineglass while his boot tapped an aggravating tune on the table leg. He muttered something about fate and destiny and Alec, not necessarily in that order.

Alec signaled the servant to fill Seymour's wineglass. "Here, drink some wine so you'll stop that infernal mumbling."

"What's wrong, Belmore?" Downe asked, innocently staring into his glass. "Worried about the future?" He looked up at Alec, his real concern for his friend tinged with a bit of amusement.

Alec slowly sipped his wine.

"He should be worried," Seymour said. "I am."

"You worry enough for all of us," Alec replied nonchalantly. "I'm not worried, because there is no reason to be. Our solicitors met this morning to agree on the marriage settlement. The newspaper will carry the announcement tomorrow morning, and in a month I'll be leg-shackled."

"The arrangements, then, are clean, precise, executed without a hitch. Exactly the way you prefer things done." Downe lowered his glass and shook his blond head. "I don't know how you manage it. Lady Juliet Spencer is the perfect future duchess of Belmore. You come to town, attend one ball, and in two minutes you find the ideal woman. I'd say you had fine luck, but then, you generally do have all the luck."

Alec shrugged. "Luck had nothing to do with it."

"What did? Divine intervention?" Downe gave a sarcastic laugh. "Did God talk to you, Belmore, as he does to Seymour?"

Seymour took immediate offense. "I never said God talked to me."

"Then I was right. It was the pickled eel."

"I hired someone," Alec admitted, deftly putting an end to another of Downe and Seymour's petty arguments.

Downe sipped his wine and set it down. "Hired someone to do what?"

"To find the perfect woman."

Both men stared at Alec in disbelief.

He set his glass down and leaned back against the tufted chair. "I contacted the firm that handles most of my London business. They did some investigating and then sent me Juliet's name. It made perfect sense."

There was a long pause before either of the other men spoke. Then Downe said quietly, "I wondered how you found her so quickly that first night. For months now I've been telling myself it was just the Belmore luck. Now I understand. You paid someone to find you a wife." The earl stared into his glass for a quiet moment. "Efficient, Belmore, but cold. That's no way to choose a bride."

The earl's face flushed with anger.

"Think with your mind, not your gut." Alec calmly sipped his wine. "Cold or not, I couldn't care less. I need a wife, and this seemed like the simplest way to acquire one. It was good business."

"Good thing she's easy on the eye," Seymour commented. "You could have ended up with Letitia Hornsby."

As if uttering the chit's name would conjure her up, Richard suddenly looked ill.

"I'll leave her for Downe," Alec said, knowing that Richard was not comfortable discussing Letitia Hornsby, a girl who was so enamored with Downe that she was forever following in his shadow. Taunting his friend about the Hornsby girl was a bit of gentle revenge for the episode with the old woman outside.

Taking Alec's lead, Seymour smiled broadly and added, "That's right. Seems everywhere you go, that Hornsby brat is hovering nearby."

"'Hovering' is not the word I'd use." Downe rubbed his injured arm and scowled.

Seymour burst into laughter and Alec's eyes glittered with amusement, for they both had been at the Seftons' Christmas ball when Letitia Hornsby fell out of a tree in the garden and landed on Downe and his mistress, Lady Caroline Wentworth, who were in the process of doing that which they did best. The silly chit had dislocated the earl's shoulder.

"Actually, Letitia Hornsby ain't a bit hard on the eyes," Seymour said with a laugh. "She's just hard on your body, Downe."

After a moment Downe changed the subject back to Lady Juliet's fine looks.

Alec set his wineglass down. "Beauty was one of the requirements on my list."

"Just what else was on that list?" Downe asked, staring into his empty glass.

"Excellent bloodlines, good health, gentle ways but also a bit of spirit—the usual things a man wants in a wife."

"Sounds like you're buying a horse." Downe poured himself another glass of wine.

"I've always thought English courtship ritual wasn't much different from horse trading—just longer and more tedious," Alec replied, remembering the rides in the park, the balls and fetes he'd had to attend while courting Juliet. In his opinion it was just a nuisance, a way of announcing to the nosy world of the ton exactly what one had planned. "Is Almack's or some chit's presentation ball any different from the Newmarket auction? Each season's new batch of females is paraded in front of prospective buyers, and you check the bloodlines, the gait, the color, and you look for enough spirit to keep you from getting bored—just as you'd do before buying a horse. Once you've found a suitable one, you buy it and ride it."

Downe choked on his wine and Seymour laughed out loud.

"Did you check her teeth?" Downe asked.

"Yes, and her withers and hocks," Alec added, never cracking a smile as he picked up a deck of cards. Downe and Seymour were still chuckling when he deftly dealt the cards.

An hour later the note came.

A footman stood at Alec's left holding a silver tray with a vellum note in its center. As Downe dealt, Alec casually opened the note, noticing that Juliet's initials were pressed into the wax seal. He unfolded the paper and began to read:

Dear Alec,

I thought I could do it, but I cannot. I had thought I could live without love, for you are basically a good man. I thought I could trade joy for a title. I thought I could be practical and pick fortune over happiness.

I cannot.

I realize I could not bear the boredom of life as the duchess of Belmore. For while you are, as I have said, a good man, with all to offer, there is no life in you, Alec.

You are predictable. You do that which is expected of you because of your own consequence as the duke of Belmore. The precious Belmore name is first and foremost in your life. I want more, Alec.

I want love. I've found it. Although he is only a second son and a soldier, he loves me. As you read this I will be marrying the man who has given me those things.

Regretfully,
Juliet

Slowly, with quiet precision, Alec tore the note to pieces and dropped the scraps onto the silver tray. He stared at his friends for a moment, absently rubbing his coat pocket, then stopped abruptly, as if he'd suddenly realized what he was doing, and let his hand slowly slide up and down the stem of the wineglass. He told the servant, "No reply."

Raising the glass, he sipped his wine, as if the message

held nothing of importance, then picked up his cards and stared at his hand, his blue eyes darker and a bit narrower than usual, his jaw a little tighter than before.

He played through that hand and three more in stony silence. When the deal passed to Seymour, Alec requested pen and paper. When it arrived, he scribbled a quick note, sealed it with wax and stamped it with his ring. Then he quietly instructed the footman to send the note to the newspaper.

His friends watched him curiously.

Alec leaned back in his chair, his hands steepled in speculation near the hard line of his mouth. After a minute his hands moved beneath his jaw. "It seems the filly has more spirit than I thought. She's bolted. I am no longer betrothed."

"I knew it!" Seymour slammed his fist on the table. "I knew this would happen. The old woman was right."

"Why?" All evidence of cynicism had disappeared from Downe's face, replaced by a flash of surprise.

"Nothing important. Whims of a woman." He said no more, yet both of his companions waited and watched. The duke of Belmore showed no emotion. "Deal the cards."

For the next hour Alec methodically and ruthlessly played his hands, winning every game with the calm and composed determination of a Belmore duke.

"I've had enough." Downe threw his worthless cards on the table, and Seymour followed, eyeing with envy the fifteen stacks of chips in front of Alec.

"Where to now?" Downe said.

Seymour stood, bracing his hands on the table and leaning closer to Alec as if in warning. "Remember what the old woman said? She said you will marry the next girl you meet."

"That's right. Why not pay a call on Letitia Hornsby, Belmore? Would save me further serious injury."

"It is nothing to jest about," Seymour said with indignation.

"Of course not, he's the duke of Belmore. He never jests about anything."

Alec stood up abruptly. "I'm leaving. Are you two coming?"

"Where?" they asked in unison, then followed him downstairs where they donned their coats.

"To my hunting lodge." Alec pulled on his gloves. "I need to shoot something."

Following his long strides across the foyer, Downe turned to the viscount. "I don't know why he intends to go to Glossop. There aren't any women within fifty miles of his lodge."

"Remember what the old crone told him?" Seymour said, rushing to keep up. "I'll wager he's going there *because* there aren't any women within fifty miles. Doesn't he know he can't change destiny?"

And they followed Belmore out the door.

Joy stomped on the burning paper with a vengeance. "Oh, my goodness, Beezle. Look what I've done!" She bent down and picked up the charred piece of paper, then straightened up, dangling it between two fingers. It was still smoking, and the lower right corner was completely burned off.

"Oh, my goodness . . ." Her words tapered off and her voice cracked a bit as she stared at the burned paper.

Beezle lifted his head up from his black paws and peered at Joy. His eyes darted back and forth between the paper and her sad face.

She dropped the paper on the table and with a sigh of defeat sank onto the wobbly stool, shaking her head in self-disgust. "I've done it again."

With a resigned sigh, Beezle stood and waddled across the table, then crawled onto her shoulder and wrapped himself around her neck. Once settled, he began to paw the loose brown curls that had escaped her chignon and now framed her delicate jaw.

"What shall I do now?" She looked at him as if expecting advice. He stopped playing with her hair, dropped his chin to her shoulder, and wheezed.

"So you have no answers either," she said, absently scratching his neck while she stared at the paper. Luckily her aunt had left a couple of hours ago—left with all the speed and elegance of a MacLean witch. It hadn't taken Joy long to persuade the MacLean to accept the position in America. She had wanted to do so, and Joy wouldn't have been able to live with herself if her aunt had been forced to miss this opportunity because she had to stay and play nursemaid to her niece. She was twenty-one—old enough to be on her own. And she had discovered that her aunt was right: when she concentrated—staring at the words on the paper helped—she was able to cast some effective spells.

Before her aunt left, she had stood over Joy as she copied the incantation that would send her to the cottage in Surrey. The MacLean had warned her that travel incantations needed particularly deep concentration. Her aunt listed a whole slew of techniques to use while Joy had conjured up a traveling outfit—the latest from a set of plates her aunt had picked up in Paris. Joy suspected that the clothing was the final test, but she'd passed, probably because she'd kept staring right at the color plates.

With little more than two snaps of her fingers she was wearing a lovely willow green cashmere traveling costume, a corbeau pelisse, and black calfskin half boots. In her hand was a forest green silk bonnet with pale green velvet ribbons and deep violet ostrich plumes. The ensemble had done the trick. Her aunt had smiled approvingly, kissed Joy goodbye, and left in a puff of sparkling golden smoke.

Then Joy's trouble had started. To better see it, she had held the paper with her travel incantation just a bit too close to the candle. The next thing she knew, it was on fire. Now here she was, a short time later, with part of her travel spell gone up in flames.

"I think I can read some of it. Let me see . . ." She smoothed the paper out on the table and squinted at the writing. "Snow . . . go. Speed . . . heed. Door . . . hmm. I can make out everything but the last line. I seem to remember that it had something to do with chimes . . . or was it bells?"

She'd have to guess. She plucked the bonnet off the table and put it on, tying the ribbons beneath her chin as best she could with Beezle still wrapped around her neck. She gave him a quick pat, picked up the paper, and with one last look at the tower room, her home for the last fifteen years, she began to read the incantation:

Oh, glorious night that hides the day,
Listen to what I have to say.
No witches brew with eye of newt,
Just behold this traveling suit.
I've donned it not because of snow
But since I have someplace to go.
'Tis off to Surrey with winged-foot speed,
So please hear my call, please pay heed.
When the clock strikes the hour,
The church bell will ring
Although 'tis not a time to sing.
Instead please send me out the door,
And then for good measure, ring the bell more!

# Chapter 3

Alec never knew what hit him. One minute he was walking back to his carriage from the thick woods that bordered the road, and the next, he was flat on his back, staring up at the white mist of fog, an armful of something—someone—on top of him. He tried to shove whoever it was off his chest. Whoever squealed. Female. Alec had an armful of woman, and he sincerely hoped she was not Letitia Hornsby.

The woman sat up with an exuberant bounce, driving what was left of his wind right out of him. He sat up, too, so he could breathe. She slid into his lap, her hands gripping his shoulders.

"Oh, my goodness!"

Alec inhaled a few breaths of damp, foggy air and turned toward her, expelling a relieved breath when he saw that it was not Letitia Hornsby after all, but a pert little brunette with wide green eyes and dark slashing brows. She had rosy cheeks, a determined chin, and a full mouth with a small but intriguing mole just above her upper lip. She was the most striking female Alec had seen in years, but at that moment, her attractive face wore an expression not unlike that of someone who had just been thrown from a runaway horse.

"Where am I?"

"On the duke of Belmore."

"Belmore? 'Bell more'! Oh, my—" She whipped her gloved hand to her mouth and looked left, then right, studying her surroundings, before she mumbled, "It must have been 'chimes.' "

"What?"

"Uh . . . nothing."

Alec shifted his weight slightly.

"Oh, my goodness!" Her hands tightened on his shoulders, and she stared at him, her face barely inches away from his. Their breath frosted in the cold air. Neither moved. For a brief instant time itself seemed to vibrate around them. He stiffened in reaction, drawing a deep breath.

She smelled of spring—clean, with a whiff of some kind of flower. He noticed that her waist was remarkably small. His fingertips met when his hands encircled it. He looked down to see his thumbs bare inches from her softly curving breasts. He glanced up and met her gaze. Her eyes were green, true deep green. There was little of the world in those eyes, no practiced look, no sexual awareness, just an innocence that Alec would have wagered had been lost by every Englishwoman over the age of twelve.

Breaking their stare, she glanced at her hands, which still clutched his shoulders. She flushed and released him. "Beg pardon, Your Grace."

"From our positions I would say grace had nothing to do with it."

"Oh, my—"

"Goodness," Alec finished for her. She didn't say a thing. Instead, she cocked her head slightly and watched him with a new expression on her face.

How odd, he thought. He was sure he had seen that particular expression before, but for the life of him he couldn't remember where. It made him uneasy. Dampness from the moist dirt seeped into his breeches, a wet reminder of where he was. "The ground's cold," he said shortly, his face expressionless.

"Oh, my—"

Goodness, Alec mentally finished for her and watched as she scrambled out of his lap and sat on the ground. He stood and extended his gloved hand to help her up. Just as he pulled her to her feet, she cried out and her ankle gave way. He caught her around the waist before she fell.

"You're injured."

She scowled at her foot, then looked up at him and nodded, continuing to stare. He dismissed her look as one of reverence for his title. "Where's your carriage?"

"What carriage?"

"You don't have a carriage?"

She shook her head, then looked around her, as if she had misplaced something and her hand nervously stroked the white ermine trim on her collar.

"Are you alone?"

She nodded.

"How did you get here?"

"I'm not sure. Where am I?"

"The North Road."

"Is that near Surrey?"

"No. Surrey is over a hundred miles south."

"Oh, my goodness!"

"I take it you're lost."

"I think so."

"How *did* you get here?"

She didn't say a thing, just stared up at him, her expression dazed. Assuming the pain in her ankle had made her wits go walking, Alec took matters into his own hands. "Never mind. You can tell me later." In one swift motion he swung her into his arms. He heard her breath catch in her throat, and as he moved toward the carriage she wrapped her arms around his neck and slowly leaned her head on his shoulder. The warm tickle of her sigh fluttered against his skin. He cast her a cool glance, but saw that her eyes were closed. He used the moment to take in her features once again. Her dark lashes, thick and brown as sparrow feathers, rested sweetly against her skin. And what skin—clear, fresh, virginal. Pearlescent innocence. He stopped in mid-step, wondering where the devil that thought had come from. He shook himself, feeling as if he had only just awakened. He took a deep breath and moved forward, attributing his reaction to an excess of strong wine and a lack of sleep.

The woods thinned at the roadway where his carriage stood waiting. He strode through forest ferns damp with foggy mist and saw Downe leaning against the carriage door, a silver brandy flask raised to his lips. Seymour was nowhere in sight. One of the footmen moved away from the carriage and hurried toward Alec, as if to take the girl. Alec shook his head and nodded toward the carriage. "Open the door, Henson. The lady's injured her ankle."

"Demme, if it ain't her!" Seymour's voice sounded from his left. He could hear Downe choking on a swallow of liquor.

Alec leaned into the carriage and set the girl inside, then turned to a goggle-eyed Seymour and gave him a look meant to chill him into silence. It worked, and he stepped into the carriage, settling next to the chit. Downe followed and sat opposite her. Alec glanced at him. The earl assessed the girl and apparently liked what he saw, because he gave her his best I'm-a-rake smile. Alec glanced at the viscount, who eyed her with a look one might use when confronted with the angel Gabriel. Neither reaction set well with him.

He turned to the footman who folded the steps back into the coach and said, "Stop at the next inn." Within seconds the coach lurched forward into the fog. He reached around the girl and turned up the coach lamp, then leaned back and watched her.

Her lips moved, but no sound came out.

"This is the one," Seymour whispered. "Trust me. I can feel it in my bones." He nervously looked from the girl back to Alec, then back to the girl. "You are her."

She looked at Seymour, then at Downe, then back to Alec, and with each look panic rose in her eyes. Sitting stiff with fear, she didn't answer; instead she stared at her hands. He wondered briefly if she was praying, and the thought touched some obscure concern he'd have wagered a thousand pounds didn't exist within him.

The girl was frightened witless. Alec sought to calm her. "Don't worry—" she squeezed her eyes closed and muttered something—"my dear, we—"

She snapped her fingers.

There was a frantic shout. The carriage slammed to a halt. Alec pressed his boot against the opposite seat to brace himself and then grabbed her to keep her from flying into

Downe. She opened her eyes, looking stunned and horrified, and bit her lower lip.

He released her, thinking he might have held her too hard. "Are you in pain?"

"No." Her voice cracked, and she immediately stared at her hands with a dismayed expression. Again she closed her eyes and whispered something.

The poor thing really was praying. He glanced up at his friends to gauge their reaction and heard her fingers snap a second time.

A loud crack pierced the air, followed by another shout and a vibrating thud. It sounded as if the heavens had just fallen to earth.

He wrenched open the door. "What's the trouble?"

Henson ran over, a stunned expression on his face. "Appears half the forest is in the road, Your Grace. Strangest thing I've ever seen . . . trees falling like wounded soldiers." He reached up and scratched his head. "And there's no wind, Your Grace."

"Watch for highwaymen." Alec opened a small compartment near his seat and removed a pistol.

"There's not a soul about, Your Grace. The outrider checked." Henson gestured toward the forest with his own pistol.

Alec handed weapons to Downe and Seymour, told them to stay with the girl, then left the carriage, armed. He surveyed the surrounding forest and saw nothing but trees mired in an eerie fog. He stood there for a silent moment, listening for movement. There was nothing. He walked to where the coachman surveyed the wood-piled road and another footman steadied the nervous horses.

At least fifteen alder trees lay like fallen columns across the roadway, and yet not a suspicious sound or movement came from the woods that lined the road.

"Oh, my goodness!"

Alec was fast learning to hate that phrase.

"Oh, no! It's 'alter,' not 'alder'!"

Slowly he turned around to see the girl hanging out of the carriage and staring at the roadway, an appalled expression on her face. She cast him a quick look, appeared to gulp, and disappeared inside in less time than it took to breathe. A moment later Downe and Seymour stepped down from the carriage and stood beside him assessing the problem.

"There's fifteen of them," the viscount announced.

"That's what I admire about you, Seymour. You've an uncanny ability to state the obvious." The earl's voice dripped sarcasm.

"When have you ever seen fifteen trees in the road? It's not something one sees regularly." The viscount walked over to the first fallen tree, then looked up. "Not a lick of wind."

Downe walked over to the closest stump and examined it. "Hasn't been cut. Looks like it just fell over."

"I've got a bad feeling about this," Seymour said, his gaze darting left, then right, as if he expected the rest of the forest to collapse.

"Here it comes again." Downe rested one booted foot on the splintered stump. "Seymour's gloom-and-doom speech. What is it this time? Fairies? Trolls? Ghosts? Witches?"

A gasp of sheer horror sounded from behind them, and all three men turned. The girl peered from the carriage, her color pale.

"Now look what you've done, Downe. You've scared the bloody hell out of Belmore's future wife!" Seymour rushed toward her.

"Did he just call that chit what I think he called her?" Alec stared at Seymour's retreating back.

"You heard him. He believes all that balderdash. Here, have some of the Little Emperor's finest. Dulls the cold and makes Seymour tolerable." He held out his brandy flask. "If you drink enough of the stuff he might even start making sense."

"The Seymours aren't known for their sense and sensibility."

Downe gave a snort of sardonic laughter and pressed the brandy into Alec's hand. Alec looked at the flask speculatively, then returned his gaze to the carriage where Seymour was just opening the door.

Alec strode over to the carriage, stepping in front of Seymour. "I'll take care of her." His voice brooked no argument. Seymour looked at him, glanced back at the girl, then smiled knowingly and received from Alec a cool glare that spoke volumes. Seymour stepped away from the carriage.

Alec leaned inside and saw that the girl had no color, so he assumed either her ankle pained her severely or she was as easily spooked as an untrained filly. "Does it hurt?"

She gave him a blank stare.

"Your ankle," he explained with patience he was far from feeling.

She looked at her foot. "Oh . . . yes, my ankle."

Alec took that for an affirmative, although she seemed to be thinking about something else altogether. He reached into the gun compartment and took out a small glass. He filled it with Downe's brandy and handed it to the girl. "Here, miss . . ." Alec stopped himself and frowned. "Or is it madam?"

"It's miss."

"Who?"

"Me?"

Alec took a long breath. "What's your full name?"

"Joyous Fiona MacQuarrie," she said, not looking at him, but giving her skirt a little shake before she settled back against the seat.

He nodded. "Scottish. That explains it." He placed the glass in her hand. "Take this. Sip it. It will keep you warm while we clear the road. I suspect it might take a while."

She gave the brandy a doubtful stare.

"Drink."

She slowly lifted the glass to her full lips and took a sip, then made a face and shivered.

"Trust me. You'll feel better if you drink the brandy."

She took a deep breath, apparently to prepare herself for the upcoming ordeal, then sipped again, screwed up her face, and gulped as if she'd swallowed the sins of the entire ton. It was a few minutes before she looked up at him again, her eyes tearing from the strength of the liquor, but the moment they met his gaze they grew misty with that same odd yet familiar expression.

He still couldn't place the look, but he knew one thing for certain: it made him bloody uncomfortable. He closed the carriage door and walked back to the fallen trees with Seymour trailing him like an overanxious beagle.

"She must be the one," Seymour said in a rush. "It's fate. I know it."

Alec stopped and turned to his friend. "Do you truly believe I would take a complete stranger and make her the duchess of Belmore?"

"Of course he wouldn't," Downe said, joining the two men in time to hear Seymour's comment. "After all, he hasn't yet researched her background. Have you, Belmore? She might not be duchess material. Besides which, when have you known Belmore here to do anything without first planning every single detail?"

Alec's back went ramrod straight.

"This trip, for example?" Seymour shot back, his expression triumphant.

"Are you two finished? We have business more pressing than goading each other or trying to goad me into one of your rows."

"Never works anyway," Seymour muttered.

He gave them his best ducal glare—the one that usually stone-silenced anyone within an immediate range and could send a servant into double time. He glanced at the flask, still clutched in his hand, and was tempted to take a drink, a very human reaction considering the day's events. But the duke of Belmore prided himself on not giving in to human reactions.

He handed Downe the flask and turned to his servants—two footmen, an outrider, and his coachman—who were valiantly trying to move the first of the fallen trees. With the wood green and wet the trees weighed enough to need special handling. He shrugged out of his coat and tossed it near Downe's feet. Seymour followed suit while Downe, whose injured arm rendered him unable to help, stood nearby making snide comments about fate and destiny and the predictability of the duke of Belmore.

Half an hour later, having had enough of Downe's wry tongue, Seymour suggested that he and Alec ram a tree trunk into the earl's blasted big mouth.

Alec didn't answer. In his mind he kept seeing Juliet's letter, which had contained the same unflattering word that Downe had unknowingly just used: "predictable."

For twenty-eight years, Alec had thought his behavior unquestionably suitable and logical for a man of his consequence. Life wasn't simple for the English aristocracy, and the higher the title the greater the responsibility. At least that was what Alec had been raised to believe. It had been pounded into his head over and over that ducal duty came first. Belmore traditions, the revered family name, the example he set by his actions—those were the things that mattered.

He took command but rarely lost his temper. He'd learned at a very young age that a Belmore duke did not show emotion. A duke needn't shout and therefore didn't. In his life there was no room for folly, which was fine with him; his behavior was ruled by custom, logic, social standing, and traditions that were generations old. Life had been that way for his ancestors, and now it was the same for him, and that was a matter of supreme pride with him.

But predictable? Boring? Those were not traits he relished, any more than he relished the humiliation of losing Juliet. He glanced at his coat, lying on a stump near the earl. In his coat pocket was the special license he had requested from his man of business, with a careful preparation that did his reputation justice. Marriage by special license held more than only its aristocratic allure. His wedding was to have been a quiet ceremony with two witnesses. That had appealed to him because such ceremonies were private and expedient. The frivolity of a huge wedding was something he would not embrace.

Yet now the license served only as a reminder that he had

been jilted. A wave of icy humiliation ran through him. His mind flashed with an uneasy curiosity about what Juliet's mere soldier had to offer compared to him. In her letter she had said she wanted love.

Love. He'd seen what love could do. He'd seen men shoot each other in the name of love. He'd seen perfectly sane, reasonable people crumble like week-old bread for the sake of that one elusive emotion that he was sure was either fantasy or folly.

There was a time, long ago, when he, too, had thought that love would be magical. He could remember standing before the tall rigid figure of his father, a monolithic presence to a five-year-old boy. He had forced himself to raise his eyes and look into those of his father. They had the same eyes, same face, same Castlemaine blood. His hands had grown clammy and he had wanted to wipe them on his thighs, but he'd caught himself, remembering that a marquess and future duke didn't do such things. He'd had to take deep breaths to get the words past his dry throat. Then he'd done it, told his father he loved him, thinking with childish simplicity that perhaps that was the magic phrase that would win approval. It won cold anger instead.

Love. He viewed it the way an atheist might look upon a crucifix. The word had meaning only for those fools who sought it.

He heaved a heavy tree trunk with strength born of fresh anger and frustration. The forest mist had swelled in the last few minutes, grown even damper. Dew caught in his silver-streaked hair and trickled a lazy path down his temples. The same misty moisture dripped like a child's tears from the leaves of the trees, peppering the ground and the men who worked to clear the road. The duke's motions became mechanical, routine, and he stood straighter, more rigid, lost in black thoughts and damaged pride. Before long, his blue eyes grew icy with a scorn born of the fact that the duke of Belmore had no knowledge of that elusive thing called love.

* * *

Joy sat back in the carriage, her imagination swimming not with a picture of a cottage in Surrey but with the hawk-handsome features of a silver-haired duke.

She sighed. A duke. Imagine that. His title ranked just below that of a prince. These were the men in fairy tales and girlish daydreams. At the mere thought of him, she felt a ripple of shock go through her, the same shock his touch had sparked. It was the oddest thing—as if she were truly bewitched.

This was a fantasy come true. He had carried her like a gallant knight in days of yore. She bit her lips to hold back a wee giggle of pleasure. It escaped anyway. Her back still tingled from the feel of his arm supporting it when he carried her through the forest. The faint aroma of tobacco lingered on his clothing, and his breath was warm and wine-sweet when their faces were little more than a kiss apart. And his eyes—those were the eyes of a man whose heart cried out for a little magic.

She hadn't been carried in a man's arms since she'd been a small child in the arms of her father. That was one of the few memories she had of her parents, who were long since gone. But this was much different from her memory. When the duke carried her she felt as if spring bees were swarming in her belly, and his scent had made her light-headed. It was odd, but in his arms she had felt as light and free as ribbons in the wind. When she looked into his face, she saw something unknown, intriguing, as if something inside her was calling out to him. It was an eerie feeling even for a witch—a witch who in reality needed to get to Surrey.

She gave a sigh of regret and shook off her reverie. She needed to concentrate on her witchcraft, not on the strength of the handsome duke, how it felt when he carried her, wondering what it would be like if he held her against his chest and lowered his lips to hers. . . .

Beezle wheezed in his sleep, snapping her back to the sensible world. He was wrapped like a sleeping fur around her neck and, as usual, not a wit of help in spell casting. Concentrate, she told herself, concentrate. No more whimsy, Joyous!

Of course whimsy provided an easy escape when one didn't know what else to do. And whimsy was safer, since she was certainly courting disaster. She had lost the piece of paper containing her travel incantation—not that it did her much good anyway, with the bottom burned off. No doubt it was lying on the tower room floor. With only her feeble memory to rely on, she had already tried to recast her spell, substituting the word "chimes" for "bell," but she had obviously guessed wrong. The result was fifteen felled trees blocking the road. A white witch was supposed to become one with nature, not wreak havoc on it. She took a quick sip of the strong drink the duke had given her.

"And they call witches' brew vile," she muttered, certain that a brew of speckled batwings and eye of newt would taste something like this potion. She took another small sip, thinking maybe it was something one had to become used to. It still tasted horrid and did not help relieve the feeling that this time she had really made a muddle of things. She wasn't exactly sure how to save herself in this situation, and when she thought about the duke, she wasn't exactly sure she wanted to be saved.

"Beezle!" She gave him a nudge. "Wake up, you slothful thing, you." The encouraging thought crossed her mind that maybe the weasel could miraculously become a useful familiar. Of course he had to be awake to be of use. She nudged him again.

He wheezed and twitched, then draped his paws down over her shoulder and went back to sleep.

"Useless. Absolutely useless." Joy sighed, absently scratching his head, which had nestled into the neckline of her pelisse. She stared at the glass of brandy in her other hand and frowned. She moved over to the carriage door and opened it, careful not to put any weight on her throbbing ankle. The men were busy clearing the road, so with a quick flick of her wrist she tossed the brandy into the dirt. She started to pull the door closed, but she couldn't resist sneaking another peek at the men, the duke in particular.

It was as if her eyes were drawn to him, and an odd

sweetness flowed through her at the sight of him. He had cast off his coat and stood at one end of a tree, directing the men. His shoulders were as broad as a Highland laird's, his hips were narrow, and his legs were long and powerful. His stance was all command and confidence. He seemed to know exactly what to do and the most efficient way to do it. The men moved easily, without struggling. They just followed his instructions and had managed to move half the trees already. He had power and surety of mind. He stepped right in and took control—a trait she sorely envied, considering she had so little control herself.

"You have no control because you do not concentrate, Joyous!" Her aunt's words came flooding back to her—a sure sign that she should look to her magic and not the imaginary hero of the fairy tale in her mind.

With one last wistful look at the duke, she settled back against the seat and scrunched up her face with the effort to remember. "Now what was that incantation?" she murmured. "Speed . . . heed. Door . . . floor? No . . . Bore? No. Core? For? Gore? Ho—Oops!" She clamped her hand over her mouth. She knew that word was not in the spell. What had she said? "Lore? More?" That was it! "Ring the bell more." She knew that that was wrong. That choice of words had sent her to the North Road with the duke of Belmore instead of to a cozy cottage in Surrey. What a fix. . . . She drummed her fingers on the armrest.

How was she to escape this situation? She was a witch. She should act like one. She would make up her own spell. Her face wrinkled in thought. A few minutes later she had thought up her own incantation:

> Oh, listen to me,
> I'm sorely in a fix.
> Apparently my spells don't mix.
> So please pay heed,
> and with due speed,
> in a hurry
> send me to Surrey!

She took a deep breath and chanted it out loud.

A loud crack echoed in the clearing, followed by some male shouts. There was another thud, then another, and another. Slowly, with a sense of dread and with her hands covering her eyes, she moved fearfully to the carriage door and peeked through her fingers. Three more trees lay in the road and the men, including the impeccably dressed duke, were all splattered with mud and dirt clods. They did not look pleased. Even the tall blond man with the injured arm was mud-splattered and the nervous, fidgety one was looking skyward as if he expected the heavens to fall at any moment.

Her gaze drifted toward the duke. He took charge immediately and had the men checking all the nearby trees. Control of the situation was in his hands. His voice could be heard well above the others. It was deep and strong, a voice that exuded power. Her mind flashed with the fanciful thought that with such a braw and brawny voice, the duke of Belmore would have made a magnificent warlock.

She watched a dreamy moment longer, then sighed and pulled the door closed before she slid back into her warm corner and elevated her injured foot on the seat opposite her. Settling back against the plush squabs, she looked around the inside of the carriage. The seats were wide and deep, the seat springs covered in a rich emerald green velvet. She ran her hand over the velvet, watching its pile catch and glimmer in the lamplight. Gold braid and thick-fringed tassels held back the velvet curtains that covered the carriage windows. The inside doors of the vehicle were made of highly polished burl, and the brass carriage lamps, with their crystal knobs and beveled-glass shades, glistened and twinkled like captured stars. Looking closer at the shades she noticed that a crest was etched delicately into the glass—falcons. She opened the door again and peered at the crest on the outside of the carriage. It was the same design. A custom carriage. What elegance!

Even more impressed, she closed the door and moved back into her corner, imagining what it would be like to be driven in such luxury wherever one had to go. No need to remember incantations, no need to concentrate. One could just lie back against the velvet and let the world pass by. . . .

"Are you comfortable, Your Grace?" the footman would ask her.

She would lift a hand bejeweled with emerald rings given to her by her devoted husband because they matched her eyes. Then she'd say, "Of course, Henson. I'm going to rest now. Let me know when we reach Brighton. I'm sure the prince is awaiting our arrival. You know what the prince always says, 'No ball is a success without the duke and duchess of Belmore.' "

Then the footman would close the carriage door, and her handsome, regal, commanding husband would lean forward, his hand sliding around to caress her neck, before he pulled her closer . . . and closer . . . until she could smell the tobacco, taste the sweet wine. Then his lips, cool and hard, would press against hers. . . .

Lost in her daydream, Joy had no idea that she had pressed her lips against the carriage window, until she opened her eyes—her mouth still pressed against the cool, hard glass—and stared into the stunned faces of the duke of Belmore and his friends.

# Chapter 4

"What do you suppose she's doing?"

"I cannot possibly imagine." Alec stood next to the earl of Downe, his coat slung over one shoulder. He glanced from Downe, who was frowning in speculation, and Seymour, who was suspiciously silent, back to the girl.

Her eyes were closed and her lips were plastered against the glass like pink leeches. With a quick flash of green, her eyes opened and stared right at him. Then she whipped back against the seat, her face hidden by the side curtain.

"She's Scottish," Alec said.

The earl nodded knowingly while Henson assisted Alec with his coat. Then with a flick of his hand he dismissed the servant and walked around to the opposite side of the carriage. He opened the door and leaned inside.

She looked at him as if she expected him to swallow her in one monstrous bite, and on closer inspection he saw that her color had come back tenfold. She quickly turned away.

"Are you feeling all right?"

After a long, tense moment she mumbled to the curtain, "No, I think I'm going to curl up and die."

"I doubt you'll die from a sprained ankle," he said, unable to keep the sarcasm from his tone. He had been through his share of London seasons and had witnessed the dramas that females could enact. Strange that it bothered him to think that this girl, with her odd face and even odder behavior, might be as vapid as many of the women he knew in London. For some reason he wanted her to be as different as her face. He called himself a fool and waited for a response.

None came. She sat there, one small gloved hand across her forehead, shielding her eyes. It was a gesture of someone who'd been hurt.

"Does your ankle pain you?"

" 'Pain' does not describe how I feel," she said behind her hand.

"That bad?"

"Worse than you could know."

Tired of questioning the back of her head, he reached out and gently pushed her hand away so he could turn her face toward him. Her face would tell him if she was suffering. The cheeks that turned toward him were so flushed they looked red. "Did you sustain some other injury?"

Panic flashed in her eyes, and she raised a hand to her cheek. "I think . . . I mean . . . a fever. Yes, that's it!" she said, her words rushed. "I think I have a fever."

He examined her face. "You do seem flushed."

"I do, don't I?" She patted her face as if she could feel the heat of it through her kid gloves. "The window is cold, you see . . . and . . . uh, it cooled my face." She blessed him with a smile—a bright smile, not the listless smile of someone who had a fever.

"I see. How very resourceful of you."

"Yes, I did have to think quickly."

For some reason Alec had the strangest feeling that they were talking at cross-purposes. He tried to counter his confusion with logic. "Did you think about opening the door? It is brisk outside."

She looked past him at the fog he knew hovered just a few feet above them. "No, I didn't. But that does make much more sense. That must be why you are a duke and I'm a wi—" She slapped a hand over her mouth so that Alec could see only her wide eyes. Her hand slowly slid away from her lips. "Woman."

"Your Grace, the fog's settling."

Alec turned to Henson. "Did you check the other trees again?"

"Couldn't find a shaky one in the lot. Every one's as sturdy as the London Tower. The road's safe, Your Grace."

"Fine. Tell the others we're ready to leave." Alec turned back and once again had a perfect view of the ostrich feathers on the back of her bonnet. He shook his head and glanced down at her hands, which she wrung nervously. Watching her was like watching a small soft rabbit snared in the iron jaws of a fox trap. Something about her innocence drew him, as did the aura of helplessness he saw in her. For some reason he felt an urge to put her at ease, though he couldn't remember ever having felt benevolent before. "Miss MacQuarrie."

She jumped as if pinched.

"We shall take you to an inn and summon a doctor to examine your foot." And your head, he thought, or possibly mine, since he realized he was staring at the tilt of her lips. He broke his stare and stepped into the carriage, settling next to her just before Seymour and Downe joined them. Within a few minutes the carriage had safely moved through the woods and was on the open road. The fog had thickened and now hovered a bare two inches above the ground.

Alec studied the girl, asking himself what it was about her that caught him unguarded. There were brief moments when she looked at him as if she saw some kind of wonder in him. Women had always stared at him; that in itself was not unusual. His wealth and title drew them like ants. But this Scottish girl was different, with her odd face and her uncanny ability to touch something inside him with a mere look. She was a novelty. He fought the urge to study her longer by looking out the frosty window and seeing nothing.

They lumbered along for a few silent minutes during which Downe once again took out his flask. The earl was Alec's friend, but he was of late a profligate rascal and was truly obnoxious when he was foxed—an occurrence that seemed to be happening more and more often. He was just preparing to tell him to put the flask away when Seymour gasped. Alec looked at him and saw that his eyes were riveted on the girl and his mouth gaped open. Downe stared too, the flask forgotten for a moment.

Alec looked at her, but saw nothing amiss, and turned back toward his friend.

"Did you see what I just saw?" Seymour asked Downe.

The earl's answer was to swill a drink and then watch the girl, his eyes narrowed.

Alec looked at her again but saw nothing odd.

"I'll take that," Seymour said, making a grab at Downe's flask.

"Won't help," said the earl. "I just saw it again."

Again both men looked at her.

"You need to ease up on that stuff, both of you. There is a lady present." Alec gave the flask a significant look.

"Her collar is moving," Seymour whispered.

All three men stared at her, their gazes locked on her throat. From her expression Alec could tell her mind was miles away. Probably in Scotland, he thought.

After a moment, during which the fur collar on her jacket twitched and shivered, she must have felt their looks, because she glanced up at the men. She looked at each one and said, "Is something wrong?"

"Your collar is moving," Seymour told her.

Her hand came up to stroke the fur. "Oh," she laughed. "This is Beelzebub. I call him Beezle," she said, as if that explained everything.

A small black-tipped paw flopped over her shoulder and an odd sound came from her neckline. It was not unlike that made by the hot air balloons that ascended from Hyde Park in the summer.

She looked at them and said, "He sleeps a lot."

Alec stared at the lump of fur he had thought was a collar. "It's alive?"

She nodded.

It snorted, then wheezed.

"What, may I ask, is a . . . a Beezle?"

"A weasel."

"So is Downe, but he doesn't make that horrid noise," Seymour said, laughing at his own wit, since it was common knowledge that it wasn't often he could get one up on the earl.

Downe raised one eyebrow.

"You have a weasel wrapped around your neck," Alec stated.

"Actually he is an ermine weasel, and he likes to sleep there."

"So would I." Downe's eyes rested on her neckline.

"I told you what we should have done with that tree," Seymour said, glaring at Downe, but only making him smile.

Alec leaned back against the seat and gave Downe a hard look meant to silence him. "These two gentlemen are quite harmless, actually. As I said before, I am the duke of Belmore. This one with the hot eyes and loose tongue is the earl of Downe."

"Doing you harm is the last thing on my mind." Downe gave her a wolfish smile.

"And this," Alec continued, motioning toward Seymour, "is the Viscount Seymour."

"Seymour is harmless," Downe added, "and witless, too."

That started the bickering all over again. Intending to finish the introduction in spite of his friends, Alec turned to the girl. She looked from one man to the other in confusion, then turned to him and moved her hand to pull her weasel tighter against her. He could see the apprehension in her expressive face. Some small scrap of sensitivity sparked deep inside him, from a place untouched. He started to reach for her.

She took a deep breath and began to mutter again. A shout sounded. Suddenly the coach shot forward at a frantic pace. The passengers grabbed anything they could to keep from flying into each other. More shouts and curses came from the coachman. A loud bang resounded, and a sudden scurrying noise echoed down from the box.

Alec grabbed her and held her fast against his chest, trying to absorb the bounce and shock as the carriage rattled over the rutted road. They hit something hard, and his body pinned hers to the seat. Momentum forced him to move against her. Every soft female inch of her pressed against him. Her hands tightened their hold on his coat and pressed into his belly. Her hot breath brushed in frightened pants against his ear.

Suddenly, uncontrollably, he was aware of her as a woman. Her eyes met his, surprised, then curious, then searching. Their world was silent. He fought for control over the natural urge that passed between them. Again she searched his face. With a coldness born of instinct, he covered his reaction. *Don't look too deep, Scottish, there's nothing in here for you.*

She flushed. A wistful sadness existed between them as surely as if they had spoken their thoughts. She closed her eyes and turned away. The coach hit another bump, and he tightened his grip on the cloth handle.

Downe grunted, then swore. The carriage finally slowed, then stopped. Alec wrapped an arm around Joy and sat up. The earl's angry voice echoed through the carriage interior. "Get the devil off me, Seymour! Your blasted bony knee's in my back."

Alec and Joy looked at them. The earl's blond head was wedged into a corner of the carriage floor, his booted feet were braced against the door, and the viscount was atop him, clinging to the opposite end of the seat to avoid the earl's bootheels. The weasel clung to Seymour's coat collar.

"Can't help it, Downe. I've no place else to put my knees."

There was a scuffle, then a loud groan. "Watch out for my shoulder. Bloody thing hurts like the devil."

"Sorry. Give me a moment to get this animal off my neck."

"Come here, Beezle." Joy opened her arms, and the weasel lumbered into them. Alec noticed that his arms were still around her and quickly pulled back. Seymour managed to right himself on the seat and began to dust himself off.

Alec gave Downe a hand up, and the carriage door opened. A white-faced Henson peered in at them. "Sorry Your Grace. We broke a harness."

"Can it be fixed?"

"They're working on it now."

"Are you hurt?" Alec asked Joy.

Not meeting his eyes, she shook her head, still clutching her weasel to her chest. He saw that her cheek was smudged with dirt and her hat was cockeyed, the purple plumes broken and hanging down over her shoulders. She looked like a sparrow that had fallen from her nest. He felt the urge to tuck her back inside it. Somehow he knew that this woman, of all women, should not be alone in the world.

He turned away from her. That helpless look on her face made him lose his train of thought. He climbed down from the carriage and moved toward the team where his coachman and the other footman were repairing the broken harness.

"Who harnessed the team?" Alec asked in a tone that didn't bode well for the culprit.

"Me, Yer Grace," Jem the coachman answered, but added quickly, "'Twas a brand new one. Sturdy as an elm, it were. Never seen the like. A good inch thick, an' it just broke like it were paper. Here, look here." He held up the leather strap of the harness piece.

Alec examined it. There were no cuts, no clean slices. The edges were frayed indicating it seemed to have torn in two. "How long before you can have it repaired?"

"Almost done now, Yer Grace. Took the strap off the thill line."

"Fine." Alec walked back and climbed inside the carriage. "We'll be off in a minute."

"This was a sign," Seymour whispered, wide-eyed and looking as if he expected the carriage to glow a supernatural light.

Downe choked on his brandy, then recapped the flask, slid it back inside his coat, and readjusted his sling.

As Alec settled back in his seat he glanced down at his coat and saw the fabric wadded into tight wrinkles where Joy's fists had clutched it. Then as surely as if she had reached out and touched him, he felt the girl's stare—that familiar yet elusive look. She seemed to be memorizing his face. It made him as uncomfortable as hell.

At this point, all he wanted was to reach the inn, quickly.

He treated her to a cool look, but it died when his gaze connected with hers. For some odd reason he looked at Downe's injured arm, then back at the girl. There was a link between the girl's look and Downe's arm. Henson closed the carriage door, and once again they rattled down the bumpy road, the duke of Belmore deep in thought.

A few moments later, to his absolute horror, he remembered where he had seen that exact look—Letitia Hornsby. He groaned inwardly. This odd Scottish girl stared at him with the same look of devotion that Letitia Hornsby wore when she looked at Downe—a look that held her heart in her eyes.

But before he could even digest that thought there was another shout.

When the wheel came off the carriage, Joy gave up. Someone was going to get hurt if she didn't stop trying to cast a travel spell. She rested her chin on a hand and tried to accept her fate. Experience had taught her that when her spells were this befuddled, the best thing she could do was give her magic a rest. Sometimes she did better, could concentrate more, if she waited. Whatever, she didn't want any harm to come to the men, especially the duke.

There was something more between them than just tattered heartbeats and intense looks. There was a force, a pulling force that told her he needed something from her. There was some remnant of desperation that he hid behind an icy glare. She sensed it as surely as she could sense a spring rain.

The nervous one, Viscount Seymour, leaned toward her, examining her as if she were an apparition. "You are the one, aren't you?"

Her stomach lurched at the thought that he might actually know she was a witch. She held her breath, not knowing how to reply.

"Leave the girl alone, Seymour," the earl said, disgust threading his voice, then turned to Alec. "Even if she is 'the one,' Belmore would have to call his man of business before making his move. Bloodlines, you know, and all that other . . . stuff."

Another argument ensued, so she glanced at the duke, whose hand had distractedly risen to his coat pocket. She caught the soft crinkle of paper and wondered about it. He told the men to be quiet, pinning the earl with a stare as cold as midnight. The earl stared back, which made them look like two dogs facing off. The viscount had grown suddenly quiet and uneasy.

The silent battle continued. It did not take long for Joy to realize that the duke would be the winner. She had seen the coldness in his eyes. After a few tense minutes that seemed never to end, the earl broke eye contact and raised his flask to his lips once again. The duke turned away. Then, as if she'd called him, he looked at her.

He took her breath away. His eyes held secrets that piqued her natural curiosity, like treasures buried deep and waiting for someone to care enough to uncover them. He seemed to be looking for something as he watched her, searching.

*What is it you seek? What do you need?* She wanted to ask the questions, but they wouldn't come. As quickly as dandelions in the summer wind the quest in his eyes was gone. And in its place was that shuttered look.

They had all been silent too long, living in their own thoughts. Too much time had passed in silence, Joy thought, chewing her lip and thinking. The questions would surely start again soon. She needed to think of a tale she could tell them. The one thing a witch was taught early was never to tell a mortal she was a witch. Mortals did not understand that witchcraft was not something dark and evil. One had to get to know a mortal very well before he or she could understand, and that was a rare mortal indeed, for history had proven that many would never understand because of their misconceptions about witches. The MacLean didn't trust too many. She said most mortals thought witches flew around on besoms, had warts on their faces, looked haggard, and had ragged gray hair.

Joy's paternal grandfather, a warlock, had married a

mortal—the daughter of an English peer—and the MacQuarries and the MacLeans had welcomed her, once she proved herself an exceptional human being. Of course her aunt also swore that her grandparents' marriage was the source of Joy's problem. Tainted blood, she claimed. Joy always figured it could have been worse. She could have had no powers at all. She could have been born all human mortal instead of a weak white witch.

She could tell these men something close to the truth without mentioning the witch business. Perhaps she'd inject a little hyperbole and, for spice, maybe a tad of drama to make the tale interesting. If she could hold them enthralled, maybe they wouldn't notice the things she left out—logic, credibility, truth.

The duke had turned his penetrating eyes toward her. Those eyes spoke to her, knew her, and they wouldn't miss much.

Here it comes, she thought.

"Where is your family?"

"Gone," she replied, wanting to stare at her lap, but unable to look away.

His gaze held hers.

"You mentioned Surrey. Is that where you were going?"

She nodded.

"Why?"

"My grandmother's home is there."

"I thought you said your family was gone."

"They are, except my aunt, and she's gone to—" She caught herself. "She's out of the country for two years."

"She went away without leaving you properly chaperoned?"

"I am of age," she informed him, raising her chin a bit. "I am twenty-one."

"I see." His tone was not unlike that used to humor a child.

There was a long silence.

"How were you traveling?"

"On foot," she answered in a squeaky voice. Even she wouldn't have swallowed that claim. *Stupid, daft, dumb.*

The duke cast a meaningful glance at her new half boots. Not a scar or a scuff marred them. The heels were unnicked, and the edges of the soles barely worn. The hems of her pelisse and traveling gown were perfectly clean, no signs of the muddy roads anywhere on her person. He turned his dark gaze back to hers and gave her a look that almost made her spill forth the truth. "You walked from Scotland?"

"Oh, my goodness, no!" She raised a hand to her heart in what she hoped was an innocent and dumbfounded gesture. "One could hardly walk all the way from Scotland." She smiled.

Again the silence went on, the duke giving her an I'm-waiting look while Joy fabricated a thousand stories in her furtive mind.

"No doubt Seymour's fairy of destiny just dropped her here." The earl lounged back against the carriage window with a smirk on his brandy-moistened lips.

"Oh, stuff it!" The viscount flushed with anger.

"What's wrong, Seymour? Has your feeling, right here"—the earl thumped his chest—"gone walking? No old hags, no angels, no trolls?" He looked at Joy. "Oh, I forgot, she's Scottish. I should probably say brownies and bogeys. Isn't that correct?"

"You're foxed, Downe," the duke said, giving his friend a hard stare. "I suggest you leave off—that is, unless you wish to walk.

"Wouldn't do to have one of Belmore's friends staggering down the road, now, would it? What would people think?"

"You're an ass when you drink," the viscount said, then looked at Joy. "Beg pardon, miss, but drinking gives him enough tongue for two sets of teeth."

Joy looked at the earl—a handsome man when he wasn't sneering—and asked, "Why do you drink, then?"

The carriage was stone silent. Something flickered in the earl's eyes, some vulnerability, and then they took on a closed, cynical look. "Because I like it. I've honed swilling and braying to a fine art. It's taken me as many years to perfect as it has taken Belmore to creep into favor with himself. He's as well known for his sublime sense of consequence as I am for my lack of the same. You see, I like some spontaneity in my life." He gave the duke a strange look, then added, "You know what they say: brandy breaks the boredom." He let his words hang in the close confines of the carriage. Then, seeing that his words appeared not to have affected the duke in the least, he turned and stared out the window.

She could feel Viscount Seymour's eyes on her, and she looked up at him.

He smiled reassuringly and asked, "Do you know where your grandmother's home is?"

"Outside of East Clandon. 'Tis called Locksley Cottage."

"Locksley, as in Henry Locksley, earl of Craven?" the viscount asked, looking at the duke, then back to her.

"My grandmother was a Locksley."

"Seem to remember my mother mentioning them, distant relatives of some sort. The old earl disowned his daughter after she ran off and married some oddball Scot, and . . ." The viscount stopped and gaped at her. "You're Scottish."

She nodded and watched his expression. "That woman was my grandmother."

All the color drained from the viscount's face and his finger, which he rudely pointed at her, began to shake. "See? See?" He looked at the duke. "I told you. It's destiny. Fate. You cannot fight it."

"Yes, Belmore, you needn't call your man of business. 'Tis all done for you, unless you need to check her teeth." The earl of Downe smirked knowingly, then began to laugh and laugh, as if it was the most hilarious thing in the world for her to be the great-granddaughter of an earl.

She had thought that her grandmother made her a bit more like them. A sick feeling settled in her belly. But she wasn't like them, for she would never laugh at someone so cruelly. She might be a witch, but she had human emotions. It hurt to be the object of someone's jest. The earl was still smirking at her. Her throat tightened and she turned her eyes to her lap and tried to swallow the lump of embarrassment.

Beezle, who had been sound asleep in her lap since their

wild carriage ride, opened his eyes and searched her face. He turned his head toward the laughing earl and slowly stood up. A moment later he was crawling up the suddenly silent earl's chest.

"What is it doing?" Downe eyed the weasel.

Beezle had crawled up to the earl's face and was lifting one black-tipped paw toward the earl's pursed mouth.

"Perhaps he intends to check your teeth," the duke said with utter nonchalance.

The weasel placed its paw on the earl's lower lip and pulled it down, then peered into his mouth. "Get . . . it . . . offumm . . . me."

Joy started to reach for Beezle, but the duke placed his hand on her arm and slowly shook his head. His eyes were those of a man one did not defy, so she sat back and watched with dread. For the next few minutes Beezle carefully inspected the earl's mouth, lifting his lips this way and that, pulling his mouth into the most awkward positions.

Beezle sniffed the earl's breath, turned his small furred head away, and wheezed. Then he released the man's lip and wrapped himself around his neck. With all the grace of a lame cow, he curled into the same position he had assumed on Joy, except that he hung his head down over one broad shoulder and stuck his nose into the earl's coat.

"Quit laughing, Seymour. Get it off me." The earl tried to shrug, but his injury must have stopped him because he winced.

"And ruin the spontaneity?" The duke almost smiled. "Surely not."

"I say, Alec. You're right. Makes my day." The viscount chuckled.

The duke silently watched his cornered friend. Joy had never seen two men communicate without saying a word, but these two were doing just that. And the tension was as thick, as real, as that between two warring clans.

By this time Beezle had climbed down into the earl's lap and was standing on his haunches. He rummaged through the man's coat until he pulled the flask out of his pocket. Joy watched her familiar sit back on his hindquarters and dig his sharp little back paws into the earl's thigh. The earl sucked in a breath, then tried to grab the animal, but Beezle hissed, baring his razor-sharp teeth. The earl snapped his hand back, clearly startled. The weasel watched him through eyes that were more awake and more threatening than they had been in years.

With the drunken earl at bay, the weasel held the silver flask between its two handlike paws and inspected it, sniffing the cap and blinking at his reflection in the silver. Then he held it in his teeth and waddled down the earl's long legs and up the duke's.

Joy looked at the duke's face, waiting for his reaction. No emotion registered. His angled face wore the same refined look. But it didn't matter because Beezle couldn't have cared less. The duke was no more to him than a human ladder. Without even a glance at the esteemed peer over whom he meandered, her familiar dropped the flask onto the seat, plopped down on top of it, and fell sound asleep.

# Chapter 5

Joy finally attempted to explain how she came to be in the woods, but she made sure she didn't look at the duke. She kept her eyes on her hands, folded in her lap, or on the viscount. He seemed the most receptive, nodding encouragement and looking concerned when she came to the more tragic parts of her story. She told them that her carriage had run into a ditch, and after a brief visit into the woods she returned to find it gone—an occurrence she attributed to some nefarious motive of the ramshackle coachman she had made the massive mistake of hiring. She finished her tale and watched closely her companions' reactions.

The viscount was the first to speak. "It's of no importance, Miss MacQuarrie. The whole thing was completely out of your control. Destiny, you know. Can't fight fate." He crossed his arms, then added, "The fates control everything, including the fact that you're Scottish, that I'm a viscount, and that Downe, here—apparently even the fates can make a mistake—is an earl. Mortal man has no control over what happens to him."

"The only mistake I am aware of is the unfortunate fact that you and I met, Seymour," the earl shot back. "And as far as mortal man having no control, I do believe Belmore is the exception. You are mortal, aren't you, Alec?"

Joy could feel the duke stiffen slightly. The movement was so subtle, so minute, that she wouldn't have noticed except that she sat next to him and could feel the squabs on the seat shift ever so slightly.

"The duke of Belmore," Downe went on, "would not allow anything as mundane as fate to command his life. Oh, no, quite the contrary, Alec is controlled by tradition, by what should be done for a man of his . . . consequence, and by his own plans and schemes." The earl spoke to Joy, but his eyes were on the duke. "Rest assured he will do what his father did, and his father's father, and his father, et cetera, et cetera." With that, he turned and looked out the window.

Joy glanced at the duke. His eyes were so cold that she felt a chill just watching him. He's vulnerable, she thought, and he's covering it up. She wondered what it was he didn't want the world to see.

He looked at her then. She could feel him assessing her, mentally weighing something. She wondered if he believed her tale and what he would do if he didn't. For some reason this man's opinion of her mattered very much.

He was such a serious fellow, and for all his hard handsomeness there was something lonely about him, or perhaps it wasn't loneliness but instead isolation. Something told her he was trying hard to act as if he didn't care. No one could be that cold. He had to have a heart inside him, because it called out to her. As surely as she knew the sun would rise in the east, she knew this man was more than what he allowed the world to see. Her eyes dropped to the grim line of his lips, and she gave him a small tentative smile.

The duke of Belmore looked as if he needed a smile.

His face changed, took on a look of curious interest, but he did not return her smile. She wondered if he knew how. She watched him for a moment, trying to picture what his face would look like if he did deign to smile. No matter how hard she tried, she couldn't picture it. Finally she gave up and stared out the window at the fog. It had dropped lower, and now the road was barely visible.

As if summoned to do so, she turned back toward him. His look had become even more intense, but she didn't believe that anger was the cause. There was something else, something intimate. She could feel her face flush under his perusal, and she averted her eyes. Her hands were clammy beneath the soft leather of her gloves, her mouth was dry as a week-old oatcake, and she had the feeling she was melting.

Looking for something to do besides blush, she reached for the wick on the carriage lamp. If she dimmed the light, maybe he wouldn't be able to see inside her soul, for that was how she felt when he turned that penetrating stare her way.

In her nervousness she turned the wick key the wrong way and it came off in her hand. She stared at it, embarrassed, and made a fumbled attempt to put it back. A hard male hand gripped her wrist.

"I'll do it." He reached toward the lamp, and his shadow fell over her. It was dark and cold, like the duke himself, and yet she could feel his warmth, smell the raw scent that seemed to emanate from him and him alone. Like the salty breath of the sea, it pulled her in an ebbing wave. It was like a physical presence surrounding her. He put the wick key back, turned up the lamp, and started to move back, but stopped, looking down at her, his intense face barely inches above hers.

She raised her eyes to his and could almost taste his breath. If she moved just a wee bit, their lips would touch. His gaze held her frozen, locked in an instant of time where hearts cried out. She could not move, but she didn't wish to and had no regret about her poverty of will. This was like being caught in a moonbeam—the only light in a vast void of darkness. The darkness was there; his face warned her away with its tightness. But the glint in his eyes said don't go.

He still held her wrist. His grip had tightened, hard, imprisoning her. Her pulse pounded against the pad of his thumb. Her heart felt as if it were somewhere around her ears, thundering inside her head. She could feel her hand going numb and the resulting tingle—her blood turning into a thousand star-points. His eyes pierced her with their heat. She had thought his eyes cold—an icy dark blue—yet how odd that she perspired from his look. Dampness beaded and trickled between her breasts, on her arms, and on the backs of her thighs.

Still holding her wrist, he moved back, breaking the bewitching magic that felt stronger than a warlock's spell. She remembered to breathe. He stared at her wrist with an odd expression, as if he had just noticed he held it. Her fingers brushed his as if to say it was all right. His grip slackened, and she felt the blood rushing back to her fingers. It matched the feeling in her chest.

For a brief second she thought she felt his thumb gently rub her wrist, but it all happened so quickly that she was not sure that it had actually happened. An instant later he sat beside her, staring sightlessly out the window into the white fog.

Again she breathed the cooling air, and with that breath came an awareness of something other than this man. The quiet. The only sound in the carriage was the muted pounding of the horses' hooves, the jangle of harness and braces, and the occasional creak of springs as the vehicle moved along the road. It was as if her senses had come back to her. Male smells dominated the interior—damp leather, tobacco, and brandy. The air tasted stale, hard, and male in her dry mouth. Instinctively she reached for Beezle and absently scratched his fur, aware that it would be soft and plush. After that exchange she needed to touch something soft and familiar.

The loud clearing of a masculine throat cut through the air. She flinched, startled. It was the cynical earl, and she looked at him, expecting a sneer. That wasn't what she saw. As sure as heather bloomed on the moors, he watched her, but his look was speculative, and it made her uneasy—a different kind of restlessness than she felt from the duke. The earl was an odd man, and she didn't like him much. There was anger inside him, raw and festering, a wound untended. He was rude, enjoyed his brashness, seemed to wallow in it, and his smile was too practiced.

One could tell volumes about a person from a smile. The nervous viscount stared out the window and muttered under his breath. But he had smiled at her, and it was sincere. Cocking her head, she looked at the duke and tried to picture his face with a smile, but she had no luck. Even her mind's eye could not see him as anything but focused and intense.

She gave up and settled back, looking out the window as did the others, until the coach finally pulled into a timbered coaching inn. A warm yellow glow from its diamond-paned windows lit their approach with a strange eerie glow. A sign proclaiming the establishment to be the Shovel and the Boot hung at a drunken angle from a rusty cast-iron mount over the heavy oak door.

Mist hovered around an ancient mossy gray stone fence that circled the carriage courtyard, where the duke's outrider dismounted and stood speaking to a post lad. The door to the inn creaked open, and light bled gold onto a flagstone walkway, only to be blocked by the shadow of an aproned innkeeper.

At the same instant the carriage door opened and the footman pulled down the steps. The duke was the first to step down. He waved the servant away and turned back, holding his hand out to Joy. She scooped up Beezle, settling him around her neck, and started to rise, but glanced down at her foot, unsure if she could stand on it without assistance. She needn't have worried, for the next thing she knew, the duke lifted her out of the carriage and strode toward the inn door, cradling her against him and giving orders that sent those within a twenty-foot range scurrying like rats in the tower room to do his bidding.

For Joy the damp English air held no chill; the cold didn't bother her. In fact, when she was in his arms she could imagine the man inside that cold shell, and her fantasies warmed her, along with his brawny chest. He had such a wonderful shoulder, on which she rested her head after a brief sigh. Just perfect. Even through the layers of cashmere and wool, she could feel the strength of his arm behind her knees.

A burgeoning tingle picked that very instant to flutter its way from her head to her toes and then to her heart. She wondered if it was the same thrill that some witches experienced when they flew. She'd heard that flying was one of the most profound and joyous rewards of being a witch.

Yet Joy didn't know that feeling. Try as she might, she could not remember the one time she'd flown. Of course she had been forbidden to fly after she did so that once, and had the misfortunate experience of blasting herself right through the two-hundred-year-old stained-glass window in the Catholic chapel at Craignure. Her aunt had rescued her and had offered a graceful apology to the bishop, as soon as he came around. It was truly unfortunate that the poor man of God had been praying beneath that window at the time.

Joy still had a three-inch-long white scar on her left hand and a longer ragged one on the back of her neck. Her aunt told her that both scars would serve to remind her that flying was not for her. But those puny scars were nothing compared to the one she carried deep inside her—the one that reminded her she was only half a witch, and the half she had wasn't very good at making magic.

But her unflagging hope carried her through the tough times, the times when everything she did seemed to go awry. Hope was her ballast. Hope was her salvation. It made her dream her dreams and pray her prayers. Someday perhaps things would be different.

She looked up and caught the duke watching her again with that open curiosity, as if she was something foreign. I am, she thought, figuring she was probably the first witch the man had ever encountered. She smiled again, hoping to receive one in return. She didn't get it. A wall of ice frosted his look again. His guard was up.

Don't touch me, it said. Stay clear.

He was so strange. There was no smile in him. How very sad. He needed someone who would dig deep enough to find that treasure he'd buried. He needed someone with hope, because he had none. Joyous Fiona MacQuarrie had plenty of hope. She'd needed it to get this far. And she needed a purpose. Was that it? Was that what bound them in some strange way? She sensed it was, because this man desperately needed a little magic in his life.

* * *

Alec sat on a hard bench at a long tavern table and studied the piece of paper on the table in front of him.

> Granted herein, by the archbishop of Canterbury, is special license to Alec Gerald David John James Mark Castlemaine, duke of Belmore, marquess of Deerhurst, earl of Fife, the right to marry without the posting of banns and at a time and place of his convenience.

A raucous cheer broke his concentration, and he looked up at his friends, who were involved in a high-stakes game of darts. In this small inn there was no private parlor, just the common room, with its stark white plaster walls spreckled with hay and crossed by dark beams, a room filled with a thick fog of smoke, the sharp stench of ale, and the heavy aroma of greasy mutton and fresh baked bread that drifted from the back kitchen.

The innkeeper was a rotund man whose smudged and faded pink vest showed red where the seams had been let out at least three times. He stood in a crowd of locals, jolly farmers who wore the black dirt of their labors and who whooped and stomped and hawed when one of them scored over the London swells.

Downe's blond head stuck out above the crowd, and Alec watched as he threw back his fifth portion of frothy and potent ale from an old sheep-horn stein. There was no doubt in Alec's mind that his friend would soon begin another drunken attempt to prove to the world that he was an obnoxious rake who held everything and everyone in contempt. When sober, the earl of Downe was one of the best men Alec had ever known, but when drunk, a state that of late seemed more the rule than the exception, he was intent upon making everyone around him as miserable as he was.

Alec glanced at the oak plank door of the retiring room into which the local leech, who had been summoned to attend the girl, had followed the innkeeper's wife. The duke glanced at his ale, but a drink was not what he needed. He doubted it would relieve the throb in his head, nor would it do anything for the burning in his eyes resulting from exhaustion and the rancid air. The truth was he was tired. He leaned back against the wall and closed his eyes, fighting back a yawn.

A commotion sounded from his left. After a moment of trying to ignore the noise he gave up and willed his tired eyes open—just in time to see Lady Agnes Voorhees—the biggest baffle-headed busybody in London—swell into the inn with her entourage. His fatigue disappeared, replaced by the urgent need to get the devil out of there before the bird-witted woman saw him. He rose abruptly, not out of courtesy but to avoid detection, and stepped back against the wall, intending to creep toward the kitchen.

"Your Grace!"

Alec groaned.

"Imagine, Eugenia! It's His Grace, the duke of Belmore! What a small world!" The woman moved toward him faster than a dart to the board, her companions toddling along behind her.

He was stuck as surely as if the inn floor were mired yard-deep in mud.

"Why, we were just chatting about you," she said, standing directly across from him. "Henry dearest"—Lady Agnes turned to her weakling of a husband—"please go and retain a private parlor." She scowled about the room, waving a lace handkerchief in front of her beak of a nose. "The air's bad." She turned back and blabbered on. "I cannot believe the exquisite luck of finding you here. You see, Eugenia—of course you know Lady Eugenia Wentworth and Mrs. Timmons . . ."

Alec nodded to the other women—the second and third biggest gossips in London. A flock of bird-wits.

"As I was saying, Eugenia said she heard from Mrs. Dunning-Whyte, who heard from Sally Jersey, that Lady Juliet Spencer—*your* Lady Juliet—had eloped! Piffle! I said. That just was not possible! Everyone knows that Your Grace would do the thing proper. A duke of Belmore would never do anything so devil-may-care! Besides, it was my understanding that you had yet to declare yourself. Of course we were sure that you would do so any day. It was just a matter of time. But you can imagine my shock when Eugenia said that you were not the groom. Well, I just laughed. Hah-hah-hah!"

Her companions giggled.

"I mean after all, no lady in control of her senses would throw over the duke of Belmore for a mere captain, no matter what his family connections are."

Mrs. Timmons and Lady Eugenia nodded in unison.

"And the whole ton knew that you were smitten from the first moment you laid eyes on her. Why I remember that night as if it were yesterday. . . ."

The stance of the duke of Belmore had not changed, but if one looked very closely, the smallest twitch was discernible in his cheek, caused by the tightening of his jaw. As usual there was no warmth in his eyes, and he stood a little taller, a little straighter, a little stiffer than before. The more the woman prattled on, the deeper and more controlled the duke's breathing became.

Then her husband returned. "The inn has no private parlors, m'dear." He looked up at Alec. "I say, that must be why His Grace is here in the common room. What say you, Belmore?"

Before Alec could respond, Lady Agnes gasped and looked around the room. "No private parlors? Ohhhhh, I feel faint." The woman sank to the bench like a deflated balloon—a hot air balloon—then lolled against the table, the back of one gloved hand pressed against her forehead.

"Now, now, m'dear." Lord Henry plucked the handkerchief from his wife's hand and began fanning her face. "There is a ladies' retiring room."

Lady Agnes found her second wind and sat up.

"Alas, m'dear, the room is occupied now, and the hostler asked that you wait out here for a few more minutes."

She deflated. "But why must we wait?"

"Seems some poor lady received an injury, and the physician is examining her now."

She inflated again, looking perfectly healthy now that there was something to snoop into. She began firing questions at her husband faster than sticks and triggers. "Who is she? Did you ask? What's her name? Who is she with? Do we know her? Why didn't you ask?"

Lord Henry blithered his way through some answers, none of which satisfied his wife.

A moment later she was in tears. "Oh, Henry, you know how desperately I need to be needed. That poor girl, whoever she is, might need me, and you know how important it is for me to feel helpful, charity being one of my greatest pleasures in this life." She moaned—a sound similar to that emitted by a clogged fireplace bellows—and closed her eyes, then dropped a dramatic hand down on the table, right atop the special license.

Alec tensed.

At the crinkling sound of paper, one curious female eye popped open, then the other. She looked down, and her pained expression disappeared. Her hand closed over the paper as if it were her invitation to heaven. One skimming glance and she had the same feral look of Alec's hunting hounds when they were on the scent of a hare. She snapped up the paper in a wink, read it, and then eyed him over the edge of the paper. Slowly she fanned herself with the license, giving him her most ingratiating, toadying smile.

She waved the license under his nose. "Why, Your Grace, what a sly one you are!"

At that moment the innkeeper's wife came out of the room and requested Alec's presence. Wordlessly, he took the license from Lady Agnes and wasted no time crossing over to the room. But just as he opened the retiring room door he heard her whisper—the king, loony and daft and locked in his room at Westminster could have heard Lady Agnes whisper—"It's Lady Juliet, Eugenia. He and Lady Juliet are to be married. I told you that murky rumor about the soldier couldn't be true."

Alec took two deep breaths and stared at his white-knuckled grip on the doorknob. Two more breaths and he entered the room, closing the door behind him.

Joy sat in a ladies' receiving chair, not hearing one word the physician said because the duke was barely five feet away. Sensing his presence in the room, she stretched so she could peer over the physician's shoulder. He snapped his satchel closed and straightened, blocking her view.

"Just a slight sprain, Your Grace," he told the duke. "I've wrapped it tightly, and the miss, here, can stand on it and move around without difficulty." He turned back to Joy. "Can't you, my dear? Here, show His Grace." He helped her up, and she walked a short distance to the huge hearth, where Beezle slept, curled up next to a fire that crackled and burned and gave warm dry relief from the damp English air. She looked at the duke and found him looking not at her foot but at her face. Joy froze.

"Show His Grace how well you are able to move your ankle, my dear." The physician seemed completely unaware of the eerie magic that Joy felt whenever she was close to the duke. There were moments when she felt this man's gaze turned so intensely personal it was as if he were inside her for a brief instant.

She lifted her skirts to just above her ankle and glanced up at the duke again. After a hesitation, he turned his gaze to her ankle and she rolled her foot to show him her ankle was fine.

"No more pain?" the duke asked.

"No," she replied. "Not a wit. Fit as a fiddle." And she gave him another smile. "Thank you."

"She should not overdo for a day or so, but after that the ankle should be strong enough to allow her to walk to Scotland if she chooses to do so." The physician laughed, and Joy flushed, remembering the conversation in the carriage. The duke's expression had not changed. It was just as steely, just as pensive as before.

He paid the man and closed the door behind him when he left the room. Joy held her hands out toward the fire. The innkeeper's wife, Mrs. Hobson, had helped her off with her pelisse and spread it and her gloves out to dry on a narrow tobacco-brown damask wing chair close to the fire. She grasped the hem of her pelisse and shook some of the water drops off. It gave her something to do other than gape at His Grace.

"Have you had any contact with the new earl of Craven?" the duke asked.

The question caught Joy off guard and she turned to face him. "No. Why?"

"I would think that, with your family gone, he would have a responsibility to you."

"If I contacted that side of the family, my granny would rise from the dead. Believe me, Your Grace, there is no love lost there." She raised her chin, remembering the stories her papa had told her of the Locksleys' harsh treatment of his English mother. She would have been hard-pressed to believe that such a family could change radically with only the death of a great-grandfather. The whole lot of them had been cruel. Scots pride and stubbornness shone from her eyes. "I could be starving and naked and half dead, and still I would not seek anything from the Locksleys."

"I see." He said no more, but he seemed to be pondering her every word. She wondered what he was thinking, how this man's mind worked, if all his thoughts were serious or if he ever let his mind wander into the fanciful world that hers so frequently visited.

The quiet sound of his boots on the wooden floor broke her thought. She watched him walk toward her, and she didn't know if she wanted to stand there or run the other way as fast as her weak ankles could carry her. She held her breath. He rested one arm on the walnut chimneypiece and rested one booted foot on a brass andiron while he stared thoughtfully into the blazing fire.

The glow lit his silver hair and limned his profile like a halo of an archangel. He had a long, noble nose, high cheekbones, and a strong jaw dusted with the shadow of a man who had not shaved, or who needed to do so more than once a day. She found that fascinating, imagining the texture of the stubble that darkened his jaw. She decided it must be rough and masculine, and her fingertips tingled with the need to feel it. Unconsciously she rubbed her own jawline.

The air became suddenly warm, and the room seemed to

have shrunk. Sweat pearled at her temples, neck, and chest. Her gown itched. She darted around to the other side of the wing chair to put some distance between herself and the fire.

"When were you born?" He barked the question.

She jumped, startled, then answered, "Seventeen ninety-two."

"What day?"

"The twenty-seventh of June."

He was silent.

"Why?"

He didn't respond.

"Your Grace?"

"I am thinking."

"About my age?"

"Not really."

"What, then?"

He turned those eyes on her, eyes that held a tinge of regret, and he slowly moved toward her. "About the consequences of what I am about to do."

"Oh." Joy stepped back. "What is that?"

Alec moved forward, silent.

A little intimidated, she stepped back again and almost fell over the chair arm.

He caught her arms and drew her forward.

"Oh, my goodness!"

His hand slid around her neck and he pulled her mouth up to meet his. She watched, mesmerized by the eyes that pinned hers, watched the hard line of his lips come closer and closer until he was so close that her eyes drifted closed. She could taste his breath, feel it against her dry lips. She wanted this. It seemed a lifetime before his mouth brushed against hers ever so softly, tentatively, as if it searched for something.

Please don't let this be a dream, she prayed. His lips brushed against hers again and again, real, tactile, with a tenderness she would have never expected in a man who didn't smile. She was afraid the kiss might end, and she wanted just a wee bit more. When he skimmed his lips to the corner of her mouth, moving gently, she turned her head just enough so there was closer contact. His hand pressed against the back of her head so her mouth was firmly on his. She melted against his chest.

Still splayed across the back of her head, his hand held her in place, but she would not have pulled away from him for anything. She had no idea that kisses were so wonderful and warm and soft. The real thing was so much better than her daydreams. No cold, hard glass here.

His other arm slid across the small of her back and ever so slowly pressed her stomach against him, and his hand moved from the back of her head to her neck, massaging the soft tendons and muscle beneath her flesh. His lips pressed harder; his hand held her fast. He licked her upper lip, then ran his tongue along the seam of her lips. She reacted with a gasp, and he filled her mouth, searching and retreating. She chilled with gooseflesh and shivered, once, twice, and again when his tongue dueled with hers.

She thought this must be like flying, only better—like flying and feasting at the same time. He tasted of everything she'd always loved—of spicy gingerbread and sweet lemon honey, of buttery scones and tart strawberries, of fine aged wine and fresh warm yeasty bread. Her head felt light, her body weightless, and her blood seemed to speed undammed through channels within her. Her swelling heart pounded in her chest and ears and wrists. She was chilled one minute, warm and flushed the next.

This was new to her, the feeling of his tongue filling her mouth, the warm dampness of the kiss, the very intimacy of it—a physical expression of the games their eyes had played. She wondered if his heart was beating with the same urgent drumming as hers, and she tried to get closer so she could feel it. She slid the palm of her hand across his coat to the center of his chest and raised her other hand to his neck. Her knees grew weaker than her ankle, and she clung to him to keep from falling. His arm moved beneath her buttocks and lifted her up off the floor, holding her safe and secure. She dangled her feet and held on tighter, gripping his coat in her fist.

With the barest of touches, his hand moved from her head

to her neck. His fingers played with the strands of hair that framed her face, then grazed her ear, and moved down her throat, across her shoulder, and over her arm to her ribs, where he rubbed slow circles that matched the rhythm of his questing tongue.

She didn't want the kiss to end and gave a plaintive cry when he pulled his mouth away. Her eyes drifted open slowly, and she saw in the duke's midnight blue eyes—a need, a flash of desperate need—the path to the treasure. Then it was gone, hidden by the mask that kept her and the rest of the world out. The hard duke was back.

"You'll do," he said.

"Hmm?" She looked up at him, searching his eyes for another sign of that need, still savoring her first kiss, the feel of his arms. "I'll do what?"

She had no idea that her eyes held her heart.

"Never mind," he said, looking away for a pensive moment, before staring at the door.

Joy was horrified to think that maybe someone else was there. She gripped his shoulders in fear, her worried eyes following his, expecting to see someone watching them, but the door was still closed, and there was no one in the room but the two of them.

He set her down, but his hands still rested on her shoulders. His look softened, and he searched her face, spending a long silent moment staring at her mouth. His hands rubbed her upper arms and then with one knuckle tilted her chin up and looked her straight in the eye.

"Marry me."

# Chapter 6

For an eternal minute she stared up at him, unable to think, unable to move or speak. She told herself her wits were wandering. He could not have said that.

"Marry me," he said again.

"Oh, my goodness!" She slapped her hand over her mouth and stepped back. He did say that. He did. Oh, my goodness, she had died and gone to witch heaven.

With little more than his thumb and forefinger, he pulled her chin forward and kissed her again and again and again, ever so gently. "Marry me," he whispered against her mouth. "Marry me."

"I cannot." But her traitorous mouth sought his.

"Of course you can. You are of age." He trailed his lips over hers again, barely brushing her mouth.

"No, I mean I can, but I cannot."

The words were barely out before he kissed her, long and deep, wet and lazy, stroking until she forgot how to think. He moved his lips to her ear. "You'll be a duchess."

"I can—"

He silenced her with another kiss, pulled her against the length of his body. Then his mouth left hers—"I cannot"—and moved to her ear. "Marry me, Joyous MacQuarrie."

"Ummmmmm."

His tongue scored her ear, and she shivered.

"But I don't know you." She wanted to see his face and tried to pull back.

Kisses trailed down her neck. "Marriage will solve that. Trust me."

"But what about love?"

He paused near her shoulder. "Are you in love with someone?"

"No."

"Then there's no problem."

"But we just met, and only by chance."

"Marriages are arranged all the time between participants who have never met."

"But you're the duke of Belmore."

"I know," he whispered in her damp ear. "And you're Scottish."

"But . . . but . . ."

"Wouldn't you like to be a duchess?" His deep voice was so soft, so quiet.

She was lost in the dreamy thoughts his words suggested.

"*My* duchess."

She didn't say a word. His lips moved in butterfly kisses.

"Hmm?" His mouth grazed her temple. "Wouldn't you?"

"I'm not sure. . . . Well, I mean, yes . . . uh, no."

"You have no argument." His mouth closed over hers again.

She sighed.

"Marry me, Scottish."

"I'm a witch."

"Most woman are at one time or another."

"No. You don't understand. I'm a *witch*. A *real* witch."

"And I can be a real bastard. We'll get used to each other. I don't care what you think you are. I just want you to marry me."

"We cannot marry."

"We can. Now. Today."

"Now?"

"Yes, now."

"You cannot just up and get married."

"I'm the duke of Belmore. I will do as I see fit." He spoke with such conviction that Joy was stunned. He looked down at her, his face relaxed, his eyes blank. "No one will question the marriage, because I am the duke of Belmore."

She couldn't counter that argument. A duke did as he pleased.

"You shall live in Belmore Park." His thumbs stroked her jaw.

"But—"

"You shall have anything you want."

"But—"

"You would like that, would you not?"

"Well, yes, but this is too quick."

His finger ran down her jawline so softly. His lips feathered over hers, and he whispered, "Marry me, Scottish."

Her eyes drifted closed. She'd do almost anything to hear him call her that again. He kissed her again. A few long, tender moments later he pulled back. "As I said, you have no arguments."

"Marriages are always carefully planned."

He stiffened suddenly, as if something she'd said had angered him. His jaw tightened. "Not this one," he said. An instant later his mouth hit hers, hard, demanding, hot, as if he could assuage some deep anger by kissing the doddering wits out of her, which he did. His lips bit at hers. His hands gripped her head. He mastered her mouth, her senses, and gave her a taste of what passion was all about.

It was a kiss so different from before. The first had been soft. This was hard. The other kiss was seductive and lingering and persuasive. This kiss had power; it was the kiss of a duke—a duke who needed to prove something.

And he did. He proved that he could make Joyous Fiona MacQuarrie forget how to say no.

Joy sat before the mirror in the ladies' receiving room and twisted a loose lock of hair back into its knot. She picked up a hairpin and slid it back into her hair, then studied her reflection. She felt as if she were daydreaming. But this was not one of her fanciful mind-voyages. This was real.

Raising her fingers to her mouth, she ran them over her swollen lips. He had kissed her. Truly kissed her. She traced the soft pink marks on her chin and cheeks where his shadowed beard had rubbed against her pale skin. The stubble had been rough and sensual. She touched her lips again as if she expected her reflection to fade like the fleeting sweet taste of sugar.

She poked her lips. Yes, he had kissed her. She smiled, then laughed a bubble of a giggle that just had to slip out. The duke had kissed her. She took a deep breath and closed her eyes, remembering every tingle, every touch, every new sensation of those kisses.

A few long and wispy moments later she sighed and got up, then walked over to the wing chair where her pelisse still lay. The duke had left as soon as he got the answer he wanted. He said he had some arrangements to make and that they would be married within the hour.

Married. Joyous Fiona MacQuarrie married to a duke. She wondered what a duchess did and wondered if she would be any better at duchessing than she was at witchcraft. It worried her a bit, but somehow it was not at the pinnacle of her thoughts.

The duke was.

Odd how a man who never smiled could make her feel things she didn't know existed. He held her heart in his hands. From the moment she saw him, some thread had linked them together. This man needed her. He needed her hope and her magic.

He needed smiles and kisses. Everyone needed kisses. And nothing else seemed to matter, not the fact that they had just met, not their differences—the fact that he was a mortal and she was a witch—not her spells, not the worry about the future. This felt so right. Something, some intuition, made her feel certain that this was where she was destined to be, and so badly wanted to be. She'd received the gift of a fairy-tale ending. It had been placed in her hands, tied with bright ribbons of love and need and dreams that would come true.

The door opened and he entered. She took one look at his scowling face, and a sinking feeling of dread came over her. With a sadness that came from a short lifetime of disappointments, she prepared herself for the worst. She had known it was too good to be true. Nothing so wonderful had ever happened to Joy, and it was not going to happen now, either.

From his face she could see the wedding had been canceled. He looked as if he'd eaten something that had made him ill. He was preparing himself to tell her that he didn't want to marry her after all. She steeled herself for disappointment, something she knew very well.

"We have a problem."

Her heavy heart was somewhere near her feet. She rose and gripped the back of a chair, trying to will away the tears she could feel burning behind her eyes. "I understand," she said in little more than a whisper.

"Three of the ton's most voracious gossips are waiting beyond that door. Don't let them intimidate you. Do not volunteer any information. Let me do the talking. Just nod your head and agree with whatever I say." He didn't wait for an answer, but she figured one didn't need to answer a ducal order.

He picked up her pelisse and held it for her while she slipped it on. Then he handed her her hat and gloves. "If the situation gets too uncomfortable I want us to be able to leave quickly. If we must wait for the vicar, we shall do so at the chapel."

Joy exhaled with relief. The wedding had not been called off.

She smiled then, a great big brilliant smile that she couldn't have hidden had she tried. He cocked his head and searched her face, as if he saw something there he could not comprehend. After an uncomfortable silence her smile faded and she looked away, spotting Beezle still asleep by the fire. She closed the distance and picked him up.

His snoring ceased, and he slowly pried open one bored eye, then let his head fall back over her arm so he could stare at the duke, eyeing him the way a sly thief might eye a fat purse. The duke scowled and returned the animal's feral look. Joy lifted Beezle to her shoulder and he crawled up, settling into his favorite position, but instead of going to sleep, he pulled the pins from her knot of hair.

"Beezle! No!" She tried to grab the pins, but she wasn't fast enough. Her hair cascaded down her back, past her waist, and down to the backs of her thighs. She heard the duke take a sharp breath. Probably in irritation, she thought. She plucked the weasel off her shoulders and set him in the chair.

She retrieved the hairpins and then straightened, grabbing a handful of hair and twisting it into a coil around her hand. "He does that sometimes. He likes to play with hair, twisting it, braiding it, chewing it. This will take me a few minutes."

She walked over to the small dressing table and sat on the bench, watching in the mirror as she sectioned off a handful of hair and twisted it around her hand before pinning it at her neck. She was bent over, trying to wrap the very back section when she felt the duke standing behind her, watching her. He seemed fascinated by what she was doing.

"My hair is terribly long and takes so much time. I—"

"It's lovely." He reached out and lifted a strand, rubbing it through his fingers as if he had never felt hair before.

"Can you hand me that last section please, the one in the back?" She held her hand out, but he didn't move. It was as if he hadn't heard her at all. She waited, watching him and trying to read his expression. He continued to finger her hair. The only sound in the room was the crackle and snap of dry wood in the fireplace. The smell of burning oak and the stale perfume of the women who had sat here before her mixed with the scent of this man to whom she was so attuned. After a minute he glanced up and met her gaze in the mirror. He looked ill at ease, very ill at ease.

"Here." He handed her the section of hair and turned away, walking over to stand by the door and wait.

Joy stuck in the last pin, stood up, and crossed back to the chair. She put her hat on, tying the ribbons beneath her chin as she leaned to the right so she could catch his reflection in the mirror. He was just out of sight.

She tugged the ribbons into a lopsided bow and gave the crown of the hat a quick pat, watching the listing feather flop like a broken twig. The hat was a mess, but it would keep Beezle from picking her hair apart again. She picked up her snoring weasel, slung him around her neck, and joined the duke.

His back was to her, his hands clasped behind him while he rocked on his heels and stared at nothing.

"I am ready."

He turned but didn't meet her look, just reached out and, after a slight hesitation, clasped her elbow and opened the door.

A richly dressed red-haired woman almost fell through the doorway. Two women behind her grabbed her pistachio green skirt with both hands to steady her. There was a second of scuffling, the rustle of silk skirts, and then the three of them flowed into the room like a gaggle of colorful geese.

"Oh! Your Grace!" The woman took great pains to brush her brocade dress instead of looking at the duke. "That horrid room out there is too stuffy. I was so overcome with weakness that I leaned against the door for support. Your Grace caught me by surprise."

"His Grace caught you trying to get an earful," he said under his breath.

Joy glanced up at him, biting back a smile. His Grace had made a jest. She expected to see some amusement on his face. She was wrong. He gave the woman the ducal glare, but she seemed completely unaware of it and of his comment. She was staring right at Joy, and she looked stunned.

The woman quickly overcame her shock and with one determined sidestep scanned Joy from the top of her head to her shoes. Joy knew instantly that this red-haired woman could, with one wee look, gauge her weight, height, and shoe size in less time than it took a kettle to whistle.

"Why, Your Grace, I don't believe I've met your . . . your—"

"Betrothed," he interrupted, ignoring the woman's sharp intake of breath. "Lady Agnes Voorhees, Lady Eugenia

Wentworth, and Mrs. Claire Timmons, may I present Miss Joyous MacQuarrie."

"A Scot!" Lady Agnes gasped, clutching her throat as if she expected Joy to grow a second head. If it hadn't been for the duke, Joy might have tried to conjure one up for the rude woman.

Lady Agnes stepped back, and her two companions backed away, too, their faces revealing abject horror.

Joy watched them, wondering how they'd react if they knew she was a Scottish witch. She looked at the red-haired woman's nose, which was elevated so she could look down at Joy.

One wart, Joy thought. Perhaps I could just give her one wee wart.

Before she could even picture the image in her mind's eye, the duke placed her hand through his arm and rested a cool hand atop hers. "If you will excuse us, madam, we have a wedding to attend."

And he walked Joy through the doorway, pausing between the woman's two companions, who scurried aside as if met by the plague. He stood a good two heads taller than any of the three women, and he squared his shoulders and looked down at Joy. "Isn't it a shame, my dear, that your grandparents, the earl and the countess, were unable to be here."

From behind her, Joy heard Lady Agnes gasp. She stifled the urge to smile and before she could even venture a peek at the woman, the duke led her away, a distinct look of supreme satisfaction on his face. She looked up at him as they walked through the inn. He was staring straight ahead, his jaw firm with a duke's pride, his hand still rested atop hers, as if to provide some assurance and protection. At that instant it seemed to Joy as if her handsome duke had just grown a foot taller.

# Chapter 7

The little brownstone church with its high narrow white spire stood at the north end of the village of Cropsey where a small brook meandered through a deep gray copse of skeletal willow and beech trees. Framing the wide path to the arched chapel doors was a matching brownstone wall thick with frost-laden ivy, where only minutes before, a small wedding party had passed by, never noticing the cold air in their rush to start an impromptu wedding.

The same frost still rimed the surrounding grass, the trees, and the church roof. But inside, past the leaded-glass windows and the walnut pews, the gilded sconces and the white marble and brass baptismal font that sat near the mahogany pulpit, the only frost in the room was in the cold blue eyes of the bridegroom when he turned and saw the uninvited wedding guests.

Chattering like magpies they walked into the church just as the vicar began the ceremony. They settled themselves in the front pew, and the vicar raised his voice so as to be heard over the harping of Lady Agnes. By the time the intruders had quieted, the bride and groom were repeating their vows.

The duke slid his signet ring onto Joy's finger, then held her hand in his tight grip so the ring wouldn't fall off. She watched his face, but his expression did not reveal any emotion. The earl's speculative and drink-ruddied face stared at her from the duke's right side. She had caught Downe watching her more than once since the duke had called his friends into the retiring room to announce that she was to be his duchess, that the marriage would take place in an hour, and that they would serve as witnesses.

"What the Lord hath joined together, let no man put asunder."

A sob rivaling that of Sarah Siddons's Lady Macbeth blubbered from behind them. The duke's shoulders stiffened, and his jaw tightened. Joy couldn't help herself. She stole a curious peek over her shoulder at the party in the front pew.

Lady Agnes was sobbing into her lace handkerchief while her beleaguered-looking husband tried unsuccessfully to give her a bit of comfort by patting her heaving shoulder. On her other side were her two friends—Mrs. Timmons, whose most memorable feature was her skin, which was as ruddy as oat flour, and Lady Eugenia, a black-haired mouse of a woman who was so small that at first glance one thought she was a child.

Both women stared at Joy as if to memorize her every feature. She suddenly felt like a butterfly specimen pinned to a board, but she had no time to worry because the duke squeezed her hand firmly enough to get her attention. She turned back just as the vicar congratulated the duke and then turned to her.

"Best wishes, Your Grace."

Joy waited for her husband to answer. After a long silence she looked up at him. He nodded toward the vicar, who was looking at her expectantly. The duke slipped his arm around her and leaned down. "Scottish?"

The intimate sound of that name whispered down at her turned her blood to warm honey. She looked up at him.

"He is speaking to you. You're a duchess now."

Feeling her face flush bright red, she averted her eyes and mumbled, "Thank you."

"Oh! What a lovely day!" Lady Agnes wedged her way past the viscount to stand barely a nose length from Joy. "Such a pity your family could not be here." She waved her handkerchief in front of Joy's face and then leaned even closer, her face instantly feral. "Who are they, my dear?"

"Your Grace," the duke corrected her, his voice ice and steel and his arm holding Joy protectively close.

It was Lady Agnes's turn to step back. Joy was sure anyone else would have run out of the kirk in Devil-fear in the face of that cold tone. Lady Agnes had more gall.

"Why—why, of course. Forgive me, Your Grace. I know how unnerving a wedding can be, don't I, Henry dear? I have married off three daughters."

"Bought husbands for them," the earl of Downe said to the viscount Seymour in a loud whisper.

Lady Agnes didn't hear him because she was still rattling on. "And it was not that long ago that I myself was married."

"Forty years at least," muttered Downe.

"Of course my family attended the ceremony, and my mother—"

"The dragon," the earl said under his brandied breath.

"She sought to ease my nervousness, but then, your mother is not here, is she, my—Your Grace?"

Lord Henry must have seen the duke's eyes turn as lethal as a raiding laird's, because he tugged on his wife's arm and her two friends began to back down the aisle.

"This wedding is private. You may leave by those doors." The duke nodded toward the church entrance.

"Well, I nev—"

"Time to leave, dearest." Lord Henry clamped a hand over his wife's mouth and pulled her down the aisle, her indignant muttering muffled by his hand.

Only when the doors closed behind them did the duke turn back to Joy. His look softened a bit. "We need to sign the register. Then I promise we shall leave as swiftly as possible."

"Your Grace?"

"Alec."

"Alec," she repeated, the sound of his name doing odd things to her insides. "Here." She handed him back the ring. "I am afraid I will lose this."

He stared at her outstretched hand; his ring was so large it took up a good portion of her palm. He took it and slid it on his finger. "I shall see about another ring as soon as possible."

"I don't need one if—"

"You are the duchess of Belmore. You will wear a ring befitting your station." He took her elbow and led her toward the altar. She had hoped he would give her a ring; it would serve as a reminder that this wasn't a dream. A ring was real, something she could touch and hold, something that would show the world they were married.

They went up the steps to the altar and toward the right, near the pulpit, where a cleric stood with pen and ink. He wrote something, then turned the vellum book toward them. Joy stared at the entry:

His Grace, Alec Gerald David John James Mark Castlemaine, duke of Belmore, of the Belmore Parish, and Joyous Fiona MacQuarrie of Dervaig, Scotland, a Protestant, were married in Cropsey Chapel by license this day, the thirtieth of December in the year 1813

by me, Jonathan Potsworth, vicar

This marriage was solemnized between us:

The cleric handed the pen to the duke. He signed the register, then dipped the pen in the ink and handed it to Joy. Her hand was shaking like a birch branch in the wind. She was almost tempted to grab her wrist with her other hand so she could sign legibly. She took a deep breath and signed her name. Then her husband handed the pen to his friends to witness. The viscount signed and turned to congratulate the duke and gallantly wish Joy the best. She liked this man. Nervous and fidgety as he was, he had kind eyes and a sincere smile.

"Please, Your Grace, call me Neil. I'm sure we will be fast friends."

"Thank you, my lord. Neil it will be, but you must call me Joy."

"Surely a name selected by the gods, and very appropriate." He kissed her hand and smiled.

Meanwhile, the earl was weaving over the book. "Hold the bloody thing still, Seymour."

The three turned and looked at the earl. She hadn't thought it was possible, but he was even drunker now than he had been earlier. Neil grabbed his friend's shoulder and steadied him, being careful not to apply pressure to the slung arm. The earl rested the sling on the register lectern and scratched a drunken scrawl across half the page, sideways.

He straightened his back, teetered a bit, then gave her a lascivious leer while rocking slightly. "I'm Richard, and I would like to kiss more than your hand."

Alec's arm tensed and she glanced down at his hand. It was in a white fist. She looked up. His face had not changed, did not look the least concerned. His fist told her that his face lied.

A second later Richard's eyes rolled back and he slumped against a column. The only thing holding him upright was the viscount.

"Best get him to a room before he passes out. Not up to snuff, passing out in a church." He tugged on the earl's good arm.

"Need a drink." Richard rummaged through his coat with his good hand. "Where's m' brandy?"

"Gone." Neil helped him walk the few steps to the side door.

"Wait." Richard dug his heels into the carpet. "Belmore can't abandon us here." He pulled his arm out of Neil's grip and turned back, giving them an insolent grin. "What would people think?"

"He's made arrangements to rent Hobson's horses," Neil told him. "We'll ride back to London in the morning." He turned to Joy. "Have a pleasant wedding trip, Your Grace. This is destiny, you know. The fates chose you, and now everything is right." He looked at the duke. "Even if Belmore here refuses to believe it."

"I need a bloody drink!"

"Stifle it, Downe. You are in a church for God's sake."

"I don't believe in God. The only good thing he ever

created was brandy!" He jerked his arm away from the viscount.

Neil grabbed him again and helped him walk out of the church.

"Is he always like that?" Joy asked.

Alec looked at her, then glanced back at the door. "Of late. He didn't used to be. People change." He grasped her arm. "The carriage is waiting."

"Wait, please. Where is Beezle?" Joy looked around, frantic.

"Henson has him."

"Your footman?"

"Our footman."

They walked through the doors and directly to the carriage where Henson immediately opened the door and pulled down the carriage steps. Beezle clung to his back and was happily chewing away on the footman's queue.

"Your Grace," he said, bowing as if it was perfectly normal for him to have an ermine weasel clinging to him like a leech.

Joy plucked Beezle off his back. "Thank you, Henson, for taking care of him."

"Certainly, Your Grace."

Joy glanced at the footman. His hair hung loose outside the ribbon that had previously tied back his queue. She looked at her familiar. He was sleeping in her arms, innocently sleeping. Joy dismissed it, knowing how fascinated her familiar was with hair, and let the servant help her inside. Her husband barked a few orders while she settled Beezle and herself onto the seat. The duke joined them, and a few minutes later they were off.

Four long and relatively silent hours later the carriage slowed and turned, then ambled through a guarded gate and down a long drive flanked by majestic old elms and pollard trees. Joy watched with silent curiosity as they passed massive tree after massive tree.

She had studied her husband for the last silent hour, not daring to again ask if they were almost there—he had seemed irritated after the sixth time—and wondering how close they actually were to Belmore Park. To her delight he had volunteered the information as they passed through the last quaint little village. Belmore Park was right outside this village, he'd said.

She had pressed her nose to the cold window to watch the timbered houses and rustic high-roofed thatched cottages pass by. She'd caught a glimpse of a wee burn edged with hazel trees. They'd trotted past a tall white kirk high on a hill with a spreading hawthorn tree perched nearby. Black smoke had billowed into the winter sky from an open smithy where a cumbersome ancient wagon stood in disrepair behind an old and weather-stained wall. Village dogs had barked a loud, continuous harangue when they passed the village green where a group of curious children stopped playing to point and gaze in awe at the carriage.

It had been nearly an hour since they left the village children to resume their game of blindman's buff in the common, and every minute since had seemed an eternity, especially since she was so terribly eager to see her new home.

Still peering out the window, she spotted what appeared to be glassy water past the tall border of pollard trees. She moved her head, eager to get a better look, but the carriage passed a low wall, then turned through a smaller set of iron gates decorated with the ducal crest. A heartbeat later a huge home loomed before her gawking eyes.

They halted in front of a tall columned portico with cream-colored limestone steps and thick carved stone balustrades fanning outward from the steps like welcoming arms. There was a quick fluttering flash of someone in the beveled-glass sidelights that framed the enormous polished walnut doors. They opened, and a rush of green and gold liveried footmen came down the steps.

Met with all the pomp and circumstance awarded to a conquering monarch, she thought, watching as the footmen lined up like guardsmen on either side of the steps. Joy expected them to break out the trumpets at any second. Instead, the carriage door opened and her husband, the laird of the manor, descended, then turned to help her down. She placed her hand in his and paused. Just the touch of his hand could turn her heart over.

"This is our home, Belmore Park." There was pride in his voice, the first emotion she sensed that he did not try to hide.

She looked up and her mouth fell open. Completely awestruck she craned her head back to take in all of the palatial glory of her new home.

It was three stories tall and completely made of pale stone with what appeared to be near a hundred huge pillastered leaded-glass windows. Duart Castle also had glass, but nothing like this, and the castle windows were small, little more than old arrow slits in the tower rooms where she had lived. The glass, as rustic and old as the castle itself, was thick and wavy and filmed with the salt of the sea. But here there was so much leaded crystalline glass that at first glance the windows looked like diamonds set in pale stone. She wondered how this house would look in spring with the sun shining on all that glass. It would be almost like a magic spell—a thousand stars sparkling in the light of day.

"This is incredible." Her eager eyes scanned the facade and the four three-story angular bays that stood out, giving an impression of depth.

"It was built by Sir John Thynne, after the original house burned down. See the balustrade along the roof?"

Joy followed his hand to the roofline of the house where an ornamental railing bordered the flat roof.

"And those domed buildings and chimneys?"

Her eyes were drawn to the pepperpot domes, heraldic beasts, and exotic chimneys and strapwork that created the whimsical image of an ironwork ball dancing across the skyline. She counted fourteen elaborately designed chimneys with ornamental turrets with finial beasts prancing atop them. Fourteen of them visible from the front alone!

"The buildings with those domed roofs are small banqueting rooms that can be used for dinner parties."

"Dinner parties? On the roof?"

"The view is quite pleasing."

Dumbfounded, she just stared at him. After a second she looked back up at the roof. Quite pleasing? She would have wagered she could see clear to Scotland from that roof.

He led her up the steps, past the stiff footmen who lined it, and into the entry. Her stomach knotted at the sight that greeted her. Her astonished gaze followed the chessboard-marble floor to the staircase, then up and up to a gallery with an intricately worked brass banister. Decorative plastered columns rose . . . and rose and rose . . . upward to a painted ceiling surrounded by more plasterwork and tall glass windows.

"It's painted."

"Hmm?"

"The dome in the ceiling. It looks like an oil painting."

The duke followed her look. "Oh, that? It's a fresco. Louis Laguerre did them. They are scenes from the life of Julius Caesar."

"Oh, that?" he had said. As in, "Oh, that old thing?"

"The staff is waiting."

She turned and looked behind her toward the center of the great hall, where a large number of servants—close to a hundred of them, she surmised—waited to pay homage to the laird, her new husband. Panicked, she looked at him. He seemed completely oblivious to the fact that he was leading her over to meet a hundred people.

She, who couldn't even remember an incantation, was expected to remember their names? Such folly she had gotten herself into this time—and without even using her magic. She whispered, "Oh, my goodness."

He paused and looked at her, his expression puzzled. "Is something wrong?"

"How will I remember their names?"

"Their names?" He gave the eternal line a cursory glance. "They are servants. They are employed by me. You needn't know their names."

"Of course I do."

"Why?"

"They are people."

"Of course they're people, but they're servants first and foremost."

"Oh, I see," she said, even though she didn't see at all. It seemed heartless to think of them as servants instead of people. She changed tack, hoping he'd see her point. "Were they born into their positions here?"

"As a matter of fact, some of them were. It is an honor to be employed by the duke of Belmore. They are paid well and have the prestige of saying they work at Belmore."

"What am I supposed to say if I need to speak to one of them? Hallo, you? Servant?" Then she couldn't help muttering, "Slave?"

"Do not be ridiculous," he snapped. "Just ask their names and tell them what to do."

She took a deep breath and bit her lip. Now she'd gone and angered him. She sighed and followed her stiff-backed husband to the head of the line. While still out of hearing distance, she grabbed his arm. "Alec?"

"What?"

"Is part of my duty as a duchess . . . is it, I mean, do I have to run this whole house?"

"There is a housekeeper, Mrs. Watley. She and Townsend, the butler, run the household."

Joy's sigh of relief was so loud it could have echoed in the frescoed scenes of Julius Caesar.

"Come along, you shall meet Watley and Townsend first. They are at their places of honor at the front of the line."

Her relief was short-lived. There was a rigid protocol attached to this meeting, and Joy was certain it was a ritual performed generation after generation.

"May I present my wife, Her Grace the duchess of Belmore. This is Mrs. Watley."

Mrs. Watley looked as if she needed some prunes. Her shoulders went military straight. Her lips grew thinner, a feat Joy would have wagered was impossible, and she looked down at the new duchess—she was at least six feet tall—as if she found her severely lacking.

"And Townsend."

The butler resembled a peer—an earl or a marquess, perhaps. He had distinguished-looking white hair and patrician features and wore dark clothing and a white shirt as crisp as if he had dressed with the help of an expert valet. He nodded once, his brown eyes meeting hers only briefly before he turned his stare back to somewhere over her right shoulder.

Slowly they made their way along the lines, with either the butler or the housekeeper introducing each servant to Belmore's new duchess. Joy tried to find some distinguishing feature in each one to help her remember who the servant was. The only one she knew she would remember was a short, dark-haired young girl whose name was Polly and who had the most delightful and friendly smile of anyone. She and the cook were the only ones who had ventured anything resembling a smile.

"Mrs. Watley will take you to your rooms, where you can rest until dinner." With his order given, Alec turned and started to walk away.

"Alec?"

He stopped and turned.

"Where are you going?"

From his face one would have thought she had asked for his blood, every last drop. After a thoughtful moment he deigned to explain. "I need to meet with my steward. I've been in London for two months, and my business here has been too long neglected."

"Oh." Feeling unsure of herself and out of place, she watched her new husband turn and leave, abandoning her into the clutches of dour Mrs. Watley.

"If Your Grace will follow me, I will show you to your rooms." The woman's order was given with the same curt expectation of obedience used by Alec, a tone that indicated one should not dare to do anything but comply.

With one wee shrug she followed the woman up the stairs, watching the way Mrs. Watley's torso stayed as straight as a caber. She was dressed in crisp black bombazine, tightly belted, with a smidgen of a white lace handkerchief peeking out from the side of the wide black belt. A housekeeper's badge—silver rings of keys at her waist—jangled and jingled with each precise step in the hallowed stairwells of Joy's opulent new home.

Reminded of sleigh bells and chimes and fairy tunes, Joy picked up her skirts and her step and bobbed her head in time to those musical keys, mentally humming a merry ballad while her eager eyes absorbed every luxurious detail surrounding her. On the left an arched coffer served as a special place for an ancient Oriental vase. On the right stood a green and gold porcelain urn as big as Lady Eugenia was small.

They crossed a seemingly endless gallery filled with priceless oil portraits of what must have been every Castlemaine born to this earth. Three more turns, two more corridors, and five or so twists, and they finally reached a long double-width hallway with several lavishly gilded doors. Continuing down the hall she looked up at the high molded-plaster ceiling half expecting to see another fresco.

There was none. The design in the plasterwork, however, did match that of the carpet, exactly. Every so often she caught a glimpse of the ducal crest worked into the pattern—a Belmore ceiling and a Belmore carpet.

Mrs. Watley stopped abruptly, her bombazine skirts rustling like leaves in the summer wind. She unhooked one of the five large key rings, found the right key with little thought, and unlocked the door.

"Your rooms, Your Grace."

Joy stepped inside a massive room lined with carved and inlaid paneling edged in gold leaf. Trying not to gape, she untied her bonnet and let it dangle from her fingers. It was all she could do not to ask Mrs. Watley to pinch her awake. This couldn't be real.

A beautiful rosewood desk with a matching chair stood behind the wing chairs by the fireplace. Decorated with Roman gods carved into rose marble, the fireplace took up half a wall. Everything in the room was rose and gold, even the bed, with its tall canopy draped in matching rose and gold silk brocade and tied back with heavy silken tassels. Her warm gaze followed the lines of the high bed, upward, past its canopy to the ceiling.

It was painted.

"This is the dressing room." Mrs. Watley pressed a panel in the wall, and the door swung open to reveal a room filled with beveled mirrors. "Beyond that is the bath."

Joy tossed her hat onto a small tapestry chair and followed her, removing her gloves as she walked across the marble floor of the dressing room and peeked around a mirrored corner. Her gloves fell to the floor unnoticed. The entire room was made of a soft rose-colored marble—the floors, the walls, the sinks, and the tub, which was sunken like a Roman pool into the floor, and one mirrored wall was framed by rose silk draperies with hand-painted gold roses.

Mrs. Watley's heels clicked across the marble floor and, with a gesture akin to holding a dead rat, opened another door. Her thin face was as hard as that marble. "This is the water closet. It's a Bramah." The door whipped shut before Joy could get even one wee glimpse of the room.

She marched back into the bedchamber. Joy assumed she was to follow. The housekeeper turned and looked down at her. "I'll send someone up with your things, Your Grace, and a maid will be here shortly to help you bathe." She flicked a watch pin up from her chest. "Dinner is served at nine, always. You have several hours until then. Your Grace might wish to rest."

Joy blinked once in surprise, then realized she was twenty-one, a duchess who was being Your Graced to death, and she had just been told to take a nap.

"Does Your Grace need anything else?"

Joy shook her head.

"Very well." The housekeeper opened the door and paused. "His Grace likes dinner on time. Precisely at nine o'clock. A Belmore tradition." And with that command—or warning, Joy wasn't sure which—she closed the door.

Joy exhaled and spun around and around in the center of the room, her eager eyes taking in every impressive detail. Dizzy with excitement, she collapsed on the bed in a puff of plump down and smoothed her hands over the lovely brocade coverlet, feeling every silken stitch. Very carefully she sat up on the edge of the bed, letting her feet dangle near the velvet footstool, and then she bounced a couple of times to test the bed's deep softness.

"Oh, my goodness," she whispered, followed by a giggle.

She ran one hand over the gilded headboard and touched its rose velvet padding, and her other hand sank into a down pillow so soft and plump that it was like touching a cloud.

A knock sounded, and she shot off the bed as if stuck with a brooch, brushing her skirts down before she stood stiffly, small shoulders back, chin raised and slightly cocked—it was her duchess pose—and said in a deep voice, "Come in." Unfortunately her voice cracked, completely ruining her attempt to sound regal.

In walked Henson, with Beezle attached to his back again. "Your pet, Your Grace."

She rushed over to the doorway and plucked her familiar off the poor man. Henson's queue was once again in disarray, only this time the gold ribbon had been chewed until it was completely frayed. She glanced down at Beezle, lying in her arms and happily chomping away, a trail of golden thread hanging like wet whiskers from his mouth.

"Thank you, Henson." She grabbed the threads and tried to pull them from Beezle's mouth. They kept coming and coming, and she wrapped them around her hand over and over until finally she yanked so hard that he bared his teeth, showing the wad of ribbon in his mouth. After a brief tug-of-war she gave up and set him down on the thick rug. He waddled over to a rose velvet chaise longue, climbed up, and chewed and chewed and chewed before he swallowed the wad of ribbon with a gulp. He plopped his pointed snout on his black-tipped paws. His tiny ears twitched and he raised his head and belched twice. Then his brown eyes grew lazy and drifted closed. The next thing Joy knew, he was wheezing.

"Your Grace's maid." Henson stepped aside, and in scurried a nervous Polly, who tried to curtsy with her arms full of clothing and bite back her bright smile at the same time. She didn't quite accomplish either and dumped the clothing onto the floor, a wide smile creasing her rosy English cheeks. With a tsk-tsk, Henson shut the door after him.

"Mrs. Watley said I am to be Your Grace's maid until Your Grace can hire someone more experienced and suited to Your Grace." Polly bent to pick up a dressing gown and some other scanty garment, set them on a chaise longue and turned back to Joy. The maid's hands, now clasped in front of her, quivered with nervousness.

Joy stared at the top of Polly's bowed head. "Have you been a lady's maid before?"

The girl straightened up, no longer smiling. She was apparently trying hard to look as serious and dismal as Mrs. Watley. "I've helped when there's been guests at Belmore, and me aunt was lady's maid to His Grace's mum, Your Grace."

"I'd like you to do something for me, Polly."

"Yes, Your Grace?" Polly worried her lower lip.

"Will you stop Your Gracing me, please? At least when we're alone?"

That bright smile came back, bonfire bright. "Yes, ma'am."

Joy grinned back. "Thank you. And I won't be needing someone with more experience. You've more experience than I—I've never had a maid before."

"Never?" Polly's blue eyes grew as wide as butter scones. "But you're a duchess!"

Joy laughed. "I don't know how to be a duchess, Polly. I've never even met one before."

"Well, I can teach you some, ma'am." Polly suddenly stood a bit taller. "A duchess always stands straight"—she patted her chin—"with her head raised very high, and then looks down the length of her noble nose." The maid's eyes crossed as she tried to demonstrate.

Joy laughed.

Polly uncrossed her eyes and gave Joy a wide grin. As suddenly as it appeared, she tried to bite it back.

"Please don't," Joy said.

"What, ma'am?"

"Hide your smile."

Polly breathed a relieved sigh. "Oh, ma'am, thank you. Mrs. Watley's forever pinnin' me 'bout smilin'. She says I look like the village idiot, a-grinnin' and laughin' like my wits took to Bath for a holiday."

Joy laughed again.

"She says for hundreds of years Belmore servants have been"—Polly raised her chin in a haughty manner, just like Mrs. Watley, and her voice became clipped and authoritative—"dignified. She said I should be like my aunt."

"Is your aunt dignified?"

"No."

"Then I take it your aunt doesn't smile."

"No, ma'am, she doesn't, but not because she's proper or anything. She lost her front teeth when she was twelve and hasn't smiled since." Polly grinned at her.

"I don't blame her, do you?"

"No, ma'am," Polly said on a giggle, then, as if she'd suddenly realized with whom she was laughing, she grew solemn. "Would you be wantin' a bath? I can take your clothes and clean them. His Grace told Mrs. Watley that your things had been stolen. How awful, ma'am. Was it highwaymen?"

Joy could feel her blush rise. "No."

"Oh, I'm so relieved, ma'am. Can you imagine being set upon by highwaymen? I read this book about some highwaymen who held up a poor lady and stole all her things and then kidnapped her for ransom. An' the things they tried to do to her, ma'am, ohhhh, it was just horrible! That is until the leader of the highwaymen rode in on his big black stallion and took her under his protection. Then they fell in love and married 'cause he was truly an earl who had been wrongly accused of killing his father. That part was so romantic."

"What was this book?"

"Something Cook was reading."

"Sounds interesting."

"It was." Polly looked uneasy for a moment, her eyes shifting left, then right, and she leaned very close to Joy and whispered. "It was a *romantic* novel."

"Oh. I see." Joy paused, then asked, "Is that bad?"

"Oh, no! Some people say they're drivel, but I think they've never read one and don't know what they're talking about, ma'am. The stories are more delicious than . . . than"—the maid looked thoughtful, and then her eyes lit up—"than clotted cream and fresh strawberries."

"I'd love to read that book. Does the cook still have it?"

"I suppose so, ma'am. I'll try to get it for you. But if I can't, then I have three more. And Cook is now reading one about a duke."

"I think I'd like that one." Joy grinned, and so did Polly; then they both started laughing.

After a minute Polly picked up the clothing she'd brought in and held it out. "The dressmaker will be here tomorrow, but Mrs. Watley had me bring these up for you." She held out a dressing gown and nightdress. "She's looking for something for you to wear to dinner."

Joy knew she could probably conjure up something with a semblance of competence—zapping up clothing was one of her strong points. But how would she explain its miraculous appearance? She glanced at the dress she wore. "If you could clean this dress, I could wear it to dinner."

"Oh, no, ma'am. Dinner is always formal. There's enough stuff in the storage rooms to clothe the whole of Wiltshire. Besides, this being your wedding night, and all . . ." Polly blushed and gave her a shy look, then disappeared into the dressing room.

Joy followed into the dressing room, slipping her clothing off as she walked, her mind on the maid's words. She hadn't thought of tonight. She'd been too worried about being a duchess and too excited about seeing her new home.

Tonight was her wedding night with Alec. The thought brought her skin to gooseflesh, and she was suddenly chilled. Slipping into the dressing gown, she thought about what a wedding night entailed. It only took about a minute before she realized that Alec would most likely kiss her again. She grinned, then giggled, then hugged her arms and closed her dreamy eyes.

If there was one thing that her mind's eye pictured as clear as Belmore's leaded-glass windows it was the image of kissing her husband again, being held in his arms, tasting him and feeling his mouth trail over her skin, his voice in her ear, saying, "Marry me, Scottish. . . . Marry me. . . ."

And now they were married. Husband and wife. Duke and duchess. Laird and lady. Her dreamy eyes flew open. Kissing wasn't the only thing that married couples did, if what her aunt had told her when she was twelve was true. Joy's cheeks grew hot. He would make love to her.

Make love. Such a strange term. Did the act mean that the emotion was there, too? She hoped so, hoped it would grow if she lovingly tended it. She wanted to be loved, to have Alec feel about her the way she felt every time she was near him. She wanted him to need to kiss her as badly as she wanted him to. She wanted to mean something to him, to fill him with magic and love and smiles so he didn't have to hide.

Polly walked back into the room. "I've started your bath, ma'am."

"Oh, fine."

"I'll go clean these things and fetch the gown for dinner." Polly picked up Joy's clothing. "Do you need anything else, ma'am?"

"No. Thank you."

The maid shut the door behind her, and Joy started to let her robe fall away, but her eyes caught the reflection of that other door in the mirror.

What was a Bramah? She tightened the belt on the robe and walked over to the door. The handle, like all the door handles she'd noticed so far, was stamped with the ducal crest. She opened the door and stared into the little room.

There was a low seat, the purpose of which was obvious, but it sat atop a porcelain bowl painted with purple irises and pink roses and a menagerie of birds. Joy peered down it, expecting to see the usual dark hole like that of the old garderobe at Duart Castle. But this bowl contained a small amount of water.

Imagine that! Somewhat puzzled, she looked upward, following a brass pipe to another painted container above her head. It had a brass handle, the only one she'd seen without a crest, extending down, just waiting to be pulled.

So she did.

"Oh, my goodness!"

Water rushed into the bowl with the whirling sound of crashing waves. It swirled and rushed and then disappeared down the hole with a banshee wail. A moment later the room was silent.

Joy stared at the thing, then covered her mouth with her hand and giggled. She pulled the handle again, watching in pure amazement at the workings of the Bramah.

Ten minutes and twelve gurgling flushes later she let the robe fall to the marble floor of the bath and stepped into the deep tub. The water was warm and toasty and like sitting in heaven. Two huge brass handles shaped like dolphins and a matching faucet were mounted in the wall above the tub. She turned one, and cold water spilled from the dolphin's mouth. She turned the second, and hot water gushed out. Adjusting both handles so the water was perfectly warm, she took the pins out of her hair and let the water pour over her head.

Never in her wildest and most fanciful dreams had she imagined anything as divine as this. After a few minutes of decadent splashing, she lay back, completely relaxed, and closed her eyes, letting the warm water lap at her temples, jaw, and chin, imagining it was Alec's lips. Two relaxing, peaceful, and romantic minutes later her green eyes shot open and she sat up in the tub, suddenly remembering something else about tonight. Something she had to do.

Tonight was her Armageddon, and it had nothing to do with kisses or loving or intimate things. She had to tell him she was a witch. The prospect was more frightening than a malediction. This was her wedding night—the most exciting and wonderful time of any girl's life—but for Joy it was also a time for revelation. As much as she dreaded it, she knew she must tell Alec exactly what she was, before they were intimate. She had to give him an out, and she hoped with all the optimism in her heart that he would not take that out.

She'd married him because she wanted to be his wife, to be loved by him, to fill the hollows she'd seen in him. He needed her so badly even if he didn't realize it. But she had to be honest with him now. She couldn't start this marriage out with a lie.

Her hand sank into the steamy water and grabbed a piece of perfumed soap stamped with the Belmore crest. She vigorously soaped up her arms and neck, scrubbing and scouring as if she could wash away what she was, so that she wouldn't have to face the task ahead of her and take the chance of failing again.

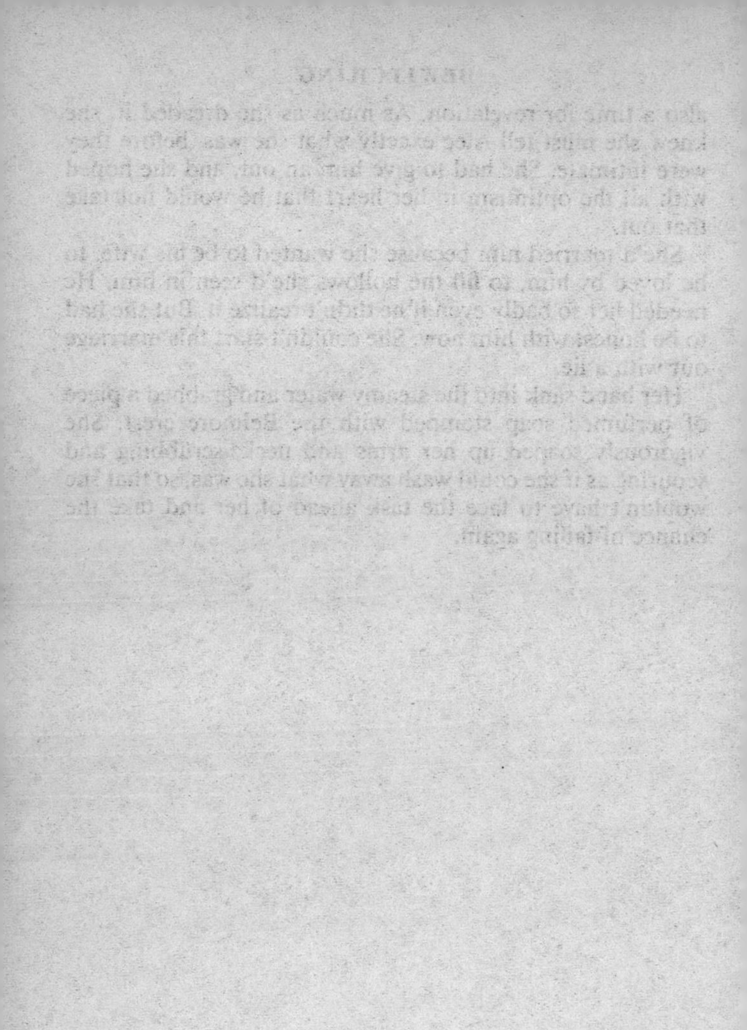

The
Havoc

**Thou art wedded to calamity.**

*Romeo and Juliet,* William Shakespeare

# Chapter 8

Joy was late. She ran down yet another never-ending hallway and heard a clock chime a quarter past the hour. Everywhere she went, she found door after gilded door and hallway after long, elegant hallway. According to Polly the dining room was on the main floor, so Joy had left her room in what she guessed was plenty of time. Polly had said to make three rights and then a left and a right and she'd see the staircase. But Joy must have taken a wrong turn, because she'd been rambling and wandering through hallways and galleries, and although she'd tried to retrace her steps, she was now hopelessly lost.

"At least a hundred servants in this place and I haven't run into a single one," she told a huge portrait of some sour-faced Castlemaine. "Where *is* everyone?" The portrait was about as talkative as her husband. She rounded the corner and stared at yet another long, empty corridor.

Another cruel clock chimed. Now she was a half hour late. Beginning to panic, she lifted up the heavy silk skirts on the outdated but exquisite rose and gold silk gown Polly had brought her and ran like a heather hellion toward the next hallway. She looked in both directions. She could turn left or right, and both were equally long corridors.

"His Grace likes dinner on time," Mrs. Watley had said. "Precisely at nine o'clock. A Belmore tradition."

"Oh, my goodness!" Her hands clenched the gown. "Why would anyone want to live in a house this big?"

She could just see Alec's face, then the image changed to that of Mrs. Watley, her arms crossed over her black bombazine-covered crow's chest, her foot tapping with impatience and her eyes glaring down at Joy. She was late, late, late, and Joy was sure that was tantamount to stealing the Belmore silver.

But, more important, being late was not a good way to start her marriage, especially when she needed to prepare her husband for her confession. Butter him up, so to speak. She stared at the clock. Its hands did not lie. The time for buttering up was past, way past. She chewed on her lower lip.

The hands of a clock? An idea began to glimmer in Joy's eyes. She closed them for a full minute of concentration, took a deep breath, pointed at the clock, and chanted, "Oh, please listen to my rhyme. Turn back the time on every clock in this home of mine!"

She slowly moved her pointed finger and the hands on the clock followed suit until it was two minutes to nine. She smiled. It had worked! Feeling incredibly proud of herself, she looked down both hallways and decided it was time for a bit more magic.

Raising her chin and hands high in the air, she closed her eyes, trying to picture a dining room. Unable to imagine what Belmore's dining room would look like, she concentrated on the food—roasted chickens and ducklings, plump roasts of beef and fresh breads, fruits and jellies and platters of delicacies so delightful that her stomach rumbled with hunger. "Oh, magic come and take me away," she chanted, "to the room where Belmore's food lay!"

An instant later she opened her eyes. Haunches of meat and plucked birds wrapped in protective salted cloth hung on hooks above her head.

This was not the dining room.

A sharp pang of ice cold air hit her. Shivering, she leaned one hand against what she thought was a wall and jerked it back.

She was in the ice house. She blinked several times in confusion. The walls were blocks of ice beneath the sacking.

Slowly she found her way to a wide plank door a few feet away. Something caught in her hair. She glanced up and then with a disgusted flick of her hand pushed a dangling chicken head out of the way before opening the door.

She stepped into another dark, dank room, and promptly tripped over a lumpy sack of onions, landing on an equally lumpy mound of potatoes. Attempting to scramble to her knees, she clutched some bound stalks of asparagus, which snapped off with a fresh pop. She dropped the stalks and managed to get to her knees, only to find herself staring at a stack of rugged-looking rutabagas. Behind them was a shelf filled to capacity with jars of orange kumquats, peaches, and marmalade, red berry jellies and deep dark jams. The jars and containers of food went on and on, stacked on labeled shelves that appeared to hold enough to feed the world. The room smelled of the sea, of raw fish, and of vegetables still coated in fresh earth.

Now she was in the pantry.

But, she thought, at least I'm on the right floor.

The door was slightly ajar and she could hear the bustle of the busy kitchen that lay beyond—the sizzle of food cooking, the clatter of bowls, the clink of crockery, and the voices of an army of servants hard at work. No wonder I couldn't find anyone, she thought. Sounds like they're all out there.

Joy struggled to her feet, brushing her hands together to rid them of asparagus tips and dirt. At least I can ask someone for directions, she thought, stepping over another bulky sack and sidestepping a barrel of salted fish so she could open the door the rest of the way. She stepped into the room and stopped.

The smells were heavenly. The rich mouth-watering scent of beef roasting on a spit mixed with that of garlic and lamb and mint. The sharp tang of cinnamon and nutmeg assailed her senses, and her stomach rumbled a protest against its empty state. Joy watched, completely unnoticed, while a dinner the likes of which she had never seen was created of the same stuff that hung so unappealingly in the pantry.

A woman stood about five feet away, kneading some dough at a large worktable.

"Excuse me," Joy said.

The woman glanced over her shoulder, then froze, except for her eyes, which nearly popped out of her head. She spun around, dough in hands, and sank into a deep curtsy. "Your Grace!"

Within about three seconds the room was silent except for the random pop and sizzle of cooking meat. Every eye in the room was stunned and on Joy.

"I seem to be a wee bit lost, and I—"

An oversized set of double doors swung open, hitting the kitchen walls with a bang. The usually reserved Henson blustered into the room. "All hell's broken loose out there!" he announced. "They've lost the new duchess!" He scanned the kitchen where every servant was looking at one solitary spot in the room. His eyes followed theirs.

Joy raised her fingers and gave him a tentative and sheepish little wave.

"Your Grace!"

Joy found herself staring at his bent head. "I'm afraid I've been lost. Would you show me to the dining room, please?"

He straightened, once again the epitome of the stiff English servant, his shoulders back, chin raised, voice controlled. "Of course. If Your Grace will follow me . . ."

Joy followed him across the silent kitchen, feeling every eye on her as she did so. A minute or so later at the end of a long corridor, Henson opened another set of double doors and announced, "Her Grace, the duchess of Belmore."

She took a deep, fortifying breath, raised her chin Watley-high, and walked into the room, where a herd of liveried footmen, Townsend, and Mrs. Watley herself were speaking to the duke. They fell silent and turned toward her, their faces all wearing the same look of disapproval.

They parted like the Red Sea. Alec stood there, handsome and broad-shouldered, dressed all in black except for a stark white cravat. His presence was so commanding. He was water to her thirsty eyes. Then she made the mistake of looking at his face—and nearly drowned. His expression was hard and disapproving.

Joy's heart felt as if it were going down for the third time.

The clock chose that exact moment to chime the quarter hour—so much for her witchcraft—and Alec frowned, glancing at the ormolu clock on the fireplace mantel. He gave it a brief look of annoyance. "That clock is broken. Have it fixed."

"Yes, Your Grace." Mrs. Watley plucked the clock off the mantel, tucked it under one lanky arm, and moved toward the doors.

The duke turned back to Joy. "You're late."

"I was lost."

Mrs. Watley passed by, still shaking her head in reproof and Joy thought she heard her mutter something about desecrating Belmore tradition.

Alec walked toward her. He offered her his stiff arm, but she would have given the world for one wee smile of reassurance.

"In the future, I will send Henson to show you the way."

She couldn't even look him in the eye. She was afraid to, so she chewed her lip instead.

After a tense minute in which she could feel him staring down at her, he added softly, "I suppose, Scottish, that this seems a cavernous old place."

He had made an excuse for her. She released the breath she'd held in her tight throat, and smiled up at him. She was forgiven.

Again his features changed into that slightly confused look. It was as if no one had ever smiled at him before and so he didn't know how to react. He turned away, his face once again stern and his eyes anywhere but on her. Look back, she thought, look back so I can chip away at that wall of ice. But he didn't.

"You will learn your way around in time." He led her toward the table. "A very short time, I hope."

Another command, to which she could only nod sadly, feeling as if she had missed an opportunity. He pulled out a chair for her at the end of a monstrous rosewood dining table that looked as if it could comfortably seat every single servant at Belmore. She sat and scooted forward, expecting him to take the chair next to her. She could not hide her astonishment when he walked down the full length of the table and sat at the opposite end.

It was what the Scots called "bellowing distance" away.

With one wave of his hand—at least she thought it was a wave, although it was hard to tell from this great distance without a spyglass—an army of footmen moved to a long buffet and began to serve the first course. Served on the heaviest, most exquisitely molded silver platters she had ever seen, the dinner went on and on, each cover more elaborate than the last—roast duckling in a silver serving dish with handles shaped like mallards in flight, a leg of lamb in a dish shaped like a sheep's head with silver curved-horn handles, asparagus in lemon sauce with sliced chestnuts on a silver plate with a raised edge of molded spring vegetables. Every exquisite serving piece matched the food that it held.

Of the seven forks, three knives, and four spoons at her place setting, only one—a small spoon placed in front of the creamy bone china plate with its gold Belmore crest design —did not have its own ducal crest stamped into its handle. It wasn't stamped because the crest design—a pair of falcons—was the handle.

Joy stared at all the silverware, then looked at her plate. Now, which utensil was she supposed to use? After a few long and indecisive minutes, Henson's gloved hand surreptitiously handed her the first fork on the left.

"Thank you," she whispered, and then began to eat. As each dish appeared, she managed with only a wee bit of prodding from Henson to move her way from left to right through the utensils.

An hour into the meal, Joy swallowed a piece of rare roast beef in a port wine sauce. The room was so unnervingly quiet that she was sure her swallow echoed like Gargantua's gulp in the high-beamed rafters of the room. She looked around while she silently chewed another piece of something her nervousness would not allow her to taste. She was uncomfortable and suddenly aware of feeling so, so alone.

Fifteen footmen stood along the walls when they weren't

catering to her or Alec. Townsend, Henson, and the duke were there, too, and yet she felt isolated in this strange new place. Nothing was familiar. Everything was beautiful, but it seemed cold and stiff because there was no enjoyment of it, no laughter, no music, nothing but the occasional clink of a serving spoon against a priceless piece of silver or the thin tinkle of a knife or fork on fragile china.

But she could enjoy the newness, the beauty, the excitement of this night. Her fanciful mind took over, and warm pleasure spread through her. Her eyes captured the bright gleam on a lovely crystal glass that shimmered in the light of a thousand candles. It was like drinking water from the stars. A huge silver candelabrum with two dozen golden tapers sat in the center of the table, and the light from the flames fairly danced on the crystal and silver tableware. Other candles glowed throughout the room, in sconces, chandeliers, and more candelabra, and the two mirrored walls that ran the length of the room caught the light a hundredfold and gave it depth and glow that made one forget that it was night and that the room had no windows.

Joy stared at the candelabrum on the table. If she moved it just a bit to the right she would be able to see Alec. With a quick glance at the servants lined up near the buffet, their eyes straight ahead like statues, she saw the coast was clear. She raised her napkin, pretending to pat her lips, but instead used it to cover her hand. With one snap and one point of her fingers, the candelabrum slid toward the edge of the table.

She hid her smile behind the fine linen napkin. Now she could see Alec instead of the candles. He raised a forkful of something to his mouth, but before he reached it he looked up, and his eyes locked with hers. There was something akin to magic whenever their eyes met. Even across a distance she could feel the spark deep inside her, almost as if she had swallowed a star.

The frightening and thrilling sensation seemed to glow within her. It grew stronger and stronger and was somehow so compelling that she could not have even used magic to break the spell, nor would she have wanted to. It was more powerful than witchcraft, more pulling than the sea tide, and held more warmth than the heat of the summer sun.

His lips closed over the fork and he slid it from his mouth, chewing slowly. His eyes were still on her, and she had the distinct feeling that the intensity he exuded had nothing to do with the quality of the food or his enjoyment of it. This was more than mere sustenance. His gaze moved to her mouth.

Slowly she lifted the water goblet, needing to feel the wet coolness of its contents. She sipped, never breaking eye contact. The water soothed her throat. Her lips parted, and her eyes locked on his mouth, the same mouth that had kissed her so intimately, had made her forget everything but the feel and taste of him.

Her breath and heartbeat sped up as if she had run for hours along the beach on Mull. He lowered his fork and lifted his wine goblet, then sipped at it as he had sipped at her mouth and neck. Time seemed to stop and become nothing but memories—his kiss, his taste, the fluttering of his breath in her hair.

An instant later the butler, Townsend, blocked her view by reaching across the table to move the candelabrum back into its proper place. Jarred into the present, she frowned at his back and waited until he had served her the next course. Then, while he served Alec, she twiddled her fingers again, grinning with happy satisfaction as the candles slid back to the edge of the table. Her magic was going well tonight.

Townsend turned around, his shoulders back, his eyes staring straight ahead. He took a few steps and paused, his attention suddenly back on the candelabrum. With a frown and an almost imperceptible shake of his head, he set the serving dish down and moved the candles back into her line of vision.

She started to twiddle again, but saw four footmen were removing dishes from the table. Figuring that patience was a virtue, she waited and waited and finally tried to catch a peek at her husband by bending down just a tad and leaning way over on the left arm of her chair. If she stretched her neck just so, she could see his dark hand on a fine crystal wine goblet. . . .

"Syllabub?"

She about jumped from her chair at the sound of Henson's voice. Flustered, she stared at her plate, waiting for Henson to point out which utensil.

"Syllabub?"

"God bless you," she whispered.

His throat cleared loudly.

*"Syllabub,* Your Grace?" He held out for her inspection a tiered glass dish with individual fruit- and cream-topped puddings.

"Oh. Aye."

He set a stemmed glass of pudding on the small plate in front of her, then handed her the spoon with the crest for a handle.

"Thank you," she whispered, and ate two bites before the coast was clear. She tried to look as if she held the stem of the pudding glass in her right hand, but she twiddled her fingers instead.

The candles slid smoothly to the table edge, and she had a perfect view once again. But it took Townsend only about a minute to move the thing back.

She twiddled again before he had taken a step. He turned back, shook his white head and put the candelabrum back. She waited until his back was turned, then moved it again. He spun around and moved it back, pulling a bit on the linen tablecloth as if he thought it was slipping.

Time to outsmart him, she decided and waited, anticipation building, until Townsend was by the buffet, supervising the removal of the courses. Every so often he'd look over his shoulder. Finally, his suspicion waned and he was busy with his duties.

Biting back a gleeful smile, she twiddled her fingers, excitedly anticipating her view.

The candelabrum moved with the speed of a lightning bolt—right off the edge of the table.

"Oh, my goodness!"

It was truly amazing how flammable that Aubusson carpet

was. It was also amazing how quickly smoke could fill a huge room with a thirty-foot ceiling, how fast fifteen footmen could douse a fire, and how quickly Alec could move. He was by her side before she could rise from her chair, and he pulled her to the doors while the footmen poured pails of water on the smoldering rug.

Despite all the smoke, the fire was out in a matter of minutes, and both of them stood in the doorway silent. She watched the smoke settle around the table like English fog. Now, staring at the black holes in the thick red carpet, she felt horribly guilty. She wondered what Alec was feeling. First she had violated Belmore tradition by arriving late, and then she'd destroyed a Belmore carpet. One tentative glance at his hard-angled face and it was obvious he felt little.

I'm sorry, she told him silently. I didn't mean to damage anything or to anger you.

He turned that emotionless face to look down at her. "You had best go on up to your room. Henson will show you the way. I shall be up shortly."

Her gaze lingered on his dark eyes, searching for something to dream of. She caught a flash of want, a need.

*What is it?*

He reached out and traced her mouth with a finger. *This and more.*

Her mouth went dry, and she quickly turned and left, her hands clammy, the skin beneath her breasts suddenly damp. He had given her a look that told her exactly what he wanted. Joy quietly followed Henson up the stairs, wondering what Alec would say when he found out what he had actually gotten.

What Alec was getting was a shave.

He sat in the shaving chair in his bath while Roberts, his valet, wiped the soap from his face. The clock in his bedchamber chimed the hour. A few minutes later the clock in the sitting room chimed the half hour. After that the clock in the dressing room chimed a quarter hour. Alec picked up his pocket watch and saw it read three-quarters past the hour.

"What the hell time is it?"

Roberts checked his own watch. "Eleven-forty, Your Grace."

"Have someone reset all the clocks."

The valet nodded and held up a floor-length green velvet robe piped in gold with the ducal crest embroidered in gold on the chest pocket. Alec slid into it, tied the belt, and left the dressing room, heading for the pipe tray and rosewood tobacco jar that sat on the deep green marble mantel in the sitting room. Alec packed his pipe, lit it, and stood near the fire, watching it burn as he smoked.

He was tense. The muscles in his shoulders and back were tight. He walked over to a walnut liquor cabinet and poured a brandy, then he sat down with his pipe and brandy before the fire. He could hear the Bramah in his bride's room, over and over.

After the fifth time he turned and stared at their common wall, frowning. Then he remembered that every time he'd looked at her during dinner she'd had the water goblet to her mouth, a mouth he found in his thoughts more often than he liked and a face that had played havoc with his digestion and had not left his mind for more than a few minutes that entire day. He couldn't remember ever having any woman remain on his mind once he'd left her presence, but she did.

He'd had a devil of a time concentrating all evening and was sure his estate manager thought he had lost his mind. In fact, he wondered if he had. He had never behaved rashly. He'd never done anything without forethought and purpose, until today. He took a long drink of the brandy.

He did not believe one word of that idiotic drivel Seymour spouted about predestination, but he still found the day's events unsettling. He had rationalized that marrying the girl was the easiest, least bothersome way to acquire a wife. After all, he had spent long months playing to the whims of society and courting Juliet, so she could lead him a merry dance and then run off with a soldier. But Scottish hadn't been given time to bolt. His hand tightened around the brandy glass.

Try as he might, he could barely call Juliet to mind. He kept seeing Scottish at the inn with all that long wavy brown hair. It had nearly swept the floor when she'd sat at the mirror. Of all the women he had known—and he'd had his share of mistresses, that being an expected part of a gentleman's life—he had never had a woman with hair that could literally be wrapped around them. In bed.

He took another drink and stared into the fire, which suddenly held the image of a pert little face with emerald green eyes, white skin, and full lips. . . .

"Does Your Grace need anything?"

"A mole."

"Beg pardon?"

"Hmm?"

"Your Grace?"

Alec looked at Roberts, then shook some sense into his usually rational head. "No. That will be all."

The bedchamber door closed with a click and at that same moment his wife's Bramah again echoed through the walls. His wife. He stared at the wall, then dismissed her actions to wedding night nerves and the fact that she was part Scot.

But she was also English—prime English. The Locksleys were one of the oldest and finest families in England, equal in stature to the Spencers. In fact, their title, like that of the Belmores, dated back to the twelfth century.

He set the pipe down, thinking about her family name. He told himself he had done suitably. He polished off the brandy and remembered her hair. He told himself he had done splendidly. He stood up and thought about her mouth. And he did not tell himself anything. He headed for the connecting door.

"I'm a witch."

No, that wasn't right. Joy locked her hands behind her back and paced the circumference of the small rug near the fireplace, pausing every so often to step over Beezle, who was asleep by the fire.

A pensive moment later she stopped, waving a hand in the air as if she were tossing off a line from Robert Burns. "I have a little secret."

Frowning, she shook her head. That wasn't right either.

More than likely her husband would think being a witch was a little bit bigger than a little secret. Drumming her fingers on the mantel, she stared into the tall mirror above it as if it could give her the answer. After a second or two she tightened the belt on her rose silk dressing gown with a determined tug and stepped back, placing her hands on her hips. She cocked her head and said to the mirror, "Alec, there's something you need to know about me."

She wrinkled her nose at her reflection. Too foreboding.

She spun around and paced some more, thoughtful and ending each stride with a dramatic turn. Finally she stopped in front of a wing chair. Perhaps she should be direct: "Alec, did you know that on a good day I can turn you into a toad?"

She sank down into the chair with a defeated sigh, muttering, "That would only work if he had a sense of humor."

Propping her chin on her hand, she hung over the arm of the chair and stared at Beezle. He snored just as the clock chimed two o'clock. She glanced up, thinking it should only have been about midnight. The delicate brass clock hands began to spin like weathercocks in a gale.

"Oh, stop it!" she said, her voice deep with disgust. The mainspring shot through the clock face with a dissonant clunk.

The fire suddenly flared up, the flames dancing as if bellowed. A door clicked shut. She turned.

Alec stood across the room.

She rose from the chair, but neither of them said a word. The fire crackled and snapped in the background.

Beezle wheezed.

Joy's heart pounded.

Alec's jaw tightened.

The clock clunked.

His gaze left hers, suddenly frowning. "What the devil is happening to all of the clocks in the house?" He crossed the room in three long strides and stood before the fireplace, glaring at the broken clock.

Joy moved back so the wing chair was between them. She gripped the wings tightly and said, "That's what I wish to talk to you about."

He turned. "The clocks? I didn't come in here to talk about clocks." He stepped toward her.

"Since you brought it up, I just thought—"

"Forget the clocks. This is our wedding night."

"I know, but there is something you should know."

"Take your hair down," he whispered, standing barely two feet away.

"I—"

"I said, take your hair down."

"Well, if you really want me to . . ."

"Scottish . . ."

At the sound of that name almost whispered in his deep warlock voice, she pulled the pins from her hair. He watched her, something akin to pleasure in his dark eyes. The distant thought crossed her mind that if she did as he asked, maybe he'd be more receptive to her confession, when she got up the nerve to spit it out.

Her hair tumbled down her back. It was so heavy that she usually threaded her fingers through it and shook her head to relieve the tingling in her scalp. She reached up, but Alec was there, behind her, and his hands closed over hers.

"Let me." His voice was right above her head and so close she could feel his breath against her hair.

Then she felt his hands running like gentle combs through her hair. He pulled her head back against his shoulder and stared down into her face. His mouth was but a breath away, one wee breath.

He kissed her. One hand held her hair while the other reached up to stroke the line of her neck and jaw with touches that were as soft and light as snowflakes. His tongue stroked her lips and she opened them, accepting his kiss with the same overwhelming need and pleasure with which her heart had accepted him as her love.

Some small bit of rationality said, *Tell him. Tell him. . . .*

But he turned her in his arms, his lips never leaving hers, and her arms slid up around his neck. His mouth moved slowly to kiss her cheeks, her jaw, then her ear.

"God, Scottish, how I want you." His hands closed over her behind, and he lifted her against him while his tongue delved into her ear.

"I need to tell you something," she whispered between hot, wonderful kisses.

"Tell me anything. Just let me touch you." His hand closed over her breast.

"I'm a witch."

# Chapter 9

"You can be anything you like as long as you're in bed." His mouth closed over hers and he walked her to the bed, knelt on it with one knee, and lowered her onto the coverlet, his arm still around her lower back so she was arched toward him. His lips left her mouth.

She pushed on his shoulders. "Alec, please . . . listen to me."

His mouth closed over her breast, pulling at it through the thin silk of her dressing gown.

She moaned, clasping his head to push it away, but she couldn't for the longest time. His free hand moved to her waist, then down her leg to pull up her gown. She felt his warm palm skim the tender inside of her thigh. She gasped and pushed his hand away.

He lifted his head, frowning.

She scrambled out from under him and knelt on the pillows, her breath coming in quick little pants. "I *am* a witch. A real witch."

His eyes narrowed. Still bent over the bed, his hands flat and pressing into the soft mattress, he did not take his gaze from hers. His eyes were dark and hot, his breath heaving with passion and anger. "This is not the time for games, wife."

"It is not a game," she whispered, her voice a bit choked. "I am truly a real, spell-casting Scottish witch."

"I have no doubt the Scot side of you thinks you are a witch."

"I'm not daft, Alec! It's true!" She could see the disbelief in his eyes. She looked around the room, searching for some way to convince him. Her gaze locked on the broken clock.

Raising one arm, she said, "Watch," and she pointed at the clock: "Spring that's sprung, go back to where you've begun."

The clock clunked, but nothing happened. Alec shook his head and pushed himself off the bed to stand beside it. He rubbed his hand across his forehead, then looked back at her, his expression kinder, more patient. "Perhaps we should slow down. You are innocent and young. I understand." He began to walk around the bed. "You're frightened, but—"

"I am not frightened! I *am* a witch!" She slid off the bed and out of his reach, standing defiantly with her chin in the air. Determined and a tad desperate, she used both hands this time: "Please believe my witch's spell. Repair the clock so all's well!"

For one brief second her eyes flashed with hope, then surprise, then pride. She smiled and pointed at the mantel. "There. See?"

One shake of his arrogant head and he gave her a look that said he would humor her, this once. He gave the mantel a quick glance, then turned back . . . and whipped his head back around so fast that just watching him made her dizzy. He shook his head and eyed the clock again.

After a moment of tense silence he slowly walked to the fireplace, never taking his wary eyes off the clock. He reached out toward it, then hesitated as if it might bite him. His hand tentatively touched the glass of the clock face.

"This was broken before." His palm pressed against the clock face. He turned back to her, his face stunned, puzzled.

"Now do you believe me?" She crossed her arms over her chest in a perfect imitation of Mrs. Watley.

"How did you do that?"

"Witchcraft."

His eyes narrowed and his lips thinned. "There is no such thing."

"The MacLean said Englishmen were hardheaded," she

muttered, looking around the room for some other way to prove what she said was true. Her gaze locked on the fireplace. "Stand back, please, away from the fire."

He moved over to grip the back of one of the wing chairs, his look perturbed.

She raised her hands and flexed her fingers while trying to concentrate. It took a moment.

"They say all Scots are daft," he said under his breath.

"I heard that," she said, never taking her eyes off the fire. Then she chanted, "Oh, fire that burns, do what you dare. Spit, sputter, crackle, and flare!"

The fire, which had been nothing but a small flame, shot up the chimney, the heat blasting its intense warmth into the room, and into her husband's shocked face. His hair ruffled from the heat blast. He stepped back, his frowning face flushed, and just stared at the fire.

You want proof? she asked silently. I'll give it to you. "Oh, flame that sprout, Go out!" She snapped her fingers and the fire was gone.

For the longest time Alec stood there, not moving, not talking, barely breathing.

"I'm a witch."

At this, he looked at her, bewildered. "This is not some sort of fairy tale. Witches do not exist." He sounded as if he were trying to convince himself.

"I exist."

"I am a duke for God's sake." He lowered his voice to an intimidating level. "The one thing I cannot abide is to be made a fool of. This is trickery—some kind of sport. I do not find it amusing. You are the duchess of Belmore." He stalked over to the adjoining door and jerked the door open, glaring at her. "I will be back in a few minutes, and I'll expect you to explain your behavior." With that command, he disappeared through the doorway.

Joy sat down on the edge of the bed with a defeated thud, an action that sent her long hair cascading heavily around her. She grabbed a handful of hair and flung it over her shoulder.

This was why witches didn't reveal themselves to mortals,

she thought, a pair of angry dark eyes the only image of him she could picture. Somehow she hadn't quite imagined it like this. She sighed, resigned that she had some convincing to do.

He slammed around in the other room. She blanched. Glass tinkled against glass; he was pouring a drink. Then there was silence. Lying back against the pillows, she rubbed her burning eyes, then closed them and waited.

At the sound of the door closing, she sat up, blinking. He held a large glass of amber liquid in his hand. She gave a wee smile. All she got for the effort was a cold stare. He moved with purpose to the wing chairs and leaned against one, crossing one foot over the other as he stood there expectantly. He took a sip of the liquor and tapped one impatient finger against the glass. "Now, wife, explain your magic trick."

"'Tis not a trick."

His eyes narrowed again. "You are lying."

With a resigned sigh she slid from the bed, her bare feet padding softly on the floor as she stepped around the bed and moved closer to him. Her gaze moved from his angry face to the other wing chair. She raised her hand and closed her eyes, trying to picture the chair hovering high in the room.

After a second of concentration she snapped her fingers. "Up!"

"Bloody hell!"

She opened her eyes and looked up.

Both Alec and the chair were five feet off the floor.

"Oh, my goodness!"

He stared down at the floor. "This is not happening."

"Yes, it is."

"It can't be, dammit!" He glared at her.

"Yes, it can."

"I'm dreaming," he said stubbornly. "Wake me up."

"Alec, I am a witch, and you cannot command me not to be."

The angry color faded from his face until he was pale with realization. "You're a witch."

She nodded.

"I am married to a witch," he stated flatly, then looked around him as if he expected the Devil himself to be hovering at his side. "A witch?" He frowned and rubbed two fingers against his left temple. He glanced down at the floor, a good five feet below him, and looked back at her. "A witch."

She nodded again.

"You're a witch," he announced to the room. Hovering above the ground, he looked at the glass and promptly downed the contents in one enormous swallow.

"Yes, I am."

He stared at the empty glass for a moment, then down at the floor. He moved his feet, watching them dangle in the air. His suspicious gaze darted left and right. He looked back at the at space between his feet and the carpet. He turned back to stare her, back at the floor, then directly at her.

"You believe me?"

"Get me the hell down from here! Now!"

Joy slowly lowered her arms and both the chair and her husband hit the floor, hard. The glass fell from his hand and rolled across the carpet.

"Oh, Alec!" she said, running over to where he was sprawled on the floor, looking very undukelike. "I'm so sorry!"

She reached out to him.

He flinched and scooted back away from her.

"Alec . . ."

He scrambled to his feet, never taking his wary eyes off hers.

She stepped toward him, reaching out. "Please."

"Get away!"

"I know this comes as a . . . a surprise, but—"

His look changed from shock to anger. "A surprise?" He spoke the words through clenched teeth.

She bit her lip.

"A surprise?" Now his neck was purple.

She stared down at her clenched hands. He was looking at

her with such revulsion that she couldn't bear to see it any longer. It hurt too much, knowing that he considered her a monster. Her throat began to ache.

"A surprise is when one finds a forgotten crown in one's pocket, wife. Not"—he moved to the fireplace and waved an angry hand at the clock—"*not* when one finds out that one's bride is a . . . a . . ." He waved his hand around some more while he tried to spit out the word.

She closed her eyes tightly and swallowed, but her tears spilled over anyway. "A witch," she whispered.

There was a full, torturous minute of angry silence.

"God Almighty . . . God Almighty!"

She opened her eyes only to watch all the angry color drain from his face.

"I don't believe this." He looked right through her. "I don't believe this. . . . I married you, in front of witnesses, in a church." He started walking toward the door, trance-like.

Hesitantly she reached out to him—a plea—as he walked by, but he gave her a wide berth and passed without even looking at her. She swallowed hard, then heard him mumble, "The new duchess of Belmore—*Belmore*—is a bloody witch."

Her throat tight, she swallowed again, her hand against her mouth as if it could keep her from crying aloud. The door clicked open. A second later, it slammed shut.

One deep quivering breath and she turned to stare at the closed door through blurry eyes. When his image finally vanished, little more than one brief memory, she turned slowly, her heart in her throat, and her chest so tight that taking a deep breath was impossible.

Wraithlike she crossed over to the bed and crawled into its center, wounded. Her mind flashed with the picture of his face, stunned, repulsed, angry. She had never told anyone she was a witch. She hadn't expected the revulsion. Tears tightened her throat. She disgusted him. Her own husband. How could someone love a monster?

Her stomach turned, churning until she thought she might

be ill with shame. She drew her knees up to her chest and gripped the silk coverlet in her fists, as if it was the only thing in the world she had to hold on to.

Her chest shook with her hurt. Her breath heaved and she couldn't control it any more than she could control the tears that poured from her eyes. The ache escaped her throat in a harsh cry, like that of a bird shot from the sky, drowning out the sudden splatter of raindrops against the window. She twisted the coverlet in her fists, tighter and tighter, until she finally buried her head in the soft cloud of pillows and hid her sobs. Outside, the rain poured down, as if the skies were crying too.

"Wake up. We need to talk."

Joy sat upright at the sound of her husband's raspy voice. A second later she grabbed the falling bedcovers and shoved her tangled hair back away from her face, then watched him, standing at the foot of her bed.

He looked awful. His hair was mussed, as if he'd run his hands through it a thousand times. A dark shadow of a beard shaded his hard jaw, and the dark blue circles of a sleepless night gave his eyes a sunken, hollow look. He still wore the long green robe, but the velvet was wrinkled and the belt was crooked, its knot having twisted over to his side, making one lapel higher than the other. He smelled of brandy.

She averted her eyes, looking toward the long window beside the fireplace. Dawn shone pink through the bedroom windows, and the room was cold, the fire as dead as Joy's hopes. He would have the marriage annulled. It was the only way out. She had figured that out about three in the morning.

He began to pace slowly, thoughtfully, not looking at her. "First of all I should apologize for shouting. I never lose control. However, I hope that, given the circumstances, you will understand my lapse."

Joy nodded. He hadn't looked any happier levitating than she had when she'd flown through that church window. But an apology was not what she expected. She had known that since this was 1813, she needn't worry about being dunked in a river, stoned, or burned at the stake, but she hadn't imagined an apology, especially when something told her that Alec never had to apologize to anyone.

"I want some answers."

She nodded again, chewing on her lip.

"Are you . . ." He waved his hand, as he did whenever he couldn't quite spit out what he wanted to say. "Do witches . . . Is death . . . Are you mortal?"

"Do you want to know if witches live longer than mortals?"

"Yes."

"No. Witches and warlocks get sick and eventually die just like everyone else."

"Eventually?"

"Just like mortals."

"I see." He seemed to be digesting that.

"But I'm only part witch." Her voice was hopeful. "My paternal grandmother was mortal."

"So that part of your story was true?"

"Yes, and I really was going to Surrey, and the Locksleys are my relatives, and they were terribly cruel to my granny." She paused and quietly admitted, "But there was no carriage."

"I see. I am not sure I want to hear this, but how did you end up on that road?"

"I made a wee mistake."

"A wee mistake? If your wee mistake was anything like your surprise, I think I had best sit down." He walked over to one of the wing chairs, turned it around, and sat down, facing her with an expectant look.

"Perhaps how one views it depends upon who one is."

"Pretend you are me."

She took a deep breath. "Travel incantations are very difficult, but if you get it right, an incantation will just zap you from one place to another."

"Zap you?"

She nodded. "I suppose I could try to show you a wee one if you want."

He held up a hand, shaking his head. "No! I have seen enough wee surprises."

It seemed to Joy that he was taking this pretty well, considering his reaction last night. He was not shouting. She could take his sarcasm.

His arms were propped on the chair, and he raised his steepled hands to his mouth and was quiet for a thoughtful minute. "You said your grandmother was a mortal. What happened to your parents?"

"They died when I was six in a cholera epidemic. My aunt raised me."

"Is she a . . . one of your kind?"

Joy's face lit up like the dining room candelabrum. "Oh, yes! She's a MacLean witch, the most powerful of all the witches and warlocks. You should see her cast a spell. 'Tis magic at perfection. Everything she does is perfect, and she's so beautiful and commanding." Joy couldn't help but raise her chin a notch. "She is a very important witch."

"Where is this paragon of witches?" He tapped a finger against his lips.

"She went to America for two years. She had some council work to do there."

"Council work?"

She nodded and opened her mouth to speak.

His hand went up again, waving a finger this time. "Never mind. The British are at war with the Americans. I don't think I want to know that either." He stared at the fireplace, then stood and walked over to the mantel where he silently watched the clock again.

The only sound Joy heard in the room was her own heartbeat.

He clasped his hands behind his back and glanced up at the painted ceiling, then let his gaze come to rest on her, giving her a level stare. "I have reached a decision."

She waited, holding her breath, hands clasped, heart in her throat.

"We shall stay married."

"We shall?" She almost fainted from shocked relief.

"Yes. There has never been any blight on the Belmore

name—no annulments and naturally no divorces—and I do not intend any shame to start with me. I need a wife. I need heirs," he paused. "I assume that is possible considering your mortal-mixed background."

"Well, yes . . ."

"Then I do not see any problem. You will remain my wife. There will be no dissolution of this union. The marriage has been registered and witnessed. It is legal and remains only to be consummated. And if last night was any indication, I do not believe we shall have a problem in that area. You are my wife. You will remain my wife and the duchess of Belmore, *but*"—he held up a finger—"there will be no more of this hocus-pocus." He waved his hand around again.

"You mean I cannot use my magic?"

"No, you cannot." His features were as hard as his voice. "I forbid it. I will not have the house of Belmore sullied by any scandal. And witchcraft would be the scandal of all scandals. Do you understand?"

She nodded, feeling guilty for not telling him before the wedding. But she had so wanted to be his wife. And she had to admit a part of her heart was rejoicing. She had a chance to make him love her. Perhaps the mortal human in her might make her a truly fine duchess. Perhaps her magic could, in time, help him. He needed to adjust. If she tried very hard, perhaps he would come to love her just a wee bit. Then maybe her magic would not matter to him anymore.

But there was one thing she still needed to tell him, since he brought it up and since she was spilling the soup, so to speak. "You should understand that if we have any children—"

"When."

"When what?"

"*When* we have children."

"You cannot know that for certain. Children are gifts from heaven."

"You believe in heaven?"

"Of course. I am a witch, not a heathen." She gave him a look of indignation.

"What about all that Devil worship business?"

"Propaganda. A white witch will not use her magic to hurt anything or anyone." At least not on purpose, she thought, then glanced back at him. "Did you say something?"

"Nothing of importance."

"Well, as I was about to tell you, I was raised to believe that God is in everything—the trees, the sea, the flowers, birds, and animals, even in our own hearts. You believe in God, don't you?"

"I was not raised a heathen either."

"Uhh . . . well, about the children . . ." She twisted a lock of her hair around a finger.

He held up a ducal hand to silence her. "Infertility has never been a problem for the house of Belmore." He watched her twist her hair. His look was intense. He stood up and took a step toward her. "Rest assured, Scottish, you will have my children."

A moment later he was beside the bed and Joy looked up at him. He reached out to touch her cheek, then stroked her hairline, his fingers combing through the mass of her hair. He could touch her. There was hope.

"I'll see to it," he added, his breath tickling her scalp.

One masculine knee sank into the mattress, and his hand reluctantly left her hair. Then his arms bracketed her hips. He moved toward her, his eyes hot and demanding.

She swallowed and blurted out, "The children might be . . . be like me."

He froze midway to her mouth. He closed his eyes briefly. "Witches or warlocks."

The clock chimed the quarter hour and he looked at it, his glance wary, his voice cold. "I see." He turned back, and his face said he might "see," but he certainly didn't like it. He took one long, deep breath, then another, and after a brief pause he pushed himself up from the bed.

"I think . . ." He turned away from her, never seeing the mist return to her sad eyes. "I need to meet with my steward again this morning." He walked over to the connecting door and opened it. "We will talk tonight." And he left.

# Chapter 10

They hadn't spoken that night. Alec had been called away on business and had left that very afternoon. He hadn't looked too displeased about having to leave, which didn't do much for Joy's frame of mind. He had been gone five days now.

On the first day of his absence a local dressmaker had arrived at eleven and spent the rest of the day poking, nipping, tugging, and throwing lengths of fabric on Joy. By the time the woman and her assistant left, she'd felt like a hex doll.

Since then she had done little but wander around the huge estate, just as she was now doing, walking along the stone pathway that circled the formal gardens of Belmore Park. It was a gray winter afternoon, and the wind whipped her skirts against her legs and brown mottled leaves fallen from the hedgerows and hawthorn bushes skipped around her feet. The ripening red berries of a prickly holly bush scattered like bloodstones across her path as she headed for the yew arbor that graced the entrance to the gardens themselves.

Over the past four days, she had walked here many times, trying to feel at home in a place where, save for Polly and Henson, she was made to feel unwelcome. She bowed her head in pensive thought as she entered the garden and slowly walked over to the stone bench on which she had spent so much time of late.

It was a peaceful place. Two fountains spat water into the air, and as it rushed downward, pooling at the bottom, the sound was as soothing as the rush of the sea on the Sound of Mull. At least for a brief time it gentled the uneasiness that arose from being in unfamiliar surroundings, from feeling that she didn't fit in here, and most importantly from her doubts about her marriage to Alec.

One moment the image of his face would swim before her mind's eye—horror-stricken—the way he had looked at her at first, as if she were the Devil himself. The next image was that of a man who wanted her and whose dark eyes flashed once with longing, of some need that instinct told her linked the two of them together.

Or was that just wishful thinking? No, she thought, there was something else there. Something had told her on the day they met that he needed her as badly as she needed to have him love her. She still felt that was true. She wouldn't—couldn't—stay if that was not the case. But she also wanted him to love her just a wee bit. She didn't need his whole heart, not really, only a little corner of it—a small corner of heaven.

Now, for a brief moment in time, she could wish and she could dream and she could hope, while she sat in the gardens where nature was her only friend. It was here that she felt most comfortable, sitting as one with the plants and trees and sky, drawing from nature a strength that made her whole. She loved the out-of-doors—the flowers, birds, and animals, the wonderful magic that made a blade of grass grow, a flower bloom, and an ancient tree grow so tall it almost touched heaven.

It was here in the gardens where, a few days before, she had first seen the playful topiary with its trees and hedges shaped like all the animals she would so dearly have loved to see. So it was here that she came to think when her welcome seemed worn out—or perhaps it was never there.

Still lonely and a little sad, she glanced at the topiary around her, hoping to feel embraced by the whimsy of it. Her favorite was the giraffe, carved from the thick branches of a manicured spruce fir, its long neck reaching up above the lower gardens almost high enough to kiss the sky. If she had designed the gardens, she would have put it below one of the tall sycamore trees so the giraffe would look as if it had stretched its neck to nibble on the tree's leaves. It would seem less like fantasy.

Except for the topiary there was no gaiety to be found this time of year in the garden, no color. No rainbow of flowers bloomed this time of year, so the garden was dreary in its monotony of winter green. The plants were dulled by the cold, many of the trees skeletal, and there was little color except for those bright red holly berries, and those were few and could be found only along the walk outside the gardens.

She folded her hands in the lap of her mulberry cashmere gown and looked past the gardens. Nowhere on the huge lake or the small pond beyond was there any ice. The weather was not cold enough, so skating was not an option, yet it was too cold and gray and dismal for any water play or boating. The fish ponds were empty, little more than dried-up rock bowls in the garden grounds. She had walked in one of the five mazes, but had found it no challenge without someone to race to the center. It was like playing hide-and-seek alone.

She glanced past the gardens to an ancient oak. A sprawling tree, it had wide clawing branches as thick as her body. The bark was mottled and ridged by time, wind, and weather. The tree had character. Witches believed that the wonder of life flowed like a magic river through the thick trunk of a tree. The older the tree, the stronger the power.

The only other time Joy could remember feeling so sad and hopeless was after her parents' death. She stood and moved over to the tree, stopping in front of it and craning her head to look up to its very crown. She wrapped her arms around the wide trunk and laid her cheek against the bark. Slowly her weary and saddened eyes drifted closed. She thought there was something soothing about hugging a tree. It was almost like the soft touch of a mother's comforting hand, like nesting in a smile or being held close to someone's heart.

A few minutes later she sighed and pushed away from the

trunk. She turned, smiling wistfully. Perhaps things weren't so tragic after all. Walking along the garden path, she kicked a small rock along in front of her until it bounced against the base of the stone bench.

She sat down once again, looking around her. Her gaze wandered upward to the fantastical beasts that stood along the roofline. She had noticed yesterday that they were perched around the entire house. From any angle below one could look up and see them. She had fancied on first sight that they looked as if they danced across the sky—a beasts' ball. She smiled at the image that thought brought to mind.

From here in the gardens she could see an ogre hunched over the corner nearest her, but it was difficult to make out anything other than silhouetted forms and the plump top of the nearest pepperpot dome. Alec had said those domes topped dining rooms. That she'd like to see, she thought with a laugh.

Gone was the wistful sadness that had tightened her chest a moment before. Trees were truly wonderful things.

Her heart felt a bit of eagerness as a MacQuarrie idea fermented like Scotch whisky in her mind. Perhaps she would take a look at that roof. Alec had pronounced the view "pleasing." She needed a bit of pleasing now, and the roof was the one place she had yet to explore. Surely Henson could show her the way. She rose from the bench and, skirts in hand, hurried toward the house.

A short time later she followed Henson up one of the twelve staircases. Twelve! It was little wonder she'd become lost. Once again Beezle clung to the poor footman's back. Henson was terribly good about it, just going along and doing his duties as if it was the most normal occurrence in the world for him to have a weasel hanging off his back.

Of late, her familiar seemed more apt to be clinging to the head footman than to be curled up someplace sound asleep. It was the first time Joy could ever remember Beezle taking to anyone. At least she hoped he had taken to Henson the man and not just to the gold ribbons that tied back his queue. She looked closer and saw that once again the weasel appeared to be chewing on it. She flicked a finger on Beezle's hindquarter, and he turned his beady little brown eyes on her, then grinned, pieces of Belmore gold ribbon peeking out from his clenched, feral teeth.

"The roof, Your Grace." Henson opened a door at the top of the stairs. Joy reached up, plucked Beezle off the footman's back, and tucked her familiar safely under one arm. Beezle hissed his displeasure, but she wasn't intimidated, just grabbed what she could of the gold ribbon and held it up to Henson. It was the eighth ragged one in four days. "I am so sorry."

"Quite all right, Your Grace." Henson accepted the shredded ribbon with a proper bow, his face perfectly impassive, the picture of the quintessential English servant, in spotless livery except for the white ermine hairs that sprinkled his shoulders and back, and his brown hair that hung free and messy and as shredded as the ribbon.

Frowning, she looked down at Beezle, wondering how much of the man's hair was in his feral little mouth. She slung him over her shoulder and turned slowly, trying to absorb the wonder of what she saw.

"Would Your Grace care for me to wait?"

"Hmm?" She turned back to Henson. "Oh, no. I shall be fine for a wee while." She turned back to scan the view. One could see for miles—rolling green hillsides dotted with clumps of gray-green trees, the dull ribbon of river that sliced through a valley and fed the village and Belmore's lake.

Beezle whissed and began to squirm about her shoulder, drawing her attention away from the countryside.

"Very well, Your Grace. I will check back occasionally to see when you wish to leave." He started to turn away, then stopped. "It might be best not to try to find your way back alone, Your Grace."

She gave him an embarrassed smile. "Afraid I might end up in the silver closet?"

"Quite possibly, or perhaps in Mrs. Watley's room, where Your Grace might freeze to death."

Joy burst out laughing. "She is a bit of a cold fish, isn't she?"

"Quite." With no smile, but a definite twinkle in his eye, he closed the roof door, and she turned back around.

The roof, the view, the statuary—this was truly the most wondrous thing she had ever seen. "Oh, Beezle, look!"

He hissed, and she turned to stare at his ferrety face. She lifted him until her face was barely an inch away from his pointed snout. "You want to get down so you can go back to Henson, don't you?"

He hissed again.

"I'll put you down, but you must stop eating that poor man's hair. Do you understand?"

He gave her a blank, perfectly innocent stare, then blinked for effect.

One more look of reprimand and she set him down. He moved faster than she'd ever seen him move before, in a half waddle, half scamper, over to the entrance to the stairway, where he stood on his fat haunches and scratched at the roof door. One sigh for patience and she opened the door. Quicker than a frog's leap he disappeared into the stairwell.

She shook her head, made a quick wish for the preservation of Henson's hair, and turned back around. With a brief, eager look at the roofline, she ran over to the nearest corner.

The ogre stood there in life-size bronze, and to his left was Pan, complete with pipes. Two angels with trumpet and harp were poised next to a griffin perched in a prowling stance. A fairy complete with ironwork appeared to be about to dance toward a medieval knight in full jousting armor astride a magnificent destrier.

Tall and strong and imperious was the Viking who stood with his hand on one of Odin's wolves, and past him were two frisky unicorns, a centaur, and the Lady of the Lake, in all her soulful beauty. Farther on stood another knight and his lady. Three gorgons and a lonely little mermaid flanked the closest chimney stack, followed by Pegasus and a few trolls, dwarfs, and the like.

Unmindful of the cool wind that blew over the roof in random gusts, she walked close to each piece of bronze statuary, the heels of her red slippers tapping lightly on the hard gray iron of the roof, and she touched each one, seeing in her mind's eye a landscape filled with dancing, frolicking fiction, as if every fairy and wee folk tale, every fable and epic romance, every fanciful story told upon a grandparent's knee had come magically alive.

Music sweeter and more golden than summer honey filled her ears, and Joy twirled and twirled, dancing to the tunes she imagined, her eyes closed, her mind beguiled by the imagery. She spun on one toe, the skirt of her new cashmere dress belling outward, and she opened her eyes to find herself in the middle of the beasts' ball.

The angels were real, alive, with golden wings and trumpet singing, harp pinging. Pan circled around her, piping out the hearty, clear notes of a tune as lively as a Scottish jig. The knight spun by her in a deep crimson doublet, swirling his blue-clad lady in his strong arms, and the ogre and trolls and gorgons—as gray-green as the winter garden below—all moved in celebration over the massive roof.

The music grew. The beasts spun. They dipped and twirled—a unicorn, a griffin, a fluttering fairy whose steps skipped along like the notes of the music—and Joy followed, caught up in the merrymaking, becoming little more than an enchanted young girl at her first ball. She stopped at one of the domes to peer into the dark windows as she turned and glided to the music. Dancing her way to the double doors, she balanced on one toe and grabbed the handles, but they were locked, so she swirled on, arms extended, head thrown back, a smile on her lips.

She spun again and again, opening her eyes to find the other knight had dismounted and, lance in hand, bowed to her. Smiling, she held out her hand and after one gallant touch of his lips, he led her in a medieval galliard to and around the next dome room, then moved on to pay court to and collect a favor from the mermaid. The music rang out, carried on the wind, and the Viking passed by, his gold-banded arms filled with the white-clad and wistful Lady of the Lake.

Beasts danced all around her. Lost in the magic of it, she closed her eyes and swirled and twirled amid the fantasy beasts who danced their way over the roof of the most majestic home in all of Wiltshire. It was fairylike, mythical, and more entrancing than the most powerful of magic spells, and Joy was part of it, dancing in it, bewitched by it, feeling wonderfully alive for the first time since Alec had kissed her.

"Bloody hell!"

Joy stumbled to a stop. Her guilty eyes shot open.

Alec stood in the doorway, the brass handle clenched in one white-knuckled hand. The ball continued, for its magic hadn't faded; the spell hadn't been broken. Her husband's face was a mixture of shock and anger. He watched the beasts, the color draining from his face, his eyes wary. Then he looked right at her. He appeared to be taking very deep breaths.

He stepped out of the doorway, only to have Pan jeté around him in a taunting circle of skittering pipe music. Alec looked at her. She had never seen a man's nostrils flare before.

She winced and watched him stride toward her. The nearer he came the more pronounced was the tic in his cheek, the redder his neck, the deeper his breaths. It crossed her mind that for a man who professed never to shout and swear or get angry, he'd done quite a bit of both around her.

He stopped about three feet from her and glowered down at her, his jaw so tight she was amazed he could speak. "What is going on here?"

"Uh . . . well . . . I suppose you could . . . I mean . . . it's a ball."

"I distinctly remember telling you no more hocus-pocus!" He waved his hand again.

"This was an accident."

"How in the name of God could *this*"—he raised his shaking hand, still shouting—"have been an *accident?*"

A jousting lance sliced down through the air between them. "Old man! Wouldst thou wish thy head lopped off?"

They both turned to look at the gallant knight, who was glaring at Alex.

Alex's own eyes narrowed in a challenge. "Old man?"

"Thy head is gray," the knight said, unflustered by the

lethal look on Alec's face. The knight dismissed him and turned to Joy, giving a small nod of his head. "My lady, dost thou wish to have this old knave's head upon a silver trencher?"

"Oh, my goodness!"

The knight drew his sword and pointed it at Alec's neck, which had darkened from red to purple.

"No! Please!" Joy's hands covered her mouth.

The knight pinned Alec with a hard stare. "Forsooth! Who dost thou think thou art to speak thus to a lady? Be ye her father?"

"I . . . am . . . her . . . husband," Alec said through clenched teeth.

The knight relaxed his threatening stance.

"And I," Alec said rather loudly, "would like her to end this nonsense." He waved a hand around, then pinched the sword tip between two long fingers and pulled it away from his purple throat. He moved his face a few inches closer to hers. *"Now!"*

Taking one deep breath for strength, Joy closed her eyes. *Please let it work.* She flung her hands up in the air and cried, "Things are not what they seem. End the dream!"

She snapped her fingers and very, very slowly opened one doubtful green eye. A sigh of relief escaped her lips. The knight was gone. The ball had ended. All the statuary was once again bronze and back in place along the roofline.

Alec stood frozen for a moment, then blinked twice and looked around the roof, his gaze pausing at the knight astride his charger. Joy was truly amazed that the statue did not melt beneath her husband's glare.

He turned back to her, his scowl untempered.

"You're not old," she said, hoping to placate him. A brief look at his face told her that her ploy didn't work.

He took two deep breaths. "Odd. I believe I have aged a decade in the last few days."

"It truly was an accident," she whispered. Her eyes widened when, over Alec's stiff, straight shoulder, she caught a glimpse of Pan—pointed brown ears, goat horns, and all—as he peeked out from behind one of the domes and eased his way toward his pipes, which lay abandoned in the middle of the roof.

"Explain." Alec crossed his arms over his chest and drummed his fingers on one arm, waiting.

Pan skulked closer and closer to the pipes, and she knew the imp would play them if they came into his hands. She raised one hand high in the air, as if to stifle a yawn and swept one finger through the air, mentally picturing the pipes skidding across the roof and out of her husband's line of vision.

The pipes levitated instead, hovering in the air like the notes from its reeds.

Pan scowled at her, his thick bushy brown eyebrows wrinkling like brown inchworms. Then he tried to jump up and grab the pipes. Joy faked a coughing spell just about the time his hooves hit the iron roof.

He kept leaping; Joy kept coughing.

"I am still waiting for an explanation, and choking won't save you." Alex stood there, arms still crossed, jaw clenched, eyes expectant and none too happy, completely unaware of what was going on behind him.

"Give me a moment," she rasped dramatically, tapping her chest with the hand that wasn't still extended in the air.

Pan appeared to have given up and had stopped jumping up and down, but her relief was short-lived. He turned his elfin face toward her and slowly smiled—a smirk of pure mischief—and she watched in horror as he eased over to the roof door. Before she could snap her fingers, he'd opened it. With a devil's wink and a gleeful wave he stepped inside and closed the door behind him, descending into the depths of a house so huge she would never find him.

The clatter of horses' hooves sounded from the gravel drive below. Alec turned toward it; so did she. A trumpet blared, and for one brief instant Joy thought an angel was still on the loose, too. The horn sang out again, and a group of riders, led by a pair of purple and gold-liveried trumpeters, approached the house.

"Bloody hell . . ." Alec stared at the procession with the

look of a man harassed. "They're in royal livery." He rubbed the bridge of his nose. "Thank God they didn't arrive in time to see what I saw." After a long-suffering sigh he grabbed her hand. "Come along. We'd best go downstairs to see what this is about." He all but dragged her to the door and pulled it open, pausing to scan the roof. Then he looked down at her. "You may explain your actions to me later, wife."

She found herself almost running to keep up with his long strides after they had descended the staircases, Joy furtively scanning every nook and cranny in the hope of seeing pointed brown ears, horns, or goat hooves.

Alec pulled her down a long hallway on the ground floor and let go of her hand long enough to open walnut-paneled double doors. Then he grasped her hand again and pulled her into the room and over to a tufted leather sofa.

"Sit!"

Joy sank into the sofa. The room smelled like her husband, a mixture of tobacco and leather and something manly and a little exotic, like sandalwood. She watched Alec cross to a mahogany pedestal desk inlaid with brass and ebony, which sat in front of two twelve-foot-tall French doors. Through the long diamond-paned windows beside the doors she could see the green of the garden and a wisp of the silver-blue lake beyond.

Nervous and a tad fidgety, she folded her hands in her lap and chewed on her lip. Bored with that, she looked at the walnut paneling, then at the beveled-glass panes in the doors that covered some of the deeper bookcases. Except for the long windows, bookcases seemed to encircle the room. She squirmed a bit, then stood so she could rearrange her skirts, which had bunched up under her when she sat down.

"Stay!"

She sat back with a start. "But—"

"Quiet!"

She frowned, wondering if he would now command her to fetch. Too bad he had no sense of humor, else she might have barked. She bit back a smile, sensing that bursting out with nervous laughter would give her more trouble.

A curt knock sounded at the door.

A moment later the tall clock chimed seven times.

"Bloody hell!"

Joy's eyes widened. She looked at Alec, who glared at the clock.

It was three o'clock.

Alec turned toward her. She winced and shrugged.

There was another, much louder knock.

"Come in," Alec snapped, standing at the desk with the glass doors behind him and the afternoon glow spilling through the glass and limning him in sunlight. He looked even more intimidating, even taller, even angrier.

Townsend opened the door and entered, clearing his throat and announcing, "Messenger of His Royal Highness Prince George."

Alec nodded and the butler opened the door wide. A footman in full formal royal livery entered and walked to the desk, where he bowed and handed the duke a cream-colored envelope. "For His Grace the duke of Belmore."

Alec took the message, glancing up at the butler after looking at the official seal. "Townsend, I'm sure our prince regent's loyal servants would like some refreshment. See to it."

"Thank you, Your Grace." The footman made another bow. "I am required to await a response."

"Fine," Alec returned in a clipped voice. "You may await my answer in the kitchen with the others."

"Certainly, Your Grace." The door snapped closed.

Alec stared at the doors, then slowly sat down at his desk, slicing open the message with a letter opener that he held like a dagger, which was not reassuring since he had a look of dread on his angled face. He scanned the letter and swore, leaning back in his chair and closing his eyes as if the letter carried his death sentence.

"We've been summoned to Carlton House."

Joy looked at him with wide eyes. "We have?"

"The prince wishes to meet the new duchess of Belmore."

"Me?" Joy pointed to herself.

"Yes, you. Seems I have the privileged honor of introducing His Royal Majesty the Prince Regent to my wife, the witch." He rubbed a hand over his forehead and mumbled, "Who turns statues into live things and dances with them on my roof."

"What is he like?"

"Spoiled, demanding, fat, imperious, and superstitious enough to do more than lop off both our heads if he should witness something like I did today." He leveled her with another stare of reprimand.

Joy was too stunned to notice. She was going to meet the prince regent, old Prinny himself. "Oh, my goodness." She glanced at her husband and could have sworn she heard his teeth grind together. "How did he know of our marriage so soon?"

"There's no doubt in my mind. It had to have been that meddling witch—"

Joy gasped.

He looked at her and waved his hand while he searched for another word. "That harpy, Lady Agnes, and her two bird-witted friends."

"When do we have to leave?"

Still staring at her, he drummed his fingers on the desk. "Tomorrow morning."

"That soon?"

He stood, but didn't answer. Instead, he walked over to her.

She looked up at his serious face.

"You have to promise me—no more witchcraft."

She just stared up at him, seeing his eyes shuttered with coldness. Oh, Alec, she thought, you need my magic.

He broke the spell by taking her shoulders and pulling her up to face him. "Can you promise me that?"

She looked at his face, so serious, so worried, so close. She wanted to touch him, and placed a hand on his chest, near his heart—the one she wanted a wee piece of. She would have promised him anything. "Yes."

"No more of that business with the clocks."

"No more clocks."

"No more"—he waved that hand around—"zapping."

"No more zapping."

"No more things or people floating in the air."

"No more floating."

"No more dancing statues?"

Her mind flashed with the image of Pan's impish face. Well, they were leaving and what Alec didn't know wouldn't hurt him. "No more dancing statues." Then she added, "From this moment forward."

His hands rubbed her shoulders ever so slightly and he seemed to be looking rather intently at her mouth. His eyes flashed with want, the same way they had before he'd kissed her. He hadn't kissed her since she told him she was a witch. She wanted him to kiss her, now, in here, to show her he didn't think her a monster, to end the aching isolation.

She lifted her hand from his chest and reached up to touch his mouth. At the same moment he lifted his hand toward her face. He paused. Her hand pressed flat against his chest. He seemed to be mentally weighing something, fighting with himself. His breathing grew deeper. His hand cupped her chin, his thumb stroking her jawline. He still watched her mouth.

*Kiss me . . . kiss me. . . .*

He was so very close. If she leaned just a bit forward . . .

She did. He didn't.

A bloodcurdling scream echoed in the distance.

They jumped apart, the spell broken, and looked at the door.

The hand that had caressed her jaw only a moment before fell to his side. "What in the name of God was that?" Alec crossed to the doors and she followed. They stepped into the hall and heard a commotion near the grand staircase. She had to run to keep up with him, then all but skidded onto the marble of the grand foyer.

Mrs. Watley lay in a six-foot-long dead faint in the middle of the floor. Servants bustled back and forth, and Townsend knelt at her side. Henson strode in from another hallway, Beezle stuck to his back and a glass of water in his hand. Polly came on his heels, hartshorn in hand.

"What happened?" The servants parted to let Alec near.

"Don't know, Your Grace. There was that frightening scream, and when I came in, she was like this." Townsend lifted the housekeeper's head and shoulders, and Polly held the smelling salts under her nose.

The woman's eyes opened. She blinked and pushed Polly's hand away from her nose as she mumbled something.

"What is it?" Alec asked.

Her face was gray. She pointed a shaking finger toward a marble statue in an alcove near the front doors. "There. Horns. Ohhhhh . . ." Her eyes rolled back into her head, and she fainted again.

Every eye in the room turned toward the corner. There was nothing there but a statue of David. Joy chewed on her lower lip.

She felt Alec's gaze and made the mistake of looking up. His eyes had narrowed in suspicion, and he stared right at her.

One deep breath and she shrugged, hoping the guilt she felt didn't show in her eyes and praying that Pan wouldn't pop out of a corner any second. After a good long stare, Alec turned back to the servants. "Send someone to the village for the physician. Tell him to come immediately, and take Mrs. Watley up to her room." He turned to two of the chambermaids. "Don't leave her alone."

A troop of footmen lifted the tall woman and carried her toward the back of the house. Alec turned to Henson. "We leave for London in the morning. Make ready." He turned to Polly. "Pack Her Grace's things and your own. You'll travel with Henson and Roberts in the fourgon. I want to leave by eight. Understood?"

"Yes, Your Grace." Polly curtsied and was gone in a flash.

Alone in the foyer, Alec turned to Joy. "What did she see?"

She winced and raised her fingers to her lips and chewed a nail.

"Answer me!" he said in a hoarse whisper.

"Pan."

"Pan?" he gritted.

She pointed to the roof and nodded.

"Alive?"

"Aye," she said quietly, watching his color deepen from angry red to livid crimson.

"Find him! Before we leave. Do you understand me?"

She nodded.

He turned with military sharpness.

"Alec?"

He turned back with a look that said "what now?"

"Must we leave so soon?"

"We need to be in London as soon as possible. The prince doesn't like to wait and we only have a few days to prepare you. If we leave early that will enable us to stay in Reading tomorrow night, and should put us in London in two days, instead of three." Alec dismissed her with a cold look, but Joy stopped him.

"Where are you going?"

"I shall be up all night going over the accounts with my steward. Twice I have come home only to have to leave again." He paused, his jaw tight, then added, "Find that . . . that thing!"

She nodded.

He started to turn, but stopped as if forced to. "Can you find your way to your chamber?"

"Yes," she said to his stiff back. "I mastered that the second day."

"Fine." He turned and walked down the hallway, all cold, hard duke.

She watched his back until he turned and was out of view. Then she listened to his bootheels clip on the marble floor until the sound faded to nothing. Finally she sighed and slowly turned to go up the stairs, her mood suddenly listless.

She walked across the marble floor, stopped, and looked up at the painted ceiling. All this opulence surrounded her—marble pillars and staircases, gilded balustrades of intricate iron work, vases that were as old as dirt, furniture so glossy one could use the surface for a mirror—and yet this place seemed as cold and lonely as the depths of Fingal's Cave.

And now this was her home, a home in which she didn't fit. She closed her eyes and swallowed, then turned to look back at the empty corridor into which Alec had disappeared.

Clinging to her hope, she lifted her chin and squared her shoulders. Determination made her eyes brighter. She would fight. She would be the best duchess Belmore had ever seen. She was unwilling to accept defeat. After all, she too had English blood, aristocratic blood. If she became a proper duchess, Alec would be proud, perhaps even as proud of her as he was of his name. That would take care of half the battle, she was sure of it. If she could make him proud that she was his duchess, then surely love would follow.

A bright smile lit her face as she let her fanciful mind imagine a day when Alec would look upon her with pride. Lost in thought she ascended the stairs, humming a love ballad and swaying to the tune until she reached the second landing and happened to glance wistfully upward, her mind's eye seeing her husband's proud face, his lips descending to give her a kiss for all the world to see. Her dreamy eyes focused upward. It wasn't the image of her husband she saw.

A mischievous, elfin face, complete with goat horns, grinned down at her from the third-floor balustrade.

"You wee Devil's spawn!" she hissed and raised her hand to zap him just a second after his head disappeared.

Skirts in hand, the duchess of Belmore charged up the stairs as if the hounds of hell were after her instead of somewhere above her—and ahead of her.

# Chapter 11

"Bloody hell. Now it's snowing." Alec glared at Joy as the carriage plodded along the icy road.

She raised her chin in defiance and pulled the carriage robe a bit tighter around her in an attempt to keep warm. "It is not my doing. I told you that when the fourgon broke down. I have not done anything. These are real accidents. I had nothing to do with that broken axle."

His eyes filled with skepticism.

"And," she said, "a witch cannot control the weather."

"Remind me to get a list one day in the very near future of what a witch can and cannot do." He turned to glare out the carriage window at the falling snow. "Damn, it's cold."

"Is this the only blanket?"

He looked at her and nodded.

She bit her lip. "I can help."

"No."

"But why should you be cold when I can whip up another blanket, or even a down coverlet?"

"I said no. No witchcraft."

"But isn't this an exception?"

"No."

"Dire circumstances?"

"No."

"If it were, say, something life-threatening, could I use my powers?"

"This is not—I repeat, not—a life-threatening situation." He turned back to the window. "It is a small snowstorm, that's all."

"But it's awfully cold."

"I will not discuss it."

"You brought it up."

His breathing became very controlled, and loud.

"Just one wee snap of my . . ." She caught his look and mumbled, "Never mind."

After a long moment of his scowling silence, she turned and looked back out the window. It appeared to be solid white. She could see little, since the glass had begun to fog up. In an attempt to see better, she swiped at the glass with two gloved fingers, but pulled them back after a minute. The glass was so cold she could feel it through her leather gloves.

The carriage slowed, lurched, then jerked after the sound of the coachman's snapping whip. After three more jarring lurches, Alec's expression changed from annoyance to worry and he stood and tapped on the coach roof, then reached up to open the coachman's window in the overhang above her. "How bad is it out there?"

Old Jem shouted back, "Colder than a witch's tit, Yer Grace."

Joy couldn't bite back her offended gasp.

There was a long moment of silence. Alec didn't move, didn't speak, although Joy had the distinct impression that her husband wanted to say something. She glanced up but found herself staring at his gold brocade waistcoat.

Jem's gravelly voice echoed down from above. "Beg Her Grace's pardon. The duchess being so new an' all, I forgot about 'er."

Alec cleared his throat then asked, "How bad is the road?"

"Snow's about a half a foot, least it were last time I could see. Couldn't see the gates o' hell in this." The carriage slowed again and the sound of whickering horses carried inside. "Team's having a bit o' a hard time of it, Yer Grace."

"How far to the next inn?"

"Maybe a mile, maybe ten. Can't see a bloomin' thing—"

The carriage lurched again and Alec put his knee on Joy's seat to steady himself. A string of gravelly curses echoed down from the driver's box. "Beggin' Yer Grace's pardon, but the bloody lead nag can't stay to the road."

"Any sign of Willie?"

"Not a flea nor flicker, Yer Grace."

"Tap on the roof if he shows."

Jem grumbled his assent, and Alec closed the front trap and turned to the rear trap that opened to where the footman rode in the carriage hood. "All's well back there?"

"Cold, wet, but tolerable, Your Grace."

"Fine." Alec closed the trap and settled back in the seat across from her. The temperature inside was dropping quickly and even with her woolen dress and pelisse and the woolen carriage robe, Joy could still feel the gooseflesh on her skin.

"Aren't they freezing out there?"

"They are Belmore servants and as such wear only the best winter clothing—heavy caped leather coats with fleece inside. They're are probably much warmer than we are."

"Oh." She pulled the robe tighter around her and still shivered.

"Are you warm enough?"

She nodded, trying hard to keep her teeth from chattering.

"Quite sure?"

"I'm sure." She held herself stiff to keep from shivering.

They were silent for a time. Then she could feel her husband's look.

"Scottish?"

She glanced up, the sound of that name doing funny things to her belly.

"Come sit over here." He patted the seat next to him with one hand and held out his other to her.

She paused, biting her lip, her eyes wary.

"To keep warm."

She took a deep breath and placed her hand in his, letting him draw her over to sit so close beside him that their bodies touched from shoulder to knee. His arm slipped around her shoulder.

After a quiet minute she looked up at him. "Who's Willie?"

"The outrider. I sent him on ahead after the fourgon broke down, but that was before the storm hit." He looked out the window again, but could see nothing through the foggy window but the mist of falling snow.

"I truly had nothing to do with the broken axle," she whispered.

He was silent, watching the snow, his face unreadable.

"Do you believe me?"

After a moment he conceded. "I realize you wouldn't jeopardize the servants."

She shook her head in agreement and joined him in watching the snow fall. The carriage lurched and slipped and the sound of the coachman's cursing and the team's whickering was all they could hear. "Do you suppose they're safe?"

"Who?"

"Polly, Roberts, and Henson." She paused. "And Beezle." She took a deep breath and watched the snow, hoping the servants weren't caught in the same storm, in a broken carriage.

"We went past the turnoff to Swindon just a few minutes before the axle broke. There's an inn little more than a mile from that turnoff. By now they're surely inside that warm inn waiting for the carriage to be repaired. I had left instructions for them to meet us in the inn in Reading. That's where I thought we'd be staying tonight."

"How far is that from here?"

He was silent, then said, "I'm not sure. We're somewhere on the edge of the Cotswolds. It's hard to tell how far we've traveled in this weather. There are no villages for miles on this stretch of road."

An instant later the carriage swayed. The driver shouted. His whip snapped. The horses neighed just as the carriage rocked forward, then listed to one side.

"Bloody hell." Alec gripped Joy's arms, and his leg pinned her to the seat. They slid to one side and a loud crack echoed about them.

The carriage settled at a sidewise slant, and all was silent. Alec pushed himself upright and settled Joy in the seat. "Are you all right?"

"I'm fine."

"Stay here." He climbed over her and moved to the door. "I have to check on the others." He opened it and snow drifted inside. A second later the door slammed shut.

She could hear him talking to the footman; then she heard Jem swearing. From the voices she could tell that they were unharmed. She looked toward the window but all she could see was white. Their voices drifted off and she snuggled down deeper into the carriage robe.

It was truly cold and when Alec had opened the door it became even more so. She shivered and closed her eyes, finally feeling her lack of sleep from the night before when she had wandered all over the house in search of that rascal Pan. She'd spent hours combing hallway after hallway and even a brief time in the Bramah where she tried to conjure him up. But it was all to no avail. She'd never even caught a glimpse of him.

In desperation she had gone up to the roof again, after receiving directions from a footman who rushed to take one of her trunks downstairs. On the roof she picked up the pipes, thinking she could use them to lure Pan out from wherever he hid. Then she'd taken another precious ten minutes to wander down the halls off the grand staircase, playing the pipes off-key and hiding them behind her back when any servant chanced by. She couldn't find Pan, though, and no spell made him appear.

Finally she found him in the pantry, stuffing his little fat face with kumquat jelly and an entire pan of freshly baked honey buns. It took her two incantations to restore the wee devil to his rightful place on the roof. On her first try, they both ended up in the stable. A slip of her tongue—"hoof" instead of "roof."

But she'd finally crawled between the cool sheets and

managed an hour of sleep before Polly awakened her with breakfast, *sans* honey buns, which Polly said had disappeared during the night. . . .

That thought brought to mind the safety of her maid, Beezle, and the others. She hoped they were tucked away in some warm inn.

The coach shook, and something banged against it. She could hear the horses and the jangling of the harness. Then there was some more talking, but she couldn't make out any words. A few moments later the door opened, snow spilling inside like flour from a fallen barrel. Alec entered and closed the door behind him. His face said everything. There was something wrong.

He tossed some things on the seat and sat down. "The horses are skittish, and the lead veered into a rut. The wheel's broken and the snow is coming down at about an inch a minute. It's a blizzard out there." He slipped his arm around her. "The coachman and footman have taken the horses and gone in search of help. They seemed to think there's an inn not too far from here."

"We shall stay here in the carriage?"

He nodded. "There's no way you would last out there in those thin clothes."

"I could do—"

"No."

She wiped the window clear and tried to peer out. "I cannot see anything."

"It's snowing very hard." He shivered, then squirmed a bit in the seat as if he was trying to disguise it.

"Please, Alec . . ."

"No." He grabbed the things he'd set on the seat and shook them out. "Here, put this on." He held up a wide cape and a heavy leather jacket.

She slid her arms into the jacket, which was miles too big, and he slipped the cape around both of them and pulled her against his body.

"We shall wait here until help comes." He sat there stiffly, holding her but acting as if he didn't want to.

Very slowly she lowered her head onto his shoulder and

took advantage of the chance to snuggle against him. He was so warm.

He cleared his throat loudly, then shifted a few times finally adjusting his long legs so they rested against the carriage door.

She shivered again.

"Lie down here beside me."

She stretched out so she was almost lying on top of him. "How long do you think it will be before they rescue us?"

"Not long," he answered confidently. There was no anger in his voice, just calm and control. She gave in to the warmth of having him hold her, even though she knew he didn't want to. She felt so right in his arms, as if she'd found the lost half of her. They were married and he was hers —sort of. At least he would be someday, and that meant there would always be someone there for her. The thought warmed her even more than his body. She closed her dreamy eyes and said good-bye to the cold and to loneliness.

"Scottish."

Joy wrapped her arms tighter around Alec and burrowed deeper against his chest and wiggled her legs between his. "Hmmm, your legs are warm."

He groaned then said, "Wake up, Scottish."

"No. So cold," she muttered.

His arms tightened around her. "I know. That is why you must wake up." He shook her, but she didn't care. It was too cold to open her eyes.

"Joy! Wake up! Now!"

Her eyes shot open at the sound of his raised voice.

"That's better," he said. "We need to talk."

"I'd rather sleep." She snuggled against him and let her heavy eyelids drift closed.

"You cannot." His knuckle lifted her chin from his chest. His finger stroked her lips. At that gesture she had to look at him. "It's too cold to sleep. We must stay awake." His arms closed around her and he lifted her as he sat up, then pulled her into his lap and adjusted the coats around them both.

"I'm sure help will be here soon, but in the meantime we must stay awake."

"Why? Is something wrong?"

He gave her a long look, as if mentally weighing something, then shook his head. He was silent, his face unyielding, his eyes less sure than before.

She looked at the white windows, shivered, and felt him do the same. "You're as cold as I am."

"I am fine."

The MacLean was right. Englishmen were hardheaded.

"Help is on the way," he said again.

"Then why can I not go back to sleep?"

"I don't think it is a good idea."

"Why?"

"Because help will be here soon."

"How long has it been?"

"A while."

"I can help . . . now."

He didn't answer.

"You woke me up to talk. Now you won't speak. Why?"

He rubbed his hand across the bridge of his nose.

"Are we in dire circumstances?"

All he did was breathe deeply.

"Is this a life-threatening situation?"

He sat more rigid in the seat, but said nothing.

"Well, if you are not going to answer me, I shall go back to sleep." She leaned against him and started to close her eyes.

He grabbed her shoulders, hard, and shook her once "You cannot go to sleep. If you do, you might not ever awaken." His expression was almost angry, it was so intense.

She scanned his face, reading the worry in his dark eyes. "Please, Alec, let me help."

"No witchcraft."

"Would you rather die here?"

He continued to pin her with a hard stare.

"Would you?" she countered. "No one is about. No one will know about the witchcraft except you and me."

He looked at her for a minute, then glanced at the white window. The carriage was buried in snow.

She shivered once. "Please."

Frowning, he looked at the other white window.

"I can zap us both to the nearest inn, with one wee incantation." She watched his doubtful face. "Please."

He looked at her, reluctant resignation on his face and said, "I suppose we have no choice." Straightening a bit, he looked down at her, his face all arrogant duke. "But only this once."

She nodded, her mind already whipping up the words she would use. "Do you know which inn is the closest?"

"No."

She paused for a thoughtful minute. "Then I shall try something general. Here, take my hands."

He pulled his hands out from under the cape and straightened his shoulders, every muscle in his body taut, his jaw set. She gripped his hands. One glance at his stiff, pale face told her that he was about as ready for this as the prince regent was to meet Napoleon and his army in Paris, unarmed, alone.

"Close your eyes, please."

He gave her one last leery look, then did as she asked.

Determined to get her magic right and impress her husband, she raised her chin and pictured a country inn like those they had passed before. Her mind filled with timbered buildings and wide windows that spread a warm yellow glow of welcoming light on the drifting snow. She saw a stone fence that separated the inn from a row of old elms and a clear icy path that wound its way through the meadow beyond.

She stopped, suddenly losing her concentration when she realized that she needed to snap her fingers, something that was impossible while Alec was holding her hands. She opened her eyes and found herself looking at her husband's taut face. His eyes were closed, his expression similar to that of someone who had severe stomach ague.

"You need to hold my wrists so I can snap my fingers."

Eyes still closed he moved his hands to her wrists and grasped them tightly.

Once again ready she closed her own eyes. Now where was

I? she asked herself. That's right . . . elm trees and the winding icy path. "All 'round us is the snow," she chanted. "We must find somewhere else to go. Take us both as quick as a flea to the place that I now see!" She snapped her fingers.

"Bloody hell!"

And she felt Alec's hands slip away.

"Alec!" Joy frantically searched for him in the snowy landscape.

"Over here!" came a hoarse shout.

Still huddled in the leather coat, she made an awkward turn toward his voice. A group of snow-covered old beetled elms stood among the huge white snowdrifts; they looked like ghosts clawing their way toward the clouds. The snow-laden elm branches rustled and a flurry of white snow tumbled to the ground. Alec's frosted gray head appeared as he made his way around the huge trees, his leather cape catching on the low branches.

Joy could hear him mumble. His boots suddenly slid in the damp snow and ice, and he grabbed ahold of a low branch.

The sound of wood cracking echoed in the winter silence, followed by swearing.

"Oh, my goodness!" Joy covered her mouth with a shivering hand and watched him skid the rest of the way down the embankment on his ducal posterior, the tree branch still gripped in his hand and the cape dangling from the tree branches above him.

He sat there for a moment, apparently stunned. Then his eyes scanned the area, finally stopping to glare at her. "Where . . . is . . . the inn?"

Joy looked around, seeing only white hills of drifting snow, frosted trees, and the icy path on which she stood. She bit her lip and peered upward, over the clump of trees in the hope of seeing a roof, a chimney, or smoke. There was nothing but a snow-clouded gray sky. "I'm not sure."

"What the hell do you mean, you're not sure? I thought you were going to zap us to the closest inn?"

"I was," she said, her teeth beginning to chatter.

"Then where is the bloody inn?"

"Well, you see, Alec, sometimes my spells get just a tad mixed up."

"What?" he shouted, bringing down a clump of wet snow on top of his head.

She winced and watched him shake the snow off his head with all the vigor of a wet hunting hound.

"A tad mixed up?"

She nodded.

His breathing became very controlled, very deep, and very loud. After a tense moment he glanced down at the tree branch clutched in his fist and tossed it aside with a look of disgust. The look was still there when he turned back to her. "Explain this, wife."

"Sometimes I make mistakes."

"Mistakes?" He struggled to his feet.

She nodded.

"Did it cross your mind that this is one devil of a time to tell me?" He appeared to shiver and looked around at the endless drifts of white snow.

"I wanted to please you."

He rubbed a gloved hand over his forehead. "I see." He looked as if he was counting, just like the MacLean. He stopped counting and Joy thought she saw him shiver. "You thought to please me by zapping us in the middle of nowhere?"

"I'm s-sorry," she whispered, the cold seeping into her skin too. "I'm sure the inn is-is nearby. I pic-pictured it perfectly before."

"Pictured it?"

"Well, you s-see . . . uh . . ." She rubbed her arms and looked at all the cold wet snow with a sense of dread.

"Speak! Now!"

One look at his face and her words spilled forth in a rush. "I have to picture the place I'm going to in my mind first and—"

"Bloody hell!" he shouted, dusting the snow off him with

angry strokes. He looked at her, then at the snow around them and muttered, "No wonder we're in this fix. A Scot's mind."

"I resent that."

"And I resent being subjected to this . . . this . . ." He waved his hand around in the air and hit the hem of the cape. He glanced upward, scowling, and jerked the cape out of the tree with a fierce tug. "I'm the duke of Belmore. The duke of *Belmore!*"

"'Twas only a mistake. I was trying to save our lives!"

He flung the cape over his shoulders, shivering again. "Now, why don't I feel saved?" He took a threatening step toward her. "Are we in a nice cozy warm inn? No . . . We're in the middle of a—"

Another loud cracking sound pierced the quiet air. It wasn't wood this time. It was ice.

"Bloody hell!"

Alec sank up to his thighs in icy water.

Another crack sounded and his head shot up, his gaze following the ice crack that etched a path toward where Joy stood.

"Don't move, Scottish!" He raised a hand. "Whatever you do, don't bloody move!"

Joy watched in horror as the icy path on which she stood began to break away, piece by broken piece to reveal the deadly water beneath.

In desperation she closed her eyes, pulling the leather coat closer and trying hard to picture the bank and Alec.

"Don't!" he shouted. "Don't try your magic!"

It was too late. She snapped her fingers.

The ice beneath her cracked, loud and sharp.

She opened her eyes wide. The ice gave way.

His hand reached toward her. His other held the tree branch, inches away.

She sank into the icy water, her coat catching on the ice, her gloves slippery as she tried to grab something—anything.

Freezing water rushed through her clothes to burn her

skin with an icy fire. She couldn't feel her legs, her arms, her body.

"Alec!"

Icy water licked at her chin.

She reached out . . .

*Oh, God!*

The last thing she saw was her husband's panicked face.

# Chapter 12

As if called forth by the Devil himself, the wind came up, icy, cold, flecked with snow that rimed the tall, cloaked figure trudging through a wet white sea of knee-high snowdrifts. The duke of Belmore hunched over, protection for himself but mostly to protect his duchess—the shivering wet bundle in his numb arms.

"Talk to me, Scottish. Do not go to sleep." He shifted her weight, and his boot slipped. He stumbled, slipped again, instinct making him pull her damp, shivering form even tighter against him. He managed to regain his footing.

"Scottish!" he shouted. It seemed as if he'd shouted continually for however long it had been since he'd pulled her from the frigid river. He felt her stir, thank God, and slowed his snow-silent steps, finally stopping so he could look down at her face. He pulled aside the cape in which he'd wrapped her.

Her eyes were closed and despite his attempts to cover her face, her eyelids were frosted with snowflakes. Her lips shivered, as did her small wet body. He shifted her so he could touch her face. She didn't move. The snowflakes on her skin didn't melt, she was that cold.

"Wake up!" he shouted to her, the sound all but swallowed by the thirsty winter wind. He shook her once, twice.

"S-s-so co-cold," she said on a convulsive shiver.

The wind howled and keened around them like the wail of mourners.

*We're not bloody dead.* Alec went on, shoving his way

through the snow, spurred by anger, spurred by sheer will. That same bloody wind sliced like an icy ax through their wet clothing. Snowflakes swirled in a sudden spiral gust, and tree branches swayed and cracked under the weight of the wet snow. He felt her shiver.

"What's your name?" he shouted. He knew he had to keep her talking, keep her lucid.

"Hmm?" she muttered.

"Your name!"

"Scottish." Her voice was little more than a ragged whisper, its sound wind-stolen.

"Who are you?"

"Scottish," she repeated. Then her breathing slowed, grew shallow and even, like that of one who was sound asleep.

"Wake up! Now!" He shook her. She didn't respond. He shook her harder. Still she didn't move.

"Bloody hell," he muttered and scanned their surroundings. Everything was white—cold, icy white. He'd managed to find the road—at least he hoped it was the road. One couldn't see a bloody thing in this storm. He had stumbled in a rut and fallen into a deep drift of snow that all but buried both of them. She had been lucid then, had argued with him to let her walk. He'd ignored her, setting her aside while he dug around in the snow until he felt the impression of wheel ruts.

A few minutes later he had stood and turned to where he'd left her sitting on his cloak in the snow just a few feet behind him. She was not there. Moments later he saw her stumbling down the road, her wet coat undone, hanging off one shoulder, and flapping in the icy wind. He knew she was chilled to the very marrow of her bones. He ran after her, unable to believe someone could be freezing and not doing anything about it.

Since then—a few minutes ago, a few hours ago, he had no idea which—he continued to carry her trembling wet body snuggled against his chest in the hope that she would garner some warmth from him.

A small clump of trees stood to his right, and he moved toward them. He needed to awaken her. In the lee of the trees he found respite from the biting wind and lowered her feet to the ground, his other half-numb arm holding her upright, the cape still wrapped around her.

She sagged against him. He gripped her shoulders and shook her hard. Her head flopped forward like a flower whose stem had broken. But then she moaned. He shook her again. "Joy! Wake up!"

"Not Joy," she murmured. "Scottish. Alec's Scottish."

"That's right. Who's Alec?" he asked.

"Alec?" Her eyes opened, clear and green and so suddenly conscious he thought for a moment that he'd imagined it.

"That's so silly," she said, looking right at him. "You are Alec." She smiled up at him and placed one icy stiff hand on his heart. "My Alec."

He could feel the frost on her glove. It was like ice on his chest. He studied her face for a pensive moment, surprised that she could become clear-headed so quickly. "That's right." Then he tested her: "Who are you?"

Her chin went up, high. She seemed to be trying to look down at him. "I am the duchess of Belmore." She struggled to stand on her own and did so with a burst of strength. She gave him a regal nod that would have done the princess of Wales proud.

He sagged back against a hoarfrosted tree and wiped the snow from his eyes. Thank God. He glanced down the road, little more than a solid, seemingly endless plain of white. He took deep, cleansing breaths that he hoped would warm him and give him the strength to go on. He had no idea where they were, if help was near, if anyone was near.

Something hit his leg—a shoe!—and he turned around.

His wife stood ten feet away surrounded by cold white snow. She stripped off her one remaining shoe and sent it soaring through the snow-filled air. It hit him in the arm.

"What the devil are you doing?" He stumbled and fell forward when his boot hit the slick wet leather of her discarded coat. A stocking landed in the snow in front of his hands. He got to his knees. The other stocking plopped in front of him.

"Stop!" he shouted and watched in stunned horror as she

shoved her soggy dress down and stepped out of it. He scrambled toward her shouting, "Where the hell are your wits, woman?"

She grabbed at her chemise and moved away from him. He slid in the snow and heard the sound of tearing silk. She struggled out of the torn garment. He tried to reach her, but slipped again, cursing. The snow had gotten wetter, heavier, and deeper, and he shoved and slid his way through it.

What rational human being would strip herself naked when she was freezing to death? God Almighty, she wasn't a rational human being. She was a witch. Was this some ritual? He shook the snow from his head. Damn her!

He pushed his way through the thickening snow. "Stand still!"

She turned and smiled at him, sweetly, as if this were some coy game, and stepped away, completely naked, her ripped chemise dangling from one bare hand.

"Scottish! I demand you stop!" He slipped and fell again, but was thankful when he heard her voice. He knew now that she was delirious.

"Her Grace is going to see Prinny. Spoiled, demanding Prinny. My husband Alec is demanding, too." She gave a little nod, apparently to emphasize what she said.

Alec tried and failed to reach her in the slippery snow.

"What else did he say about Prinny? Oh, yes! He's fat." She shook her head. "Alec isn't fat. He's imperious." She held one finger to her lips, then whispered, "Alec is imperious, too much so. But . . . back to superstitious old Prinny! He went to Paris alone, you know, Prinny did. But I shall save him from Napoleon. Then he won't lop off our heads. Alec needs his old gray head."

Alec regained his footing and eased his way toward her.

She threw the chemise at him. "Here, catch!"

He ducked and lunged at her, falling deeper into the snow and grabbing her legs. She went down with him, kicking.

"No! No! I'm a good witch!" Her eyes looked through him, unseeing. Her breathing was raspy, haggard, and loud, getting louder because she was fighting him, squirming in the snow. Her bare foot slammed into the side of his head.

"Damn!" He grabbed her flailing foot in a tight grip. "Stop it!"

"It burns my skin! Don't burn me! The fire! My skin is on fire! They're burning me, Alec! Help me!" Despite her delirium she squirmed to get away, kicking out at him with the other foot. "Help me, please help me. Don't let them burn me, please." Her breathing changed to sobs.

"You little idiot! You're going to freeze to death!"

"Can't freeze. On fire, on fire . . ."

"Hold still!" He pinned her down with his body. "You're not on fire!" She kept twisting beneath him, then as suddenly as her sobbing started she was still, quiet—deathly quiet.

He shook her. "Wake up!"

She flopped in the snow, limp, her skin cold.

"Scottish! Wake up!" He pulled her against him, wrapping his own wet arms around her and rocking her. "It's me, Alec."

She didn't move.

"Your Alec." He spoke softly, but he shook her again.

Still nothing. He placed his cheek against her bare breast. It was as cold as ice. He held his breath, listening for a heartbeat. All he could hear was his own racing heart. He tried again. Nothing. He closed his eyes, concentrating hard, listening for a sign of life.

There was a slow, shallow beat, and a trace of what he prayed was a breath.

He struggled toward her clothes, awkwardly, on his knees, the duke of Belmore with his limp, naked duchess clutched with one cold and fast-weakening arm against his heaving chest. The snow grew thicker, quieter—as eerie and frightening as the silence of his frozen wife.

He wondered if she was going to die, then if he was, too.

He forced that thought from his head. A duke didn't die while lost in the bloody snow. At least, not the duke of Belmore. Neither would his duchess. He grabbed her snow-covered and torn chemise, and shook it so hard it snapped like a gunshot in the air. He slid one of her arms into the chemise and then struggled to get the other one through it. Grasping the ragged edges, he pulled them together.

Next came the sodden wool dress. He slipped it over her head and tried to get her arms into it. Her hair was soaked and little more than a lump of thick brown ice. Her skin had a blue tinge to it.

Get her covered, he thought, and quickly. He wrenched the leather cape from the snow and wrapped it around her small body. Now he was shivering so hard he could barely hold her and still remain on his knees. It was then that he realized she had stopped shivering some time before. Instinct told him that was not good.

He crawled with her to where her stockings lay—limp frozen rags in the snow. He shook them out and tried to get them on her feet and up her stiff legs. His hands shook.

He searched for her shoes. The snow fell harder, faster, thicker. He couldn't see those shoes. She needed her shoes . . . he knew that. He crawled near the tree, sat back on his heels, and laid her across his lap. Then he bent over her, pinning her between his chest and thighs while he dug in the powdery snow.

The hole grew, three feet deep, four feet wide, before he found one small leather shoe, emptied it, and tried to slide her stiff foot into it. He cursed his shaking hands, sure that was reason he couldn't do something so simple, so important.

It was then that he noticed her feet and legs. Though her body was limp, flaccid, like a rose wilted by the wind and weather, the muscles in her legs and feet were inexplicably taut. He rubbed them over and over, trying to get them to relax, then tried again and managed to put the shoe on.

Once again he dug in the snow in a frenzied, desperate search, as if the lost shoe symbolized their chances of survival. He had to find it . . . he had to . . . had to. . . .

The wind whipped the snow from the trees. It tumbled down, filling the hole. He swore, loudly, a shout in the sharp air, at God or at the Devil, he didn't know which. All he knew was he needed that shoe.

His clawing hand closed over it, and he almost cried out in relief. He dumped out the snow and massaged her small foot again, then forced it into the hard, frozen leather. He pulled back the cape and looked down into her face, so still.

"Don't die. You cannot die. You are the duchess of Belmore. Do you hear me? You will not die." He struggled to his feet, shifting her in his arms, and a frigid moment later he stumbled down the road, wading through enough snow to bury all of London.

The flurries ceased. Alec moved up a hill, the snow now waist high. His teeth chattered, he shivered, yet the exertion of plodding half frozen through the deep snow had him sweating. He could feel the sweat seep down his head, his arms, and his back. It froze on his skin and made him even colder.

He wanted to call out, but he was a duke. A duke didn't, couldn't, needn't, show emotion.

The wind was still a lethal whip of iced air. It was colder than anything he could remember feeling, colder than the coldest thing he'd ever encountered—his father's icy hard voice.

"You are the heir, Alec. You!" his father had said. "You will be the duke someday. A Belmore duke does not cry. Stop it, Alec! You need no one. Understand? No one. A Belmore duke does not laugh. Laughter is for fools. A duke does not need anyone or anything. Do you understand? Do you? Emotions are for weak fools. You are a Belmore. No Belmore is a fool. You need no one. You are a Belmore . . . a Belmore. . . ."

Alec stiffened, that cold voice echoing in his mind as if his stoic father still stood before him. He sucked in a deep breath of windswept air. He opened his eyes, expecting to see his father's face. He saw a white blur. It was snowing again.

His lungs felt suddenly tight. His head hurt. He was tired, more tired than he could ever remember being. He could not, would not, sleep or stop.

He made the top of the hill and collapsed, falling on his back in the snow and sliding down another incline, his wife a deadweight on his chest. Still he clung to her until he stopped sliding at the base of the opposite hillside. He sucked in a ragged chestful of air and closed his eyes, his head sagging to the side, and succumbed to exhaustion and the elements.

The odd distant sound of a bell pierced what little consciousness he had left. "Here," he whispered what felt like a shout into the snow. "Belmore . . . we're over here." Might be help. He needed to open his eyes, but they were heavy and cold. He wanted to swallow but couldn't find the strength. Even the inside of his throat was dry and cold.

Again he heard the bell. The bawl of a cow. Distant voices. A song, a quiet laugh, so faint he wondered if it was only in his mind. He tried to lift his heavy head. He couldn't feel his neck muscles. He couldn't move.

They would die.

His arm lay across his wife—little more than a still, wet weight atop his drained body.

The duke and duchess of Belmore, frozen to death in the middle of nowhere.

Somewhere in the depths of his mind a part of him fought the inevitable, a part of him refused to give up. If he gave up, he was little more than the weak child who would never live up to being a Belmore duke in his father's cold and unforgiving eyes.

He managed somehow to turn his face an inch more and he bit into the wet snow. It melted in his mouth, trickled down his dry throat, reminding him that they were still alive. In one last effort, one last attempt to survive, he lifted his heavy head from the ice-flaked ground and willed his eyes open.

He saw little, only blurry white.

Again he thought he heard a cow bell. He took a breath and gave a weak shake of his head. Snow fell in a sodden clump from his eye sockets.

Then he saw it—golden yellow light spilling from the narrow windows of an ancient daub-and-wattle inn, its plump thatched roof blanketed with snow.

"God Almighty, Scottish, the inn . . ." He pulled his wife tighter against him and lurched upward, only to fall backward again. He turned, still clutching her to him and crawled a few feet toward the inn. His weight packed the snow enough for him to dig in his boots, to get his footing. He stumbled to his knees and fell forward atop her.

She moaned, a weak, small thread of a moan, but it was a moan.

"We've found the inn. Wake up! Damn you, wife, wake up!"

He rose to one knee, holding her tighter than he'd ever held anything in his life—and he managed to stand.

He limped. He stumbled. But he moved forward, closing the distance to the inn door, the last hundred feet, his breath coming in heaving pants that fogged in front of his face, his body numb, cold, and functioning on only God knew what.

His shoulder rammed against the solid door. It didn't open. He could hear muted voices, laughter and music. He raised one foot and found the strength to kick it open, then stumbled into the suddenly silent tavern room in a flurry of ice and snow.

"Help us," he said, unable to focus on anything but the massive stone hearth and the blazing fire within it. "Cold . . . fire . . . my wife . . ."

Alec moved toward the fire, Scottish in his frigid arms. At the feel of the heat he dropped to his knees, his arms still gripping her tight. Just before he collapsed, he rasped, "You are the duchess of Belmore. You will not die."

A pair of hard, strong hands grasped his shoulders. "Steady, I've got ye," came a rough dark voice.

Someone tried to take Scottish from his arms, but he refused to let go. "No! I have to make her warm. The fire . . ."

"Leave off. I 'ave them both," the dark voice said. The hands stopped pulling his wife away. The dark voice said, "Fetch some more blankets 'n' stoke the fire upstairs."

Alec heard the scurrying of feet, the creak of stairs, a door slamming, the crackle of the fire, and then those same scurrying feet in some room above him. Then he felt himself being lifted by some massive body, and the intense heat of the fire hit his face. It burned his skin and sucked the breath from his lips, but he knew it was what she needed. He held her tighter.

"Here. Sit. Ye'll 'ave to let me 'ave 'er."

"No!"

"Calm down, Yer Grace."

The heavy ice-crusted cape was lifted from his shoulders and replaced with a thick warm blanket. "Forget about me. She needs to be warm."

"Ye 'ave to let go o' her. Best get her out o' them wet things."

Alec looked up toward the voice, and his blurry vision sharpened. He saw a rough, broad man with a big potato of a nose and bright yellow hair that hung to his shoulders. The man was examining him with shrewd gray eyes.

Alec's teeth began to chatter. He tried to stop it, but couldn't and he shivered. "I—I'll do it."

The man eyed him skeptically. "Can ye make it up them stairs?"

Alec nodded and tried to stand, but his legs were so cold they buckled.

The man's arms clamped around his shoulders. "Best let me 'elp ye." The man led him up the narrow rickety and creaking stairs.

"Watch yer 'ard 'ead on the blimin' beam," he warned, ducking under the timbered overhang and leading Alec toward a narrow door. "'Ere." He opened the creaking door.

The room was small but very warm from the blazing fireplace opposite the bed. Alec's wits were fast returning, as was the feeling in his numb hands and feet.

He knelt on the hearth, letting the blanket drop from his shoulders. He laid his limp wife atop it, then awkwardly peeled the icy gloves from his hands. "Send up a maid and send for a physician."

"No womenfolk 'ere, an' no leech."

"Bloody hell." Alec jerked the snow-crusted coat off his wife. His hands were still so numb he couldn't feel the cold of the coat. "She needs help." He could hear the frustration in his dry voice.

"Take them wet rags off 'er. 'Ere, I'll 'elp."

"No! I shall do it. Alone." He looked down at her, one meager blanket around her. "Are there any more blankets?" He covered her with his own.

The door creaked open and a small white-bearded dwarf came into the room, his pudgy arms laden with a stack of old thin woolen blankets. He waddled over to where Joy lay and set the blankets beside her, his eyes odd and wary. Then he was out the door again.

Alec lifted Joy onto those thin blankets, then crossed over to the bed and stripped the bedclothes off of it.

The big man eyed him speculatively, then said, "Ye need to get out o' them clothes."

"First my wife." Alec grabbed the edge of the wide straw mattress and tried to pull it off of the bed. The cold had taken its toll. He had little strength in his hands, which tingled with a thousand sharp needlelike sensations.

The huge man had joined him and grabbed one side, muttering about stubborn Englishmen while he helped move the mattress close to the fire. Alec settled Joy atop it, then stared at her white face. He sank to his knees next to her and felt another blanket cover him. He said nothing, just struggled to get the sodden clothes off her.

The big man still stood over him, watching. Alec struggled with the wet dress. He stopped suddenly and looked up, his eyes hard, his mind sharp—all duke of Belmore. "I will see to it. She's my wife."

The man gauged him for a second, then moved back toward the door. Frustrated at his awkward hands Alec stared at the sodden dress, then grabbed wet wads of it in both hands and ripped it in two.

"I guess ye will," the man muttered and opened the door. He paused and turned back. "I'll bring ye up a kettle to warm over the fire. Ye'll be needin' hot water."

Aware that he needed it, but loath to admit it, Alec looked up and nodded. The man closed the door, and Alec tore off the rest of Joy's clothes. Her shoes were ice and stuck to her poor cold feet. If it hadn't been for the stockings he would have had to cut the shoes off her. Her skin was a bluish white, what little he had glimpsed in his rush to bundle her up in the thin blankets. A feeling of complete ineptness swept through him as he stood there. Since the moment this witch popped into his life he'd felt as if everything was out of control. Nothing was right.

Watching her as she lay there, bundled in blankets, half frozen, half alive, and perhaps half dead, something wrenched inside him, something deep and unsettling, and in his confusion he had the merest glimmer of a premonition that nothing would ever be the same again. The thought did little for his peace of mind, did little to assuage this new feeling of vulnerability.

He bent down and tugged at his own frozen boots. The blond man returned with a steaming kettle of water in his hand. Alec glanced up and met his gaze. The man drew a knife from his belt. For a tense minute neither moved. Alec realized the vulnerability of their situation—an isolated inn, snowed in. Wouldn't it be ironic to have survived the frigid cold only to be murdered by some giant in the warmth of a cozy inn?

A pair of sharp gray eyes gazed back at him, assessing him, weighing him, almost reading his thoughts. Then the man averted his eyes, knelt at Alec's feet, and sliced the side of one of his Hessians. Alec relaxed.

The dwarf came in with a tray laden with bowls of steaming soup and some bread. He set the tray on the floor near the fire and then left as quickly and wordlessly as he had come. An old hinge squeaked in the silent room. "There be wood in 'ere." The blond man pointed to a deep pine chest. "We'll leave ye be, now," he said, his boots clomping like the hooves of a draft horse on the wooden floor as he went to the door.

"Thank you," Alec said quietly—words that were seldom spoken by the duke of Belmore.

"Ye be welcome, Yer Grace." And he left them alone.

Alec checked Joy, lowering his ear to her lips and listening for her breath. It was still shallow. He pulled his own wet clothing off, wrapped one of the blankets around himself, and moved on stiff and tingling feet to kneel near his wife—the witch.

The duchess of Belmore was a witch. He found the idea incomprehensible. He had thought his days away from her would assuage the feeling that he was having a nightmare.

The scene on the roof had convinced him otherwise. He was living the nightmare.

From the moment she'd convinced him of the truth, his mind had viewed her as something unreal, inhuman. Then he'd done what he always did—pushed his emotions aside and rationally thought the situation through. He realized there was nothing he could do about it. He'd married her in front of witnesses, and divorce or annulment was out of the question. He was a Belmore. He needed heirs. He needed a wife. He would deal with her the way he had always dealt with everything. He would take charge and command her to be normal. Then perhaps he could view her as a normal woman.

He looked down at her pale skin. He touched her cheek. It was cold, soft, unmoving. She was no nightmare; she was real. And, witch or no, she was his wife. He could not change that, and God help him, some small strange part of him didn't want to change it.

Although he was loath to admit it, he was drawn to her by some strong elusive cord of desire that he had never encountered before and that he could not command to go away. He had stayed away from her, thinking himself drawn to her by some spell, by witchcraft.

Until now. There was little life left in her, let alone any magic power. Still he felt that compelling need to stay close to her, an overwhelming urge to touch her.

He rubbed her damp hair between his fingers, remembering it full, brown as mink, and waving clear down to the backs of her thighs. He touched her cheek, her lips. Yes, she was real. This was no nightmare. He'd married a witch with the face of an angel. He looked at that face, touched the cold softness of her cheek.

She didn't react to his touch.

He tucked another blanket around her and sat there, watching her pale lips, sodden hair, weak breathing. He had no idea how much time went by. He just sat there watching her shallow breathing as if he expected it to cease should he look away.

Such foolishness for an English duke.

He forced himself to move then. He checked the water in the kettle. It was warm. He dipped a few rags into it, wrung them out, and lightly bathed her face and neck—a task he had never performed for anyone.

The color came back to her cheeks after a few soft strokes of the warm cloths. He wrapped one around her cold wet hair and then moved to her hands, aware that the extremities were the most vulnerable to frostbite. He bathed each small hand, staring at the unique lines in her palms and her fingertips, at the pale nails and small feminine fingers, so different from his large hands. He had never noticed a woman's hands before, but he noticed hers, and he had another truly odd reaction. He felt awkward, different, and was suddenly aware of his size, his sex.

He moved to her feet, washing them, holding them, really looking at them, and realizing how small and how human his wife really was. And never in his twenty-eight years had Alec Castlemaine, duke of Belmore, felt so completely out of his element.

# Chapter 13

At the request of Neil, Viscount Seymour,
chapter thirteen has been omitted.
Bad luck, you know. . . .

# Chapter 14

Joy drifted between two worlds—that of consciousness, where it was cold and where pain abounded, and that place where she felt nothing, no pain, no cold, but where there was also no life, no warm sunshine, no fresh-smelling pine trees, no bright-colored flowers. No Alec.

"Scottish."

She tried to tell him something, anything, but her voice wouldn't work. She felt him near, his warm breath on her face. It soothed her. She tried desperately to move her lips. They were too cracked and dry.

"What?" he said. "I cannot hear you."

"Alec . . ." The word scratched her throat.

"I'm here."

She tried to lick her lips, but couldn't.

"Wait a minute," he said, then she felt a warm wet cloth bathe her mouth.

"Cold, so cold," she whispered.

"I know." The cloth touched her as gently as his gruff voice spoke to her.

"Hold me."

She felt his hesitation, then heard the rustle of a blanket, and he was next to her. He lifted her and held her against the length of his body. She could feel the strength of muscle, tendon, and bone, so different from her own softness and so very warm. He wore no shirt, and she threaded her fingers through the hair on his chest. He covered them both with his blanket, then wrapped his arms around her, holding her in a protective cocoon of strong male flesh.

Alec, this time I need your magic, she thought. A second later she felt warm and real and vibrant, as if the life had poured from him into her.

He was warm—her sunshine. She breathed in the scent of him, clean and sharp—her pine trees. She willed her eyes open and looked into the deep midnight blue of the season's first Canterbury bells. Bells, she thought, her heart smiling because her lips couldn't. Bells, Belmore, Alec . . . Suddenly Joy wasn't so cold.

"Better?" His hand brushed her face.

She tried to answer, but nothing came out.

"What?" he asked. Again his breath was in her hair.

She placed her icy hand over his heart and rasped out a tiny whisper, "Kiss me."

He stared down at her. She could feel his pause, his look. Then his knuckle touched her chin, raising it, tilting it near her mouth.

His lips touched hers, so softly, little more than a lingering of lips.

She moaned in protest.

He pulled back, a question in his eyes.

"Like before," she whispered, patting his heart. "Makes me warm inside."

He kissed her deeply. And she tasted what she loved—her Alec.

Some time later Joy stirred, not wanting to let go of her dreams, dreams of sparkling fairy tales that ended with the princess and her gray-haired prince dancing across the roof of his castle to music played on an angel's harp and Pan's pipes.

She was warm, truly warm, all toasty inside, but she wasn't sure if the toasty feeling was from the fire or from the memory of Alec's kiss. It was the last thing she remembered clearly, his kissing her, for she'd tasted all she loved just before she fell asleep in the tight secure ring of his warm arms and slept soundly, lost in her dreams.

After a few more moments of quiet memories, that drifting of the mind where the world was exactly the way one wanted it—filled with the sweetness of dreams and hopes and wishes. Half asleep, half awake, sensing that Alec was nearby, she opened her eyes. Her vision was nothing but a blur. She blinked a few times, then turned her head.

Covered in a veil of fair moonlight he stood at a narrow window across the dark room. He stared outside. The tail of his white shirt hung outside his buff breeches, which were smudged with dirt and had a ragged rip at the back of one knee. His fine polished boots had been slit down the inside of his calves and flopped open. The gold tassels that trimmed them were now ragged and skimpy threads, as if Beezle had been chewing them.

One long arm reached upward and his hand gripped the top of the window frame. The other hand held a cup or a mug, something from which he would take an occasional and thoughtful sip. She stared at his stance, remembering warm masculine hands stroking her face, pressing warm wet cloths against her cold skin, a rough beard-stubbled cheek against her chest as he listened for a heartbeat, a deep voice telling her she was a duchess and as such she could not do anything foolish, like die.

She remembered trying to tell him that she was just tired, not dead, but after a few mumbled words that refused to form on her dry lips, nothing had mattered but the flavor of the salty broth that he spooned into her mouth. She remembered the taste of bread soaked in soup and the sound of her husband's voice commanding her to eat.

It was hard to picture the duke of Belmore playing nursemaid. Her gaze drifted back to him, and she used the opportunity to watch him. He appeared to be deep in thought, and she wondered what he was thinking. Of course she always wondered what he was thinking. Since his face seldom showed any emotion except anger—she'd seen that one once too often—she could never gauge his thoughts.

What would a duke think? Her mind flashed the image of him standing thigh-deep in icy water and asking her where the hell the inn was. Then she remembered the look of horror on his face when he realized she was truly a witch. That image gave her an answer: he was probably thinking that she was a problem—a big problem.

A little defeated, a little ashamed, she looked down at the mattress on which she lay, seeing the small sprigs of hay and straw that poked through the worn ticking. She fingered one small piece of broken yellow straw that was lying all alone on the sack ticking.

Joy felt like that piece of straw. It had foolishly slipped out of its tight and safe little world, only to end up broken and in vastly unfamiliar territory. With a sigh she tossed the straw aside. It landed in the fireplace and was gone in a flash of hot blue flames. She frowned, not liking the analogy that crossed her mind—straw consumed by fire.

All she had really wanted was to impress him with one incantation that would transport them to a warm, cozy inn. That didn't seem like too much to ask. Sometimes her spells went so wrong that she wondered at her purpose in life. Then she glanced up at him. Was he the reason she existed in this mixed up world of happiness and heartache?

With a sad sigh, she pulled the heavy, warm blankets tighter against her chin. Her bruised and aching muscles protested even those small movements, and she winced. Her body felt battered—like the time she'd fallen down the tower stairs while chasing a broom, which had been running at the time. She had brought the thing to life in a misguided attempt to magically clean up the tower floor—a chore that had been her punishment for some other ill-begotten mistake.

There had been so many mishaps at that awkward time in her life that she could only recall the most memorable and painful. And painful that one had been. She had carried the blue bruises for weeks after her rough tumble down fifty stone steps.

It wasn't easy being a young witch, even if one's skills came naturally. In Joy's case, the rose of youth was blue—black-and-blue. And so, it would appear, was the rose of her womanhood.

She looked back at Alec and all the years of mistaken

spells and shameful accidents faded away like fog in the sunshine. This was so right—the two of them together. She knew it as surely as if someone had handed him to her on one of Belmore's silver platters and said, "Here, this man is yours—your purpose, your reason for living. He needs you."

On that last thought her eyes drifted closed and a smile teased her lips. Once again she escaped to her world of wonder, that place without aches of the body and heart, an enchanted sleepy world where a witch's spells worked perfectly, where a handsome gray-haired duke smiled and turned her night into day, and where dreams might indeed come true.

Alec was truly living a nightmare.

He was sure of it. The giant and the dwarf had bloody well disappeared. He had searched, called out to them, waited, but no one was there, and from the looks of things no one had ever been there.

There were no clothes in the clothespresses, no signs that anyone lived or had lived there. The standard inn furniture was there along with pots and kettles in the kitchen, but no people or personal possessions. He knew he had seen the two men—bloody hell, he'd felt them. Someone had tried to pull Joy from his arms. He had spoken to the giant.

His puzzled gaze moved to the narrow window. He saw nothing but white snow and foggy windowpanes. No one would have left in this weather. But the men were gone.

He walked over to the hearth and looked around the tavern dining room. There were old splintered tables and chairs, but no signs of any drink. There were no barrels of ale or beer, no mugs or steins, nothing but an unoccupied room with tables and chairs, a fireplace, and a small pile of chopped wood by the hearth.

Alec could have sworn he had heard bells, laughter, and voices, and the cow. Those sounds had drawn him to the inn. He crossed the room and rubbed the foggy window, then bent down and tried to see out. He knew he had heard that cow, so there had to be a barn or a stable; this was an inn.

He caught a glimpse of a dark shadow some distance away. It was hard to see through the falling snow, but he dared not venture out until Joy was awake. And truthfully, he was not eager to go tramping through the snow again anytime soon. He moved away from the window and went into the open kitchen behind the rickety staircase.

A pot of soup hung unattended and cold in the kitchen hearth. There was little left, not even a bowlful, but Alec did find a small hunk of bread left. Near the kitchen hearth stood a large water crock, and the small pantry held a few dirt-crusted turnips, carrots, rutabagas, and potatoes, a burlap sack of coarse flour, and half a crock of lard. That was the only food to be found, and being a duke, he hadn't the slightest idea what to do with it. He had never cooked a thing in his life. In fact he'd been in a Belmore kitchen only once or twice, when he was a child.

He walked over to the shelf and eyed the rugged-looking vegetables with trepidation. He was an intelligent man, he reasoned. He ran estates, argued points of law in the House of Lords, and was an eminent peer of the realm.

But peasants cooked. Women cooked. Peers of the realm did not cook.

He pondered that thought for a minute, then came to a perfectly logical masculine conclusion. He was a duke and a man. Surely he could do as well, no doubt better . . .

"You need to eat, Scottish. Wake up."

Joy groaned, then felt Alec lift her so she was once again against his chest, and such a nice warm chest it was, too. She placed her hand over his heart and drifted back to sleep.

"Do not go back to sleep. I will not allow it."

"So tired . . ." she managed to mutter.

He gave her a little shake. "You must eat."

She sighed and opened her mouth, then took the opportunity to slide her arms around him and snuggle a bit closer.

"Good."

Yes, she thought, very good. She placed her hand on his heart and sighed just a bit.

"Now, here's some soup."

She felt the warm metal of the spoon against her lips, then the trickle of warm broth filling her mouth.

She gagged, turning away from his warm chest. Then she coughed and swallowed and coughed some more. She took a deep breath and, grimacing at the foul taste, looked at him, unable to believe he could be so cruel.

He sat perfectly stiff and eyed the soup for a moment. "You need to eat."

"I don't want it." She slumped back down on the mattress and pulled the blankets tighter around her.

"You must eat."

She shook her head. "No."

"You are my wife and I command you to eat."

"It tastes like dirt."

He stiffened, but she was too tired and too weak to argue. He could be as arrogant as he wanted, but she would not eat that vile brew. She told him so again and closed her eyes, missing the offended look that crossed his face as he looked into the soup bowl. After a very silent few seconds he placed a hunk of bread next to her and, bowl in hand, left the room.

Joy awoke to the smell of woodsmoke. She peeled her eyes open and watched the flames of the nearby fire lick a blue-orange path up the stone chimney. It was a big fire that sent waves of undulating heat over her. She turned toward the window, hoping to see Alec. He was not there. Instead her hopeful gaze was met by white daylight that melted through the frost-framed windowpanes.

She sat up, wincing as her muscles ached in protest, and looked around the room. He was not there. She pulled the blanket tighter around her, feeling suddenly very alone and vulnerable and very naked beneath the blankets. She scanned the room again and spotted her clothes stacked atop a wood chest near the window. She tried to stand, a foolish act that sent the pain of unused muscles speeding through her feet and legs as if they were filled with swarms of bees.

She plopped back down on her bundle of blankets, feeling even more helpless. She rubbed her bare feet until they felt somewhat normal and then tried again to stand, successfully this time. With the awkward gait of a drunken duck she waddled, still wrapped in a bundle of heavy blankets, over to the stack of her clothing.

As quick as she could, she rummaged through the clothes, only to find her chemise a torn, gaping rag. She stood back a bit, one hand holding up the blanket and the other pointed at the chemise. "Oh, silky garment with ribbons of blue," she chanted, "go back to original form anew!"

The chemise disappeared in a pop! Joy stared in shock at the place where it had lain. She stepped closer, and saw a white cocoon the size of a robin's egg. Bending over the cocoon, she watched the tiny silkworm moving inside.

"Not that original form," she muttered.

Try again. . . . She closed her eyes, mentally picturing a new chemise: "I need an undergarment just for me, exactly like the one I see!"

She snapped her fingers for good measure and opened her eyes. The torn chemise lay there just as it had before. She sighed, reasoning that she was still a tad weak and her magic, which was not that strong anyway, must be suffering.

She picked up the chemise, looked at it for a moment, then, being a frugal Scot through and through, she put it on backwards, figuring it was better to do that than to go without. A few minutes and many stumbles and struggles later, she had dressed in the wrinkled and torn green cashmere dress haphazardly pinned together with two hairpins, the stiff once-white stockings, and the crusty hard viridian slippers. She pulled her hair from its tangled knot and ran her fingers through it, wincing. Finally giving up, she wrapped the whole mess around one hand and jabbed in a few hairpins.

Quietly, she opened the door, expecting to see the narrow hallway of a typical English inn. Instead she faced a small landing and a steep staircase. She stepped outside, quietly closing the door when she heard the muted sound of Alec's voice from below stairs. She gripped the rough handrail, and slowly and carefully on somewhat wobbly legs made her way down the narrow stairs. Little more than halfway down she could make out his words. She stopped, and listened.

"The duke of Belmore stuck in the middle of God only knows where. Not a bloody servant to be found. What the hell kind of inn is this?"

Joy waited for an answer. None came. Who was he talking to? There was only the loud banging of something metal. She crept down another few steps, ducked under a low beam, and saw Alec's broad back hunched over the kitchen hearth. Except for him, the room was empty.

"Here one minute, gone the next." He shook his head and muttered something strange about disappearing giants and dwarfs.

The duke of Belmore was talking to himself—Himself. She heard the scrape of metal against metal, then the gritty high-pitched scraping of a flint . . . a loud *whoosh!*

"Bloody hell!"

Hot blue flames shot like Easter bonfires up the brick chimney. He stood back from the blasting hearth, staring at the fire—giving it the ducal glare, no doubt. The oven door burst open with a blast of hot air and banged against the brick. Flames shot all the way up to the bread oven.

It looked like one of her magic spells on a really bad day. But it was nothing compared to how he looked.

His ears, his neck, his rolled-up sleeves, his forearms, his shirtfront, his chest, the brown leather apron that covered that chest, and a good bit of his hair were dusted white with flour. His hands were caked in lumpy dough. His Grace, the Right Honorable—and overly proper—duke of Belmore, was a mess.

She couldn't help it. She giggled.

He looked up at her. The second their gazes met his face flashed with an instant of surprise, then a snatch of something that made her breath catch. He actually look pleased, very pleased, but the look of pleasure was gone so fast she wasn't sure she'd really seen it. He had almost seemed happy to see her. Joyous hope in her heart, she searched his dark eyes, but she saw only his usual cool expression.

"You're well." He took a step toward her, his face unchanged.

She nodded, then descended the last two steps and returned his look. After a moment of serious staring between the two, she smiled. His face was streaked with flour where he'd obviously wiped his brow a few too many doughy times. He hadn't shaved, and his chin and jaw were dark with stubble and dusted with flour. The scowl, however, was very familiar.

"What are you doing?" she asked, looking around him.

His shoulders went back—his I-am-the-duke stance—before he announced stiffly, "I am preparing a meal."

She took a few steps closer and saw a wooden worktable in one corner. In its center was a huge white slab of something that, with a mountain of imagination, might have passed for bread dough. It was the size of a bagpipe, and it lay in state—a sad state—amid a good inch of coarse-milled wheat flour.

"I see."

He stood as stiff and still as a Celtic stone.

"Bread?"

He turned back and stared at the slab of dough. It was the first time she'd seen his self-assurance slip. He looked uncomfortable and not the least bit confident. Her proud husband didn't have any idea what he was doing, so she offered to help, figuring she might be able to convince him to let her conjure something up.

"Ah, you can cook." His voice was tinged with relief, although she could not see any change in his expression.

Now, Joyous Fiona MacQuarrie Castlemaine, the duchess of Belmore, part Scot, part English, part witch, was anything but stupid. She would not pass up such a perfect opportunity to impress him. After all, her chances up until now had been few and far between.

She only hoped her expression didn't show the wee fib she was about to spill. She couldn't cook, but she could usually zap up a good meal. One deep breath, her eyes wide, and out it came. "Aye."

"Good."

It appeared that he couldn't get out of that apron soon enough. Joy bit back a grin. He hadn't moved that fast since she set fire to his dining room carpet. He glanced at her and she struggled to look properly serious. From his expression she was certain she'd failed. He stood a touch straighter—very ducal—then tossed the apron on the worktable, where it landed in a puff of flour.

"I shall see to the fire," he said.

Joy looked at the blazing fire in the kitchen hearth. His gaze followed hers.

"The fire in the great room." He made a military turn and left the kitchen. A few moments later she heard the thud of logs on a grate.

She turned back to the room and stared at the mess and at the meager supplies. She crossed the room and examined the vegetables. It seemed vegetable soup was destined to be their menu. If only she could use her magic. But there her husband wouldn't be fooled.

She crossed to the table, shook out the apron, and tied it on, then put some of the vegetables on the table. Flour was everywhere. She looked around the room and spotted a willow broom propped against a butter churn in a dark corner.

Should she? She was feeling stronger, and she'd finally managed to master broom control last year. She stretched her neck to see what Alec was doing. His back was to her and he was fiddling with the fire.

Quickly she looked at the broom, narrowed her bright eyes, and said, "Come." The broom took two wobbly leaps toward her then stopped, standing all by itself. Closer, she thought. She gave another furtive glance in Alec's direction and deepened her voice, "Come!"

The broom slammed into her and clattered against the table.

"Are you all right?"

She winced at the sound of Alec's voice. She stretched to

see him again. He still knelt by the fire but was looking her way.

"I dropped something."

He nodded and went back to work.

She looked at the broom and grinned, then bent down and whispered, "See the flour, stone ground? Sweep it into one big mound. Do your work without a sound, and stop the instant Alec turns around."

The broom swept the flour from the table in a few puffs of white, then did a tidy little dance around the table, sweeping the flour into a pile. Joy smiled, then dropped the vegetables onto the table top next to Alec's bread dough. She eyed the lump, then turned to the bread oven above the hearth. She turned back and tried to pick up the dough. She could only hold half of it, the other half flopped over her arm. She set it back down, pointed at it and twiddled her fingers.

The dough crept like an inchworm to the edge of the table. Must be too heavy for twiddling, she thought. She raised one hand and said, "Up!"

"Bloody hell!"

*Oh, no . . . not again!* Grimacing, she looked into the great room, expecting to see her husband in midair.

Alec stood on the solid floor, bent over the small woodpile near the fireplace. "The blasted wood won't light. It must be too green."

Joy let out a relieved breath, then saw the dough still hovering above the table. She pointed at the oven and whispered, "Go! Cook yourself!"

The bread flew into the brick oven and the iron door slammed shut with a loud clank. She heard Alec's boots on the plank floor. The broom stopped its sweeping and stood in the middle of the room. She grabbed it just as he walked past, heading for the staircase. "Is everything all right?" he asked.

She nodded and gave him what she hoped was an innocent smile.

"I have to get some dry wood from upstairs," he said, then paused at the bottom of the stairs, giving her an odd look. "Is something wrong?"

She tried to smile more broadly. "No." She shook her head. "Just cleaning up a bit." She lifted the broom.

He nodded and went up the stairs. She watched his split boots disappear and sagged back against the table. From the ceiling above, she could hear him entering the upstairs room. Work quickly, she thought, then frowned at the pile of flour and snapped her fingers. "Disappear!"

The flour was gone in a blink. Smiling proudly, she rubbed her hands together and decided to try her hand at the vegetables. She was just thinking up an incantation for vegetable peeling when Alec came back down the stairs.

He bent under the upstairs overhang, his hands gripping the stair rail, and looked at her strangely. "The firewood is gone."

She looked up at him, an uneasy feeling settling in her stomach like a lump of dough. She stared at the ceiling above her.

His eyes grew a wee tinge suspicious. He waited a moment, then asked, "Did you see a stack of wood up there when you awoke?"

"I don't remember," she said, her mind swimming with the picture of the nice neat stack of wood that had been by the fireplace. "Did you see a knife in here anywhere?" She turned her back to him and began rummaging through the kitchen, closing and opening cabinets with a dramatic flair.

There was a long silence. Then he answered, "No. What do you need a knife for?"

"To peel the vegetables," she said, poking inside a drawer but still not meeting his questioning gaze.

"Peel them?" he said under his breath. "Who would have ever thought to peel them?"

Joy glanced up and saw him frowning at the pile of vegetables on the worktable. His gaze met hers and his shoulders went ramrod straight just before he turned away. "I have to get some more wood," he said and left the room.

She paused and looked up at the beamed ceiling, breathing a thankful sigh of relief that the whole upstairs hadn't disappeared.

Finally after rummaging through another cabinet, she found two knives. She took the smaller one and crossed to the table. She looked at the vegetables and knew that she had to do this without the benefit of any more magic. She had a feeling she was already under suspicion. She washed the vegetables in a basin of water from the barrel, then dried them on a small piece of flaxen toweling she'd found in her search.

She peeled the tough skin off a turnip, humming a song from her childhood and thinking about the wonderful dinner they could have had if only she could have used her magic. She could have conjured up a roast duckling with honey and orange sauce, braised carrots with tiny sweet onions, creamed potatoes, and rich, buttery scones.

*Hmm.*

Suddenly Joy was starved. Butter, she thought. Now, that was what their bread needed. A frown creased her face. No doubt he would notice if she contrived some. She turned toward the old butter churn in the corner. She tapped a thoughtful finger against her chin, then walked over and dragged the churn into the middle of the room.

Wiping her hands on her skirt, she left the room and found Alec. "Come see what I've found."

He set a stack of wood down and pinned her with a look that said, "Now what?" She smiled. He finally shook his head and silently followed her into the kitchen.

"Look. It's a butter churn." She waited for his response.

"Yes, I suppose it is," he conceded, obviously not impressed.

"We can make butter!" She rubbed her hands together in anticipation.

"I don't remember seeing any cream."

"Isn't this an inn? There must be a barn, or maybe there are cows in the stable. Don't all inns have stables?"

"I'm certain this is not like most inns."

"Have you looked outside?"

"I believe you are the one who should look outside."

Joy crossed to the window and cleaned the glass. All she saw was snow, white mounds of snow, and it came almost up past the window ledge. Her shoulders slumped with defeat and she turned back around. "I just thought your bread would taste better with butter." She stood there quietly. She could feel him watching her and glanced up to search his hard-angled face.

He took a deep breath and ran a hand through his hair, muttering something about freezing to death again. A second later he strode across the room, where he picked up the cape they'd used in the carriage. He slid into it and crossed to a side door.

"Where are you going?"

"There's a building across the carriage yard. I suspect it's a barn or a stable or a combination of the two. I heard a cowbell when I found this place, so maybe your cow is out there."

"Oh, good!" She followed him at a half-skip. "Where's my coat?"

He stopped suddenly and slowly turned, looking down his noble nose. "You shall stay here."

"Why?"

His face said he was looking for patience. "Because the snow is deep and you have only been up for a few minutes."

"But I want the butter, so I should go with you."

"No."

"It's only a few yards."

"No."

"But—"

"I am not used to having my commands challenged." Gone was the man who had eyed the bread so doubtfully, and back was the arrogant duke. He reached for the doorknob.

Remembering that one weak moment in the kitchen she switched tactics. "Can you milk a cow?"

He stopped mid-motion, his hand tightly gripping the doorknob. It seemed a lifetime before he said, "Your coat is across the room."

Smiling at her success, she took the bread out of the oven,

then rushed across the room and donned the coat, anxious to get going before he thought to ask her if she knew how to milk a cow.

They stepped outside. The snow was so high that it was past her waist. Not one to let a little snow stop her, she walked into it.

He grabbed her arm, and she started to protest, until he swung her up into his arms—her favorite position. Her heart picked up a fanciful beat, and she clasped her arms around his neck and rested her head on his shoulder, smiling and resisting the urge to hum.

He was so wrong. She'd never freeze to death as long as she was in his arms.

A few dreamy minutes later they were inside the dank stable. He set her on her feet and shook off some of the snow while she looked around. It smelled of musty, damp hay mixed with the sharp sting of cow dung and the stench of chickens. She wrinkled her nose, while her eyes adjusted to the lack of light. She could hear the mumbling cluck of several chickens. "Look! We can have eggs."

His gaze followed her pointing finger to a broken wagon piled with hay that made perfect nests for a few scrawny brown chickens. A plump white cow lumbered out from a dark corner to the dull tune of a clanging cowbell.

"Oh, look! It has a bell. I love bells, don't you?" She sighed with a dreamy smile and thought of kirk bells and wedding bells and Canterbury bells and best of all a Belmore duke's warm arms.

The cow stood there, staring at them, blinking. It bawled. Joy sighed and pushed her fantasies from her mind. She turned to Alec. He looked at her blankly. The cow blinked. No one moved to milk it.

Finally he shrugged out of the coat and hung it on a peg near the door, then helped her off with hers.

"Tell me what you need," he said, "and I'll see if I can find it."

What she needed was to know how to milk a cow. She fidgeted, then reached out to stroke the cow, figuring they should get acquainted. After a few strokes she summoned up some Scots determination. "I need a pail."

"Fine." Alec began to search the stable.

Joy leaned over to the cow. "I could use some help here," she whispered.

The cow cocked its head and stared at her through huge gray bovine eyes.

"I want to impress my husband, so it would be very nice if you would cooperate for me," she said, as she patted the cow's wide back. The animal twitched its ears.

There was a loud clunk and the tooth-jarring ring of tin. "I found your pail. And a stool."

A stool? "Oh, good," she said, then whispered to the cow. "Please." She gave it one last pat before Alec joined her and set down the stool and pail next to her.

Joy tried to look confident as she sat down on the stool, then flexed her fingers, as she did just before casting an especially complicated spell, which she might have to resort to if this didn't work. She peered under the cow's full belly, then set the pail under the animal's udder.

"Mind if I watch?"

Joy jumped at the sound of Alec's voice over her shoulder. "No." She reached way under the cow and grabbed hold of two of those dangling spigot-things. Her arms were so short that her cheek rested against the cow's silky white hide.

The cow bawled and she jumped. She pulled. Nothing happened.

She squeezed. The cow swished its tail.

"Nothing's coming out," Alec said.

"I haven't milked a cow in a long time." She squeezed again and nothing happened.

"How long?" His voice was suspiciously quiet.

Joy turned her head away and muttered into the cow's hide, "Twenty-one years."

After a moment he said, "It's still not working." He bent

down to look under the cow. "Did you have many cows in Scotland?"

"No."

"How many did you have?"

She didn't answer, but could sense that he was now aware of her ploy.

"You said you could milk a cow."

"Not exactly." She pulled her hands back into her lap, folded them prayerlike, and stared at them. "Actually, I asked you if you knew how to milk a cow."

"I assumed that meant you did know how to milk one."

She shrugged. "I thought it would be easy," she admitted. "I could try my magic if you—"

"No!"

"But—"

"No, I said!" He paced a short impatient path behind her, mumbling something about curdling the milk. He stopped and squatted down beside her. "It can't possibly be that difficult." He rubbed a finger over his lip while he thought about it. "Are you squeezing them?"

"Yes," she answered. "Watch." She gripped the spigots in her hands and squeezed. "See? Nothing happens."

"Try it again."

Again nothing happened.

"Maybe they're plugged up," she suggested and bent her head down alongside his. She turned one of them upward so she could see the tip. "Can you see anything?"

"No." He leaned closer.

"Neither can I."

Joy turned the other one up. "How about now?" She gave a wee tug.

A white stream of milk spewed straight past her.

"Oh, look!" she said, her voice filled with glee. "I did it! I did it!" She turned to Alec.

The duke of Belmore's noble face dripped with milk.

"Oh, my goodness." She covered her mouth with a hand and watched with dread as the milk dripped from his aristocratic nose, his arrogant chin, and his jaw—which was clenched so tight his cheek had a wee tic—and drops of milk dribbled down his neck.

She couldn't help it. She giggled.

He wiped the milk from his eyes.

"I'm sorry." She giggled some more. "I truly am. I didn't . . . I mean, you look so . . ."

He scowled at her, his whole body stiff with damaged pride. "So . . . what?"

Even his arrogance couldn't keep her from laughing. "So silly. Oh, Alec!" She couldn't keep it in. "It just squirted right past me and *splat!* And you looked so serious and all, but even a duke can't look serious with milk dripping from his face, and I just . . . I just . . ." She stopped laughing and looked straight into his proud eyes. She placed a hand on his and patted him. "I just like you, even with milk on your face."

An odd expression of surprise and curiosity shone from his face. He just watched her, the tic slowly disappearing from his cheek, the anger draining away. The pride was still there, but his look changed to one that held a breath-catching moment of naked longing.

She was so happy to see it that she smiled. He needed her, and that fact had just hit him.

He reached out to graze her cheek with his fingers. His eyes locked on her mouth and grew serious. He rubbed her lips, touched the mole above her upper lip.

She knew that look, and her heart picked up its beat. *Kiss me . . . kiss me . . . kiss me. . . .*

She knew he wanted to. The air almost vibrated with it. Her lips parted in anticipation, and she leaned forward just as he slid his hand behind her neck, pulling her mouth up to his.

Sliding one arm around his neck, she placed the other where it belonged, on his heart, feeling it beat in time with hers. At that same instant their lips touched. Their mouths opened at the same time, and his arm slipped around her and pulled her flush against him.

His other hand moved to cup the back of her head and

hold her mouth against his. He tilted his head and his tongue sank inside, filling her mouth.

He kissed her. The monster was gone.

The cow shifted, and she heard the bell ring, but little mattered in this instant because she knew this was right where she should be.

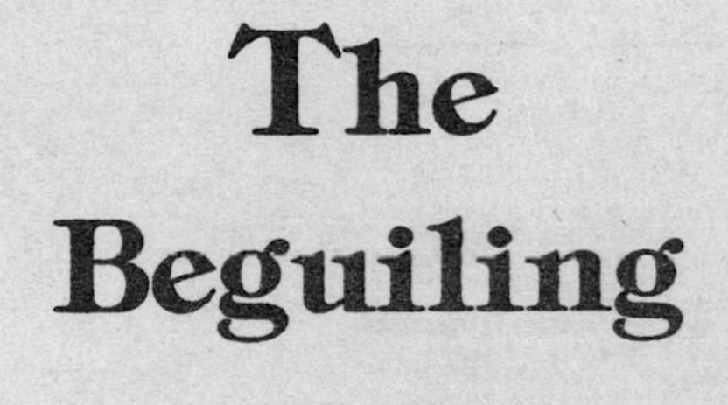
The
Beguiling

**To bed, to bed. . . . What's done cannot be undone. To bed, to bed.**

*Macbeth*, William Shakespeare

# Chapter 15

Alec heard the bell and knew this was not where they should be. He abruptly broke off the kiss, steeling himself to ignore his wife's little moan of surprise. Her eyes were still closed, her lips parted and moist. He felt the pull of her so deeply that he wouldn't have been surprised to see a chain linking them together. That thought sent him into another deep breath. Then he stared into a pair of dreamy gamine-green eyes. Unable to resist, he lifted a finger to her mouth, traced the line of her lips, then touched the little mole above them. With a smile she made him forget so much so easily.

"Not here." He did his best to ignore the blatant disappointment in her expression. Disappointment could not come close to describing what he felt. He would have liked nothing better than to make her his wife then and there, with the hay as their marriage bed—but they were in a bloody barn. The duke and duchess of Belmore would not couple in a barn.

With a steel will bred of too many empty years, he ignored his thoughts and nodded toward the cow, who still stood nearby, chewing her cud and swishing her tail. "We have a cow to milk."

That made her smile. She looked up at him worshipfully. He glowered back at her. He didn't want to be worshiped, dammit!

She averted her eyes and began fiddling with a piece of hay.

He was being harsh, but he had his reasons. His reaction

to her galled him, because it wasn't something he could control with a command. And he couldn't make it go away, either. It was as if with one look she could lure him into her strange world, a world he did not understand any better than the one he lived in.

A sick thought hit him like a fist in the belly. Had she done this to him? Had she used her magic to cast a witch's spell? Was that why he couldn't control this odd need for her, this lust? He watched her for a minute, still feeling that taut chain of need. "Did you cast a spell on me?"

She cocked her head, her face registering surprise. "No."

"Then why is all this happening?"

"All what?"

"Every time I look at you I want to . . . to behave strangely. I do believe you have cast some love spell over me. I want you to remove it." He crossed his arms and waited. "Now."

Her eyes brightened. "A love spell?"

"Yes. Get rid of it."

"But—"

"I command you to remove the spell."

She looked at him for a long time. He could see her furtive little witch's mind working. Her eyes flickered with it. Finally she sighed, giving in, and whispered some mumbo jumbo and waved her hands around for a very long time.

He waited for the feeling to fade. It didn't. She walked over to him very slowly, her eyes locked on to his. She stopped in front of him, her face suddenly serious, and said, "I have to kiss you to remove it."

He stiffened, not knowing what to expect. "Go ahead."

She slid her arms around his neck and slowly rose up on tiptoe, her mouth and that damnably sexy mole closing in. Her hands moved from his neck to his cheeks just as her lips touched his. He counted in Latin, and it was working until her small curious tongue traced his lips. He groaned, and her tongue darted inside his mouth, stroking him and making him feel the magic. He tried counting in Greek, then conjugating French verbs, anything to fight the urge to wrap his arms around her and take her right there in the hay.

She finally pulled back, slowly, took a deep, calming breath, and said, "I'm done."

"It's gone?"

She started to smile, then bit it back. "Yes."

He didn't feel any different. "No more spell?"

"No more spell," she confirmed, then gave him one of those smiles that made him forget reason.

He drew himself up and said, "Never again. You are to never again cast any love spell, especially on me. Do you understand?"

"Yes, Alec." She stood with her hands clasped meekly and her head bowed.

"Fine. I'll milk the cow," he told her, expecting an argument. "You can gather some eggs."

She raised her bright eyes to his. "Oh, good! I've never gathered eggs before, have you?"

"No."

She acted as if he had just given her a special gift. He expected her to clap her hands any minute. It amazed him that she could find delight in the least little thing. He did not understand it, or her, so he gave up trying and set about the task at hand and sat on the milking stool, scowling. Within moments the only sound in the barn was the clean ring of milk hitting the tin pail.

"You do that very well." She hadn't moved.

He glanced up, his first urge to order her to do as he'd told her, but she was smiling again, and some weak part of him told him not to spoil the blatant happiness that shone in her bright face.

"Are you sure you removed the spell?"

"Witch's honor." Her face suddenly serious, she held up a hand.

Taking a deep breath he opened his mouth, but no words came out. He had to search for those sharp angry words that in the past could flay the skin off the person to whom they were aimed. This time those words didn't come easily. He had to search for them, and when he looked at her pert little face, he couldn't say them. He'd seen her happiness fade before and remembered feeling as if he'd kicked a kitten.

"Why did you ask?" she said. "Do you still feel it?"

"Yes."

"Oh. Well, perhaps it takes a while to wear off."

He grumbled, "It had best hurry."

"Well," she said, bending back to dust the straw from her backside. "I have eggs to gather, don't I?"

He watched her hand sweep across her bottom, and didn't answer because his mind was filled with the flash of an image of Joy with her hair undone, swinging down over that same area she'd dusted off, and on down to the backs of her thighs, her naked thighs.

The ring of milk quickened. He concentrated on the task at hand with narrowed concentration and deep control—a control that had been drummed into him at a young age and that, since his marriage, had been slipping far too often.

The duke of Belmore worrying about wounded kittens and handfuls of hair? He took a deep breath and forced himself to think of his estates, of which fields should lay fallow, of the problems with his tenants and with poachers, of the latest Whig maneuver in the House of Lords, of anything but the happy tune his wife was humming across the barn.

"Oh, Alec! Come see! I've found something!"

"Bloody hell," he said under his breath and stared at the pail of milk.

"Hurry!"

Resigned, he wiped his hands on his thighs and stood up, then walked around the cow only to have his wife run up to him, grab his arm, and tug him over to a dim corner.

"Look there."

His gaze followed her pointing finger to wooden crates of books and a straw-speckled trunk.

"What do you suppose is inside this trunk?" Her voice was as eager as if she had just found buried treasure.

"No doubt something no one wanted."

"Where's your spirit of adventure? Let's open it."

The flush of rapt anticipation on her bright face was more than even he could ignore. He bent down and moved aside the crate of dusty leather-bound books and released the brass latch on the trunk. The hinges creaked like hungry cats as he lifted the lid, and his wife's curious head suddenly popped into his line of vision.

She gasped. "Oh, my goodness! Look!" She pulled out a huge red velvet hat, the size of a large hunting saddle, with more plumes than a herd of ostriches. He had to back up to keep from getting the feathers in his face as she turned it this way and that, inspecting the monstrosity the way a child might inspect a new toy. She plopped the hat on the back of her small head and raised her chin, tying the frayed ribbons.

She stepped back and struck a pose. "How does it look?" She gave the hat, which was made to set atop a full pompadour, a jaunty pat. It sank down over her small nose, the feathers flopping downward over the front of the brim. She blew the feathers away from her mouth and said, her voice muffled by the hat, "I believe it's a tad too big."

Before he could control it, let alone think about it, a bark of laughter escaped his lips. He stiffened immediately and swallowed the next one.

She pushed the hat back, her eyes wide, green, and curious. "What was that?"

"What?"

"That noise."

"I didn't hear anything."

"Well, I surely did. Sounded like the selkies on Iona Reef."

"Selkies?"

"Seals."

He cleared his throat gruffly and tried to look suitably serious. "Impossible."

She pushed the hat back off her head and moved her inquisitive face closer. She searched his eyes. "Alec . . . is that a smile?"

"Hardly."

"I think your eyes are smiling."

"Dukes do not smile with their eyes or with anything else."

"Why?"

He turned away.

"Why won't you smile?"

"Village idiots walk around grinning, not dukes. Laughter is for fools." He heard his father's coldness in his own voice and he tensed inside and out.

"I believe that laughter is a gift."

"Don't you want to see what else is in the trunk?"

"I want to see you smile," she muttered.

"And I want to finish this nonsense so we can go back inside."

"Nonsense?" She was suddenly quiet, too quiet. She gazed at the trunk. All the delight had drained from her expressive face. Biting her lip, she turned away from him, her shoulders drooping a bit, her head down as if she was embarrassed or, worst yet, ashamed. She sighed. "I'll just look at these books. You can look inside the trunk."

He watched her shoulders heave slightly with her deep breaths. He searched the tips of his boots for kitten fur and stood there feeling like a cloddish oaf.

Bloody hell! He heard her deep sigh and ignored it. Finally he looked at her bowed head and the damned word slipped out: "Scottish?"

She turned those wide, defeated green eyes up at him. He almost smiled for her, almost, but managed to stop himself. What the hell was wrong with him? After a strained minute during which he felt as if she had swallowed him, he said, "I'll bring the trunk inside so you can go through it."

"You will?" She grinned up at him. "Thank you."

He released a breath he didn't even know he'd been holding. "Are you sure you removed that spell?"

"Cross my heart. There is no love spell on you."

He saw no deception there, which frustrated him even more.

"Do you think we could borrow a few of these books, too?"

"Fine." He took his cape from the peg and shrugged into it. "Just put aside the ones you want while I take the trunk in."

"And the tub?"

"What tub?" He turned back, fastening the cape.

"That one." She pointed to another corner where an old tin hip bath was filled with hay.

"And the tub," he said, walking over to close the lid on the trunk.

He lifted the trunk and had to stifle a groan. The bloody thing weighed a ton. He moved toward the barn door, his thighs and arms feeling every pound. He felt a small hand on his arm. He stopped, taking a breath in the hope that he wouldn't drop the damned thing.

Joy stared up at him. "You do that well too."

"Do what?"

"Carry things," she said with pride in her voice. She gave his arm a pat and ran back to the corner.

Alec stood there for a moment, the muscles in his arms taut and straining from the weight of the trunk and his shoulders and back quivering with the strain. He took another deep breath, searching for extra strength, and found it from some miraculous place. Head high, shoulders back, and face unchanged, he strode through the doors, bloody well determined to haul the damned trunk to the inn.

"The dark and dangerous duke of Dryden reined in his huge frothing stallion and searched the foggy marsh for a sign of the Gypsy girl. He spotted a flash of red and slowly edged his mount toward a misty pile of rocks. He intended to find her, by God! The wench was destined to be his! The shadowy mist suited his black mood, for she had pricked his pride, and he would exact revenge by taking her to his bed. . . ."

"Oh, my goodness." Joy slammed the book shut and stared at the title: *The Dastardly Duke.* "I think I need this one, too," she muttered and placed it on the stack of books that seemed to grow with each volume she touched. She looked at the other titles—*Tom Jones, Moll Flanders, Fanny Hill, Robinson Crusoe*—novels she had never read.

Then she turned to her discard stack—Shakespeare. The MacLean had forbidden her to read his plays, calling him an upstart Sassenach who didn't know the first thing about Scottish witches.

Joy shrugged and walked over to the tin tub. She tipped it over, emptying the hay, then dragged it over to her stack of books. She stood back and dusted off her hands.

Alec came back inside and looked at the smaller stack of books. "I see you like Shakespeare." He began to put the wrong books in the hip bath.

"Oh, no. Those are the ones I don't want. The other stack is what I want."

He scanned the spines, frowning. He picked up the top book. "*Tom Jones?* I think not." He tossed the book into the corner.

"But I looked through it. It's about a poor foundling."

He ignored her and picked up another. "*Moll Flanders?*"

"Her mother was imprisoned for stealing food, before she was even born. Poor wee thing. She was sold to the Gypsies. It was her first recollection." That too went the way of the others.

His voice grew louder. "*Fanny Hill?*"

She blushed. "That one looked . . . very intriguing."

And louder. "*The Dastardly Duke?*" He all but choked on the title.

She winced, but wisely remained silent.

"You will not read these." He picked up the last book and read the title. "You may read this one." He handed her *Robinson Crusoe.* "And the plays of Shakespeare." He picked up the books from her discard pile and put them in the tub. He straightened, then said something about retrieving the milk and crossed over to the cow.

Joy stared at the one book in her hand. She glanced at him, seeing he was behind the cow. Quickly she picked up *The Dastardly Duke,* rammed it under the stack of Shakespeare, and placed the sanctioned book on top. Just for good measure she put the small basket of eggs atop that, then scooted away and stood there, hands behind her back, waiting and humming and trying to look innocent.

He came around the cow and set the milk pail in front of her. "Do you think you can carry this?"

She tested the weight of the pail. "Aye."

He helped her on with her coat, then lifted the tub of books in his brawny arms, and they left the barn.

Joy halted the moment they stepped outside. The wind had ceased and all was silent—that utter stillness that seeps often settled in after a snowstorm. It was as if the world had stopped and there was nothing but silence within silence. Icicles dripped like white crystal beards from the steep roof of the inn, where snow lay in a thick puffy icing atop the thatch. Standing between the innyard and the frozen silver river were tall trees that the storm had powdered with clean white snow. It was almost as if they'd been dipped in sugar.

A rabbit hopped across the snow, its footprints the first sign of life in a white and silver world. It paused to look at them, its whiskered nose sniffing the air for a sign of danger, then twitched its long ears and darted off behind the trees in a trail of scattering white.

"Oh . . . isn't it lovely?" Joy said in a whisper of awe.

"What?" Alec shifted the tub and searched the area.

"The snow." She couldn't believe he didn't see it. "It's winter's gift."

"Hardly a gift. More like a coffin. We almost died in it."

She set the milk pail down. "But look around. Can't you see the beauty of it? It's almost as if we're in a silent fairyland, all white and silver and sparkling. Do you suppose heaven could look like this?" She lifted a handful of fresh white snow and held it up. "If you hold it up and look through it—see?—the light shines through and the snow glitters like diamond dust."

Alec frowned.

"Look," she insisted.

"All I see is water running down your arm." He walked past her without a glance.

She looked at the melting snow in her hand, tossed it away, and watched his back as he carried the tub down the path. "Hardheaded Englishman," she muttered. "Thinks I cast a love spell over him." Frustrated at his inability to be anything but rigid, she grabbed a handful of snow, packed it, and flung it right at his hard head. It felt so good.

He stopped walking, set the tub down, and slowly turned around, brushing the snow from the back of his neck. He stared at her as if she were daft.

She hurled another snowball. It hit him smack dab in his scowling face.

She giggled.

"Bloody hell! What do you think you are doing?"

"Hitting you with snowballs." She nailed him with another.

"I do not find this amusing."

"I do."

"Stop. Now."

Her answer was to take aim and throw another, hoping he'd loosen up and throw one back.

"Stop it." He wiped the snow from his face.

She remembered the cocky way he'd tossed her books aside. Her patience waning, she packed the snowball tighter, then wound back her arm, and got him right in the chest. Her magic should be so accurate.

"I said cease, at once!"

Then she remembered the arrogant way he'd told her to remove her love spell. She packed the snow in her hand. There hadn't been any love spell. She wadded the snow as tight as she could. If she could have cast such a spell on him, she would have done so. That would have been a whole lot easier than trying to teach this man about love. She heaved the snowball, hard.

He ducked. "I command you to stop this."

"Haven't you ever played in the snow?" She tossed another well-packed snowball from one hand to the other, deciding which body quadrant she should aim for.

"Dukes don't play."

"I meant when you were a wee lad."

"I was never a wee lad. I was the Belmore heir." His voice was hard, and his stance became stiffer. She could see the tension in him, but couldn't see the child in him because he had never been one.

She stared at his unyielding expression, knowing he had never sneaked down to the kitchens to raid the pie shelf in the pantry, never skipped stones across a lake, never played hide-and-seek or blindman's buff or any other child's game. The air grew quiet and a little sad. She looked at the snow splattered on his coat, then at the snowball melting in her hand. Something told her that snow would melt a great deal sooner than her husband would.

With a sigh of defeat, she gave up for now, dropping the snowball into the snow. She could tell by his look that he would become angrier if she continued. She picked up the milk and carried it toward the inn.

As she walked past him, his voice became ice and he said, "You are not some child. You are the duchess of Belmore."

"Not really." The words flew out of her mouth before she could blink. She walked by and opened the inn door.

He followed her inside and dropped the tub with a loud thud. "What the hell is that supposed to mean?"

"I am not truly your wife." She set the milk down in the kitchen and turned around, hands on her hips. She was fed up enough to challenge him. "I think you are afraid of me."

It worked. She caught a quick flash of pricked pride in his face, and a second later he pulled her, none too gently, into his arms.

He looked down at her, still angry. "What can you possibly do to me that you haven't already done? I am not afraid of you."

"There was no love spell, Alec. I cannot control my magic well enough to cast one."

"You made me out the fool?" Suddenly something more primal than anger shone in his eyes, and his mouth closed over hers. There was fierceness in his kiss, and passion. He met her challenge, rose to the bait. But passion rose faster, and their lips did not break apart until he had carried her upstairs. He kicked open the bedroom door, and it crashed against the wall.

"Alec," she whispered against his stubbly jaw.

His answer was to kick the door shut, hard.

"Alec," she repeated softly, and placed her hand on his heart as she looked up at him.

He turned furious eyes on her.

"See?" she said, patting his chest. "You do carry things well."

He was so quiet, didn't move, except to close his eyes. He took deep, calming breaths. He opened his eyes and said nothing. His face was that of a man who was fighting to keep some demon down. His jaw tightened, his hands were tense, his mouth thinned.

Don't fight it, love, please, she prayed, please. . . .

He struggled. She could feel the rhythm of his heartbeat against the palm of her hand.

She touched his jaw. "My Alec," she whispered.

All the anger drained out of his face, melting like snowflakes in a warm spring rain. He bent over and kissed her, his lips barely touching hers. He tasted her with his mouth the way one might sip fine wine. She had known this tenderness was there, underneath that icy veneer he wore like his pride. He set her gently on the mattress before the fire, and then she was in his arms again.

The duke of Belmore kissed with the same command, the same confidence and assurance that had first drawn Joy to him. She adored his flavor, the erotic feel of his tongue stroking and filling her mouth. It made her want something more, made her feel as if she needed to somehow get closer to him.

The roughness of his tongue against hers, against her lips and teeth and the roof of her mouth made her warm and tingling. Nothing in the whole wide world could have been more wonderful than being held by Alec, kissed by him, loved by him.

After little more than one passionate kiss his hands opened the buttons on her dress and stroked her back through the torn gap in her chemise the way a breeze might caress the leaves. His mouth moved to her ear, the rough stubble of his beard grazing her cheek and jaw and raising gooseflesh on her neck and arms. He raised one hand and touched the tender skin along the side of her neck. She opened her eyes and watched him.

He answered the question in her gaze quietly. "So soft. Your skin is so soft. Are you as soft and sweet inside, Scottish?"

"Alec . . ."

"You are my wife, my duchess, in every way but one." He licked her ear and whispered, "Now, Scottish. I want you now."

She moaned a yes, and his mouth wet a path down her neck. At the same time, he pushed her dress off her shoulders. The torn chemise went with it. The air hit her bare breasts. She sucked in a breath and tried to hide her chest against his.

"No. Let me see you." He held her fast while his mouth and tongue moved across her collarbone and down to a breast. "Let me taste you, watch you pearl for me."

His mouth closed over that taut breast, sucking, his rough tongue flicking across the tip. She groaned and held his head against her while he took more of her into his warm mouth, sucking harder and harder, and with each pull of his mouth she felt something deep inside that most private part of a woman. Such unimagined ecstasy, this thing between man and woman. She closed her eyes and let sensation overtake her.

He went on and on until there was little conscious thought left in her, yet she had never been so alive, so aware of things inside her body that she'd never experienced. She could almost feel her blood thicken and flow honeylike through her, feel the differences between them—male versus female.

His skin was rougher, but that roughness was tempered by the stroking tickle of the thick dark hair that curled on his arms. She ran her hands up them, feeling that warm soft hair. His muscles were firm and hard, his skin darker than hers. And there was some kind of exotic thrill in those differences, and an excitement that was as old as time.

His tongue stroked the crest of her breast sending chills skating over her skin. Her breath rushed out like the tide. His mouth created a mist of kisses over her ribs, the undersides of her breasts, her collarbone. Then he sank into her mouth. She didn't know what it was she wanted, but she wanted something and held him tighter, moved against him with some distant yearning.

As if he knew her need, he ran his hand down her thigh, his teasing touches like wind-kisses, then slid up and under her skirt to stroke the length of her inner thigh with his palm, each time moving closer and closer to the heart of her.

He touched her then, and heavens above, she found what she had craved. She buried her face in his neck and whimpered, half embarrassed and half relieved. He moved his fingers through her private hair, combing until he touched a small damp bud. That touch sent a jab of pleasure through her so sweetly that her eyes misted. She cried out.

"Scottish. Spread for me."

She did, and he rubbed more, making fuller circles first, then using two fingers to press against and between her nether lips, fondling her flesh so intimately that she knew he was the only one destined to do this. After an eternal stroke of time, stroke of pleasure from his knowing touch, he cupped her and kept pressure against her most sensitive point with the heel of his hand, fingering and playing with her. Never would she have believed a touch could be so intimate, but it felt so very good that she wouldn't have stopped him for all the magic in the world.

"Unbutton my shirt," he commanded in a whisper, then moved a finger deeper, massaging along and between her nether lips, flickering the point of her with each stroke.

"Alec." She pushed his shirt aside and down his arms. Her sensitive breasts touched the thick curly hair on his chest and it was his turn to groan. In reaction he pushed his finger into her inch by wet inch, pulling back, only to dip deeper the next time.

Her knees began to quiver, and her breath came in hurried pants. Instinctively she rubbed her breasts against his chest.

"God Almighty." He filled her mouth with his ravaging tongue. He used the arm that held her to pull her tight against him. His other hand, the one that was damp with her, tore at the buttons on his breeches. He fumbled with his clothes, kicking off his boots and pants and shrugging out of his shirt, the whole time he held her. He tossed the shirt behind her. "Stand up."

"I can't. My legs won't hold me."

He swore and pulled her clothes down her hips and knees until he could lift her free of them. His hands gripped her buttocks and held her against his waist. He used one hand to lift her leg around him.

"Lock your legs around me."

She did, and instantly felt herself open, felt the coolness of air against the place his touch had melted. He sat back on his heels and she felt his hardness, the full length of him. He reached between their bodies and opened her flesh more, so the hardest part of him nestled along her. Then he shifted, using his male strength, the hard length of him, to caress her as his fingers had, and to rub against that tender bud.

Her arms were linked around his neck, her mouth fused to his, his tongue filling and retreating with long, slow strokes. His hands gripped her bottom, separating and lifting her as he moved his hips, sliding up and down the length of her nether lips in the same rhythm, the same slow movements, the same thrusts as his tongue.

She dewed against him, could feel his heartbeat, and her own sounded like drums in her ears. She strained toward him even though his hands on her bottom were controlling the movements. She wanted something more.

"Please," she begged against his mouth.

He groaned a response she didn't hear. Gone were the senses of sound and sight. She could taste and she could feel, but no more. He followed her down to the mattress, his hard length still spread against her damp womanhood. He pulled back, and she cried out, but an instant later his fingers separated her and she felt the tip of him penetrate her, enter inside her, and widen her with its thickness.

She stilled. "It hurts."

"Don't move." He stopped, and his breathing increased.

Then he filled her more, and more, until something stopped him. She winced when he gently pushed against it. "No more," she said. "It doesn't fit."

He pulled back a bit. "I'm sorry, Scottish." He thrust hard.

She screamed, then bit her lip to keep from doing so again. She shoved at his heavy shoulders.

"Easy. I won't do any more until you're ready."

"There's more?" She couldn't keep the squeak of horror from her voice.

He took another deep breath and swore softly.

"It hurts."

"I know."

"If it hurts you too, why are we doing this?"

He groaned something, then shifted just enough to place his hand between their bodies. He rubbed the very point of her, but it wasn't the same. She still burned deep inside, and she ached from the fullness of him. His mouth moved to her ear where he whispered to her, calmed her with that deep voice. His finger moved in fast circles, and soon she felt a wonderful shimmer inside, building up higher, and she strained against him.

He shifted then, slowly, with purpose, and she thought he was finally going to leave her body. He didn't. He edged back into her, in eternal inches, then slowly out, his finger stroking and flicking against her the whole time. The pain subsided, and only deep pressure remained, pressure and a shimmer of something that grew and grew.

Soon, the more he thrust, the stronger the glow within her, the more it spread until it didn't matter that he no longer used his finger because each long stroke of him inside her was pushing her closer to the edge of something so wonderful she begged to touch it for even one brief instant.

Her hands grasped his shoulders. The muscles were hard and tense and moist. She wanted to see him, but her eyes wouldn't open, so she called his name over and over in tempo with his quickening thrusts.

A second later it was as if she were finally flying. Her body soared with a pulsing ecstasy that rose from deep within her. Her body clutched the hard, thick length of him over and over while pleasure flooded her soul. It seemed as if it would never stop, and she didn't want it to, was still savoring it when her body finally quieted. Her heart lay open, floating on the wealth of love within it, love for this man who, in one elated magical moment, had shown her the other side of heaven.

He kept on moving within her, faster and deeper as if driven to touch her soul. She was sure he had, just before that wonderful soaring happened again, so fast, so strong, taking her even higher than the last time. She heard her own muffled cries and couldn't stop them, didn't even know what she'd said.

With each slick thrust into her she pulsed again and each time harder than the last. She felt the tickle of something feather-soft floating onto her skin. His touch, she thought, then realized his hands still held her bottom as he continued to drive harder and deeper.

He swore, loudly, just before he pushed once more and held himself inside her, filling her with the warmth of life, pulsing and throbbing as she had.

She clung to him then, their bodies moving as one, time not moving at all. It could have been a few minutes and it could have been a lifetime; she didn't know, and at that very second, she didn't care.

Slowly but vibrantly her senses came alive again.

She smelled roses—wonderful, sweet-scented roses. The air was filled with the sweet tangy fragrance of them. She felt a featherlike touch again on her arms and her face. She opened her eyes.

Hundreds of pink rose petals floated down from nowhere.

She stared at them, stunned, but she could say nothing because her body was still humming from the pleasure of him so buried so deep within her.

She blew a few petals away from her face and listened to their bodies. Her breath came in deep pants and so did his. It sounded so loud in the silent room. His heart beat against hers in a throbbing rhythm. She watched the petals light upon their bodies, drifting down from the same magical place his body had taken her.

He lay resting, possessing the depths of her, their bellies pressed together. Her whole body felt damp and wet. The musky scent of them mixed with the tang of rose petals, the most bewitching fragrance she'd ever breathed. His head lay beside hers, his breathing finally slow and deep. She brushed some petals off his damp back and idly stroked him. She turned her face toward his and whispered, "Now I understand."

He groaned. "What?"

"Why we were doing this."

Alec felt his wife wiggle her hips beneath his.

"Now it fits," she said brightly.

It took him a moment to find his voice. "I'm not sure that's a compliment, Scottish."

"I just wanted you to know that you don't have to stop. It fits just fine now."

A million comments went through his mind, most of them cynical.

"That was very kind of you." She patted his shoulder gently.

"What?"

"Shrinking so you wouldn't hurt me."

He laughed out loud. He couldn't control that sharp foreign sound that came from his throat.

"You laughed. Oh, Alec, you *can* laugh! I'm so glad." She was quiet for a blessed minute. Then she said, "I'm not sure what you found so amusing, but that doesn't matter. You laughed." She gave him an impish grin.

He shook his head and searched for an explanation, then laughed again at the thought of how she would react to the truth of how their bodies worked. She was watching him, trying to understand. He could tell from her silence. Then she sighed sleepily and snuggled her face into his neck.

She should be tired, he thought. She'd been talking incessantly for the last few minutes. She'd even thanked him. He remembered her yelling the word into his ear after she'd peaked the first time, then saying something about flying. After what he'd just gone through, he should have been thanking her.

He closed his eyes at the thought. The intensity of their joining made him feel like an inexperienced youth. When he looked into her face he felt things too deep to be real. Every time she smiled up at him the freedom of that smile touched a place he had thought didn't exist, and each time it was more captivating than the last. A part of him wanted to curl inside that smile of hers and stay there.

Such foolish thoughts didn't set well with him. He searched for some sense of control; he took a deep breath, and another. God . . . she smelled of roses, in the middle of winter. He'd noticed the scent earlier, but it seemed even stronger now. He wondered if she had some rose perfume on her skin and thought perhaps the exertion of their lovemaking had brought it forth.

He moved his lips to her neck, but it wasn't skin his lips touched.

It was the velvet feel of rose petals.

He raised his head and saw layer after soft layer of petals. He looked over his shoulder. His whole naked body was covered with pink flowers. He gazed back down at his wife, who looked up at him as if he had just given her every star in the sky.

Odd that he felt a sudden burst of pride at that look of hers. He should have been able to ignore it. He turned away for a moment and saw more petals on the mattress. "There are rose petals everywhere. Pink rose petals."

"I know. Don't they smell wonderful?"

"Why?"

"Why do they smell? I'm not sure. I think—"

"Why are they everywhere?"

She was very quiet; then her face reflected something akin to guilt. "I don't know."

"It is the middle of winter. Roses do not bloom in winter. I am not a fool. Did you think to impress me by conjuring these up?"

"But I didn't! Not on purpose, anyway. They just came out of nowhere." She turned her head aside and took a deep breath. "I cannot always control my magic. 'Tis the curse of the MacQuarries." He could hear the shame in her voice when she quietly added, "I'm sorry."

He watched her fight a silent battle with her own demon and felt something that bonded them, something other than blinding sex. Without a thought, he raised his hand to trace her hairline, something he'd never done to a woman in his life. He touched her hair, brushed the petals away, then pulled the pins from it. It was little more than a rich brown knot of tangles. Slowly he unraveled it, combing it with his fingers, watching the rose petals cling to it. It was so long that when he spread it out beside them, it spilled over the edge of the mattress.

She watched him, seemingly fascinated by what he was doing.

"It's so long, Scottish. I've never seen hair so long."

"It's tangled."

He fingered it, felt the weight of it in his hands. He looked at her then, at her odd face and those deep green eyes that saw the world so differently than he did.

She saw diamonds; he saw ice. She saw fairies; he saw death. She loved life; he despised it.

He closed his eyes and blocked out all that confusion, at least for now. He opened them again and saw that her white skin was flushed and there were pink marks from his rough beard on her chin and lips and—he looked downward—on her breasts. He ran his mouth along the marks. They were the signs of his possession. She could no longer claim that she wasn't his wife, because she was. But it wasn't the power of possession that made his blood flow now; it was pride.

And at that very moment he didn't give a bloody damn about witchcraft or anything else, because he could feel his desire again, feel the tight knot of it in his groin. He rolled over, taking her with him in a shower of petals. She gasped at the sudden motion.

Above him now, surrounded by the sweet scent of roses, she gave him a curious look of innocence, a look that belonged only to her. He kissed her, ran his hand through her petaled hair, and let it spill over them. The deeper he kissed her, the more she responded, and the tighter his desire became. He could feel her hair spill down over their hips in a silky caress of pure sensation. Then she shifted, and it fell between their legs and brushed against the sensitive flesh of his stones.

He buried his tongue in her warm mouth and tasted his wife. She moved her small plush body atop his, opening her mouth wider for him. She learned quickly. He gripped her buttocks, and his hands filled with soft warm flesh and the occasional velvet texture of roses. It was the most sensuous experience of his life.

She moved her hips over the length of him, brushing his hardness with the feminine mound of downy nether hair. He moved then, edging closer to her center.

She pulled back, her eyes wide and worried. He tried to kiss her again, but she held back. "Alec."

He stopped trying to kiss her and took in her worried face. "What's wrong?"

"Can't you shrink it a wee bit?"

He lifted his mouth to her ear to hide his smile. "Don't worry, Scottish, I'll make certain it fits." And he did.

# Chapter 16

Two blissful days passed during which Joy marveled at the way Alec could control and command his body, swelling and shrinking at will. It was the same command with which he did everything else. She had told him so, too. He had laughed again, once. Since then she had carried the memory of that raspy foreign sound cupped like precious fairy wishes deep within her heart.

They'd talked for hours, with her prodding, and he had told her what London would be like, but she couldn't believe that it was as horrid as he said—after all, this was the man who couldn't see the beauty of the snow. He had told her repeatedly what would be expected of her—which mostly boiled down to not doing anything that remotely resembled magic.

However, he did admit that he had been wrong about the contents of the trunk. He'd told her that when he was brushing her hair dry after a bath in which more water ended up on the floor than in the tub or on the two lovers within it. It seemed odd to her at the time that a duke would play lady's maid. But as he slowly drew the brush through her hair, she could see from his face he did not consider it a chore. He seemed to have some fascination with her hair, and the act soon became a prelude to being locked in deep love with her husband.

Afterward, he claimed the brush had been quite good luck, so had the man's shaving kit and an old game of draughts painted on a faded flat piece of tin. He had never played the game, but it was one of her favorites, which was why she had conjured it up along with the brush, his razor, and some other things she felt they needed. She had made a few mistakes, but he had assumed the sack of mush, the knife blade, and the incomplete deck of playing cards were more of the trunk's cast-off contents, and completely useless.

She figured what Alec didn't know wouldn't hurt him.

Now she stood in the kitchen, preparing dinner the mortal way. It was a shame that she couldn't conjure up dinner, but she knew he wouldn't swallow that. She winced . . . bad pun. She gave the inn door a quick glance, wondering how long he would be gone. He had stepped outside to bring in some more wood and feed the cow. She smiled. The duke of Belmore feeding a cow—imagine that.

During the past few days he had not been so hard edged, so wrapped up in the illustrious Belmore name. His voice was less tense, every phrase did not sound like an order. He was more approachable; their time together not strained. It was almost as if he thought that being married to a witch wasn't so bad a thing after all.

Joy liked him that way. She could see glimpses of that hidden part of him she'd sensed was there from the moment she looked into his eyes, that hollowness that needed to be filled, that heart untouched, that part of him that needed her, even if he didn't realize it yet. She could feel it every time he held her, every time he loved her.

She'd find some way to make him understand. She'd given him her heart and her body in love. And Joy wouldn't give up on someone she loved, even if that person was a hardheaded English duke.

She sighed, which dried her throat, so she swallowed and winced at its soreness. It burned and was scratchy, and her ears ached. She ignored them, figuring a busy mind would make her forget she wasn't feeling up to her stifles, and checked the soup on the fire and then turned around to look at the turnips on the worktable; they needed to be peeled.

Next to them was a bowl of separated cream waiting to be churned into butter. She decided to save the vegetables until after she churned the butter. Wiping her itchy nose on her sleeve, she moved to the churn, filled it, then stood there plunging the shaft up and down stopping only to wipe her runny nose.

The novelty of the task lasted only a few minutes. Then her arms began to ache and her mind began to wander. Sweat beaded at her temples, but she kept working. Butter couldn't take too long. With her lip between her teeth and determination in her eyes, she plunged the shaft over and over, then checked the reserve, expecting butter. There was none.

She kept churning until the sweat dribbled like rain from her hairline. Churning butter was the most tiring and boring task she'd ever performed. She checked the reserve again, but the cream had hardly thickened. She stretched her sore arms upward, then planted a fist on her hip and contemplated the pale contents of the reserve, frowning.

She could whip up the butter with a wee bit of magic and without all this silly work. Alec wouldn't like that. But then she didn't particularly like doing the job his way. She rubbed her sore arms.

What she was needing was some kind of compromise. She stared at the shaft, then looked out the inn window. No Alec. Her eyes twinkled with an interesting idea, and she smiled. Why not do both?

With a twitch of magic, she left the churn to agitate under witch power, doing the work the mortal way with a bit of witch's ease. She watched the shaft agitate. Then, bobbing her head in time to the drumming beat of the churn, she crossed the room to see if the bread had cooled yet.

Humming a Gaelic ditty she felt the warm loaf and decided that the bread was doing just fine, so with a song on her lips she spun around, intending to dance across the room to begin another chore. After all, as the old Scot saying went, there wasn't much guile in a heart that was singing.

Her skirt caught on something and she stopped. Beside the hearth was the stack of books from the barn. She'd had no time to read, having spent every minute with Alec. And what wonderful moments they had been. She smiled, thinking back over the days, the hours, in his arms, remembering his willingness to accept the sweet scent and shower of rose petals as part of their lovemaking.

Joy sneezed. She wiped her nose, cleared her scratchy throat, and stared at the chores still facing her. She frowned. Then, as if drawn by magic, her gaze turned to one of the books: *The Dastardly Duke.* She turned away, willing herself to finish cooking. Willpower was not her forte. She slowly turned back to the book, wondering what happened to that Gypsy girl. A second later the book was in her hand, a gleam of anticipation in her eyes, a smile on her lips. She opened the book: "The raven-tressed beauty cowered against the curtain of his massive bed, her green Gypsy eyes sparkling like fiery jewels. He moved purposefully toward her, holding her in his raw power with a dark look from his devilish black eyes, his riding crop tapping against the black leather of his boot. He could see she wanted to run. She was frightened beyond reason. By God, he wanted her that way!"

Joy exhaled in a whoosh of tight air. "Oh, my goodness." She searched the room with guilty eyes. The soup bubbled innocently on the fire and surely needed stirring. The turnips sat abandoned on the scarred worktable; they still needed peeling. But Joy needed to read that book.

She lifted one hand and, with a stream of sparkles in its wake, twiddled a spoon in the soup pot. A couple of quick spins of her fingers and the spoon stirred the soup on its own, swirling and dipping into the liquid like a dancer on a ballroom floor.

The turnips were next. She intoned a simple command: "Oh, knife so real, cut away the peel on the turnips for our meal!"

She gave a slight grimace. Not the most impressive of spells, but it did the trick. The closest turnip levitated and the small knife followed, swaying into the air where it pared the vegetable in midair, the purple and white turnip peeling dangling downward like a bouncy curl.

Joy sat on a stool, gave her runny nose a good blow, and opened the book again: "The duke of Dryden stalked closer to the girl on the bed. The closer he came the wider her eyes grew, the more intense her shivering fear. A tambourine jingled in her shaking hand. He smiled rapaciously. 'Twas the smile of the Devil himself. He expected fear, submission. She raised her chin defiantly, her lips as red as summer roses. . . ."

Joy turned the page and exhaled at the same time. She took another deep breath, sneezed into her hankie again, and read on: "He lifted his hand toward her, unaware he still held the crop, so mesmerized was he by the challenge he saw in the verdigris of her eyes. The tempestuousness of the chit! Her eyes darted to the crop and she gasped. He wanted her, and by God, he would have her! Bent on ravishment, he let the crop fall from his hand, and he grasped her up. The tambourine fell to the bed. He pulled her against his huge rock-hard chest, knocking the breath from her rose-sweet lips. . . ."

"Bloody hell!"

Joy slammed the book closed with a bang and jumped up, staring at her husband and his purple neck.

"What in the devil are you doing?" His eyes locked on the butter churn; the bloody thing was pumping all by itself. He looked up to see a wooden spoon stir the soup on its own power, and there were bloody turnips—turnips?—floating around the room pursued by a flying knife.

Shaking his head, he closed his eyes, then opened them again. He took one look at his wife's guilty face and crossed the room in two long angry strides, grabbing her shoulders. "You promised no more . . . no more . . ." He waved one hand in the air, searching angrily for the word—that damned word.

"Witchcraft," she whispered.

"That's right! Damnation, woman!" He gave her a little shake—a hell of a lot littler than he would have liked. "You cannot *do* this sort of thing—especially in London." He looked into her face. "Don't you understand? Don't you?"

She stared up at him, guilt and fright battling in her eyes. "I'm sorry."

The fright was what did him in. He took three deep

breaths, then released her shoulders and turned away, running a hand through his hair and pacing while he tried to think. He had to make her see that she couldn't do this.

They had to go to London, snow or no snow, witch or no witch, duke or no duke. What the Prince Prinny wanted, he got. He turned back toward her and stopped cold.

Purple and white blocked his vision. He stepped back. A turnip hovered in the vicinity of his nose. He took another deep breath, seeking patience from somewhere, somewhere nonexistent.

He ducked under the turnip and dodged the bloody knife, then lost the little control he had. "God Almighty, look at this!" He pointed to the butter churn, then the spoon. "Look! This isn't England! I'm in a bloody . . . bloody"—he looked out the window while he sought the word he needed—"fairyland!"

Joy said something.

"What?" Alec spun around, fuming.

"Nothing."

"I want to know what you said."

She sighed, which made him want to wring her neck.

Control, he needed control. He straightened up to his full height and crossed his arms, staring down at her. "I'm waiting."

She didn't speak, so he moved a step closer.

"I said fairies don't live inside. They live outside, under the dewy green—Alec, I think you had better sit down. Your face is awfully red."

He held up his hand, a signal she shouldn't touch him at that very moment, and took in deep breaths as he counted.

"I'm sorry," she whispered, staring at the toes of her crinkled leather shoes. She stood there silent, then looked up and searched his face, staring at him as if she could see inside his head. "Are you counting?"

"Yes, dammit!"

"I thought so," she muttered with a sigh, then righted the stool and sat on it, hooking the small heels of her shoes on the rung before resting her chin in her hand. "Let me know when you reach a hundred."

Another turnip drifted past him. "Get . . . rid . . . of . . . the . . . turnips. And! The flying knife *and* the spoon *and* the . . . the—"

"Butter churn," she supplied, moving toward the open corner of the room where she mumbled something and waved her hands around, then stopped suddenly and blew her nose.

A turnip conked him in the back of the head, twice. "Wife!"

"Oops. Sorry." She tucked her hankie away, closed her eyes, and snapped her fingers.

In a flash all was normal, if his life could any longer be called normal. He rubbed the back of his head.

"Did it hurt you?" Searching his face, she moved closer to the narrow stairs.

"No!"

"Oh." She waited a moment, her hand nervously rubbing the newel post, then added in a hopeful tone that did little to assuage his anger. "We could always look on the bright side."

"There is no bright side."

"Aye. There is."

"I cannot wait to hear this bit of Scottish enlightenment."

"It could have been worse."

"Impossible."

"It might have been the knife."

He looked at her upturned face, dumbfounded. He'd married a crackbrain. He closed his eyes for a moment, unable to see anything other than the dire consequences they could face if she did not heed his warning.

She muttered something about jests not working unless one had a sense of humor.

"This is no jest." He stepped toward her, angry and frustrated that she couldn't comprehend the seriousness of their situation.

Her gaze never left his, but something flashed in her expressive eyes and suddenly her chin shot up dramatically.

Alec stopped and stared at her, confused—his usual state of mind since his marriage.

The look she gave him was all defiance.

"What the devil is that look for?"

She raised her chin higher yet, wiggled her nose, and sniffled some nonsense about a Gypsy just before she sneezed twice.

"Bloody hell!" A riding crop was in his hand. He stared at it for an unbelieving moment, then looked up at her, then back at his hand, then back at her.

"Oh, my goodness."

He slowly lifted his hand, the crop lying across his open palm. He looked into her surprised face. "Explain."

She winced and sniffled.

He took a deep breath and rubbed his free hand over his pounding forehead, then looked up, expecting to find her in tears. Her eyes were moist, and she dabbed at her nose, but it wasn't red from crying. She grabbed her linen hankie and covered her nose just before she loosed a huge sneeze.

An enormous vase of blood-red roses appeared behind her.

"Roses" was all he could say. He pointed at them with the riding crop

She spun around, her hands pressed to her cheeks. "Oh, no, not that!"

"Not what?" he shouted and walked slowly past her, asking himself why her words had the same effect on his stomach as did the ague. He paused, then looked into the great room. There were red roses on the tables, red roses on the chairs, red roses on the counter. A rose bush—red—grew near the hearth as if it had been planted years ago. He looked up. Red roses sprouted from the bloody lanterns.

With more constraint than he'd used in an entire London season, he slowly turned back to her, trying to comprehend what was happening. This was no longer the world he knew, the one he could control.

"Ah fink ah haff a code." The hankie was still pressed against her nose and mouth.

He couldn't speak; he couldn't move; all he could do was breathe.

Ah . . ." She raised the linen to her nose. "Ah . . . Don't let . . . ahhhhh . . . sneeze!" She gasped, then sneezed anyway.

Alec's arms were suddenly filled with roses—and a tambourine. For the first time in his life, the duke of Belmore panicked. He dropped the roses as if they'd burned his hands. The tambourine clattered to the floor with a tinny crash that seemed to symbolize the end of his orderly world. He stood there completely confused. Very slowly he turned and looked at his wife. "You sneeze roses whenever you have a cold?"

She shook her head.

"What do you mean, no? There are roses everywhere. More of them materialize every time you sneeze!"

"Ah sneeze whatever is on mah mind."

"God Almighty . . ."

With the hankie pressed to her nose, he could see only her worried and helpless green eyes.

Visions—nightmares, really—played before his eyes: the hands of the clock tower at Windsor Castle spinning faster than Boodle's roulette wheel; the Greek and Roman statuary in Hyde Park dancing across the promenade at precisely five o'clock; the prince regent levitating; the patronesses of Almack's standing near the gallows to watch his hanging, their arms filled with unexplained roses.

The duchess of Belmore sneezed whatever was on her mind.

Without a word, he turned and walked slowly away, as if he could walk away from what had turned his world upside down.

"Alec?"

He didn't turn back.

"Ah'm sorry."

He didn't stop until he reached the door.

"Please."

He opened the door and paused. He turned back. Roses were everywhere, and his wife was looking at him with bewilderment in her eyes, but he could see only chaos.

He couldn't look any longer and turned away to stare out at the ice and snow. Odd that he didn't see the cold frigid air, the bitter white ice that had almost killed them. He saw only solace and peace and escape. He stepped outside and closed the door without looking back, seeking something, anything, but the confusion behind him.

# The Mistake

**All creatures have their joy and man hath his.**

"Man's Medley," George Herbert

# Chapter 17

Silence, as barren and desolate as the misty moors of Scotland, made the room almost unbearable. Joy sniffled, but she hadn't sneezed for the last hour. She rubbed her itchy nose, then picked up their meal and carried the two plates of food, barely touched, to the kitchen. She stared at the uneaten food. The vegetables were congealing in stew broth, the butter she'd craved was now little more than yellow fat that turned her already tight stomach. The bread was as hard, dry, and crumbly as the basalt cliffs on the isle of Staffa; the absorbent heat of the inn's fires had sucked it dry. Her mouth and throat felt equally dry. Unfortunately, her eyes didn't.

It was a head cold, she told herself, not her heart breaking. She cast a forlorn glance at the chair where Alec had sat through their meal in stony silence.

Perhaps it was her heart after all. She bit her lip and sniffed. She would not cry.

Turning away from the plates, she swallowed hard and stood there, alone in the kitchen where the savory aroma of food had aged into pungent odors and the only sound was the occasional sharp snap of burning firewood. Try as she might, she couldn't keep from looking back into the great room where Alec sat staring into the fire, his elbows on his knees, his face golden from the warm glow of the fire—an illusion, because there was no warmth in his face. He'd said little since he came back inside, but his actions, his face, his rigid stance, told her everything she needed to know.

The cold, hard duke was back.

They'd had two idyllic days together. He had softened a tad. His guard had been lowered, and she had caught more than mere glimpses of the man she sought. Now, as she watched him, her hope curdled inside her.

He must have sensed her look, because he glanced up for an instant, just long enough for her to reach out one hand toward him, to take one step, to say a quick prayer. He turned away. No emotion, no words. Nothing.

She could have taken his anger, but the silence, the silence tightened into a clenching fist that seemed to cry out failure. She took a deep breath for solace, then another. There was no solace. She moved around the kitchen, her refuge, cleaning and trying not to look at her husband.

There was none of the natural bounce to her step, no humming, no lilting tilt of her head. To anyone who would chance a look at her, she appeared a small, solemn figure who seemed to carry the weight of the world atop her defeated shoulders. If Alec had looked, he might have seen that she was not as ignorant of her actions as he thought. But he did not look.

So when Joy turned back for one more hopeful glance she saw what she had seen before—he just continued to stare, unmoving, into the hypnotic colors of the fire.

*Don't kill the wee sparkle of magic we had.*

But there was little magic in the tense silence of the room. She bit her lip and slowly turned away, knowing if she looked any longer the tears would flow. She went on about her work, dredging up some bit of hope from the dark pit inside her.

Half an hour later, with the kitchen clean and the fire banked, she bent to pick up her book. Slowly she straightened the pages with a reverent touch of her hand, pressing the bent corners and crinkled, thin paper. She closed the book then ran her fingers over the gold embossing on the letters: D-u-k-e.

With the book clutched to her chest she tiptoed out of the room and started to climb the stairs, figuring to leave her husband to his brooding silence.

"Joy."

She stopped, one hand holding the banister, the other still hugging the book. She closed her eyes in dread. He had called her Joy, not Scottish. Her fingers tightened on the railing. "Aye?"

"Come here."

She closed her eyes and made her wish: *Please let him say all's fine. Don't destroy the magic because of one mistake.* One fortifying breath and she turned, looking down as she descended those few stairs and tried to summon up the courage to look him in the face.

Her fingers whitened from her tight hold on the ragged leather-bound book. She didn't notice. She moved unseeing, one small foot in front of the other, and too soon she was but a few feet away.

She waited, stared at his gray head, which was still bent in thought. His elbows rested on his thighs, his strong dark hands were clasped and hung between his knees, and his thumb tapped impatiently against a knuckle.

"Sit down." He didn't look at her, just gave a curt nod to the small willow chair nearby.

She sat down quietly, the book now flat on her tightly pressed knees, her damp hands folded atop the embossed letters. She waited for him to speak.

If there had been a clock in the room it would have ticked and ticked and ticked. As it was, she heard only the anxious thrumming of her pulse.

A burning log tumbled from the grate with a loud thud. She jumped. The fire sizzled and crackled and sparked. She wondered if his anger did the same.

He picked up the poker and shoved the log back onto the grate, jabbing and poking it into place far too fiercely. She had her answer.

"You're still angry."

He didn't confirm her statement, but the look he gave her could have frozen the river Tweed.

"I don't suppose counting would help this time, would it?"

He didn't deign to answer.

Still no sense of humor. She stared at her hands. Maybe he was counting. She cocked her head and tried to see if his lips were moving. They were. She chewed on her lip, then counted the knuckle lines on her folded hands. Her throat felt dry and her nose itched again. She rubbed it and waited.

One quiet sigh, then another. She hated the waiting, sitting there so close physically yet emotionally as far apart as two people could be.

An impatient thought hit her. She truly wished he would just get it over with and say what was on his mind.

Then she sneezed.

Hands cupping her nose, she opened her watery eyes. A strange look passed over Alec's face, as if a turnip had conked him again.

What had she been thinking? Oh, my goodness! She had wished he would speak his mind. She looked up, panicked.

He shook his head once and stood up abruptly.

She mentally groaned.

He clasped his hands behind his back and—*Here it comes*—began to pace and talk. "I don't believe you understand how serious this situation is. We have been summoned to London because the prince regent, our ruling monarch, such as he is, wishes to meet the duchess of Belmore, not some Scottish witch!"

She winced at the volume of his voice. "Alec, you're shouting."

"Yes, I know, and it feels good." He gave her a stern look and went on, "There are some two thousand members of the English ton, most of whom thrive on gossip and the misfortunes of others. Like Lady Agnes Voorhees they seek out any tidbit they can find. Think about it. Think about what I have been exposed to in the last two weeks. Put yourself in my boots. What do you think would happen if they saw any of your . . . your *zapping?*" His eyes pinned her.

She opened her mouth to answer. His hand shot up to silence her. Her mouth slammed shut.

"I'll tell you what would happen. They would lop off our heads quicker than any pompous knight." He scowled at her.

She chewed her lip, remembering the intensity of the glare he'd planted on that statue. She glanced up. Oh . . . it was back. "Well . . ." she began.

"Or perhaps they'd hang both of us. That's what they'd do. The duke and duchess of Belmore—*Belmore!*—but that would be after the trial, after the entire ton had chewed up our reputations and spit them out, and then . . . then the rest of London could start in!"

"But—"

"For seven hundred years!" He spun on his bootheel and shouted at the ceiling. "Seven hundred years we've been known as one of the finest families in England! The Belmore title is that old!" He turned back to her. "Do you realize how old a dukedom that is? Do you?"

"Well, the MacQuarries are—"

"'Tis old, I'll tell you that. The title is and has been more a part of England than the crazed Hanoverian House. For all those hundreds of years our family has been revered, respected, known for our . . . our . . ."

"Arrogance," she muttered, too softly for him to hear.

"Prestige!" He raised one finger. "Yes, that's the word I was looking for. The first duke of Belmore was . . ."

Same thing, she thought and watched him purge his mind some more. She shook her head and wondered what would happen if his friends could see him saying exactly what was on his mind. She watched the animated way he moved. He spoke with fervent zeal instead of cool anger or disdain. She had known there was deep passion within this cold man. She had seen it whenever he loved her and then in his anger. It was in his eyes somewhere, just a wee flicker. But one had to look past all that pride and arrogance. She also knew that his supreme arrogance was one of the things that made him the man he was. No one she'd ever met had so much pride, and that was what gave him such confidence and strength, what made him Alec, her Alec. Even if sometimes he was hardheaded and a bit of a prig.

He said something about the third duke, who, according to Alec's diatribe, went on a quest to the Holy Land in search of the Grail. Silly, silly mortal men. That third duke couldn't have been successful, she thought. Every witch and warlock knew the Lord wouldn't have let the *Holy* Grail be hidden in the *Holy* Land. That would have been much too obvious. She shook her head and listened and listened, until her mind drifted a wee smidgen.

He paced; she watched. He paced and spun; she watched and got dizzy, so she focused on his face. There was more emotion on it than she'd ever seen, than she had even imagined in her most fanciful dreams. Of course it wasn't exactly the emotion she most wished to see, that being love, but at least it was an emotion. And a strong emotion at that. She listened to him lecturing. One might even have called it ranting, although she doubted he would have used that word. Surely the duke of Belmore would never rant. At that thought she chewed back a smile.

"And the fifth duke of Belmore . . ."

Now, what number had he said he was? Joy tapped her chin thoughtfully, trying to remember. Twelfth? No, that didn't sound right. Thirteenth? No, that was an unlucky number, and being married to Alec was the luckiest occurrence of her life, so that couldn't be right, either. He must be the fourteenth duke. She watched him pace, noting that he took a breath with each turn.

She sniffed and waited.

He turned.

"What number Belmore duke are you?" She spit out the question so rapidly she almost became tongue-tied.

"Fifteenth," he answered distractedly, then went back to the family history.

For ten more minutes Joy did her wifely—duchessly—duty and listened to every word of her husband's monologue, but his pacing was making her tired. She almost wished she could sneeze and hush him up. Her eyelids grew heavy. Her throat was still dry and scratchy. She sniffed, searching for a sneeze.

Nothing. She rubbed her eyes and blinked twice in an effort to listen.

". . . All because of me, my pride, my foolish pride." He ran a hand over his forehead and continued. "I had to rush into marriage with some strange Scot. And why?" His hands shot into the air. "Why? Because she was beautiful!"

*Beautiful?* Her head popped up, her eyes suddenly clear and awake.

"I've never done anything so hot-brained before. And what happens? What?" He spun and raised one hand in the air. "She turns out to be a witch. A bloody witch!"

"You think I'm beautiful?"

"Yes," he snapped.

Joy grinned. "Really?"

"But that is not the issue here. 'Tis not important."

"It is to me," she murmured around her smile.

"Every clock within a mile of you breaks. You levitate me. I'm your husband, not some hot air balloon."

"No one ever told me I was beautiful before." She sighed.

"You almost get us frozen to death."

"Wonderful," she murmured.

He didn't hear her and ranted on. "Turnips fly around the room, and roses appear out of nowhere." He spun around. "God Almighty, woman"—he struggled with his words—"you sneeze and produce whatever is on your bloody mind!" He ran a hand through his gray hair and paced again.

"Yes, I do."

"And you dance with statues—*statues,* mind you—on my roof, where anyone, including the royal messenger, could see you!"

"Don't forget the rose petals," she added absently, her mind still chanting, *beautiful, beautiful, beautiful* . . .

He stopped, his face less tense, his expression thoughtfully reminiscent. "I rather like the rose petals."

"You do?"

He grumbled a yes, then added, "But at this moment I don't know whether to wring your foolish neck or make love to you until you're too tired to cast any more spells."

"Oh, Alec!"

"Bloody hell!"

"You can make love to me," she suggested quietly.

"No. I cannot." His voice was firm.

"But you just said you wanted to."

"I cannot. I will not let myself fall into that trap again.'

"What trap?"

"Making love to you. It muddies up my mind. From now on, I intend for life to resume some semblance of order. I need control. Now."

"I see," she said quietly, wondering how she could live with him and not have him make love to her. Those were the times when she felt closest to his heart. She'd have to work on that.

He looked back into the fire, his expression utterly baffled. "I don't know what's going on here. Nothing is the way it should be. Damn, I'm confused. I've never felt like this."

"You haven't?"

"My life will never be the same." He sat back in the chair.

"Do you love me?" she asked in a small voice, hope in her eyes, feeling as if her heart was in her throat.

He stared at the fire. "I don't know what love is."

"I could teach you," she whispered and rubbed her itchy nose.

"Don't try."

"Do you think you could . . . ?" She wiggled her nose. *Not now!* she commanded herself. *Don't sneeze now, just when he's baring his heart.*

"Could what?"

She sniffed again, then felt the traitorous sneeze coming. She pinched her nose and tried to talk.

"What?" He frowned.

She tried again.

"I cannot understand you."

She released her nose and sneezed, hard.

Alec shook his head, and she heard him softly mumble, "Ninety-three, ninety-four . . ."

A few seconds later he looked up at her. The cold duke was back. "I thought I told you to sit down."

Joy stood there for a confused second. Then she realized he didn't remember anything. He'd told her everything he'd been thinking; he'd spoken his mind, but he didn't remember doing so. She didn't know whether to laugh or cry.

"Can you not obey me in anything?" He scowled up at

her. "I can see that the past week has changed our situation, but you are still my wife and you must obey me. You must understand how serious this London trip is. It is not some game. You cannot be a witch in London."

"But I am a witch."

"You are also the duchess of Belmore and my wife. I order you to behave as such." His face and his tone brooked no argument.

But it wasn't his tone or his command that was on her mind. She'd realized he was fighting very hard not to change. Which meant he was changing. Which meant there was hope—more hope than she'd thought. She thrived on hope. She felt a wonderful sense of victory begin to flutter inside her. She could live with his rules. Yes, she could. She would try very hard to be the duchess he wanted. She would, truly, because perhaps she was only a hope away from a gift more precious to her than the ability to cast a perfect spell—her husband's love.

She smiled then, unable to squelch it, and caught his stunned look. Still clutching the book to her chest, she patted him on the shoulder. "Yes, dear." Then she started to climb the stairs, pausing halfway up to look back at him. His face held surprise and something akin to suspicion.

"I'll leave you alone," she said, ascending the rest of the stairs. Her mouth curved into a knowing smile. "I'm certain you have a lot on your mind."

Whatever thoughts, dire or dreamy, occupied the minds of the duke and duchess of Belmore, they were interrupted the next morning when a familiar shout heralded the arrival of the ducal coach and the lumbering fourgon. In a sloshing splatter of melting snow, old Jem reined in the carriage team just ahead of the baggage wagon, and in a wink Henson, Polly, and the others were gathered inside the great room.

Alex had just extracted another promise from his wayward wife, the witch, that she would behave herself while they were in London. Despite her wide-eyed seriousness, something told him he still needed to worry. He looked at his staff with mixed feelings. Their arrival meant the routine would return to normal. But it also meant the roads were clear. It was time to go on to London, to Prinny, to the nosy ton. Not an enjoyable prospect.

It was time to face whatever cruel destiny fate had conjured—Alec mentally groaned, *bad choice of words*—in store for him. He rubbed a hand over his pounding forehead. God Almighty, he was beginning to sound like Seymour.

Old Jem tramped in, stomping the ice and wet snow off his heavy boots. Alec gazed at Roberts and Henson and said, "We were to meet in Reading. How the devil did you find us?"

Henson and Roberts exchanged worried looks, but Jem, who was never intimidated by the duke, spoke up. "Five of us rode through the bloomin' storm. Took us near four hours to find the carriage, Yer Grace. Buried in the snow it were, deep as the King's pockets." The old driver paused, then looked Alec in the eye. "We thought Yer Graces were under the hatches fer sure."

The room was quiet for a moment, then Henson said, "A giant of a man with an odd little mute dwarf came into the inn at Swindon, Your Grace. Said you were well and had taken refuge here. He gave us the direction of this place."

Alec nodded, half-relieved because he'd been beginning to wonder if the man and the dwarf had ever existed. "We need to leave as soon as possible."

A moment later Jem closed the door behind him, Henson straightened, the perfect ducal servant, and Polly stood near his wife, fretting and talking excitedly to her mistress. The outrider, Willie, brought in a large trunk and another footman, at Roberts' direction, had set up a makeshift ducal dressing room in the kitchen.

Alec took a deep breath. Things appeared to be returning to normal. Then Henson turned, that snoring weasel hanging off his stiff collar like a long white queue.

"Beezle!" His wife plucked the rodent off his footman's back and then tried to tug something out of the animal's mouth. Alec could have sworn the thing was sound asleep.

Still tugging on whatever, she glanced up at Henson. Her

wide eyes and her concerned face gave him fair warning that something was amiss.

"I'm so sorry," she whispered.

Alec's narrowed gaze followed hers. Henson's queue, tied with a shredded riband, was little more than a nub the size of a walnut, and there were two bald spots behind the man's ears. Joy jerked the rest of the gold ribbon from the weasel's mouth and gave the animal a look of reprimand. The fat vermin had eaten his footman's hair.

Commendably, Henson remained composed, his face holding nothing but respect for the duchess even though the remnant of the ribbon dangling from his head held little hair. Joy scowled at the weasel—whatever its name was. Alec seemed to recall that it appropriately had something to do with hell. He watched her take the thing upstairs with her, Polly clucking and following her wake, a stack of fresh clothing in her hands.

"A half an hour," Alec reminded them, watching his wife pause at the top of the stairs. She gave him a silent nod then disappeared in the bedroom. He turned, another order on his lips, but Henson had already anticipated his command. Dignity unflagging, Henson turned and went outside, leaving Alec to stare at the pink-skinned twin bald spots on the head of his master footman.

A strange sense of beleaguered camaraderie hit Alec. It was the first time he could remember feeling that he had something in common with a servant. Taking a quick swipe at his still abundant gray hair, intact behind his own ears, he made a mental note to increase Henson's yearly stipend substantially.

The duke of Belmore's traveling coach and wagon rumbled down the icy road. Inside the carriage hung the silence of two people who had been fighting—he fighting her hold on him and she fighting to hold on tighter. In a matter of minutes the ducal vehicles disappeared over the rise, and the lonely, quaint little inn that served as their refuge slowly faded into nothingness. The magic had gone.

* * *

Seven hours later the duchess of Belmore sat in the carriage, her pink cheek pressed against the cold window, her bright eyes as eager as those of a kitten with a dish of fresh cream. Her unflagging enthusiasm should have annoyed the hell out of Alec. Instead of asking himself why it didn't, he gazed out the window and tried to quell the recurring visions of scaffolds and nooses and roses.

"I once read that London was 'the flower of Cities all.'" She turned to him with rapt anticipation on her face.

"I do not smell the scent of flowers." Alec stopped pulling at the nooselike tightness of his cravat. "Muck, yes. Stagnant water, yes, but not flowers. But I suppose Londoners can be a foolish and loyal lot."

Her smile dimmed, and she turned back to the window. "'Twas a Scot who called London so."

Alec grunted a response, choosing not to metaphorically step on her tail and tell what he thought about Scots. She was wonderstruck by, of all things, the outskirts of London. London. He pinched the bridge of his nose and tried to will away the thoughts of what could happen should the ton discover their secret. Seven hundred years of dignity and distinction—gone in a puff of magic smoke.

She turned her pert little face toward him, distracting him from his dire thoughts, and the brightness in her eyes changed to concern. She tilted her head and placed her small hand on his forearm. "Can you not see it, truly?"

"See what?"

"Out there." She tapped the glass. "Look."

"I've seen it all before."

Her lips thinned into a stubborn line and she crossed her arms. "Then tell me what you see."

"London."

She sighed the exact long-suffering sigh he wished to heave himself. "No. I meant right at this moment. Look outside and tell me what you see."

"Why?"

"What else have we to do?"

"Pray you don't sneeze."

"I have not sneezed for over three hours."

"The coaching house at Pilldowne Crossing will never be the same."

"No one noticed," she said quietly. "'Twas only a little smoke. Truly, you heard them. They thought something was stuck in the chimney."

The clamor of horses' hooves on the paving stones rang out in the tense silence. "Satisfy my curiosity and tell me something," Alec said.

She nodded.

"What were you thinking about when you sneezed at the coaching house?"

Her face flushed with guilt, and she turned to the window and mumbled something.

"I cannot hear you."

She sighed again, then turned back. "I was thinking that all those horrid plumes of choking chimney smoke were blowing on the poor wee post laddies and the horses outside the building. You saw it and heard them cough. One could hardly breathe. And I didn't do it on purpose. It just happened."

"Next time you feel a sneeze coming, do me a favor: don't think." Alec could almost feel the noose growing tighter and tighter around his neck.

The carriage made a sharp turn and rumbled onto a cobbled street. Daylight had just begun to fade into the distance, and she turned, her face cast in pink light for a brief instant. She watched him. He could see the urge to speak itching at her lips.

"Spit it out, Scottish."

Her face broke into that smile, young and eager and bright enough to dull the sunset and make his chest tighten.

"Isn't it the most wonderful thing?"

"What?"

"London. The sights, the sounds. Listen to that."

He frowned, hearing only the annoying clang of bells, the sharp tinny trumpets of the gazetteers, and the jibberish of hawkers calling out their cheap wares. An irritatingly squeaky hackney rattled past, a child screamed, horses clattered by. There was nothing but the harsh city din.

"Did you hear? They sell gingerbread on street corners. Imagine that . . . gingerbread." She gave him a wistful smile. "I love gingerbread, with currants."

Alec grunted a response.

"Whenever I eat it I think of All Hallows Eve." She leaned over and whispered to him, "Witches always eat gingerbread on All Hallows Eve, you know."

He hadn't the foggiest notion what gingerbread tasted like, but knowing it was connected with witchcraft did little to inspire him to sample the stuff. They'd probably serve it to him as his last meal, near the gallows.

She began to hum a bright lilting ditty.

The mournful strains of a funeral dirge played in his head.

Alec stared at her. The duchess of Belmore was humming. Better than sneezing. She wiped the fog from her window and swayed her head to some tune only she knew.

She looked at him, smiling, her head still swaying. "Don't you hear the bells? I love bells. They remind me of Christmas and sleighs and"—she froze, as if to cut off what she was about to spill—"and the things I love."

It was there again, the look that made him feel as though he held the fate of her heart in his hands. He didn't want to feel anything. It was safer.

He looked at her, hoping to see something to help steel his reserve. That face. That strange, odd little face. She derived glowing pleasure from the most minuscule and ordinary things. Joyous.

She turned her face to his as if she'd heard his thoughts. "I've never ridden in a sleigh. Have you?"

"Yes." He stiffened, inexplicably irritated by her question and the path of his thoughts.

"Was it wonderful?"

He tried to think back, but could feel only the tension that was coursing through his body. "I have no memory of it. I suppose it was cold."

"Oh." She stared at her folded hands. "There weren't

any sleighs on Mull. It only snowed once, and then but a tad."

In an effort to cut her off, he stared out the window, looking at London but not seeing it because he had to think of some way to get them through the next few weeks without the ton finding out that the duchess of Belmore was a witch. The only solution he had been able to come up with was to hide her, keep her away from the nosy ton until it was absolutely necessary to reveal her. Perhaps he could pretend she was ill. Yes, that might do it. Just until she met the regent. Then they could get the devil out of London.

He stood and tapped on the driver's box above her seat. The trap slid open. "Jem, take the river streets to Belmore House, and use the back entrance."

The carriage whipped into a sharp right turn. Alec grabbed the back of the seat and braced his legs. Joy fell forward and clung to his left thigh, her face level with the buttons on his trousers. He glanced down and stopped breathing. The image that filled his mind was blatantly erotic. Then she righted herself, looked up at him with that innocent face, and apologized. He closed his eyes and stood there for the longest time. *Control yourself. Control.*

He pushed away and sat back on the seat. She is a witch, he thought, watching as she turned to look out the window. There was nothing he could say, nothing he could do. He might be a duke, but he couldn't change the past or the weather. He couldn't give her rainbows and stars and diamonds in the snow and all that other rot. He had enough trouble not giving her a piece of him, of not letting her smiles and sighs and rose petals bewitch his heart. Bloody hell. He hadn't even known he had one.

He looked at her face and the unbidden thought of making love to her came to mind so strong that he had to take a deep breath. His rational mind told him their lovemaking had been at the root of his downfall. Perhaps he was only suffering from a good healthy dose of lust. He'd gone through it once before, at eighteen. But he was older now, more seasoned, smarter. Lust he could fight and control. It was something with which he was familiar.

For the next ten minutes they rode in silence—his stony, hers enthralled.

She squirmed in the seat, casting covert glances his way. She wanted to ask him something. Finally she found her voice. "What do you see when you look out the window?"

He looked outside. "Fog and dirty snow."

"Is that all?"

"That's all there is."

Her voice held a tinge of sadness that made him want to look away. "The fog is like the mist at home. The Scots say that a thick mist is just a wee bit of heaven drifting down to earth." She looked outside again and a few minutes later quietly asked, "Do you suppose there's enough snow for us to take a sleigh ride?"

Annoyed by all the talk of sleighs and bells and gingerbread—things he knew little of—he gave her the answer he assumed she sought. "Perhaps in the park."

But she continued to wait, her face expectant. He looked away, casting a covetous glance at a prime team of bays. Horses fit for a prince.

"What did you just see that so pleased you?"

He turned, startled that she could read his expression. He waited, then answered, "Horses."

"Oh."

Even Alec could hear the disappointment in her voice. He had little time to ponder that. After a few sharp turns and a shout from Jem the carriage ground to a halt in back of his tall and elegant town house.

"Oh, my goodness!" Her hands flew to her mouth.

"God Almighty, don't sneeze!"

"I wasn't going to," she said, her palms now flat and, like her nose, pressed against the glass. She tilted her head back and looked upward.

"This is Belmore House." Alec stepped down from the carriage and turned back.

She gave him one of her awestruck stares.

How in the name of God could he turn her loose among the ton? He didn't know who needed more protection—her or them.

He shook his head resignedly and took her hand. "Come along, Scottish. You have more servants to meet."

# Chapter 18

"What the devil do you mean, there aren't any servants?"

Joy blanched at the sound of her husband's icy voice in the next room. She had been abandoned in the salon and had spent the last few minutes tilting her head this way and that, trying to decipher the scene in the high painted ceiling above her. A man with a lyre and a wispy maiden frolicked in a forest amid a cluster of wood nymphs. The Pan-like creatures immediately brought to mind Mrs. Watley, all six uppity feet of her, in a dead faint.

"Most of the help went home to the country for the Christmas holiday, Your Grace. The weather has delayed their return."

"Then find some more."

Snapped from a vision of goat horns, an impish face, and a man-sized woman hitting the floor, Joy heard the servant nervously clear his throat. "We tried, Your Grace, but none are available."

"This is London, Carstairs. There have to be servants available. Contact all the agencies."

"I did so. There's no one available. They've all been hired out, Your Grace. Too many people stuck in town because of the bad weather. I tried, but—"

"Who's missing?" Alec's curt voice filtered through the fireplace grate.

Joy stepped closer and heard Carstairs rattle off a list of names.

Alec swore again. She blanched. He'd need a whole

armful of heavenly forgiveness for that word. Chair legs squealed across a wooden floor; then she heard the echoing sound of him pacing in the next room—thud, thud, thud, turn. "So we are, with no butler, no cook, seven . . . no, eight missing footmen, and approximately five absent maids." She could picture him, eyes hard, head bent in thought, hands clasped behind his back, his long-legged strides eating up the floor. Her experience had taught her that he always started a sentence on a turn.

"And the stable master," added Carstairs.

"Jem's here, he can fill that position." He must have turned, she thought.

"Henson and the others can fill in," Alec continued, "but the cook . . ."

"Two of the maids can prepare plain meals, and I heard there's to be a hiring fair tomorrow. Normally I wouldn't hire from a fair, but in this case I suppose we have no other choice."

Joy grinned and her eyes brightened. A fair! What fun. She had never been to a fair.

"Fine. Do what you must, but I want this house adequately staffed by tomorrow night."

"Yes, Your Grace."

A door closed and a moment later the sliding mahogany pocket doors rumbled open and Alec strode into the salon. Wordlessly he walked past her, and she heard the clink of fine crystal behind her.

While he poured his drink she looked into the next room and saw another salon, larger than this one and done in darker tones of deep claret and rich hunter green. The strong, warm scent of tobacco and sandalwood drifted from that room. It smelled of Alec, she thought, catching a glimpse of a hunting scene above a small nook where a carved card table and heavy leather chairs formed an intimate playing circle. "What room is that?"

"The gentlemen's saloon."

She tried to see if the ceiling was painted, but the wall that encased the doors blocked what must have been another three-story room. After a tense silence during which the only sound was the splash of pouring liquor, she said, "I couldn't help overhearing."

Alec looked up at her, still scowling. "Bloody weather." He leaned against a small gilded cart. He glanced down at his glass, then up at her. "Would you like something? A glass of sherry?"

She shook her head. After the last time she didn't think she wanted to drink any amber-colored liquids. She toyed with a pale blue glass figurine atop the marble chimneypiece for a thoughtful moment. "Alec?"

"Hmm?"

"Who were you speaking to?" She set the figurine down, crossed to a stiff-backed chair, and traced the carved wood that edged it.

"Carstairs, my secretary."

"Oh." She strolled over to a sofa, picked up a tapestry pillow, and fiddled with the gold fringe while she leaned against the carved arm. "What do you do when you're in London?"

He seemed surprised by that question. "The Belmore dukes have always had a seat at government. I sit in the House of Lords."

"What else?"

"Attend balls, go to my club, ride in the park—the usual things done by English peers." He glanced up and must have read her face because he added, "It might sound frivolous, Scottish, but most of England's laws are formulated and decided not in Parliament, but at social events." He took a drink. "Why?"

"I was just wondering." She fondled the pillow, then asked the dreaded question: "When do I meet the prince?"

He set the glass down and took an envelope from his coat. "This was awaiting us."

"What is it?"

"An invitation to the prince regent's ball. Seems he's decided to celebrate some monumental occasion—probably the birth of a new litter of hunting hounds." He dropped the envelope on the table between them, and she picked it up and sat down.

The ball was to be held in two weeks. A wee smile tickled her lips. A ball! A prince's ball. "You seem upset. Don't you like balls?"

Alec glanced up at her. "I didn't plan to stay in London that long."

"Oh." She stared at the invitation in her hands, then asked, "What does a duchess do when in London?"

"She doesn't cast spells."

Frowning, Joy set the invitation down. "You keep saying you expect me to behave as the duchess of Belmore should. How can I behave as such if I have no idea what is expected of me?"

He sighed. It had a defeated sound. "I'll have to teach you." He took another drink, then said something about frozen hell and training witches.

"I'm sure there's someone else who can show me what I need to know," she said in a cold tone.

"I said I'd do it."

Pride made her sit erect. She folded her hands in her lap and lifted her chin a notch higher than normal. "What are my duties?"

He took another sip of brandy and said, "Planning balls, dinners, and other social affairs. Basically you will be a hostess."

"Is that what most duchesses do?"

"Yes. Some ladies hire the servants and oversee them."

Aha, she thought. There might be a way to see a fair and a ball all in one trip. Her face lit up like the lanterns at Vauxhall. Now, Joyous, she told herself, you need to work this just right. . . .

"The Belmore women have done both," he continued. "I understand my grandmother was quite a tyrant with the help."

"Who runs this household?"

"The butler did"—he paused again—"does . . . will . . . oh, hell, whenever he returns."

"Would you like me to take care of the servant problem?"

His eyes narrowed. "How? You have no experience."

She gave him a weak smile and snapped her fingers.

"God Almighty, no witchcraft!" He took a drink, then added, "And whatever you do, don't sneeze some up."

She'd known he would react that way. On to her next ploy. "Well, since using my powers isn't an option"—he grumbled something—"how about the fair?"

His head shot up, his eyes suspicious. "What about it?"

"Can I go?"

"No."

"But I'd like to hire the servants. 'Tis a duchess's duty."

"No."

"You just said it was."

"Yes, I did. Yes, it is, and no, you cannot go to a hiring fair."

"You said I should attend to my duties."

"Not this time."

"But—"

"No."

"You don't believe I can do it."

"No."

"You keep saying no."

He lifted his glass in a gesture that said, "You're right."

"You're not even listening to me." She was quiet for a minute of thought. "How am I supposed to learn to carry out my duties if you won't give me any?"

"No."

"Aha! I caught you! That was the wrong answer. It wasn't a yes-or-no question."

"No, it wasn't, but no matter what you ask, the answer is still no."

"I thought you were a just man. You haven't given me a reason."

"I have my reasons."

"But it's a fair."

"This is not the kind of fair you think it is."

"Then why do they call it a fair?"

His eyes narrowed in frustration. "Someday I'll take you to a fair, but not this one." He stood and poured another drink.

"You could take me to this one."

"I have business to take care of tomorrow, and you are not ready to be on your own in London."

"I could take Henson."

"No."

"And Polly."

"No."

"And Carstairs."

He just leveled a glare at her.

She sighed. Englishmen were hardheaded. She drummed her fingers on the sofa arm and looked around the room. After the silence had stretched on for too long, she glanced at Alec. He broodingly stared into his glass. She had tried repeatedly to get him to respond to her. She wanted to unlock her husband. Since he'd walked in and caught sight of the broom and churn and roses, he had been harder than ever. It was as if the ice around him had thickened.

But she was not going to give up. She intended to melt him, magic or no. She was not a quitter, and Alec needed her; he was just too hardheaded to admit it. Little did he know that he had declared war the minute he said he would not make love to her. She intended to find a way to reach him, and so far, their lovemaking had been the only time he'd let his guard down. She would keep chipping away at him until she won. She stood up, intending to plan her strategy. "I'll go up to my room."

"The rooms are not yet ready. I told Polly and Roberts we'd wait in here." He glanced up at her. "Are you hungry?"

She shook her head and sat back down. They'd eaten a large meal at the coaching house where she'd tried to fix the chimney. She rested a small chin on one hand and relived that misadventure. So much smoke. She shook her head.

"We have no cook and no butler," he said, "so it's just as well you're not hungry, I suppose."

"You could always cook," she suggested with a smile.

He scowled at her.

Still no sense of humor. She sat there idly twisting the pillow fringe and looking at the green and gold room. The pale green sofa and chairs formed a circle atop a deep green Aubusson carpet that matched the malachite bordering the dark wood floors and trimming the hearth and mantel. The room was more formal than the salon at Belmore Park, more fragile and stiff. Sitting on the sofa was akin to sitting on a block of Aberdeen granite. She cast a quick glance at Alec. He didn't look any more comfortable than she felt, but she wondered if it was from the hard furniture or the awkward silence in the oppressive room.

She craned her neck and squinted at the ceiling.

"Orpheus and Eurydice," Alec said in an offhand manner.

"Hmm?"

"The scene on the ceiling." He stared at it, too. "Remind me not to look back."

"Hmm? Look back at what?"

"Nothing."

She searched for something to say to fill the awkward silence. "You mentioned your grandmother. What was she like?"

"I never knew her, only of her. She died before I was born."

"And your mother?"

"What about her?"

"What was she like?"

He seemed surprised by the question, then stared into his glass before answering, "Regal, efficient, beautiful—the perfect duchess."

His mother was the perfect duchess. Everything Joy was not. She bit her lip and tried to summon some pride. It was somewhere near her toes.

When she glanced up again he watched her over the rim of his glass. She was reminded of their distant dinner at Belmore Park. He was staring at her mouth. His eyes grew uncomfortably dark and penetrating. A moment later he looked away.

He wanted to kiss her, she realized and closed her eyes in thanks. The power between them was still there. She could feel it; she could see it in his eyes. It's my move, she thought. This is my chance. She stood up and slowly walked toward him. "Would you like another drink?"

He raised his tense face to hers and was silent.

"Your glass is empty." She pointed to it. "I'll refill it."

He looked at it, but before he could answer she plucked it from his hand and sauntered over to the brandy cart, refilled it, and sauntered back. She held out the glass. *Look at me, Alec.* He took the glass without a glance.

So stubborn. This called for drastic measures. She reached up and quickly pulled the anchor pins from her hair.

"Oh, my goodness!" Her hair tumbled down, and she heard his soft intake of breath. She looked at him. He held the glass halfway to his lips, his motion frozen. "I've lost my hairpins. Do you see them?"

"No." He took a deep drink.

She shook out her hair so it floated behind her. "They must be here somewhere."

He stared at the wall, taking deep slow breaths, and she bit back a small triumphant smile, then knelt on the floor in front of him and crawled around searching, making sure her hair swished over his bent knee. "They couldn't have just disappeared." She sat back on her heels and flung her hair back.

His knuckles were white.

She reached up to touch her hair and watched his gaze follow her hand. He raised the glass to his lips. Don't fight it, my love, she pleaded silently. Please, please, kiss me. She watched the battle being waged between his obstinate will and the hot pleasure that burned between them. He closed his eyes, and she held her breath, thinking she'd lost again.

He set the drink down.

"Do you suppose the pins are in your chair?" She reached over and started to put her hand down the side of the chair, giving her head a shake so her hair fell over his hand.

He grabbed her wrist.

She smiled.

He didn't.

Witchcraft should be so intense, she thought. She could feel the physical pull of this man as if an iron chain bound their hearts together. So powerful it was that she wondered for a brief instant if she had started something that even the strongest witchcraft couldn't handle.

He rose, never letting go of her wrist. Kneeling before him, she raised her face and looked up at him. His other hand moved toward her face and traced her cheekbone, then her jaw. She felt as if he could see inside her, see her heart open and needing, see the love she felt for him, her quaking knees, her pounding heart, and see her fear—the weak part of her that was afraid he'd never love her.

He paused to touch the mole above her lip, then ran his fingertip along the seam of her mouth. Her lips parted. His finger slipped inside and touched her tongue. His eyes grew dark and hotter. They touched—hard male finger to soft and damp female mouth. They were two feet apart, Joy kneeling, Alec standing. Their breathing increased; they exhaled slowly. This force, this magical gift that existed between them, was everything.

Her body was damp, her blood flowing thick. Her heart drummed along to its own excited beat. The tip of his finger tasted salty, like the air off the wild Scottish sea. She was home.

He drew his fingertip back, turned away and dipped it into the brandy, then brought it back, letting the droplets fall like honey onto her lips. "You are a witch," he said, then pulled her to her feet, and his mouth closed in, his tongue stroking out for a quick taste of her brandied lips. He groaned a deep growl of defeat into her mouth and drove his tongue inside, filling it thickly.

Her arms curled around his neck, and she pressed her body against him, needing his touch. She could taste the bitterness of the brandy, but it was sweetened by the flavor of Alec. Her Alec.

She breathed in his scent. His hand closed over a breast, and he grumbled another groan of male pleasure into her mouth, a deep primal sound that she could feel clear down to the heart of her womanhood.

He whispered something against her lips, then flicked open the front buttons on her gown, one by one by one. His hand dipped into her bodice and cupped her, his warm rough palm rubbing circles against the tip of her breast. She pearled in response, then threaded her fingers through his hair and moved down to touch his ear and trace the hard length of his strong neck. It was damp. She could feel the abrasive stubble of his beard, feel the hard lines of his jaw, the warmth of his skin—everything that proved he was real, that he was male.

Her hand slid downward and stopped over his heart, then she was lost in the thrusting rhythm of his deep kiss. His hand left her breast, the other hand left the back of her head and he gripped her bottom and lifted her up off the floor and against him. He rocked his hips slowly.

"Now," he said. "Here. Now."

She nodded against his neck.

He walked her back against the closed doors and pinned her there with his hips. His hands slid to the backs of the thighs, and he placed her knees on either side of his rocking hips. His hand slid down the fabric of her skirt and then up underneath.

She moaned when his warm hands slid over her stockings and touched the bare skin of her thighs. The dress rose with his hands, with the tender touch and stroke of them.

His hips moved and she slipped down the door. He raised his hips, sliding her back up. "Tighten your legs around me."

She pressed her knees against his hips and his fingers found the heart of her and plied their magic. He touched her, stroked her, played with the core of her until her body seeped tears of response.

His hand left her to open his trousers. A moment later she felt his power, his strength, the thick fullness of him sliding into her as smoothly as if they were and always had been one.

She gave a ragged cry.

"Hush." His voice was hoarse, his head bent, his breathing labored.

Her eyes drifted closed, and she savored their joining, knowing this was the ultimate gift between man and woman. His lips moved across her face like light summer rain. Slowly he circled his hips and rocked, filling her, then pulling back.

"Too slow," she murmured against his lips.

"Never too slow, Scottish. You'll see. It's never too slow." His tongue stroked her ear, and he inhaled. Chills ran down her neck and over her arms and breasts.

She pulled at his shirt, opening it, wanting to feel his chest against hers.

He thrust deep, and she tightened her knees, gripping him. She pushed his shirt aside. He thrust again, agonizingly slow and deep. Their chests touched.

It was his turn to groan.

His hands slid higher and rubbed and gripped her bare bottom, then stroked her from the point where they joined backward, touching every bit of her private flesh with the tip of one male finger. Every time he moved into her he plied that stroke so privately that her need unfolded, spiraled, slowly with each penetration, with the stroke of that finger, and now the thick hair on his chest played havoc with her breasts, teasing and tickling and making her pucker with life.

His hands gripped her bottom tighter and he moved in hard slow circles that pressed her nether lips even tighter around him. He groaned into her mouth, something private, earthy, and male.

And stopped moving.

"No! Don't stop . . . please."

He said something, but she couldn't hear, couldn't do anything but feel. He pulled back and thrust deep, again and again, suddenly moving with the speed she craved. Her pleasure spun upward with each thrust of his driving hips. Harder and harder he moved, faster, and the door thudded with each plunging stroke of him, over and over and over. . . .

The beat picked up more and more, deeper, stronger, rattling the door hinges. He bent his head again and kept on thrusting, the meter unchanging. It started then, the glimmer that grew and grew with each motion of him within her, that wonderful journey to ecstasy. Higher and higher she rose. He moved deeper and seemed to swell within her. The noise of door hinges, the deep thudding movements faded, and that delicious glimmer grew bright until she screamed into his mouth and pulsed so hard around his shaft that she almost ached with each throb.

A moment later she smelled roses.

"Damn, but this is good," he growled in response and pulled her knees higher and sent her over the edge again and again until she could hardly tell one release from another. She opened her eyes and saw pink petals raining down, hundreds of them.

"The roses," he rasped against her lips and circled his hips faster and faster.

The petals lit on his bent head, stuck to the dampness of his neck and back, where his muscles grew taut and bulged with the drive of his motions. Still he rocked inside her until finally he pulled almost out of her and drove inside with a shout of triumph. An instant later his life pulsed into her.

Then there was nothing but time, seconds and minutes that went by unnoticed. Her fingers loosened their grip on his damp shoulders. Crushed rose petals drifted down to join the layers on the floor around them. Her heart still sped, and her breath still came in panting gasps, and just as it had before, the air smelled spring-sweet and autumn-musky. She let her head fall back against the door and just breathed.

She felt Alex stir against her, for the first time in many minutes. His hands relaxed their tight grip on her bottom and moved to her hips; then he slid his palms down to her knees and tenderly lifted them from around him, and her legs fell free. He slowly lowered her to the floor, her cheek sliding from his damp shoulder to the center of his chest where his heart pounded a rhythm in her ear that was almost as hard and strong as their joining.

He finally raised his head. She saw his face. He seemed to be clinging to some desperate sense of isolation he found necessary to his being.

Let it go, my love, please, she thought.

He was quiet for a moment. Then he stared at her mouth

with avid hunger in his eyes. He kissed her again, parting her lips and tasting her before he moved his mouth to her ear and told her what she felt like inside and how he wanted to feel that again.

She smiled, but it was hidden by his warm damp neck.

He lowered his head to kiss her.

The door resounded with a firm knock.

The kiss continued.

The next rap was harder.

He pulled back, then whispered against her mouth, "Our rooms must be ready." He righted his clothing and stepped back, then helped her button her bodice and brushed the rose petals off both of them.

"My hairpins." Joy pointed at the rug, which was layered with rose petals.

He looked at her through heated eyes and reached out to lift a long hank of her hair. A stray petal fell, drifting down to the floor in the utter silence of the room. Now that he'd given in, it was as if he didn't care about anything but the two of them. It was a beginning.

The knock sounded again.

"Yes, yes! In a minute!" He dropped her hair. "Leave the pins and the petals. We'll finish this upstairs." Grabbing her hand, he jerked open the door and started to pull her along behind him.

Somewhat red-faced, Henson cleared his throat loudly. "Your Grace, the earl of Downe and the Viscount Seymour."

Joy bumped into Alec as he ground to a halt. He muttered a swearword.

Stunned, she glanced up at him and followed his gaze to Neil's embarrassed face. Hers must have flooded just as red.

"Welcome to London," Richard drawled, leaning against one wall of the long entry hall, a knowing look on his cocky face.

Mortified, Joy glanced to Alec for help.

He stood as straight as a Highland pine. "How long have you been here?"

Richard turned to Neil, whose sheepish stance told her

exactly how long they'd been there, and he pulled out his pocket watch and gave it a cursory glance. "Ten minutes or so. Long enough."

No embarrassment showed on Alec's face, only arrogance and displeasure. He turned, blocking her from their view. "Go on upstairs."

"Where?" she whispered. She had no idea where their rooms were, but was almost willing to chance getting lost again just so she could get away.

"Fifth door on the right. I'll join you later."

Richard said something about his use of the word "join" that made Alec's hand tense on hers. She sucked in a breath. He released her hand. "Go."

She hurried up the stairs. Just as she made the first landing, she heard the earl's sardonic voice.

"That's fifty pounds you owe me, Seymour. That was definitely a door banger."

# Chapter 19

The morning of the hiring fair dawned crisp and cold and icy. The ice prevented the physician from arriving at Belmore House until almost noon—the ice and the measles epidemic. He departed an hour later, leaving instructions for poor Carstairs and two of the maids—the ones who could cook—to remain in bed until the spots faded. Since the duke had left even earlier, fate had given the new duchess her first duty.

Wedged between Fishmongers' Hall and the Wharf House was a small and drafty brown brick building where a straggly group of misfits stood upon a platform, each holding a sign proclaiming his or her occupation. Amid the prospective employers stood the duchess of Belmore, her chin high, her small shoulders back, and her green-gloved finger pointing at a black man at the end of the line.

A bewigged Henson leaned toward Joy and said, "Begging Your Grace's pardon, but I don't believe that . . . uh . . . one"—he took a second look, frowning for a moment before he continued—"is exactly what His Grace has in mind."

"You don't?" Joy eyed the huge man who dwarfed the scruffy and pitiful men and women standing on a platform before them. She tapped a finger against her lips. Except for the one man, the prospects did not look promising. If the truth be told, most of them were frightening. The men appeared hard-edged and dirty, and many looked at her as though they were intent on mayhem and murder. There were only two women, both slovenly, and they had eyed poor Henson with the same ferity with which Beezle eyed his hair.

She felt a gentle tug on her skirt and turned to her maid. The girl looked at her in wide-eyed horror. "Oh, ma'am, you cannot hire that man! He's . . . he's—"

"The sign he's holding states he can cook," Joy said, trying to judge exactly how tall the man actually was. Despite the short black beard that framed his wide lips and covered his chin, the man was clean, and there was something about him that belied his massive size, something that said he wouldn't harm a soul.

Polly leaned over and whispered, "He looks like a pirate, ma'am, a huge black pirate. I read a book about pirates, and they're cruel. They drink rum and make people walk the plank—even womenfolk. And they kidnap orphans, they do."

Joy had to agree that the billowing white shirt, black breeches, and high black boots made him look dangerous, but she sensed this man had a good heart. "There haven't been any pirates in England for years, Polly. It's just the big gold earring that makes him look like one."

"But, ma'am, what about his hair?"

"Different, isn't it?" She raised a finger to her lips again and inspected him. "I don't think I've ever seen a man with a braid that long."

"But the rest of his head is bald."

"Quite possibly he's been with Her Grace's pet weasel." Henson eyed the man's shiny head, then fingered his own white periwig.

"I am so sorry about your hair, Henson."

"Quite all right, madam. I have always preferred a wig. Gives the livery more distinction."

Joy had wanted to conjure up some more hair for Henson, but Alec had loudly forbidden it. She turned toward Polly. "Didn't you tell me that at Belmore Park the cook was always complaining about not being able to reach the tall shelves? This cook won't have that problem. Besides, he's the only one whose sign says he can cook. So we have no choice." Joy turned to Henson. "Do any of the others claim they can cook?"

"I believe Her Grace is correct." Henson tugged on the curled queue of his wig.

"And look!" Joy pointed. "See there? He's even got his own chicken. Do you suppose it's dead?"

A choked gasp came from her maid.

"Don't those look like chicken feathers to you, Polly?"

"Yes, ma'am, but I don't see a chicken—just the feathers, I do."

"There, you see. Let's go speak with him before someone else snaps him up."

"Somehow I doubt that will be a problem," Henson said, but Joy was already moving forward, leaving her two servants no choice but to follow. She reached the platform and turned back just in time to see Polly genuflect, mutter something, and cross herself.

"I didn't know you were Catholic," she said when Polly joined her.

"I'm surely not, ma'am, but from the likes of him I'd say the Lord's Prayer isn't enough." She leaned closer to Joy and whispered, "What do you suppose he does with those feathers?"

Joy shrugged, then looked up at the man. Judging from the lack of lines in his face skin, she was positive he wasn't old, and he certainly looked able-bodied. He was even broader and taller than Alec. A yard-long braid dangled like a tail from high on his shiny black head. In addition to his pirate clothes, he wore a wide thick belt studded with metal. Small beaded gourds, a hank of hair, and a clump of feathers swung from one side of the belt. If she hadn't known that the world's last genie was tightly corked in a bottle somewhere in North America, she'd have guessed this man was he.

"Her Grace, the duchess of Belmore," Henson said to the agent who stood next to the platform. "She would like to speak with that one." He nodded toward the black giant.

Joy shook out her skirt, raised her chin so as to look appropriately duchessy, and tried to make her mouth haughty, but it was difficult to purse one's lips when one's neck was so strained. Somehow she didn't feel like a duchess at all; she felt like a trout surfacing for flies.

The agent called out a number, and the man nodded, then stepped forward, the gourds rattling at his side.

Joy craned her head back to look up at him, and her attempts at haughtiness, lip pursing, and nose elevating were lost to the sheer wonder she felt when she took in his size. One deep breath and she found her voice. "The sign says you can cook."

The man nodded, pinning Joy with a stare that was serious but held no malice. "I cook with the ship *Black Magic* five year." His voice was as deep as a barrel and heavily accented.

"Where are you from?"

"The Caribbees."

"You need to address the duchess as Your Grace," Henson informed the man.

The pirate turned his black eyes toward Henson, then looked back at her. He smiled then, showing his white teeth. "The Caribbees, You Grace."

Joy knew then and there she would hire this man. His smile was real. "What are you called?"

"Kallaloo. John Kallaloo."

"Well, Mr. John Kallaloo, what can you cook?"

"You Grace, call me Hungan John. Hungan John can cook anyting." He stood even taller, his face as proud as Alec's. "You Grace like langosta . . . lobster? Crab? Cocido de riñones?"

She nodded, sure that the duke and the ton would like lobster and crab. "What is cocido de riñones?"

"You say kidney stew."

Polly chanted a prayer to Mary, the mother of God.

Joy nodded. It sounded good to her, and she remembered the English liked kidneys.

"Hungan John Kallaloo cook You Grace the best. No

mon, no womon, cook better. You see." He swelled his chest out a bit, which was something to see, considering its size to begin with.

She thought him perfect for Belmore House. He had as much pride and self-assurance as her husband. "I'd like to hire you. Would you like to cook for Belmore House?"

Polly let out a wee squeak of protest, but nothing changed on Henson's face, ever the loyal and imperturbable servant.

"You'll have to excuse my maid," Joy said. She leaned closer and whispered behind one gloved hand, "She thinks you look like a pirate."

He pinned poor wee Polly with his black-eyed stare and slowly bent his head closer and closer to the maid, who was frozen in fear. He closed in until he was but a few feet from her horrified face. "Boo!"

Polly screeched, her panicked fingers digging into the arms of both Henson and her mistress.

Hungan John's laughter, as deep and thundering as the fabled Scottish battle drums, echoed in the hall—a wonderful sound. Still grinning, he looked right at Polly, who was still clutching Joy's arm, then took a circlet of white chicken feathers from his thick belt. He hung it around Polly's neck. "Fetish necklace. Keep away the pirates, little girl." Then he patted Polly's head. He turned his gray gaze back to Joy, and the grin faded from his dark face. Very quietly, he said, "Magic."

*He knew.* Joy's breath caught in her throat. Somehow, some way, this man knew what she was. She returned his look.

He smiled then. "Good magic, You Grace."

They stood there exchanging knowing looks, judging and liking what was there.

"Mr. Kallaloo will be perfect," she said to Henson.

"There's a wagon outside behind Her Grace's conveyance," Henson told the new cook. "Gather your things and load them into the waggon. We'll leave shortly."

Hungan John paused. "You Grace need more servants?"

Joy nodded.

"You need a butler?"

"Why, yes we do. Do you know someone?"

"Old mon called Forbes. He was a butler for fifty year. Master die. Old mon tossed out."

"There now, Henson. Hungan John has found our butler for us."

Henson straightened his wig and eyed the platform. "They all appear ready to slice our throats, Your Grace. Which one is Forbes?"

Hungan John pointed behind him.

Standing near a dingy curtain was a small white-haired man with bright red cheeks and thin lips. His blue satin coat was tattered and dusty, and his breeches looked to be as ancient as he was. His dingy white silk stockings were ripped and snagged, and one sagged around his ankles like elephant skin. He wore unmatched shoes—one black satin with a tarnished buckle, the other brown kid with a slightly higher heel—and they appeared to be on the wrong feet. His wire-rimmed spectacles were as thick as thumbs and magnified his pale blue eyes.

The poor wee man had no home. It didn't matter to Joy that he looked as old as the Tower of London. He seemed to need them even more than they needed a butler. Doing her best imitation of a duchess, Joy threw back her shoulders, raised her chin, and looked at the agent. In a voice she hoped was as commanding as Alec's she said, "We'll take Forbes, too."

Alec strode up the front steps of Belmore House, only to find the door locked. He pounded on the door. Nothing. He pounded again. Nothing. His face a mask of aggravation, he turned back around, but his carriage had just disappeared around the corner of the house.

"Bloody hell," he muttered, pacing back and forth on the steps. "Blasted weather. No servants, no footmen, no butler. Forced to eat cabbage for supper last night—*cabbage!*" He shivered at the memory of the vile stuff. He stepped back and looked upward, searching for some sign of life inside. Nothing.

Frost edged the windows, and the London air was freezing

cold and damp and seeped right through even the many capes of his greatcoat. "Damn, it's cold." He knocked again. "Where the hell is everyone?" He slammed his fist against the door.

The bolts clicked and the door cracked open. One ancient, wrinkled, and suspicious blue eye peered out at him from behind thick spectacles. "Who be ye?" came a shout as loud as a battle cry.

"I am—"

"Eh?"

"I said I am—"

"Speak up, there!" the old man shouted. "Can't hear ye when ye mutter!"

"I said," Alec shouted back, "I am His Grace—"

"What's wrong with yer face?"

"Not my face, you idiot! His *Grace!*"

"He's not here!"

The door slammed shut.

The Belmore crest on the door stared back at Alec. He waited, counting, for the door to reopen. Nothing. He pounded on the door again. It opened a couple of inches.

"I . . . *am* . . . the duke . . . of Belmore, and—"

"The duke don't need yer ham!"

The door slammed shut.

Alec stared at the door, then took great pleasure in making a tight fist and clouting it. After the fifth bang the lock clicked. The door cracked again.

"Be gone with ye or ye'll have to face the duke himself!"

"I am the bloody duke!" Alec bellowed, his fists so tightly knotted his whole body shook.

A gasp sounded from behind him, and he spun around to see the horrified faces of his neighbors, Lord and Lady Hamersley, staring up at him. Taking a deep breath, he collected his wits and tipped his hat. "Good evening, Lady Jane. Hamersley."

They nodded, whispered something to each other, and hurried toward their home across the square as if running from a raving lunatic.

Seething, Alec turned around and took a step toward the entrance.

The door slammed closed again.

He saw nothing but a red haze. He spun around and strode down the stairs and along the carriage path toward the back of the house. His boots crunched in the snow with every sharp, angry step. He jerked the kitchen door open and ground to a halt.

Blackbeard was in his kitchen. *Blackbeard.*

He stepped back outside, took two deep breaths, and tried again.

"Put the lime in the coconut." The man's long black braid swung from side to side as he sang in a voice as deep as if it came from a cannon.

Alec's stunned gaze moved from the man's shiny black head, past the earring—he needed a brandy—to the hammy black hands poised over bowls. First he squeezed the lime, then a lemon.

Speechless, Alec moved through the wide space that separated the kitchen from the larder and ascended the stairs toward the person responsible—his wife, the bloody witch.

"Oh, Alec!" Joy spun around in the foyer when she spotted her husband. Relief in her voice, she ran to him, her hands patting his chest and arms. "Are you injured? Forbes said—"

"Forbes?"

"The new butler. He said someone came to the door looking for idiots, and then he said you were bloody." She searched for wounds. "Where are you hurt?"

He removed her hands from his chest and threw off his greatcoat. "Follow me," he ordered in a voice as icy as the London air and strode into the drawing room. "You went to the hiring fair."

She followed him inside. "Yes, but—"

He slammed the doors and spun around. "I told you you could not go."

"But Carstairs is ill and—"

"I don't care if he's dead! And he might be when I get through with him."

"He has the measles," she whispered and watched him pace.

"You disobeyed me."

"But we needed servants, and you were gone, so I thought as the duchess of Belmore I should hire them."

"Do not disobey me again."

"I'm sorry." She searched, but the only blood she could see was the blood red color of his angry face. "Are you all right?"

"No! I'm bloody mad, or going mad!"

"I thought something terrible had happened," she said.

He spun around, his face cold with rage. "Something terrible did happen. I married you."

She stood frozen; her hand flew to her mouth. His words were so cruel they robbed her of breath. She stared into his face, then escaped his coldness by closing her eyes. When she opened them, the room was nothing more than a mist of tears, the dark blurry shape of her husband the only thing visible.

She found her breath, but it labored in her chest where her heart had died a sudden death, where her shame had begun. She turned, pulled open the doors, and ran out of the room and up the stairs, the sound of her small feet and one broken sob echoing in the cold marble hall as, outside, fresh snowflakes fell on the windows of Belmore House.

Brandy glass clutched in his hand, Alec opened the door to his bedchamber just as the clock struck one. He checked his pocket watch, a habit he'd acquired since his marriage. It was indeed one in the morning. He raised the glass to his lips, but stopped in mid-motion.

A small table sat in the sitting room near the smoldering remains of the fire, a chair on either side. He crossed over to it, doing his best to ignore the apprehensive tightening of his stomach. He looked down at the table.

It was set with the Belmore crystal, china, and silver—

two places little more than three feet apart. Two small silver candleholders stood on either side of a bud vase filled with pink roses.

He closed his eyes and took a deep breath. As if drawn by a chain, he faced the door to the adjoining room. He continued to stand there, looking at the door, his eyes hard and unseeing, his mind a jumble of thoughts and something else . . . some emotion. Alec didn't like this emotion. One could temper anger, hide grief and fear and jealousy. He'd been trained to do so from a young age.

But guilt was too hard to control.

All evening and into the night he had tried to summon up some anger. Anger would have been justifiable, considering what he had gone through recently. But all he saw was the image of his wife's stricken face the moment those cutting words were out of his mouth. He had made cutting remarks before and never felt a moment of remorse. But those he cut had deserved it.

Something deep inside him knew that Scottish didn't. Whatever she had done, feeble-brained as it might have been, there was no malice, no mean intent in her actions. Most everything she did was done with the innocence of good intentions.

But all the good intentions in the world wouldn't change the fact that she was a witch and had the power to ruin both of them and the Belmore name as well.

He sat heavily in a nearby chair and stared unseeing at that damnable table.

Guilt. Guilt. Guilt. The word became a litany in his mind with each tick of the clock. His harsh words had crushed her, hurt her so cruelly that he cursed the tongue that had spat them. His anger had been real, but he wasn't sure whether he was angry about the servants she had foolishly hired or angry because she had gone out and, worse yet, gone out without him to keep a watchful eye on her.

His jaw tightened as he faced another sharp and foreign pang of guilt. Worse than the odious words he had said was the knowledge of what her reaction would be if she knew he was hiding her.

The duke of Belmore was hiding his wife.

What an ironic twist of fate. He had hired the best solicitors in England to find him a bride, and then he'd married in haste after Juliet damaged his pride. He ran an impatient hand over his brow. And now the duke of Belmore was hiding his duchess.

How noble.

His anger came back, but it was self-anger. Then, as if drawn by some obscure need to do so, his gaze drifted back to the small supper table, then to the connecting door.

He set his drink down, rose, and walked toward the door, even got so far as to grasp the handle, but then he stopped.

What would he say to her? I'm sorry I said those things? I'm sorry you're a witch? I'm sorry I married you? I'm sorry I'm hiding you? I'm sorry I'm an ass?

An apology was not something that readily formed on the duke of Belmore's lips, especially when he wasn't sure what he was apologizing for.

He turned away, saw the table, and turned away from it too. He crossed to the leather chair and sat down, his hands clasped behind his head, his boots crossed at the ankles atop the matching leather ottoman, and his hard eyes glaring up at the luxuriously painted scene on the gilt-molded dome ceiling.

Wealth provided many things: painted ceilings, expensive town homes, imported silk dresses. Wealth provided sparkling jewels that would buy forgiveness, but somehow a gift of jewelry seemed as cold as his words. Money, clothes, and expensive trinkets might appease other women, but not Scottish.

He glanced at the table, thinking of his wife, of the stunned and shy look on her face when she sat atop his chest in a foggy English forest. He remembered her frozen and half-dead and the aching frustration he'd felt as he looked down and saw the deadly shroud of ice on that odd yet beautiful face—the same face that could emit the sensual glow of a woman he had satisfied, the only face in which he ever saw innocent love.

He closed his eyes and leaned back in the chair. It was

there again—the guilt. The air went stale with it. He stood up, his gaze locking on the brandy glass he'd left on the table. He moved toward it and as he did so, his damned traitorous mind flashed with the image of a pair of misty green eyes, eyes that held the innocence of the world. He looked at his brandy glass and reached for it, but his hand moved past it, choosing instead to finger the softness of a pink rosc.

Joy awoke to the darkness of her bedchamber, her eyes burning and sticky from spent tears. Her throat was dry from the sobs that had robbed her mouth of moisture. His words echoed in her mind and heart. Sickness threatened, a thick wave of it rising from her belly like Satan from hell. Her breath caught in her throat.

She had failed. The blinding hope that drove her on in the best and worst of times had shattered like a broken mirror under the cruelty of her husband's words.

"Something terrible did happen," he had said. "I married you."

No muddled spell, no dwindling magic, no failed witchcraft, could crush the soul with more potency than rejection by the one you love. That was a lesson hard and painfully learned this evening. No magic could make the hurt go away.

So this was the dark side of love. This was the ache that could consume like a gargantuan beast, devouring every hope, every dream, every star-wish a girl could have. She turned over, staring sightlessly at the canopy above her lonely bed. Her eyes flooded, and she just let the tears flow in rivers of the pain of broken dreams and the hurt of hope gone dead, damp streaks that symbolized the fact that all of her wishes on all the twinkling stars in the universe would not make love grow where there was none.

The fresh snow that had fallen on the cobbled streets and icy lancs of Town stopped by midmorning, about an hour before Polly burst into Joy's bedchamber, saying she needed to get her mistress dressed and ready, for the duke himself had ordered it.

Eyes still burning from the sharp sting that bespoke a night of tears, Joy sat up in the plump bed and tried to summon up the energy to rise. She could hear Polly rummaging through the adjoining dressing room, hear the creak of trunks opening, the thud of them closing, the muttering of her maid as she searched for whatever it was she sought.

Donning a lovely gown would not lighten her mood. She wondered if Polly had packed any sackcloth and ashes. Sometime in the middle of the night, when awakened for the fifth time, she had thought about what her dismal future held. As surely as he who buys land gets stones, she knew Alec would send her away.

So an hour later, dressed in a heavy cream pelisse and a fur hat and muff, she descended the stairs with all the anticipation of the condemned. The heels of her leather half boots tapped, dirgelike, to the front doors where Henson and Forbes stood waiting.

"Good morning, Your Grace." Henson made a bow.

Forbes rammed a bony elbow into him, then shouted, "There's nothing wrong with her face." He made his bow, still scowling at Henson.

"Good morning, Henson, Forbes. Where is His Grace?"

"What's a disgrace?" Forbes adjusted his spectacles and scowled down at his livery, straightening his gold waistcoat, which was on backwards, and tugged at the waistband of his knee-length velvet pants. "These clothes fit me fine." He glowered at the footman. "Ye said so yerself, Benson."

"He's awaiting you outside, Your Grace."

Joy moved toward the front door.

Henson cleared his throat. "Out the back, I believe." Henson crossed over to a narrow doorway near the stairs.

"What's on my back?" Forbes, who had followed Henson, craned his white head over an aged shoulder, trying to see the back of his coat.

Henson opened the door, effectively pushing Forbes back into a corner where he could yank at his clothes with less noise. "If you'll follow me, Your Grace."

Still uneasy, Joy followed Henson down the stairs into the almost stifling warmth of the kitchen. Hungan John moved around the kitchen with practiced ease for someone whose head almost reached the ceiling beams.

"Chop those apples, little girl," he said, grinning at a small maid. "Make Them Graces the best apple chutney this night." Then he began to sing a lively song about apples in the Garden of Eden.

The maid smiled and began chopping to the beat. Hungan John's long black braid swung from side to side as he crossed to where a jack slowly turned a leg of lamb on the spit.

Joy followed Henson down the last step. A flash of white sped past her. An instant later Beezle hung by his teeth from Hungan John's braid.

"Beezle!"

Henson grabbed his wig.

Joy rushed over to the cook, who spun around, sending both his braid and the weasel clinging to it in a free-swinging circle. Joy caught Beezle just as the braid swept past her.

Lying on his back in her arms, Beezle glared up at her through narrowed brown eyes and hissed.

"You were locked in my room. How'd you get loose?"

His brown eyes turned innocent, but were soon eyeing the cook's braid again. His wee pink tongue slipped out and licked his snout.

"What's that?" Hungan John looked at Beezle.

"Her Grace's pet," Henson said, having released his death grip on his wig.

"He ate Henson's hair," she said.

The huge cook leaned over and examined Beezle. He touched Beezle's fur, then looked at the fire. "That fur would burn plenty fast."

Beezle hissed, loud and long, but Henson's mouth held a hint of a smile.

"Hungan John could change the menu. Make weasel ragout. Hmm." He rubbed his stomach and winked at Joy, then laughed that deep, echoing laughter before turning back to his duties.

She handed her pet to a maid and told her to take him back upstairs and make sure Polly locked him up. Beezle climbed over the girl's small shoulder and began pulling the pins from her hair. Two pins pinged onto the stone floor, and Beezle looked up at Joy, guilt all over his sly face.

"Stop that," Joy mouthed as the maid carried her familiar up the stairs. The last thing she saw was Beezle chewing.

Henson opened the back door, and Joy tentatively stepped forward, her stomach a tight knot of apprehension, her throat clogged. The bite of cold air hit her cheeks. Her eyes misted with tears again. She hadn't thought she had any left. She took one deep fortifying breath and stepped outside.

Her vision was blurred at first and she saw nothing but misty white. She willed the tears to stop flowing. She did have a wee spark of pride left. She lifted her small chin and focused her eyes. Everything was still covered with snow, white and clean and fresh now. But standing in front of the stable doors was a shiny black sleigh with Jem in the driver's seat and Alec standing at its side.

She froze, unaware of the joy that shone from her face.

A shaft of pleasure flashed in Alec's dark eyes. She'd expected anger. She had expected a lecture, a reprimand, a denunciation. She had expected to be sent away. She hadn't expected one of her fanciful dreams to come true. But better than the sleigh, better than the bells that hung from the team, better than the realization that she was not to be banished, was the hint of an apology on her husband's face.

"Are you planning to stand there all morning or do you want your sleigh ride?" He pulled the brass catch and opened the door.

She hurried down the steps, but instead of taking her hand, Alec lifted her onto the seat. Her heart picked up a beat, and she held her breath for an instant, then settled into the plush leather squabs and adjusted her skirts and coat around her. An instant later Alec was at her side, his arm across the back of the seat, his legs alongside hers. He looked down at her. "Ready?"

She gazed up at him, not knowing that excitement and love and relief glowed from her face. He watched her for a moment, silent, pensive, and seemed about to say something important. She cocked her head to try to read his intention, but she couldn't determine his thoughts from his face.

"Where to, Yer Grace?"

Joy looked up and caught Jem's expectant and impatient look.

"The park," Alec answered, his hand coming to rest on her shoulder.

And with a snap of the whip, the sleigh lurched along the snow-covered drive.

# The Change

**Excite the mortified man!**

*Macbeth*, William Shakespeare

# Chapter 20

On most days London rang with the noisy shouts of street hawkers and piemen, the music of flute-pipes and hurdy-gurdies, and the incessant clatter of iron wheels and clopping hooves upon cobblestones, but not this day. As if struck by a Sabbath pause, even Hyde Park stood deserted. It was a dreadful shame that most of the ton snuggled deep in the warmth of their fur robes or sought the melting intensity of hot coal fires after the steely English sky had deigned to sprinkle the rolling park lawns and lanes in a silent magical blanket of fresh snow.

Along the drive a double avenue of oaks arched in a fleecy white canopy. The normally clamoring hooves of the prancing team fell silently, like snow upon snow. But the sleigh bells rang clear and clean in the frozen air, the chiming melody dimmed only by the lyrical notes of the duchess of Belmore's delighted laughter.

"Look Alec! We're the only ones here!"

"I know."

Joy pivoted in the seat to see the landscape—an unfettered ivory wilderness in the center of town. "Doesn't it take your breath away?"

"What? The fact that no one is here?" His look told her there was little that the duke of Belmore would lose his breath over.

"No." She waved a hand around. "This!" Then she saw from his expression that he had no idea what she was talking about. "Look around you and tell me what you see."

"Snow."

"What else?"

"More snow."

"What else?" she said on an exasperated sigh.

"The park."

She stared in thoughtful silence at the muff in her lap and wondered what kind of person saw only the shell of things. Tilting her head she studied him. He was perfectly serious. But somewhere beneath that cold exterior lived another man. She'd seen glimpses of him. In fact she wondered if that wasn't what she had first seen in Alec—a soul locked up. It was almost as if he didn't know how to live life, as if he somehow didn't quite fit in, so he kept himself aloof.

She placed a hand on his arm, hoping for a wee glimpse of the other man she knew was there, the man who only a little bit earlier had managed to wear an apology on his face. "Look at that long loch and tell me what it looks like to you."

"The Serpentine?"

"Is that what it's called?"

"Yes."

She looked at the long silvery snake of ice and understood the name. "Describe to me what you see."

"I see frozen water—a lake, or loch as you Scots put it."

"Do you notice anything special about it?"

"No."

"What color is it?"

"Gray."

"What do you think of when you look at it?"

He shrugged. "I don't think about it."

"Just try."

"I see gray ice. Nothing special." He turned his cynical gaze toward her. "I'll bite, Scottish. What do your eyes see?"

She looked at the glittering loch. "What do my eyes see? 'Tis not only my eyes, but my mind, too." A wispy smile played at the corners of her mouth. "I see a ribbon of shimmering silver, as if its surface has been painstakingly polished for hours."

Alec frowned, staring in puzzlement at the lake.

Her gaze drifted upward. "And look up."

His eyes followed hers.

"See the sky? How silvery gray it is, too? Except where the sun glows through those clouds. I know it's the sun shining, but see the way the dark clouds break and every so often there's a wee bit white of light? I think it looks like moonlight."

She turned back to look at the Serpentine. "That's what I see—the miracle of moonlight shining in the daytime." Her eyes grew misty as she lost herself in the wonder of the scene, but she came back down to earth when she felt his gaze. She smiled, thinking to describe it in terms more familiar to him. "I see a dinner table."

"Pardon?" He gave her a look that said he thought her daft.

"I see a silver lake that reflects the color of the sky and shines like polished serving plates. I see trees dressed in crisp white ice, standing like waiting footmen. I see pure white clean snow that has never been touched or trod upon or dirtied. To me it looks like the finest damask linen atop a table, and I think that if I held some of that snow high in my hand, up to the light, I'd see it glistening as the cut-crystal goblets do when they are near candlelight during a dinner at Belmore Park." She turned to him and smiled. "Now can you see it?"

His stubborn jaw tightened, and he exhaled in a way that said he thought her description silly. "I see what's there. A plain gray lake and cold snow, nothing more. It's monotonous and dull."

She watched him put up that shield of his, but instead of warning her off, it did the exact opposite. Through narrowed eyes she watched him, thinking he'd have to do better than that to discourage her. "Look! Over there, beneath the snow." She pointed to her left. "I see bits of color—the orange and yellow leaves of pollard oaks peeking through the snow. And there! If you really look, you'll see snippets of red—holly berries," she said with a nod of her head. "And next to them, in the hedgerows, look closely and see that poor wee bird?"

"Where?" He squinted at the bushes.

"There, tucked inside that hedgerow as if it's trying to get warm." She pointed at a hole in a hawthorn bush about the size of a Scottish golf ball. "A wee spot of blue. See it?"

The bird fluttered, and Alec grunted something she took for a yes.

She faced him again. "Those are the things I see. If you look closely, you'll see them too."

"Why would anyone want to take the time to see things that aren't there?"

"But they *are* there. That's my point. How can you appreciate anything if you don't really look at it? To imagine that the moon is shining in the daytime makes the day seem special, different from yesterday and probably different from tomorrow, which means one can only enjoy today . . . today." She watched him shake his head in disbelief. "Alec?" She touched his arm. "How will you ever have any memories if you don't create them?"

He seemed to think about that.

"Didn't you ever make things up when you were a child? Pretend you were a knight, a soldier, a king? Make believe that an apple was magical, that a stick was a broadsword or a horse, that a dog was some fierce beast out to gobble up the world and only you could save it?" The moment she finished the question she saw the change in him and knew she'd said the wrong thing.

There was no child in him and there never had been. And no, he'd never done those things.

Jem turned around and gave Alec an odd look. Alec turned away. His eyes scanned the area. After a pause he said tersely, "I suppose 'tis how one views things. I have no time for whims and fancy, no time to weave tales about nothing."

"What do you have time for?"

"I found the time to take you for a foolish sleigh ride."

The sleigh lurched forward with a strong jerk. "Sorry, Yer Grace. Hit a hard rock." Then Jem muttered something about a head.

She swallowed hard and stared at her hands, then whispered, "If you consider it foolish, why did you do so?"

He didn't answer, but she saw that his own hands had tightened as if he was once again struggling to speak or searching for the words. Without looking at her, he finally said none too gently, "I don't bloody know."

Neither said another word, but the sleigh jangled onward, around the drive and on toward the dell, over a wee hillock and down a stark white path where the snow was as virginal as a new bairn.

After long minutes of tense silence, she gave up. "You may take me home now."

"You wanted to ride in a bloody sleigh, so ride in it." He spoke through clenched teeth and glared at the park so angrily that she wondered why the snow didn't melt.

One glance and the urge to speak became too strong for her to quell. "I imagined it would be . . . different."

"So did I," he said under his breath.

After another tense interval she asked, "How?"

"How what?"

"How did you think it would be different?"

He said nothing, but continued to look out his side of the sleigh. His hand tightened on the rim. "I thought 'twould please you." He spoke the words quietly, like someone admitting a dreaded sin.

She stared at his tensed hand, at his straight stiff shoulders, at the too-proud lift of his head, and knew the struggle it had taken for him to make that admission. Perhaps there was still hope. At least they were talking. Also, that was probably the closest thing she'd ever get to an apology.

She reached out and placed her hand on his forearm. Under her fingers, his muscles tightened in response. "I had hoped to please you, too."

He faced her then. "How?"

"When I hired Forbes and Hungan John."

Frowning, Alec ran his hand over his forehead. "I take it Hungan John is the cook."

"Have you seen him?"

"One couldn't miss him."

"Forbes is the butler."

"So you said last night."

Again the silence, both of them thinking of the night before. Neither one comfortable.

"The deaf butler."

Joy winced at his tone. "He's only a tad hard of hearing." She watched Alec to gauge how angry he still was. "And we did need a butler." She paused, then said, "And if you could have seen him. Poor wee old man was thrown out on the street after fifty years of faithful service. He needed us too."

"I've no doubt he needed us. There must be thousands in London who need us, but no one needs a deaf butler, Scottish."

She stared at her hands again. "But that's exactly my point." She touched his arm again. "He has so much pride. Surely you of all people can understand that?"

"Was that supposed to be a compliment?"

She ignored him and went on. "He stood on that hiring platform, his head high despite his tattered old livery. Couldn't we give him some of that pride back? Please?" She stared straight at him, watching his eyes as the mental battle continued within him.

He tore his gaze away. "Just keep him away from me, and the front door."

"Their lordships, the earl of . . . eh? What was that name again?"

The drawing room door slammed shut, only to open again a second later.

"Their lordships, the earl of Town and the viscount . . ."

The door slammed again.

A few seconds later it cracked open. "What do ye think I am? Some numbskull? Not announce yer presence, for God's sake!"

Another voice said something.

"What's wrong with yer face? I don't see anything wrong with yer face! Ye can't go in yet! Let go of that door! Eh? Benson! *Ben-son!* Oh, there ye be! Their lordships forgot their names. Do ye know them?"

The door opened slowly and Henson stepped inside. "Their lordships the earl of Downe and the Viscount Seymour."

"I need brandy." Downe moved past Henson and headed straight for a decanter on a table near the wall.

"Where's Seymour?" Alec asked.

"Still trying to get that paper scull of a butler to say his name right." Downe sipped his drink, then turned back around. "He never knows when to give up."

Seymour came into the room. "I say, Alec, odd choice for a butler. The old fellow can't hear a bloody thing."

"Really, Seymour? How observant of you. I'm sure Belmore here hasn't figured that out yet and truly needed you to tell him his new butler—and I use the term loosely, considering the man's as old as Methuselah—is deaf."

Alec stood by the chimneypiece, ready to fend off the usual round of bickering. Downe had poured his second drink, moved to the closest chair, and slowly lowered one hip onto the arm with a groan.

"What ails you?"

Downe winced again, then scowled at the room in general. "Nothing that murder won't cure."

"Whose?"

"Letitia Hornsby's," Seymour answered, grinning.

"Feather-skulled, bacon-brained child from hell," the earl muttered.

"What happened this time?" Alec glanced from one friend's brooding face to the other's grinning one.

"One word, Seymour. One bloody word and I'll call you out," Downe threatened.

"Should have been there, Belmore. 'Twas better than the Christmas Ball. Downe never saw it coming."

"You're a dead man."

"Only if I manage to stand too close to the Hornsby chit," Seymour goaded with a laugh. "And her dog."

"The beast should be shot, along with its mistress."

"Her dog bit him on the ass."

"Dawn tomorrow, Seymour."

"That's what got you into this in the first place. If you

hadn't gotten in your cups and called out Hanford this never would have happened."

"Speaking of asses. Who's the ass who told her?"

"*I* didn't tell her. She was hiding behind a potted palm at Maitlands' ball and overheard the whole thing. Destiny, you know."

"He doesn't know when to quit and he doesn't know when to shut up." Downe's face turned redder with each comment.

"You wish I'd shut up because you don't want to hear about your own follies. Hanford's a crack shot, Downe. You know that as well and I. 'Twas a stupid move. Your hand was shaking so badly from your excesses the night before I doubt you could have hit a tree at three paces."

"And I doubt you can keep your mouth shut for more than five minutes."

"Letitia saved his drunken hide," Seymour told Alec, then added, "Although from what I saw, the hound's teeth had a good hold on most of it. Surprised the animal didn't get the hiccups."

"Hudson Green, Seymour."

"Do you suppose the beast is hung over?"

"At the crack of dawn."

"You're not going to call me out, Downe. I'm the only one willing to be your second."

"A pound of good you did me when I met Hanford at dawn." The earl turned to Alec. "Seymour was crawling around on all fours searching for a bloody four-leaf clover."

"Found it too," Seymour said, stroking the rabbit's foot on his watch fob, "just before the chit's hound came bounding up the hill." A thoughtful look crossed his face. "Do you suppose that's prophetic?"

"No doubt it was planted there by the dueling fairy." The earl swigged down his brandy, then frowned at the empty glass.

Alec watched in pensive silence as his two friends glared at each other. He gave the earl's glass a significant look and said seriously, "If you don't stop swilling that stuff, all of

Seymour's charms and fairies won't help you. Something or someone worse than a dog is going to put you out."

Downe drilled Alec with the look of the damned. "What I do is my own bloody business, Belmore. Stay out of it."

Alec and Neil exchanged a glance, and the viscount shook his head to indicate that talking to the earl did no good.

The tense silence was broken when the doors to the drawing room opened with a bang and Joy rushed inside, the deep ruby red of her skirts swirling and swishing and rustling, her face eager and expectant, as if the most wonderful experience of her life was occurring this instant. Alec had seen that look before—whenever it rained rose petals.

Her ruby silk dress was the finest his wealth could buy, yet something told him she would look just as vibrant in a ragged gown of drab flannel. Her heavy mass of shimmering brown hair was swept up on one side, away from her expressive face, elegant and formal, but a cascade of long curls fell from the other side, framing her flushed cheek and flowing over a pale feminine shoulder. Diamonds and deep rubies sparkled at her ears and neck and on the toes of her slippers, but no one would notice because her smile outshone them.

Her appearance suggested what she was—a bewitching sprite of a woman who found adventure in a walk through the snow or a sleigh ride in the park, a woman so untouched by cynicism that she saw the essence of all things in the smallest leaf and in each crystalline granule of snow. She was an unusual beauty whose eyes at times could make Alec forget he was duke.

He watched her greet his friends—Seymour with a genuine welcome, Downe with tolerance mixed with apprehension. Then she scanned the room, her gaze seeking and finding his, then pulling away when Seymour spoke to her. Downe had stood when she entered and raked his gaze from her head downward, randomly stopping to stare at prime parts. Alec had to quell the urge to cuff him. His hand tightened on his own drink.

Henson announced dinner, and Alec acknowledged him with a curt nod, while his friends escorted his wife toward the dining room. He tore his brooding gaze away from the empty doorway.

He'd married for convenience and gotten none. He'd gotten a witch. He almost laughed at the irony. Almost. He took a drink and looked back to the spot where she'd stood, wondering if protecting the Belmore name was his only reason for hiding Scottish. He set down his glass and pushed away from the wall with more force than necessary. Then he followed them, and not liking the answer his conscience gave him.

During the next few busy days, Joy learned social behavior under the tutelage of her frustrated husband. It took her a whole morning to master the royal curtsy; her knees ached from the ridiculous and unnatural position in which they'd been bent. When she suggested that Englishwomen must have knee joints different from those of the rest of the world, he countered that she was part English. She decided her knees were Scot.

She'd learned forms of address, proper responses, and who was who among the ton, and she'd been cooped up in Belmore House until her need for nature had made her as fidgety as a child on Christmas Eve. 'Twas then that dear Neil and Richard had suggested an outing and now all four of them were in the carriage just pulling away from Belmore House.

"Are you warm enough?"

Joy looked at her husband and nodded. "I'm fine, truly." He settled back in the carriage seat, then absently rubbed a hand over his arm. That was the third time he'd asked the same question, so she asked, "Are you cold?"

"No," he answered too quickly, as if she had asked him something so personal that her question offended his masculinity. He looked out the window. "Must be the damp air."

Half an hour later, the team's hooves clattered with a

hollow sound as they passed over London Bridge. For the first time in over a century the Thames had frozen. The river was now alive with milling dark-clothed crowds enjoying this wondrous event—the Frost Fair. Between London Bridge and Blackfriars Bridge the river was known as Freezeland Street. There, enterprising watermen were charging an ice toll of twopence to walk along the ash-covered aisles.

A few minutes later, Joy and Alec followed Neil and Richard through the wooden entrance to the icy walkway. At river-level, bright pennants and banners—yellow, green, and blue—red and white flags, and multicolored swagged bunting were strewn from booth to shopkeeper's booth, each proclaiming the fair's best goods. Crusty beef pies and roasting mutton warmed the bitter air with their sweet scent while tavernkeepers emptied hogheads of frothing ale to sell to the hordes of fairgoers.

"I don't know how I let them talk me into this," Alec said under his breath, his glare pinned on the viscount and the earl.

Joy whipped her head from left to right trying not to miss one exciting thing. "You promised to take me to a fair."

"You attended one, without my permission, and that's how we ended up with a deaf butler whose voice could wake the dead and a Caribbean cook who sings his recipes."

"You said yourself that dinner was superb."

"I happen to like lobster."

"So did your friends."

He grunted some kind of response, frowned, and fastened the brass frog on his greatcoat.

"Alec, are you sure you're not cold?"

"I'm fine."

"I say, Joy. Need some advice, here." Neil waved them toward a booth at the west end of the ice aisle. "Which do you think I should purchase?" The viscount held up a small vial of blue oil and a watch fob made of ivory.

"What are they?"

"This"—he held up the bottle—"is protection oil."

"Protection from what?" the earl asked.

"Ghoulies, ghosts, goblins, and the like," the shopkeeper said, then added, "and witches."

"I believe I could use that," Alec said dryly, and Joy frowned up at him.

"No harm in being safe, Belmore," Neil said seriously. He held up the other item in question. "And this is a tooth from a hellhound."

"What, no garlic ropes?" The earl leaned against the corner of a booth.

"Over there, yer lordship, next to the hex dolls and the bogey charms," the wiry little shopkeeper said with a gap-toothed grin. "The garlic's fer bloodsucking vampires."

"I've known a few bloodsuckers in my time, but haven't seen any vampires. I'm certain, however, that Seymour has."

"Have not. But this morning I saw you fight off a hellhound." He dangled the fob in the earl's line of vision.

"Don't remind me." The earl winced and rubbed his hip.

Neil turned to Alec and said, "I daresay, Downe needs the hair of the hound that bit him." Then he chuckled and asked, "What do you think he needs, Belmore?"

"I think—" Alec stopped in mid-sentence. "Bloody hell. I thought you said none of the ton would be here."

Neil turned to follow Alec's scowling look.

"Oh, look who's here! Eugenia! Claire! Look! If it isn't His Grace!" Lady Agnes skittered toward them like a foraging squirrel to plump nuts. "What a small world!"

"Too small," the earl commented while the three gossips sidled through the crowd.

Joy clutched Alec's arm. His hand moved to rest atop hers just as a cheer cracked through the icy air and the crowd shifted to gather around a circle of gamblers who were winning at *rouge et noire*.

"Hurry!" Alec pulled her through a space between the booths, the earl and viscount following. They wormed their way past a fat grinning kettledrummer and a dancing fiddler, then ducked behind a makeshift stage where a small crowd of fairgoers watched a Punch and Judy show.

"Quick thinking, Belmore. Now I can enjoy my ale without having to listen to that noodle-headed woman and her gaggle of gossips." The earl tossed an ale seller a coin, then paused and, in a completely surprising move, ordered a hot mulled wine and handed it to Joy with a gallant bow. Smiling at her stunned expression, he leaned indolently against the stand, sipping ale from a foamy tankard.

"I say, Downe, 'tis a small world—and fast becoming even smaller," Neil said, his voice suddenly amused. "Look there, over your right shoulder, by the skittle alleys. Isn't that . . ."

The earl turned, then finished in a groaning voice, "The Hornsby hellion."

Joy would have not have thought it possible for the earl of Downe—rake, cynic, and borderline drunkard—to panic at anything. But he did. His handsome and cool features became a grimace, and there was true dread in his usually shuttered eyes. He quickly stepped between the booths, trying to hide behind a swag of bunting and the shoulders of a puppeteer.

She followed the direction of Neil's amused eyes and saw the infamous Letitia Hornsby. The girl was one of the most harmless-looking women she had ever seen. Neither tall nor short, she had a bright and serious English face. She'd unfastened her rich blue pelisse and underneath was a pale blue cashmere dress with dark blue flounces and a bodice line of bright gold anchor buttons. To Joy she appeared to be completely harmless and totally incapable of creating the havoc of which these men accused her.

The girl turned suddenly, searching, her hand raised to shield her eyes as she swirled, the reticule on her wrist launching into the air like a Greek discus.

A nearby gentleman stopped it—with his open mouth. He yelped and wiggled a front tooth while he danced in ringing pain atop the ice, sprinkling ashes upward with each bootstep.

Poor Letitia gathered her startled wits and tried to apologize, reaching out to the flailing man. Like precisely aimed arrows two of her fingers poked his stunned eyes. His holler could have been heard in Glasgow. She grasped her cloak and stepped back, obviously fearful of the man's rage. With a dull thwack, he fell flat on his back, losing his beaver hat in the crowd of onlookers. His shiny black-booted feet—which had been standing on the hem of her cloak—were now pedaling the air in time to his bellowed curses.

"Oh, my goodness," Joy whispered, trying not to giggle.

"Good God!" Neil grabbed his good luck charms and stared at the supine man who was Letitia's current victim.

"What?" Alec and Richard said in unison.

Neil pointed at the man who was still lying on his back. "That's Brummell!"

# Chapter 21

The party of fairgoers arrived back at Belmore House two hours later. Laughing at the banter between the viscount and the earl, Joy blew into the foyer in a flurry of wet snowflakes, followed by the bickering lords and Alec, the only one of the group who was scowling.

"I say, Belmore," Neil said, while handing his outerwear to Henson. "You've been glowering since this morning. No fun at all."

"'Twas bloody cold," Alec said, waving off Henson in favor of the drawing room fire where he stood for a few minutes of warming before he removed his gloves. "See that the fire in the saloon is stoked up, Henson, and close those doors. This place is freezing."

"I'm not cold." Neil looked at the earl. "Are you cold?"

"No."

"Been acting strange all day, Belmore."

Alec didn't answer, just glared at the viscount and backed a bit closer to the fire.

"We weren't ready to leave, you know," Neil went on. "The fun was just starting."

"Unless you were Brummell," the earl added, sinking into a wing chair and stretching out his long legs, his hands unusually empty of drink.

"I say, wasn't that the strangest thing you've ever seen? The Beau with no voice. One minute he was bellowing at that chit and the next nothing but a croak and then silence."

"Even I felt sorry for that hellion," the earl commented.

"Brummell can cut to the quick with that rapier tongue of his."

Joy moved toward the door. "Well, I think I'll leave you gentlemen to your—"

"Wait." Alec's voice, sharp and cold as the sting of frost, stopped her just before she made her escape. She turned.

His back was still to the fire, and the light glowed a golden outline around him. She couldn't see his features, but the stiffness of his stance, the angle of his head, told her exactly how he felt.

"I will speak to you. Alone."

Joy didn't dare move. He knew, as sure as cream crowdy had rum, he knew what she'd done. She swallowed and tried to look innocent. She opened her eyes wider and hoped it worked. "Me?"

"You."

"Whatever for?" She hoped that sounded innocent.

His silent look gave her the answer.

"Where?" How in the world had her traitorous voice cracked on a word of one syllable?

"I say, Joy," Neil cut in, unaware of the tense exchange going on between husband and wife. "Before you leave you must promise me a dance at Prinny's ball."

"A dance?" She turned to him with the eagerness of someone seeking shelter.

"A country dance or a minuet. Prinny still insists on opening and closing his balls with minuets. I turn a fine leg, if I do say so myself."

"Turn an ankle would be more the truth." The earl gave him a smirk.

"I'm afraid I don't know those dances," Joy said quietly, reminded how out of place she really was.

"Bloody hell."

She turned toward her cursing husband.

"Egad! How can you go to the ball if you can't dance? What are you going to do, Belmore?"

Alec said nothing.

"She can learn now," Richard said. He flipped open his

pocket watch and added, "We don't have to be at the club for a few hours."

"Winning idea, Downe. We shall be her dance instructors."

Surprised, she faced the earl. She would have expected such a favor from the viscount, but not the acidic earl of Downe. Unwittingly, he had saved her from an angry husbandly lecture. Joy could have kissed the man, even though she still wasn't sure she particularly liked him. He was a strange cynical man, and she had thought he had a cruel streak of his own. Yet she had seen another side to him today. Today he'd been sober. And most uncharacteristically gallant.

Complain as he did about Letitia Hornsby, he was the one who had finally spirited her safely away from the ranting man who rang such a cruel and embarrassing peal over the poor girl. Joy had noted how Letitia's eyes had moistened and her face had flushed with the threat of tears, yet bravely the girl had refused to let herself cry.

'Twas then that Joy had twiddled her fingers, robbing the cruel man of his voice. She'd hoped Alec had missed it. Now that hope was dead.

"I assumed you knew how to dance," Alec said to her, his voice still too controlled for her peace of mind.

"What say you, Belmore? To the music room?"

Alec crossed the room and stood next to her. The look on his face killed any hope she'd had that he'd forgotten about the incident at the Frost Fair. She wanted to step away, and he must have read her thoughts, because he placed his hand on her arm in a gesture that had nothing to do with husbandly affection and everything to do with keeping her within reach. "We shall follow you."

The two men left the room and went up the staircase. Joy started to follow, quickly, but Alec held her arm firmly so she could do little but walk by his side.

"Tell me, wife. What do you suppose happened to Brummell's voice?"

"Perhaps the cold weather. I heard once about—"

His grip tightened on her arm. "I told you: no hocus-pocus," he whispered through a clenched jaw.

"He was humiliating that poor wee girl," she whispered back.

"That is none of your affair."

"I couldn't stand by and watch that kind of cruelty, Alec."

"London thrives on cruelty."

"The girl did not deserve such unkind treatment. That man should count himself lucky," she added fiercely. "It could have been much worse."

"I don't see how."

"I could have made him spit toads."

He ground to a halt and turned, his face livid. He grabbed her shoulders, his face a mixture of anger and panic. "If you ever make anyone spit toads, I'll . . . I'll—"

"He was too cruel, Alec."

He just glared down at her as if he couldn't believe she was arguing with him, as if no one ever argued with him.

"Sometimes words can cause greater pain than physical blows," she said with quiet seriousness.

His mouth tightened into a thin line. Both of them remembered his own cruel words to her. She expected his face to tighten with displeasure. She was wrong. His eyes had narrowed, but not in anger. There was a distant look in his eyes, and he seemed to be thinking back far beyond a few nights ago. There was vulnerability in his expression—something she'd never thought to see in the duke of Belmore.

When he focused again, he searched her face, as if seeking something so elusive that he despaired of ever finding it. His eyes reflected defeat—now, that was something Joy understood. This was what she had first seen in him, this need, this vulnerable side to the cool aristocrat seen by the rest of the world. So she and Alec were both cursed by a sense of failure, only each dealt with it differently. She accepted it; he didn't. She tried to compensate; he fought it with a will so strong it formed his being.

She wished she could conquer his demons with her magic. But she couldn't even conquer her own. He had her heart and a part of her soul; she had his name and his protection. But she'd have given those away along with her powers, weak as they might be, for a loving smile from this man.

"Belmore! I can't remember which blasted room is the music room."

Alec watched her a moment longer, then blinked once and answered, "Fourth door to the right." He loosened his grip on her arms and silently led her up the second flight of stairs.

Two hours later, while Alec played the piano, Joy moved through a lively Scottish reel, partnered first by the viscount and next by the earl. She finished the last step with a dainty spin and a merry laugh. She dropped onto a brocade settee and said, "You've worn me out, my lord."

"The pleasure was mine, Your Grace." The earl bowed over her hand and held it just a bit longer than seemed necessary.

"I say. We've taught her all the country dances—the ecossaise, minuet, contredanse. I believe that is everything."

"Except the waltz," the earl said.

"Do you suppose there'll be any?" Neil asked. "You know Prinny prohibited the waltz at his last ball."

"Our regent changes with the whip of the wind. Talk was that Cathcart's ball was a blinding success because Lady Jane dared to play waltzes all night. I suspect Prinny will have a waltz or two, and I'll be happy to offer my services to teach Joy to waltz."

"Stuff it, Downe. You had the last dance. 'Tis my turn."

"Stop!" The pianoforte keys banged in loud discord.

Joy turned toward Alec, who had risen like an angry specter. "I will teach her."

No one said a word, but she thought she saw a look of pleasure cross the earl's face.

"You can play," Alec said to the earl, who sauntered over to the piano and sat down, clearly amused by his friend's outburst.

Joy looked up at her husband, who stood in front of her so tall and rigid, and placed her hand in his outstretched one. His skin was hot, and she cast a quick surprised glance at their joined hands. He had been strangely quiet since they'd entered the music room. She had assumed he was still angry and didn't want to dance with her, partly because she was so unschooled in social graces.

"Put your hand on my upper arm." He slid his warm hand around her waist. "Come closer," he said, pulling her forward until she was too close. "'Tis three-quarter time, like the dance with the allemande. Do you remember?"

She nodded.

The earl began to play the loveliest melody she had ever heard. It caught her off guard and she turned to watch him play with more feeling than any musician she'd ever heard. "He plays wonderfully."

"Yes, he does. It's one of the few things he still appears to take seriously." There was a look of pity in her husband's eyes that she knew would have sent the earl into another bout of careless drinking had he looked up from the keys at that moment. Alec's hand squeezed her waist. "Ready?"

She nodded, her head filled with music as wonderful as that at her beasts' ball, and a magical moment later she was swirling across the marble floor in the strong and steady arms of her love.

"I say! You caught on quickly!" Neil called out.

The music played on, sweetly, gently, the notes flowing like satin ribbons in the air. She looked up at her husband, seeking his approval. His face was stone serious; the light in his eyes said he was fighting some silent battle, and losing. If this had been a dream, she would have hoped he was fighting a battle with his heart, but this wasn't a dream. Surely the battle was with his anger, or possibly with his shame at his choice of a wife. "I'm sorry," she said quietly.

From the expression on his face, she knew her remark had confused him.

"This must be humiliating for you," she clarified.

"Why would you think so?"

"Because you've had to teach me how to act around your friends."

"The members of the ton are not my friends, Scottish."

"Oh," she said lamely and was surprised when he pulled

her even closer, then closer still, until her breasts just grazed his chest with each swirling turn. His hand flattened against her back and inched downward until it rested scandalously low. His warm fingers tightened on hers, and his breath brushed her forehead.

She stared at the studs on his shirt, wanting to look up but unable to do so. The heady scent of him, the almost scorching heat of his hand, the sound of the music, and feel of his breath ruffling her hair filled her senses until there was nothing in the room but the two of them. She finally raised her gaze to his and saw a need that made her heart catch in her throat.

His silver hair looked like moonlight in the golden glow of the chandelier, the shadow of his beard showing just enough to make her remember the rough and erotic feel of it on her skin. His hand moved slightly, a mere inkling of a stroke across her waist. It was like dancing into a dream where the air was a living, breathing thing and the music a tune to make love by.

Her eyes drifted closed and in her mind she relived her intimate moments with Alec: his head bent as he took her breast into the depths of his mouth and his rough tongue over the tip of her; him above her, his skin damp and glistening from the thundering movements of his body inside hers; the feel of him filling her so full that she wasn't sure where her body ended and his began; that one magic moment in which nothing existed but the wonder of them together.

He pulled her closer and spun, then dipped, and her eyes shot open in surprise. He was looking at her mouth, intensely. She looked at his, remembering the feel of his lips and the taste of his tongue.

Kiss me, she thought, kiss me and end this yearning.

As if her wish had come true, he lowered his head slowly, watching her, daring her to break eye contact before his mouth met hers so softly, just a sweep of his lips, a tease. Her own lips parted in surprise, for she had expected passion of the same vibrant intensity that his eyes promised.

Silently he was asking her if she wanted more. She did, and her fingers tightened on the hard strength of his upper arm. A second later his lips, as hot as fire and moistened by a quick flick of his tongue, were on hers and he pulled her flush against him, never once breaking step, never once missing a beat.

If anything their spins were faster, their dips deeper, each anticipating the other's motion before it happened. The tempo of the music increased and the volume grew. With each turn, his tongue flickered over her lips, with each dip it sank into the depths of her mouth, filling her in a perfect imitation of the way his body filled hers. The mood of the music changed, the pitch descended. Then the melody changed, climbing higher and higher, swelling in volume and intensity until it reached a peaking crescendo.

It was the kiss of a lifetime, but it ceased a brief moment later.

The music had ended.

"Scottish," he whispered her name in an aching plea.

Joy opened her eyes.

And Alec lost consciousness.

"The measles! Impossible!" Alec arrogantly raised himself up in the bed. "I cannot have the measles."

Joy sat in an overstuffed chair near her husband's bed. She was terribly relieved, but her husband's sharp tone and scowling fevered face told her that he was not the least bit pleased with the physician's diagnosis.

"And take that bloody candle away from my eyes. You're going to blind me with that thing."

"Does the light bother Your Grace?"

Alec looked at the physician through bloodshot eyes that narrowed in suspicion. "Why?"

With a small shake of his head, the physician pulled the candle away and gestured to his patient's chest and belly. "The rash is the measles. Once it spreads, Your Grace's fever will drop." He set the candle down on the bedside table and picked up his case.

"I have never been ill a day in my life," Alec said to the

room in general, as if by making this announcement he could make the illness go away.

"If Your Grace had had measles as a child, Your Grace would not have them now," the physician said with infinite patience. "This is a rather severe case, I'd say, considering the high fever and the widespread rash." He closed his case with a snap. "Keep warm and stay in bed until the coughing ceases."

"I haven't been coughing." Alec's tone was so belligerent that Joy winced.

"You will. Your eyes will stop tearing, and your nose will stop running. Recovery will begin a day or so later." He turned to her and said, "In the meantime please keep him warm, Your Grace."

She stood. "I will, thank you. We'll take fine care of him." She ignored her husband's unaristocratic snort and walked with the physician into the sitting room. "Is there anything else I should know?"

"No. As I said before, it is imperative that he be kept warm." He gave her a look of pity. "I suspect he won't be a very cooperative patient."

"I'll make sure he stays warm." She gave him a warm smile, hoping to make up a bit for Alec's poor manners and thanked the man again as Henson escorted him out.

She reentered the bedchamber. Although she would have thought it impossible to look arrogant when one was ill, Alec managed it. He was enthroned among the monogrammed pillows, his chin up, his arms crossed in a manner that said, "I am a duke and therefore I am not ill." His expression, to say the least, was not pleased.

She sat on the edge of the bed. "I'm sorry you don't feel well."

He just glared at her.

She tried again. "I was very frightened, you know. One moment you were standing there and the next you had collapsed."

Silence.

"'Twas the fever, I suspect."

Brooding silence.

"You should get some rest."

"I am not tired."

She sighed and reached for the bellpull. "Should I have something sent up to you? Water? Soup? Are you hungry?"

He coughed, once, twice, then tried to suppress the next one.

"Alec, you do have the measles."

He blew his nose. "I know, dammit!"

"Are you warm enough?"

"No."

She shook open a blanket and added it to the pile already on the massive bed. "There. Is that better?"

He grunted a response she assumed was a yes.

She stood there a minute, then shook her head and gave up. "Well, since you don't need me—"

"Don't go."

She stopped and turned around, surprised.

"Read to me." He pointed to a book on the table.

She picked up the book and read the title, *The Gentlemen's Guide to Selecting and Breeding Prime Horseflesh.* "This?"

"Yes, the page is marked." He leaned back into the wealth of pillows and waited expectantly.

She opened to the marked page and began to read. Half an hour later, Joy had learned that horses can be cow-legged, bowlegged, or pigeon-toed, that a sloping croup means lack of power in the hindquarters and a straight croup means less power in jumping, and that horses suffered from such afflictions as ringbone, seedy toe, and bog spavin—which sounded like something a witch might use to cast a black spell.

"I've been thinking," Alec said, cutting off the latest tidbit of information. "I realize I have been rather rigid about your . . . your problem."

"My problem?"

"Yes."

Now he's going to bring up that incident at the Frost Fair again, she thought, deciding that if he did she would not hit him with the stack of blankets Roberts had supplied.

"I realize you cannot change what you are any more than I can change what I am."

She nodded and waited for the rest.

"I suppose if your magic can do some good, 'twould be acceptable, every so often, for you to use it."

She clamped her gaping mouth shut.

"Not in public, of course, but in private, behind closed doors, when only you and I are present." He looked at her expectantly. "Like now."

"I don't understand," she said.

"I am giving you permission to zap the measles away."

For a second she had to think to make sure she'd heard him right. Then she burst out laughing. "Oh, Alec!" She collapsed onto the chair in a fit of giggles. "You can be such a hypocritical prig sometimes."

"Me?"

She bit her smile back. "Yes, you."

He looked down his nose at her, then winced and scratched his chest. "I'm waiting," he said.

"I cannot."

"What do you mean you cannot?"

"A witch cannot just zap an illness away."

"Why the hell not?"

"'Tis not one of our powers."

"Bloody hell," he muttered, then sank back against the pillows.

Well, husband, she thought, you might never have been a child, but today you are acting like one. She forced herself to keep from laughing and asked, "Shall I continue reading?"

"Yes," he barked, then leaned his head back and closed his red-rimmed eyes.

Halfway into the next chapter he was sound asleep, and Joy was thumbing through the pages of the first interesting and enlightening chapter: "What to Look for in a Breeding Stallion."

Joy's face haunted the duke's fevered dreams.

Alec could almost feel her touch, the way her fingers combed his hair and tugged it when she became excited. Her finger grazed his ear, circling it with featherlike softness. He could feel her warm breath, feel her mouth nuzzle the back of his ear.

"Scottish," he groaned and turned toward her.

She wheezed.

He froze. His bloodshot eyes flew open.

Two beady brown weaselly eyes stared back at him.

"God Almighty . . . my hair!" He shot upright, grabbing his scalp, picturing in his mind the pink skin on the back of Henson's head. He bolted from the bed like a man crazed, not stopping until he reached the looking glass in his dark dressing room. He fumbled for a flint to light a lamp, his hands shaking from the heat of his fever. He struck the flint and lit the lamp, then leaned close to the mirror, turning his head this way and that.

Although it was tousled from a fevered sleep, his hair appeared to be all there. No bald spots. He picked up a hand mirror and turned, angling it upward so he could see the very back of his head. A second later he sagged in relief against the dresser.

Now more angry than ill, he turned and strode back into the bedchamber, plucked his wife's snoring rodent off his pillows, and crossed to the adjoining door. He opened it, crossed the sitting room, and went into Joy's bedchamber. The plump little weasel lay back in his arms and watched him through sly eyes that slowly moved from his face to his hairline. As if reading the duke's mind, the rodent licked its lips.

"Don't even think about it."

The animal wheezed; then its lips curled in what Alec supposed was a grin. Resisting the urge to drop it, he put the damn weasel in its basket and turned, but he stopped short of leaving.

The room was dim, the drapes drawn over the windows, but the bed draperies were open, hanging loose near the carved bedposts. A flicker of light from a guttering candle twinkled from the lamp at the bedside table and he moved closer. His wife lay sound asleep atop sheets that glowed almost golden in the candlelight. That long curtain of deep brown hair fell to one side and spilled down over the side of the bed. It drew him like silken threads of need that bound him to her, as it always did, as it had the first time he'd ever seen it.

It was odd that he noticed things about her that he could not remember noticing about other women. In his eyes, women were either beautiful or not beautiful. He had never noticed a woman's eyes or nose, the wistful tilt of her lips, a determined chin, the thickness of her brows, the delicate shape of a small ear. Yet he had with Scottish. And it hadn't stopped there. He'd noticed the motion she made with her hands, hands that he had held and rubbed and examined so closely when he had thought they were frostbitten. It leveled him somewhat to realize that he even knew the pattern of the lines on her palms, whereas he could only guess at the color of Juliet Spencer's eyes.

He closed his eyes and found himself longing for those old familiar times before Joy had entered his life. What had happened to the man he used to be? Little more than a few weeks ago everything had been simple, predictable, routine; there were no surprises in his life back then, and no complications. It had been so simple.

Looking back at his sleeping wife, he knew that nothing would ever be simple again, and he wasn't certain how he felt about that. He had to ask himself what he really wanted.

He wanted Scottish. Yes, he wanted her, wanted her with a need so strong that many times he had turned away just to prove to himself that he could fight it.

But the fact remained that he was drawn to her as if she had cast a spell that somehow linked them together. He didn't want to admit it. But he knew it. It was there to haunt him every time he felt a sexual need. It wasn't lust, but he wanted it to be, because lust he could control. This elusive thing that bound him to her was something he could not control, because it was not something he could name.

She breathed in the deep, soft pattern of one who was sound asleep. A book, tented across her chest, rose and fell with each whispering breath. He bent forward and picked it up, giving the cover a cursory glance: *The Dastardly Duke.*

He knew he should be angry with her, but he wasn't. He shook his head at his own inability to be what he thought he should be, what he had always been—a man who prided himself on his control.

He started to turn away, but stopped and looked down at the book in his hand. He bent over the bed and picked up a small silver bookmark that lay in the tangles of her hair. He marked the page and set the book on the bed table.

His still feverish head began to throb with the pain of an illness that had the audacity to strike the duke of Belmore. He blew out the lone candle and returned to his own room, where he could wish for a simpler time and regain the strength he needed to control his marriage and the strength he needed to fight his unreasonable need for a small Scottish witch.

The evening of the prince regent's ball arrived on a frozen wind. Spindly winter birch branches scraped and scratched like grasping fingers against the eastern wall of Belmore House and a liquid fire of golden light poured down from the windows, spilling over the tree trunks and onto the icy flagstones below.

But in her upstairs dressing room Joy saw only darkness.

Her head was trapped in a hoopskirt of waxed calico over stiff whalebone. "Polly!"

"Sorry, ma'am. One more tug and . . . There!"

The hoop slipped down over her bodice and finally clumped onto the wooden floor. Joy gasped for air while Polly tied the waist ribbons, then glanced down at the hoop. It was very narrow at the sides, presumably to allow one to walk two abreast, and full in the front and back. She picked up the skirt and looked down. "It drags on the floor."

"Here, you need the slippers, ma'am." Polly held out a lovely pair of golden slippers with small squat heels that, like the toes, were crusted with sparkling diamonds and deep emeralds. The maid slid them on Joy's feet, then stood back to judge the effect. "The heels are just the right height." Polly pointed at the cheval mirror.

"I don't want to look until I'm all dressed."

Polly grinned. "Your Grace has been sayin' the like at every fittin'."

"And *Her Grace* hasn't changed her mind, so will you stop Your Gracing me."

"I can't help it, ma'am, this night being so special and all. Look at what you'll be wearing. Someone who's wearin' that fancy court gown should be Your Graced."

"I am looking at what I'm wearing, and I don't see the sense in it." Frowning, Joy poked at the hoop, which bounced like a well-sprung curricle. "What's next?"

"The emerald green satin." Polly unhooked a long full skirt and held it up. "See this? Oh, ma'am, isn't it the loveliest thing you've ever seen?" The rich green color was set off by golden falcons with emerald eyes embroidered on the hem.

Polly came at her and once again Joy saw nothing but green darkness, and no sooner was that skirt in place than another deep green tulle overskirt with a golden lace furbelow at the hem slid over her head. Finally Polly tucked into place a short top skirt of gold-spangled tulle, arranging it so that the golden falcons in the Belmore crest showed in the tuck openings.

Joy looked down at the layers of clothing that formed the English court costume, plucked at them, and muttered, "No wonder they call Englishwomen 'skirts.'"

Polly picked up an emerald green plumed Carberry headdress with emerald-studded combs, paper-thin gold leaves, and golden tassels that dangled like Beezle down the back of Joy's head. She fit the combs into the elaborate piles of her mink brown hair, then lowered her arms.

Joy wobbled, grabbing the back of a chair. "I don't think I can stand up in this thing, let alone dance in it." She felt as if her chin were in her collarbone.

Polly stood back. "What if you held your chin higher, ma'am?"

Joy shoved her chin up with one hand. The muscles in the back of her neck strained. "I doubt even Mrs. Watley could hold her chin up with this on." Her neck felt like soggy bread. She tried to stiffen but managed only to contort her face into a grimace.

Polly giggled.

Joy took a wobbly step and hunched forward. "If I have to wear this thing I surely won't have to worry about anyone calling me Your Grace. No one is that blind." She could feel her disappointment on the rise. Forcing herself to try to stand erect, she took two steps, and had to grip the chair again. She tried three more times under Polly's nervous eyes and finally said, "Let me practice for a few minutes, please. Will you check on Beezle for me?"

"Yes, ma'am."

The moment the door closed, Joy sagged into a chair. The back of the hoop caught against the chair. She sat down, and up went the hoop. Green satin and tulle bounced into her face. She felt a cold draft on her thin silk stockings and shift. She shoved the yards of fabric aside and batted the hoop away, but it bounced back in her face. How did women sit in these things without having the hoop fly upward? She wondered how many ladies had given the world a private view. Again she tried to smash the hoop down but finally gave up. Her neck ached so, even when she was leaning back, that she rested her chin on a hand and stared at the sea of green.

This night was terribly important. She wanted to be the perfect duchess, but she doubted she could walk, let alone waltz. And she so wanted to waltz with Alec. Perhaps she could recapture that magical moment.

With this headpiece, waltzing would be impossible. She could, however, lighten the headpiece in her own way. She bit her lip. Just one wee incantation. One little bit of a spell. Of course if Alec found out he'd be very upset, but she was behind closed doors where it was very private, and those had been his conditions. Also, he had been willing to allow her to use her magic to cure him, and she would have if that had been possible.

But this wasn't impossible. There was also the fact that if she didn't do well tonight he'd be even more upset. When she rationalized it that way—the what-if, against the sure—she had her answer. She'd do what came naturally—witchcraft.

She stood, or wobbled, upright, then shimmied the hoop back down and sat again. She raised her arms in the air, but raising her chin was impossible. Her eyes locked on the carved mahogany legs of her bed. Her line of vision wouldn't reach any higher. Suppose her magic was weak from lack of use?

*Since when has your magic been strong?*

*Don't remind me.*

To her this was a dire circumstance, and perhaps her magic would be stronger because it hadn't been drained by overuse lately. She liked that rationale. Flexing her fingers for good measure, she closed her eyes tight and concentrated, really concentrated, on creating an incantation:

Oh, night so dark,
Oh, wind that blows,
Hark! Hark! Hark!
Help me with these furbelows.
Ignore my pelisse,
But hear my plea.
Make this headpiece
As light as can be!

Satisfied with her creation, she chanted the words aloud, then opened her eyes.

"Ahh." Joy sagged back against the chair in relief. She straightened a moment later and walked toward the cheval mirror, her headpiece now as light as air. "My powers are not so rusty after all," she muttered, tilting her head from side to side and watching the plumes bounce.

A few feet from the mirror she raised one hand shoulder-high, then held the other about where Alec's hand would hold hers, then she began to waltz, "One, two, three. One, two, three." Around she turned, swirling as if she were in her husband's arms, twirling and gliding and wishing she could look up into those midnight blue eyes and see his very heart.

Her skirt swirled with the hoop and felt wonderfully elegant—there might be something to this garment after all, if one wasn't sitting down—and she laughed, gliding over to the mirror, where she stopped with a gasp.

"Oh, my goodness." She stared, awestruck by the woman who stared back at her. "I look like a duchess. A real duchess."

"Yes, you do," came Alec's deep voice.

Joy's heart skipped a beat. She turned to face her husband. He stood in the connecting doorway, looking like the title he so proudly bore. He was dressed in a tailcoat and knee breeches of a dark green velvet that almost looked black, and the points of a gold-embroidered waistcoat extended downward exactly two inches, as superb taste demanded. Shimmering in the perfect folds of his stark white cravat was an emerald and gold stickpin.

Her gaze returned to his face. "How long have you been there?"

"Only since your oh-my-goodness."

Thank heaven.

"Why?" He closed the distance.

She stared at the wee sparkling stones on the toes of her slippers and tried to look as if she hadn't cast a spell in years.

He lifted her chin with a knuckle. "There's no need for modesty, Scottish. I've seen you in much less."

Not recently, she thought, his illness having kept them apart. In fact this was the first she'd seen him since he'd recovered. She knew he'd been avoiding her. But now he stood barely a foot away. He still held her chin atop a strong knuckle. She searched his face, looking for a sign of his thoughts. He stared at her mouth again and she almost sighed, but held her breath instead. She could feel his gaze as surely as if it could stroke her flushed cheeks. Uncomfortable, she stepped back, holding out her skirts. His look started at the headpiece and moved downward, so slowly it seemed she stood still for eternal minutes during his perusal.

She held her breath. For the first time in her life she did

feel beautiful—fairy-tale beautiful. Remember, she told herself, he thinks you are beautiful. And the excitement of the night, of her first ball, of the promise in his look, made her blood race through her veins. It made her feel alive and giddy and . . . well, just magical, as if they should walk with a trail of stars in their wake. She smiled. "So you approve, then?"

"No."

Her smile died. She closed her eyes against the sharp jab of disappointment that pierced her chest.

"You need these."

She willed her eyes open. Though the view was misty she saw that he held out a velvet box embossed with the Belmore crest. The mist cleared, and she cocked her head and studied the box. It was green with gold embossing. He snapped open the lid, revealing emeralds so deep and pure and clear a green that they appeared to have been conjured up by the perfect spell. "The Belmore emeralds," he said.

She took a step toward them, unable to believe they were real and fascinated by the way they were designed. Every gold setting formed the outline of the ducal crest, and each clasp was an intricate figure of a falcon—the Belmore crest. There were earbobs composed of three square-cut emeralds set in the intricate gold crest pattern, a brooch shaped like the crest, three bracelets, a necklace, and a set of combs.

"Everyone will surely know I'm the duchess of Belmore."

"Of course. The Belmore emeralds were designed for the fifth duchess and were thought to rival some of the crown jewels. I believe Henry the Eighth tried to purchase them from the tenth duke. But the settings are unmistakable and the stones are as much a part of Belmore as the crest."

Still no sense of humor, she thought, but enough pride for all the English. She laughed inside, but her smile was small and bittersweet.

"Turn around and face the mirror."

She turned and watched him in the mirror. He placed the heavy necklace around her neck and clasped it. The gold was cold and hard against her skin. He handed her the earbobs and she put them on and stared in wonder at the woman who looked back at her. She put a hand to her lips and did something a duchess would never do. She giggled.

"Scottish."

Summoning up some proper seriousness, she composed herself, trying to look suitably arrogant, then met his eyes in the mirror.

"Turn back around."

She did, expecting him to put the bracelets on over her gloves.

A second later she was in his arms, his lips parting hers and his tongue burrowing into her mouth with that dark, desperate passion he hid so well from the rest of the world. He tried so hard to control that passion . . . and she delighted in making him lose his control of it.

"Oh!" Polly's voice sounded from somewhere far away.

Alec gave a small groan and broke off the kiss. Joy wanted to groan herself. Their gazes locked and the moment swelled between them. He started to reach for her but stopped himself, then shifted his gaze to the doorway where Polly still stood. Joy turned.

"Beg pardon, Your Grace." Polly curtsied and backed out of the room.

"Wait!" Alec held up a hand, then picked up the jewel case and held it out to the maid. "Here. See to your mistress." He crossed the room in long strides and paused at the door. "The coach will be waiting. I'll be downstairs." He left without a backward glance.

# Chapter 22

"The duke and duchess of Belmore!"

The royal servant's imperious voice echoed in the formal hall like a battle cry in the Highlands. On the arm of her husband, Joy followed a footman up one side of the double staircase of Carlton House. The distant hum of voices and music drifted down from above, but she barely noticed, for her eyes were too busy taking in the room, which was all crystal and golden light. Candles glimmered in a majestic dance of flames on the massive chandeliers that hung from the heaven-high ceiling. Walls of mirrors flanked the stairs and captured the light, reflecting it like white moonlight on the glassy midnight sea. She saw gold—everything was gilded or sparkling. It was as if they'd entered the palace of Midas.

Their own reflections shone in the mirrors. She couldn't tear her gaze away. That was her looking back from that mirror, covered in satin and jewels and sparkling from her toes to the top of her head. But best of all she was on the arm of Alec, her Alec.

Her hand rested atop his forearm, and she could feel his muscles tense. She glanced up at him, noticing the taut jaw, the wee spark of tension in his dark eyes, and with Scots determination she whispered, "I'll try to make you proud."

He seemed stunned by her comment, and something that looked like guilt flickered across his face, but her husband had nothing to feel guilty about, unless it was his marriage to her. Her throat tightened in reaction, but she refused to give in. She cast him a glance and saw that nothing in his stance suggested that he felt guilty or ashamed. He looked as proud as ever.

She summoned a small shred of confidence from somewhere under all that satin and tulle and thin skin, and a second later they ascended the last two marble stairs that led to an enormous room filled with a sea of elegant and suddenly curious faces.

Tonight she wasn't Joyous Fiona MacQuarrie, the Scottish witch. Tonight she was the duchess of Belmore, on the arm of her proud duke.

She felt Alec's warm hand cover hers. "You look beautiful, Scottish."

It was as if he knew the exact words she needed to hear. A slow smile spread like warm honey across her face, and her confidence became real. "I remember. You told me."

"When?"

She stopped cold and cursed her loose tongue. "Uh, just now."

He frowned at her, then shook his head and guided her down the hallway.

She stuck her duchess chin up another inch or so and squared her small shoulders, her skirts gliding around her, waving and floating with each step she took. Her mental clock ticked, making her nervous and excited and feeling as if it would take years—aeons maybe—for them to enter the ballroom. She peered upward, above the heads of the crowd, catching the glittering light that spread from the open ballroom doors at the end of the wide corridor. Music grew louder, truer, and sweet, and it was only the thought that a duchess probably didn't sway her head to the music that kept her from her natural inclination to do so.

The crowd thickened as they approached, closing in and making her even more aware of how many people would be there to see her if she failed Alec. For the briefest of moments she understood his apprehension. There were hundreds of people here.

"What are you doing?" Alec looked down at her.

"Counting."

"What?"

"Forty-seven . . . jewels on the rug. See them sparkling? Forty-eight . . ."

"They fell off the women's shoes and clothing. Happens at every ball, but especially a royal ball. The servants who clean up reap the rewards." He held her elbow and steered her through a tight group. He leaned down. "Any particular reason why you felt it necessary to count them?"

"Because then I don't have to look at all those staring eyes." Her whisper reeked of apprehension.

"You had best become used to it. You're the duchess of Belmore. As such, you shall attract attention."

"Fifty-four . . . When do I meet the prince?"

"We'll be summoned in a while. This isn't a formal presentation." He looked down at her. "Scottish."

"Sixty . . . Aye?"

"No hocus-pocus."

She cast a look of dismay at the carpet. "I lost count."

His fingers tightened on her arm. "No changing the subject. No levitating. No dancing statues. No spinning clocks. And above all, no spitting of toads. No magic. Those eyes that make you so uneasy will be very alert, looking for anything to find fault with, anything about which they can create a scandal. Every eye in the place will at some time tonight be on you. Promise me—no magic."

"Tonight I am the duchess of Belmore, your wife. Nothing more," she said firmly. A small part of her was getting tired of being reminded not to use witchcraft.

"Fine. I'll be nearby."

She watched him a second, not sure if that statement was for comfort or a warning. They continued walking down the hallway toward the ballroom where a staring crowd stood in the doorway, many of the women whispering behind fans. She looked away, glancing into each room she passed for a glimpse of what was inside, seeking comfort from the furnishings because they didn't have curious eyes.

Time then seemed to change speeds, and she saw the glimmer of ballroom light. She had time for only one quick breath before they stepped through wide doors into the ballroom.

In her most fanciful imaginings she would have never thought to see such a sight. Feathery plumes of every imaginable color—crimson, fuchsia, royal blue, canary yellow—bobbed above the waves of society people and aristocrats whose headpieces were so tall and so bejeweled that she wondered at the strength of the Englishwoman's neck. From the tops of their heads to the jewels on their toes the women of the ton were a most impressive sight of ornamental humanity. They sparkled, they glowed, they glittered as if it had snowed diamonds.

"The duke and duchess of Belmore!"

Her heart stopped. A second later they stepped into the swelling crowd and an ocean of eager and speculative eyes turned toward them.

"Take a deep breath or you'll faint." Alec slid his arm out of her grip and casually wrapped it around her waist, holding her under the pretext of guiding her through the crowded room.

She gulped a mouthful of air and let him prod her ahead, walking through the throng unseeing.

"I say!"

At the sound of the viscount's familiar voice, she focused on the first friendly face she'd seen. She did breathe then—a deep, relieved breath. The earl was with him. The other men parted to make room for them, and the earl took her hand. "Your Grace." He made his bow, then looked at Alec. "Loveliest woman in the room, Belmore."

"I daresay. Downe's right," the viscount added with his own bow.

From some distance away came the grating screech of another acquaintance, Lady Agnes Voorhees. "Oh! Look who's just arrived, Eugenia! Claire!"

Joy could have sworn she heard Alec grinding his teeth.

"Henry!" Lady Agnes rammed her elbow into her husband's ribs. "Yoo-hoo! Yoo-hoo! Come along, Henry! Don't dawdle or you'll make me miss them again!"

"Bloody hell," Alec muttered, his eyes on the woman who

was blazing a trail toward them in spite of the crowd. "That woman's enough to make me faint."

"I believe certain . . . childhood ailments . . . have the same effect, Belmore," the earl said quietly, wearing that goading smirk.

Alec glared at him.

"Or possibly," the earl continued, making a mocking bow, "a fair damsel's sweet kiss." All the while he stared at Joy's mouth. She wanted to zap a pair of blinders on the man.

"Downe's right. I forgot all about that. One minute you were grinding your lips on your wife—beg pardon, Joy, but we were there—and the next, *whop!* right on the floor." Neil stopped, an idea widening his features. "D'you suppose that's what all this brouhaha is about the waltz? I must say, looked fairly risqué to me. Had me pretty uncomfortable until you scared the bloody wits out of us by hitting the floor. Tell me, Belmore, is the rash gone?"

"Judging by our friend's cold glare, Seymour, I'd say you're moving into a sensitive subject."

"You brought it up, Downe. I was just inquiring about a friend's health, him having been sick and all."

"Come along, Henry! Why, Lord Seymour, did you say someone has been ill? Who's been ill?" Lady Agnes asked, almost breathless from her rush to get to them. She all but jerked her husband to her side. As if conjured up by a conniving fate, Lady Eugenia and Claire Timmons popped up like lackeys to their Lady Agnes, both women intently awaiting a response.

Grinning, the earl leaned over to Alec and whispered, "What'll you offer me to keep quiet?"

"My word that I won't beat your bloody brains out," Alec shot back in a low but lethal voice.

"Don't tell me your poor bride has been ill." Lady Agnes slapped a hand over her bejeweled chest. "That explains why we haven't seen you about town. Now what ails you, my dear?"

"Her Grace," Alec reminded her with a cold stare.

"Oh. Why, yes, do forgive me, Your Grace. I forgot."

In a voice as chilly as the winter air Alec said, "Don't forget again."

The silence in the immediate area became a physical thing, tense and heavy. The twin gossips' eyes grew wide, and they cowered under the ducal glare. Joy thought them more prudent than Lady Agnes who, having lost only half her wind, launched onward, "Well, I cannot tell you how truly honored I was to be the one to spread the good word of your *sudden* marriage. 'Twas the talk of the ton for days." And she blithered onward.

Joy felt Alec's forearm tense. Hoping to ease the tension she leaned toward him and quietly whispered, "Shall I give her a wart?"

The look he gave her showed his panic.

"That was a jest," she whispered quickly. He seemed to relax, and she couldn't resist adding, "Perhaps just a wee one on her nose."

"I do not find that amusing," he said out of the corner of his tight mouth.

"I do." She knew he was watching her, so she turned her gaze to the woman's nose and gave it what she hoped was a speculative eyeing.

"Don't even think about it," Alec gritted in her ear.

Meanwhile Lady Agnes had gone into a new dissertation on who was present and with whom and who was absent and why. "Even Lady Juliet is here tonight," she added with a sly look Joy didn't understand. The gossips tittered, but that was the only sound within five feet.

From her husband's cold look, Joy was sure that at that moment, if he were a warlock, Lady Agnes would have the warted face of a toad. Completely nonplussed by the icy look, she turned to Joy and smiled sweetly. "Have you met Lady Juliet, Your Grace?"

"I haven't had the pleasure. Who—" she began, then almost yelped when Alec gripped her arm.

"I meant to tell you, Belmore," Neil deftly cut in. "Addersley's been looking for you. Something about that horse you've been wanting."

Before anyone could respond, the earl of Downe stepped

in front of Joy and said, "Her Grace promised me a dance, Belmore."

Joy glanced at Alec, confused at the quick change of subject and apprehensive about her first dance in public. She would rather have danced with her husband, but she could feel a hundred pairs of eyes watching her, assessing her, expecting something from her. She could feel her skin crawl.

"You go on," Alec said, placing her hand in Richard's. "I need to see Addersley." Then he gave her a warning glance that said, "No magic." Apparently satisfied at her nod, he turned and left, looking back only once, probably to make certain that no one was levitating.

The earl moved onto the dance floor after gallantly reminding her what dance the tune suggested, and a moment later she was caught up in her first real country dance. Again she saw a different earl of Downe, the man of whom Alec had spoken. He executed an allemande and said, "I'm not sure I like the look on your face. What flaw am I exposing this time?"

"No flaw. I was just thinking that I like you better when you have no drink in your hand," she answered bluntly.

"How odd," he countered in a manner too offhand. "I like myself better when I have."

"Why?"

He looked down at her, his expression a battleground. "False courage. Then I really don't give a damn."

She tried to think of some response, but the music stopped. When she looked at him, her thoughts must have shone in her face because he said, "Don't pity me, Joy. I like what I've become. It's easier." Then with that fake sardonic smile he led her through the crowd to a quiet corner where Neil stood waiting. They argued for a few minutes over what she should have to drink and who would fetch it. The earl won, but before he left, the viscount grabbed his arm and said, "Only lemonade. Nothing else, Downe."

The earl grinned and patted his empty coat pocket. With a wink at Joy he headed toward the refreshments.

"Alec should be back in a few minutes," Neil commented.

then snapped open a jeweled box, pinched some powder, sniffed it up his nose, then sneezed into a lace-edged handkerchief.

Frowning at the dusty contents of small jeweled box, she asked, "What is that powder?"

"Snuff."

"What's it for?"

"Never seen it? It's tobacco powder. Makes you sneeze. Clears the head and all that rot. And this is m'lucky snuff case. See here?" He held the case up to her just as a garden door opened and a breeze ruffled through the room, sending the fine brown powder right into her face.

She slammed a hand over her nose and mouth, trying desperately not to sneeze, knowing what might result if she did sneeze.

He snapped the case closed. "Sorry about that. Ought to sneeze and get it out. You'll feel better." He must have seen the fear in her eyes, because he patted her hand. "No need to worry about decorum. Everyone does it. Quite the thing, you know. Go ahead. Sneeze."

She shook her head and pinched her itchy nose closed. *Don't think. Don't think!*

"I say, Joy, ought to just sneeze it out."

"I hate to sneeze," she told him, her voice muffled behind her hand, her eyes tearing. She glanced up to see the earl.

"Some lemonade." He held a glass out to her and waited, and waited. She was afraid to take it.

"What's the matter?" he finally asked.

"Got some of my snuff." Neil held up his snuff box.

"No wonder she's crying, Seymour. The stuff is vile. Here." He held out the glass again. "Drink up. The lemonade should take the sting away."

Joy locked her eyes on the glass, held her breath, and reached for it, then promptly sneezed. She peeled her eyes open slowly, trying to remember what her last thought was. The two men stared at her like doting brothers, nothing unusual in their faces. She scanned the immediate area. The dance floor was filled with happy guests. The music played clear and sweet, and the crowd appeared unchanged. She looked up and saw nothing unusual. The chandeliers still shimmered gaily, nothing out of the ordinary. No roses, no riding crops, no tambourines. She breathed a relieved sigh and sipped the drink.

"I say. Look there."

Joy and the earl followed Neil's gaze.

"Where d'you suppose Prinny found lemon trees in February?" Neil asked.

"Hothouses," she answered quickly, staring at the long line of potted lemon trees.

Neil went on, "Not a smart place to line those pots up. Blocks the terrace doors, you know. I say. Look there, behind those trees. Ain't that Belmore and Addersley?"

She turned just as Alec walked inside from the terrace with another man. They parted and Alec turned, looking right at the trees. He turned back to the terrace doors, then back to the room as if to get his bearings. He frowned thoughtfully and then, very slowly, with lethal precision, his gaze moved from the trees directly to her. She tried to look innocent and must have failed, because he was obviously livid. He shoved two pots aside and stepped through them, never taking his eyes off her.

That look would have panicked even the most confident soul, which she was not at the moment. Quickly she glanced at Neil and twiddled her fingers. He turned, his face a tad dazed. "I feel the sudden need to dance with Her Grace." He extended his arm and away they went, into the intricate figures of a country dance and out of Alec's reach.

The steps took most of her concentration, but every so often she looked up and saw Alec standing at the edge of the crowd only a few feet away. Then her partner would lead her away to the swift beat of the music. The dance ended, but luck was shining down on her this night, because she was safely at one end of the ballroom while her glaring husband stood at the other. Before he could get to her, she was off again, this time to the tune of a lively schottische. Neil had mentioned that he thought the dance might be too fast for her, but she assured him at this moment she was in need of a fast dance.

For the next twenty minutes the duke and duchess of Belmore played cat and mouse. Whenever he wended his way near her, her eyes widened and she twirled away. His face revealed his frustration and a promise of retribution. She pretended not to see it and smiled at her partner whenever they moved past Alec.

Two dances later she lost sight of him, but since he had last been immersed in conversation with a small group of men, she decided he must have given up for now. She was certain he would lecture her about her behavior later, but for now she felt safe. The last dance ended, her partner made his bow, and she turned—and stared into the intricate folds of a white cravat adorned with an emerald and gold stickpin in the shape of the Belmore crest.

"Oh, dear," she mumbled just as his hands tightened on her upper arms. A second later he pulled her away to a spot where they could speak privately.

"Get rid of them," he hissed.

"But surely everyone's seen them by now."

He glanced over to where a group of guests were fingering the bright yellow fruit on the potted trees. He turned on her with a look of fury. His jaw was clenched tight, and his next words were almost ground out. "What the devil did you think you were doing? Lemon trees in February?"

"It was an accident, truly. And there are hothouses."

"Dammit, wife—"

She placed her hand on his arm and explained, "The snuff made me sneeze. Please don't be angry."

A dawning light hit his eyes. "Seymour?"

She nodded, feeling a little sheepish. "It just blew right into my face. I'm sorry."

His anger drained away and, frowning, he rubbed two fingers over the bridge of his nose. "Bloody hell. I forgot about his penchant for snuff." He looked at her, then he said, "Do me a favor, Scottish."

Surprisingly she stared into eyes that held no anger and a tinge of forgiveness, and nodded.

"Keep clear of anyone with a snuff box." He turned then,

his gaze scanning the room. A footman in royal livery chose that exact moment to approach them.

"His Royal Highness is waiting," the man told Alec, who nodded and indicated they should follow.

Utter fear swept through her. She took two steps, then came to a halt.

"What is it?" Alec asked.

"I'm frightened."

"You'll do fine," he said with an assurance she was far from feeling. "He's only another Englishman. Try to think of it that way. Like me, he's just English."

"My knees feel Scottish," she muttered. That drew an odd look from him. If she hadn't known better, she would have believed he was actually amused.

"Just curtsy. You'll be on my arm, before and after. And don't look at him or rise until he speaks."

She stared unseeing at the back of the footman. "I'll remember."

"And don't forget to breathe."

She nodded and took a deep breath.

"You're the duchess of Belmore." His warm hand slid over hers as he led her from the large ballroom into a narrow hallway. "And you look lovely, Scottish."

She smiled then, his approval doing rejuvenating things to her confidence, and as they stopped outside a set of double doors she turned her face toward his, but there was no time for words. The doors opened.

"The duke and duchess of Belmore!"

The heat from the room hit her like a blast from a bonfire. Instantly perspiration beaded all over her skin. Inside the stifling room was a group of people in full court dress. All eyes were riveted on her.

Alec's hand still covered hers and he squeezed it, then whispered, "Breathe." She did and a second later they stopped. The next thing she knew he released her hand and introduced her, and then she was in a full curtsy—head bowed, shoulders straight, her hands gripping her skirts, and her Scottish knees shimmying like aspen leaves. The silence went on. If the man didn't speak soon she was going to shame her husband by falling face down on the floor. She remembered Alec's comment and took a deep breath, knowing it was probably the last movement her wee body could make.

"Ah, my lady duchess."

Joy almost crumbled to the floor with relief. Slowly straightening, she gave him a smile, but it faltered when her knees cracked like Christmas walnuts. Even Alec heard them. She caught his wince out of the corner of her eye.

"Lovely, Belmore. We are impressed. You always did have a good eye." The prince regent studied her, rather rudely and quite thoroughly. Joy just stood there, her smile plastered to her lips, her heart pounding and her knees aching, amazed that this man was the future monarch of England. He had a large midriff, although there were no rolls of flesh bulging from his buttoned coat. He looked puffed up.

His hair was a golden red and swept upward from his wide forehead in a comblike wave. That hair, combined with his thin bandy legs, gave him the distinct look of a plump rooster. He even had a few red chins that rested wattlelike against a pinch-folded cravat.

She sneezed.

The prince regent opened his mouth. And crowed. Heads turned and stared at him, but he apparently didn't notice and kept on talking to her as if nothing unusual had happened.

Unfortunately, Alec had noticed. He did, however, keep his composure, continuing to speak quietly and briefly, his hands gripping her close. She had a feeling he had some ruthless way to stop her should she chance to sneeze again. Calmly he carried most of the conversation until the prince requested they dine at his personal table, and her husband became suddenly quiet.

"We desire to better know your lady duchess, Belmore." And with that pronouncement they were dismissed and the prince regent turned and moved across the room, an odd creaking sound following in his wake.

"What's that sound?" she whispered.

"His corset." Once they were well out of whispering distance he asked, "What the devil were you thinking when you sneezed?"

She didn't want to tell him, but his hand tightened on hers as he led her from the room. "I thought he looked like a rooster."

Once they were back in the hallway he wordlessly handed her a handkerchief. "Blow until all the snuff's gone."

She did as he asked, allowing him to use his body to hide her actions from the rest of the room. She looked up at him.

"Finished?" he asked.

"Yes."

"You're certain?"

She nodded. "No one appeared to notice when he crowed."

"The prince can sometimes be as eccentric as his mad father. I suppose we should be thankful people tend not to question royal behavior."

She nodded, chewing her lip, then looked up at him from wary eyes. "Are you angry?"

He stared down at her for a moment, then shook his head. "No. I have to admit, Scottish, he does look like a rooster." Then he actually laughed. For the first time since the inn, he laughed.

She released her held breath, and a smile of blinding happiness came unbidden to her lips. He watched her for a long time until he began to look uncomfortable, so she looked away. The moment was lost. Without another comment he guided her back into the ballroom, where they stood on the rim of the crowd.

"I do, however, believe this is going to be a long night." His face stayed taut, but he loosened his hold.

Before she could ponder what he meant, the haunting strains of a waltz rippled through the ballroom, causing gasps of outrage and titters of eager laughter. The dance floor emptied, and remained so. No one dared to move into the dance.

She watched the crowd close tighter and saw secrets being whispered behind a bevy of fans as the guests hesitated. "What are they waiting for?"

"Looks as if no one wants to be the first to begin waltzing. The dance is still considered improper in many circles."

"Are they just going to stand there?"

"Until someone throws caution to the wind, I'd say yes, the floor will remain empty."

"I suppose everyone knows that the duke and duchess of Belmore wouldn't dare be the first couple to waltz."

"Is that a challenge, Scottish?"

Her shrug said he could take it any way he wanted.

The earl suddenly appeared at his right. "May I have the honor, Your Grace?"

Alec's hand tightened on hers. "I'll dance with my wife, Downe. Find someone else." With a knowing smile the earl moved on, choosing a partner and spinning her onto the dance floor, looking as if he cared not a fig for what anyone in the room thought.

Alec watched the couple intently, speculation in his dark blue eyes, and with a fleeting wistfulness, she wondered if perhaps he might have, given a minute longer, whisked her out onto the dance floor, public opinion be damned. But now it mattered not, because others had joined the first dancing couple. Finally Alec grasped her waist and with no words, only a nod of his head, he spun her onto the dance floor.

The sweet music swelled just as before. As if the fates needed to prove life's recurring ironies, the orchestra played the same Viennese waltz the earl had played that night at Belmore House. And as before, she and Alec moved as one, sweeping across the room with movements so fluid and light that she barely felt the floor beneath her. Candlelight rained in glittering light-drops downward from the dome of the ballroom, thousands of wee flickers that bathed the dancers and the other guests in the starry luster of the moment. Her gaze was drawn upward, driven by the overwhelming compulsion to see if the glimmer was as startlingly brilliant as it felt.

If only her curious eyes had gotten that far. Once they met her husband's they were held prisoner. The impact of his look fanned memories that flashed like wind-ruffled book pages through her mind, memories of the last time they had danced just so, and the passion, the kiss. The same thoughts must have flooded his mind too, for the moment suddenly existed again as naturally as if they lived it every day, every minute.

How odd that the world could melt away so easily, with a look, the touch of a hand, the sweet kiss of a lover's breath upon one's cheek. Bewitching. The rich sound of music wafted through and around them like colorful garlands on a Maypole. And the tension grew with the notes, that incredible magical presence that seemed to burn like a flame fanned between them with the engulfing and overpowering strength of something more than mere magic, something that no one else in the world could ever know, live, or cherish. And she knew with certainty she would never experience this passionate force with another. This was theirs alone. This wonderful bewitching.

He pressed his hand against her back, and she moved inch by small inch closer. Each time they turned, each step they took, brought them together. Her skirts brushed his legs, swished and swirled and floated between them like mist. Their steps were flawless, their gazes locked, the motions little more than elegant foreplay. The emeralds on her gloved wrist caught the brilliant light, but their sparkle was dim compared to his look, open and needful for one brief instant in time.

They were so close that their bodies grazed each other scandalously, and his fingers tightened on her waist and hand. He feels it as strongly as I, she realized. But he fought the magnetic pull, fought it as the sea fought the moon tide.

*Kiss me. . . .* Her mind called out to him over and over, just as it had before. His gaze drifted to her mouth, reveled in it, but he wouldn't move closer, wouldn't close the space between them and say, "The world and propriety be damned."

Then the music ceased and they stopped, suddenly aware

that they were observed by a thousand curious eyes. Alec immediately stiffened, but before they could move, let alone speak, supper was announced to the chiming of a group of royal glass bells, and they were swept up with the noisy crowd, a heavy silence between them because neither one was in control, and they both knew it.

With a sense of impending doom, Alec watched the steward refill his wife's wineglass. She sat talking to the prince, waving her animated hands to emphasize her words —on which Prinny appeared to be hanging. The prince had insisted they attend the theater with his party tomorrow night. Alec mentally groaned at the thought. He had hoped to leave for Belmore Park first thing in the morning so he could sequester Joy safely in the country.

Her joyful laugh caught his attention, and he turned back, watching. She was a success. He should be proud. Uneasy, but proud. And pleased that they had pulled this off. So why did he feel as if the world around him danced to a different tune? He felt out of place and alone. The feeling of isolation was not comforting. It annoyed him. He had always sought solitude, preferred it to the noisy life of the English aristocracy, but now he found it unsettling. Why did he wish for something else? He sipped his own wine and asked himself what it was he sought.

As if in answer he felt the need to look at his wife. At that exact moment her eyes met his and he stopped breathing, caught off guard by the innocent hunger in those eyes, and knowing that his own mirrored a hunger that held no innocence, but instead a passionate intensity, a need to get inside this woman so deeply that the urge to couple was lost in an all-encompassing urge to touch some rare fire in her. Only her. It was intoxicating, drugging, this overpowering thing that burned so bright inside him he actually doubted his ability to live with it and remain sane.

At the thought he laughed to himself. His actions on the dance floor, the struggle to control himself in front of the entire ton—that was proof that he was no longer sane, hadn't had a rational thought since he married her. He wondered if a part of this insanity resulted from his dealings with all women lately.

His gaze scanned the room. Juliet was here; he had caught a glimpse of her blond head earlier. Odd that he'd felt little anger when he spotted her. For reputation's sake he would have to speak to her publicly, to squelch the rumors about their sudden marriages. Not that he was doing it for her sake. He couldn't have cared less about Lady Juliet Spencer, but he knew it would make things easier on Scottish if there was no speculation about their impromptu marriage.

He justified that bit of sensitivity by reminding himself that his own reputation was at stake too.

And so it was an hour later, while his wife danced on the arm of one of his cronies, that Alec found himself threading his way past the bloody lemon trees and onto the terrace, to which Lady Juliet had just escaped. He stood outside silently, watching her as she looked out over the icy gardens below, leaning against a stone balustrade and fanning herself in spite of the fact that it was freezing outside.

She turned as surely as if he had spoken. "Alec."

He gave her a curt nod. "Juliet."

The look she gave him was sad, which surprised him. "Why the sadness? Odd, for a bride. I expected to see love glowing from your lovely face, my dear." The scorn came naturally to his voice.

She looked down. "I suppose I deserve a worse cut than that for the way I handled things. I don't blame you for hating me, Alec. But I did what I thought best for both of us."

"I don't hate you."

She laughed rather cynically. "No, I suppose in order for you to hate me, you would have to have loved me. And you didn't."

"No, I didn't."

"Thank you for not lying about that."

"I never lied to you, Juliet. I thought we understood each other. I was wrong."

"He loves me," she whispered.

"I would have never guessed a romantic soul lay beneath your cool beauty." He shrugged and joined her at the balustrade.

They stood there in a kind of awkward kinship. He glanced at her, noticing for the first time that her eyes were blue. Just blue. No mischievous twinkling of green. Nothing more than ordinary blue. He leaned over the railing, resting his elbows atop it, and he watched the icicles drip. A moment later he set his pride aside and looked up at her. "Perhaps it was for the best."

She searched his face. "You married," she said, sounding as if she felt betrayed.

"Yes."

Her smile was sad and a little wistful. "I saw her."

When he didn't respond, she went on, "I saw both of you waltzing."

"Yes, I suppose everyone saw us."

"She loves you."

He turned back to her, leaning against the balustrade in a pose of indifference he was far from feeling. "It doesn't matter."

"I think it does."

Something tightened inside him as if she had just seen him naked. He watched her silently, not knowing quite how to respond.

"You see, I know what it's like to love someone."

"Ah, the exciting captain."

She smiled and shook her head. "No, Alec. You see, I said he loves me, not that I love him. I loved you, but you could never love me back, and I couldn't bear to spend my life with only half a heart. All those things I said were just a way to lash out at you." She laughed. It was sincere laughter with no malice, but it held a hint of sadness and self-derision. "Although it's true that you can be pompous," she told him with a genuine smile, "I honestly think I was angry that you couldn't love me."

He stood straight at her words. After taking a moment to

absorb what she'd said he commented, "How is your marriage to the captain any different? If only one partner loves, isn't it still a marriage of . . . What did you call it? Ah, yes, half a heart?"

"Yes."

Her face confirmed the truth of her confession, but it was strange that he felt nothing for her—no anger, no humiliation, no pity, really nothing but a certain camaraderie that came from learning to know each other on a different plane. "Then I suppose we're both settled into marriages with half a heart."

She smiled then, a smile of friendship. "No, Alec, I don't think so. You see, I saw you with your wife." She placed her arm through his. "Come along. Escort me inside. Let's give those loose tongues something to wag about." They moved toward the door and just before they stepped inside, she paused and looked up at him. "You are hardheaded, pompous, arrogant, and handsome as the devil, Alec, but your marriage is whole."

He looked at her in stunned silence.

She stepped through the doorway and delivered her parting shot, "I just wonder how long it will take you to realize it."

It took Joy only a few minutes to realize that Alec was nowhere in the room. She searched the dance floor, and threaded her way through the crowd until she stood outside the main throng. She saw the dancers gliding across the floor, watched the jewels sparkle, and found herself swaying to the wonderful music. The ball was better than she had dreamed. She had met the prince, dined with him, and except for those wee sneezes, everything had gone smoothly. She so hoped that Alec was proud of her. A feeling of success ran through her when she remembered that the prince had even asked them to the theater.

Yes, everything was wonderful, but somehow it wasn't as thrilling, as exciting, when Alec wasn't there at her side. She wanted to dance with him, one more time before they left.

She wanted to feel him holding her and twirling her, his eyes assuring her that they would finish at home what they had started on the dance floor.

The thought made her smile and she scanned the room again.

"Why, my dear!" Lady Agnes's voice came scraping out of nowhere.

Joy turned. Apparently the woman still hadn't accepted her title, and for the second time in the last few minutes she wished Alec were here. Lady Eugenia and Mrs. Timmons stood like extensions behind her.

"You look lost, standing here all alone. Where is that handsome duke of yours?" Her gaze roved over the room. "Do you see him, girls?" The gossips shook their heads in unison. She turned back to Joy and patted her arm. "You know, my dear, I thought I saw him step out on the terrace. Let's go see, shall we?" She tucked her arm in Joy's and guided her toward the wall of doors.

The crowd shifted and a group of men stepped between them only to part soon after and give Joy an unobstructed view of the terrace doors. A lovely blond woman dressed like a frost princess stepped inside, her taunting laughter ringing down to where they stood.

"Oh, there he is, my dear. See there?" Lady Agnes nodded toward the terrace. "He's with Lady Juliet. How interesting."

She could feel Lady Agnes's penetrating stare as Alec followed in the woman's wake. A smile came to Joy's lips when her gaze lit on him. She glanced at the woman with him and commented, "Lady Juliet is lovely." She turned to Lady Agnes. "Is she someone special?"

The gossips' eyes grew round and twinkled in anticipation. Then they tittered. Lady Agnes raised a hand to her chest dramatically. "Why, didn't you know, my dear?" Her voice suddenly filled with exaggerated sweetness. "She and His Grace were to be married."

Joy whipped her head back around, suddenly aware of Alec and Lady Juliet as a couple. They were a perfect match, her golden blond hair and his black and silver, their bearing, the instinctive lift of their chins, their noble breeding. She stared at the striking couple. They were as regal and well matched as possible, and in reaction, her stomach sank and landed somewhere in the now black depths where her hopes and dreams had once lain.

Lady Agnes continued, "She cried off and married someone else . . . the very day before you were married."

There before her eyes was the fairy-tale ending, real and standing across the room for the world to see.

Everything around her seemed to fade into a bitter mist. She felt a sharp and painful realization about her marriage —one that even she, with all her hopes and dreams and wishes, couldn't make go away. Even her witchcraft was useless. She could never win Alec's heart because it was a prize already won by another. Her hopes along with her heart died a slow and withering death.

Appropriately a chill wind swept around Carlton House, bending trees and bushes and suddenly rattling the terrace doors. The skies rumbled as if pained, and a second later it began to rain.

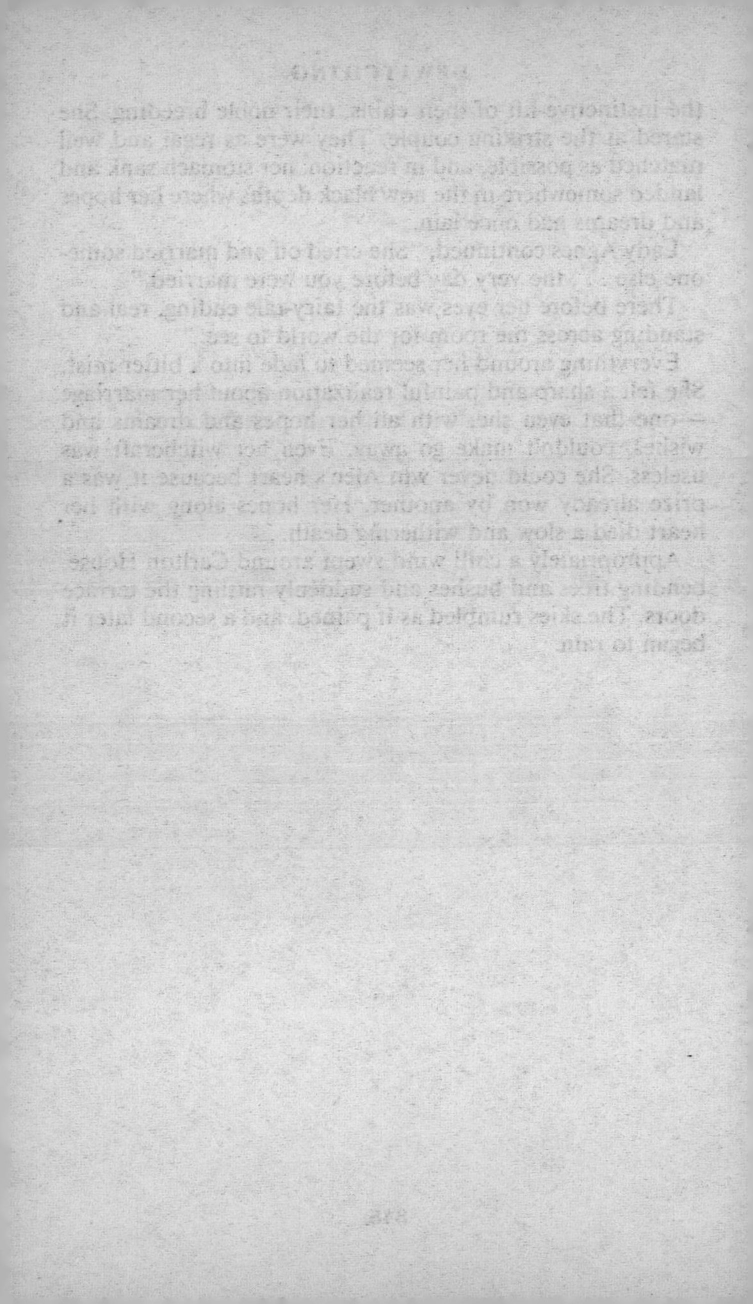

# The Heartache

**Nothing in love; now does he feel his title.**

*Macbeth*, William Shakespeare

# Chapter 23

Joy sat in the window seat of the rear drawing room and watched the rain sprinkle rings in the dark puddles on the flagstones below. The rain had continued on and off since the night before, the night that had begun with excitement and wonder and ended in emptiness. 'Twas all she could do not to break into sobs once she'd learned the truth. Only her pride had kept her from falling apart at the ball in front of all of English society.

Alec had seemed equally pensive. Alec, Joy thought. Even the thought of his name could bring back a jab of heartache. Juliet's Alec. Something vital deep inside her twisted so tightly she felt the room spin. She took another breath.

From the moment he parted from Lady Juliet he'd worn a troubled air. She was sure she could name the trouble: his wife wasn't Lady Juliet, his love, but instead a Scottish witch who made his life chaotic. His mood had only served to drive home the painful realization she cradled where her hope used to be—he loved someone else. His heart was not untouched; it belonged to Lady Juliet, who didn't want it any more than Alec wanted Joy's heart. She'd been caught up in wishful foolish dreams.

Oh, God . . . She couldn't even fall in love right.

She wiped the tears from her eyes once again, amazed she had any left, and tried to summon some Scots pride. Sitting here blubbering wouldn't change what was. She took a deep breath that quivered traitorously in her tight chest. Her gaze drifted to the trees in the walled garden below. Winter had turned the birch trees as skimpy as her pride. The rain had stopped, but the sky still hung gray. With the rain had come the warmth of approaching spring, and the snow and ice had been washed away when the skies cried with her.

Standing in the back corner near a small hawthorn bush where ivy twined with dormant honeysuckle up a stone wall was a proud English elm. She pressed her tear-blotched cheek to the glass and looked up at the sky. The heavy rain clouds had moved on. As surely as if it had called her name, she looked back at the tree. She needed a tree now, needed to feel the warmth of nature cradling her, soothing and healing her.

She plucked a paisley shawl off a coat stand, wrapped it around her, and went out through the French doors, descending the stone steps and sidestepping the deeper rain puddles. A minute later she stood in front of the great tree.

Elms had character, even if they were English. Their trunks were mottled, as if wrinkled with the knowledge and wisdom of age and time. Even the bark was gray. But instead of reminding her of age and knowledge and wisdom, it brought to mind her husband's silver-streaked hair.

She placed a hand on the rough bark. "I'm Joyous, and I need your strength, your life, because some of mine's died. Please help me."

Slowly she slid her hands around the thick trunk and pressed her cheek and chest against it, feeling the bark cut into her softness but needing desperately to be very close to it. She shut her eyes and let nature take over.

Alec sat in his study and stared at the letter opener he had just used to slit open the royal reminder. As if he could forget his obligation to spend another night under the scrutiny of society. He intended to return to the country tomorrow, royal command or not. The servants were already making ready. Tonight was the last trial. What an appropriate choice of words. Brought to mind witch trials, something he was trying to avoid.

He twirled the opener in his fingers, aware of the mesmerizing effect of the lamplight catching the brass blade. Married to a witch, and no one knew it. He wondered if Juliet would have changed her romantic ideas about his marriage had she known the truth. At first he told himself that she thought thus only because she was a woman, and naturally driven by emotion. But his behavior gave the lie to that excuse. Still, he was disturbed by her perception of his marriage. A love match, she'd implied.

He doubted if any Belmore marriage had ever been a love match. His parents' certainly wasn't. His father had made that clear at the same time he'd made clear that the Belmores were above that sort of drivel and that no son of his, and certainly not the heir, would let his life be mucked up by such foolishness. Then he'd taken Alec's tutor aside and made certain that all future history lessons would revolve around the stupidity and dire outcome of love matches. He was to study the fallen kingdoms, lost wars, and vain politics that were the direct result of affairs of the heart.

Alec had learned that love led only to destruction. But he had also learned, and learned quickly, that the only way to win his father's approval was to think like him, live like him, act like him. The lesson soon became a way of life.

Odd that he'd only recently learned his pride, too, could produce disastrous results. Without much more thought Alec realized he had done the one thing he'd so proudly warned Downe of: he had let emotion rule his actions. His hurried marriage was a direct result of wounded pride. He had married in haste because he was worried about what people might think. That was quite a weakness for the duke of Belmore to admit to; it rated right up there with hiding his wife.

He turned the letter opener again, still mentally justifying his actions and trying to ease his guilt. His wife was a witch, something he had nothing to do with. He wondered if divine retribution was involved, if being wed to a witch was his punishment for using her. He had known when she gave him that first wide-eyed worshipful look that her heart was his to do with as he pleased. And in those circumstances he had chosen to marry her, for his own convenience, knowing full well that she wouldn't turn him down. It was a way to salvage his pride.

But his awareness of his actions was something he intended to carry to his grave. He didn't want Joy to know he'd been so foolish as to give in to a weakness like wounded pride. Some part of him liked the way she adored him, took pride in fact that he could fill her dreams. He didn't want her scorn. He wanted her respect, perhaps even more than he wanted respect from the ton.

For the first time in his life his name and title, his role in life and society, had nothing to do with how someone felt about him. She called him her Alec—not her duke, her husband, or anything else. Just her Alec. His dukedom was not the driving force between them. His wealth and bloodline and title didn't matter, and oddly enough neither did her heritage or her witchcraft. They were bound by something deep within, uncontrolled, something he couldn't name, but knew existed. And it scared the bloody hell out of him.

"Belly to belly. Back to back. This is the way I cook the rack. . . ."

Joy stood in the doorway of the kitchen watching Hungan John spit a side of lamb. He set the spit into place, then wound the jack and went back to the counter, singing in his deep voice a nonsensical two-quarter song, his long braid swaying behind him. The two kitchen maids had taken up the beat and one pounded her fist rhythmically into a mound of bread dough while the other chopped onions in the same two-quarter time.

Hungan John finished the song, then took a deep drink from a bottle and started anew. "I work all day on a drop of rum! Dah, dah, dah, dah, dah-dah, dah, dum!" He lifted the bottle, but stopped mid-motion, suddenly spotting her. "You Grace." Ignoring the maids' startled gasps, he made a gallant grinning bow, his teeth sparkling like the ring in his ear.

"Please," Joy said, raising her hand. "Don't let me interrupt your work. I was a wee bit hungry."

"No wonder. You Grace ate nothing this day." His black eyes gave her a shrewd, knowing look. He walked over to a table in the corner and pulled out a chair. "You Grace sit here. Hungan John fix you up good."

She sat, and he began to clear off a work surface, grabbing the bottle. He eyed the inch of rum at the bottom, drank it down, and plucked up the cork, and rammed it into the bottle neck, then hooked the bottle to a chain on his wide belt. He caught her look and winked, giving the bottle a pat. "Best bottle. Strong cork."

He laughed and laughed as if that were the best of jests. She watched him move around the kitchen, singing out orders to the maids, who responded rhythmically. A few minutes later there was enough food to feed the whole household sitting on the table.

"Just a wee slice of bread and butter would have been sufficient."

"You Grace keep eating like the hummingbird, will soon look like the hummingbird. You miss breakfast, you miss tea. You won't have supper till late tonight." He set a glass of milk on the table. "Here, drink this."

She sipped, and her eyes opened wide. "This isn't milk."

He nodded. "It be coconut milk with pineapple and rum. Magic." He winked at her. "Drink up."

The concoction was truly delicious. She drank the first glass and two more while she ate. An hour later she wasn't sure if it was the strength of that old elm tree or the food in her stomach that made her almost float upstairs, humming a catchy little tune, another magical rum drink in her hand. Suddenly things didn't seem quite so bleak.

Polly dressed her in a lovely gown of midnight blue silk trimmed with pearls and glass beads, and she wore slippers of blue with glass heels. Tonight there was no required hoop as in the court dress. She felt light-headed as she waltzed around the room before Polly's delighted eyes. She had just donned her white gloves when a footman knocked to say the carriage and His Grace were waiting below. Polly quickly fastened the set of sapphires and pearls that Alec had sent up earlier, then left to fetch her reticule.

Joy stared at her reflection. Yes, once again she looked like a duchess. She raised her glass and finished off her fourth coconut fruit drink. She could easily have had another, but there was little time left. She licked the sweet foam off her upper lip and looked at herself again, her hand touching the cold jeweled necklace.

She assumed Alec had sent them as an order for her to wear them. A wee part of her rebelled at that and if it weren't for the prince she would have refused to wear the jewels. There had been no note, and no husband to fasten them on her and end the task with a passionate kiss, as he had the night before. She turned away from the mirror and the memories, and the room spun. She gripped the back of a chair and took a couple of deep breaths. The room stopped.

My, my, my, she thought. Maybe I overdid the tree hugging. She shook her head, then frowned for a dizzy moment. Mean old Alec wormed his way back into her scattered thoughts.

She looked into the mirror and didn't like the face that stared back. She looked gloomy. She found her Scots pride, and stuck up her chin, staring down her nose at her reflection. Better, she thought. Much better. Now, having spent so much time thinking about her situation, she decided it was time for action. No more nice witch. All she'd gotten for being nice was a broken heart.

Alec had asked her to marry him. She hadn't forced him. In fact, she had tried very hard to say no, but he wouldn't let her. He had wanted to marry her. Of that she was certain. But why? That was what had her thinking, and she intended to find out why before this night was over. That was her goal.

Juliet might have his heart, but Joy was his wife—a wife who knew her husband had used her. It had been a painful thing to accept, and she had gone through all the stages of mourning—the tears, the hurt, the shame that made her ache.

But now she felt angry, because Alec had done her such an

injustice. A good part of her wanted to pelt him with snowballs again—two or three hundred to start with.

One of the few things that set fire to her anger was injustice—like the poor post laddies at the coaching inn being forced to breathe smoke, like pitiful old Forbes being thrown out after years of faithful service, and like the poor clumsy Letitia Hornsby being subjected to an obnoxious man's public ridicule. Joy was now in the same predicament. And for the first time in a long time she was angry in her own behalf. Good and angry.

The Belmore carriage edged along behind the crush of conveyances in front of the Royal Opera House at Covent Garden. Alec watched his wife with thoughtful eyes. She was quiet, unusually so. Last night after dinner she had told him with gleeful anticipation that she had never been to the theater, so he'd expected her to have her face pressed to glass, trying to see the many lanterns that lit the gardens, or squirming with anxiety and asking him every two minutes if they were there yet. Instead she sat stiffly, her hand occasionally gripping the armrest. This cool woman across from him was the perfect duchess, but she was not Scottish.

"Are you feeling unwell?" he asked.

She turned to face him, blinked twice, and nodded, only to take a deep breath and turn back. Her face held no animation, just a comely flush. He'd asked her something. She had barely answered, just a clipped yes or no. She reminded him of all the Englishwomen he had known, and he didn't like it.

The carriage stopped and a footman opened the door. Alec stepped out and turned to help her down. She wouldn't meet his eyes. She just placed her hand in his, allowed him to assist her, then snatched her hand back so abruptly that she wobbled and almost fell. She made a big to-do over shaking out her skirt and never once looked at him.

His curiosity was piqued. He gripped her elbow and guided her inside. He'd seen a flash of anger in her eyes only twice—once when he confronted her about what she did to Beau Brummell, and again just a second ago. He moved to where the wide staircase to the private boxes was roped off and three royal footmen and two others stood guard. On sight a footman released the rope, handed him a printed program, and led them up the stairs.

Twice she almost fell, and only Alec's arm had stopped her. When he started to question her she had stuck her chin up regally and continued on as if nothing had happened. At the top landing he paused and pointed out Rossi's statue of Shakespeare atop a pedestal of rare yellow marble. She gave it a cursory glance and walked on. A few minutes later they greeted the prince and were seated at the front of the box—in the seats of honor at the prince's right hand.

Silently they settled in. After a moment she finally deigned to look at him and asked, "What play are we seeing?"

He hadn't even thought to ask or to look, so he glanced at the program and felt all the blood drain from his face. He stared at the title in disbelief.

The word *Macbeth* stared back at him.

He didn't groan. He didn't think. He didn't do anything but say, "Shakespeare."

She made a face, then turned back to the stage. The prince leaned over and said, "My lady duchess, being Scottish, you will surely enjoy this production. We have persuaded Sarah Siddons to return for a special performance of her most acclaimed role, Lady Macbeth."

A second later the curtain rose to whistles and jeers and shouts from the noisy crowd. An actor walked onstage and shouted, "Scotland! An open place."

Prinny smiled and nodded at her, and Alec watched closely for a sign of her reaction. The requisite crash of thunder and flashes of lightning streaked across the stage, and the witches entered.

This time Alec did groan. He'd forgotten how haggily garbed and made up they always were. The prince with his impeccably rotten timing said, "See there! The Scottish witches. Ugly as sin, ain't they?" Everyone around him nodded. Everyone except Joy.

She turned from the prince and took another long look at

the warted faces, at the wild straggly white hair, at the ill-fitting black gowns, at the sheer ugliness of the Three Weird Sisters, and slowly turned a pair of angry green eyes toward Alec.

He leaned over and warned, "Remember who you are and whom you are with." He gave a quick nod toward the regent. For the next few acts, she watched the play. He didn't. He watched her. She appeared to accept the play, stiffening only when the witches plodded onto the stage to deliver their dire predictions, and he felt somewhat relieved, until one of the later acts.

He should have taken the thunder as warning. The witches came out, hovered around a bubbling cauldron, and chanted, "Double, double toil and trouble; fire burn and cauldron bubble."

A moment later the cauldron skidded across the stage, leaving the witches with stirring sticks in hand and stunned expressions on their faces. He had to look twice to assure himself he'd seen it. The witches exchanged confused looks, then ran over to the cauldron and went on shouting ingredients and pretending to drop them inside. "Scale of dragon!"

A column of flame burst from the cauldron, causing the witches to shriek and back away. It continued to bubble and steam and sputter.

"Tooth of wolf!" the most stalwart witch continued, standing back an extra few feet before pretending to toss a tooth into the pot.

A wolf howl echoed louder than the thunder in the theater's rafters. Alec whipped his head around to stare at his wife. She looked innocent. Her hands were folded in her lap and her eyes were narrowed, but she was staring straight at the stage.

By the time Alec turned back to the stage, Macbeth had entered saying, "How now, you secret, black, and midnight hags!"

The actor took two steps and tripped over thin air, landing face down on the stage. The audience gasped and Alec grabbed her hand and squeezed it. "Stop it."

She gave him a false smile. "Stop what?"

"You know what."

Macbeth managed to regain his composure and shouted, "Though you untie the winds and let them fight—"

Joy coughed and a blast of air whipped across the stage, forcing all the actors to grab ahold of the cauldron. Wigs blew off, costumes were plastered against their bodies, and props skittered around like leaves in a whirlwind.

"I said stop it!" Alec said through his teeth.

The wind died suddenly.

"I haven't the faintest idea what you mean," she said.

Macbeth straightened his clothing with a sharp tug and jammed his wig atop his head. He stood straight, arms in the air, and said, "Though castles topple—"

The set behind him clattered to the ground in a cloud of dust. The audience began to laugh.

Alec grabbed her just as Macbeth finished his lines in a whisper, his worried gaze darting left then right.

A witch cried out, "Pour in sow's blood!" He felt Joy wiggle, then giggle, and he looked down at the stage. Three pigs waddled onstage to join the fray, snorting and wallowing, knocking over the cauldron and snorting around Macbeth.

"Is that what you meant." She giggled against his chest.

"Damnation, woman," he whispered tightly, his arm clamped viselike around her. He shifted so he could speak to the prince. "My wife is ill, Your Highness."

The enthralled prince was laughing so hard he barely looked at them. "Yes, yes, whatever, Belmore." He dismissed them with a wave of his hand.

But by then Alec was dragging her out of the box, doing his best not to kill her with his bare hands. He pulled her over near the statue of Shakespeare and he shook her. "What the devil were you doing?"

"Teaching them a lesson about Scottish witches." She smiled, then hiccuped, whipping a hand over her mouth and looking at him through eyes that held only mischief.

He studied her. The gleam in her eyes did it. She hiccuped again. He sniffed her mouth. "Have you been drinking?"

"Coconut milk," she answered. "'Tis delicious with a

wee"—held up two fingers to show him how much—"spot of rum."

She was sotted. As if to confirm his conclusion she hiccuped again, then fluttered her eyelashes at him. At the sound of another round of laughter from the theater, she gave a wave of her hand. "They seem to like it."

Livid, he scooped her up in his arms—a gesture that held no romance, but only the desperate need to get her the hell out of there—and he stormed away.

"Mr. Shakespeare," she called out over his shoulder. "Double, double toil and trouble!"

"Be quiet," he ordered and strode toward the stairs, never seeing the warts break out on the statue's face.

The bedchamber door banged against the wall, eliciting a healthy scream from Polly, who was snoozing near the fire. Despite the fact that Joy was still in her husband's arms and still a tad tipsy, she gave Polly a little wave.

"Leave us. We need to speak privately," Alec said, glowering at the room in general.

She looked at the wide-eyed maid. "You'll have to excuse His Grace. He's a wee bit upset." Then she grinned up at him. "Aren't you?"

His neck turned purple. He spun around, glared at the awestruck maid, and shouted, "Out!"

As Polly scrambled out of the room, Joy waved a hand around dramatically. "'Out, damned spot! Out, I say!'"

Through clenched teeth he said, "Shut. Up."

"Still no sense of humor, Alec." She shook her head, but stopped when she looked up and saw that he had two of those arrogantly noble Belmore noses. She squinted to try to focus her eyes.

"There was not one wit of humor in what you did tonight."

"The audience thought so," she argued, pressing one finger to her lips in thought. "I distinctly remember them laughing. I felt the pigs were a nice touch. My magic worked rather well, don't you think? Perhaps it was the rum."

He tossed her on the bed.

She bounced and giggled, staring up at his angry face with a delighted grin of mischief. "That was fun, Alec. Let's do it again. I can put my arms around your purple neck, and you can throw me on the bed. Then we'll count how many times I bounce. I'll let you do the counting, since you've had so much practice."

She watched his anger peak. His hands shook with it. Seething in his usual cold silence, he spun around and crossed into the sitting room. Barely two minutes later he appeared in the doorway, brandy in hand, and glared at her.

She gave him a sugary smile. He mumbled some swear-word that made her want to goad him again and she quipped, "Fee fi fo fumble! Listen to Alec, he's starting to grumble."

He stiffened for a shocked second, glanced left, then right, and pinned her with his ducal glare.

She ignored him. He stalked toward her, placed the brandy on her night table next to her book, and slowly placed his fists on the mattress, leaning intimidatingly close. She tossed her head back in brave defiance. He would not intimidate her.

He almost spat out the words, "Did you just cast a spell on me again?"

"No." She returned his look. "If I cast a spell on you, believe me, you'll know it."

"What the devil is the matter with you?"

"I'm upset."

"Why?"

"You tell me why. Why did you marry me?"

"Is that what tonight was all about? You wreak havoc on a public play, in front of the prince, because you want to know why I married you?"

"No. Because I *do* know why you married me."

His eyes narrowed for an instant; then he jerked her up against him. "Because of this?" His mouth covered hers in a passionate kiss. The kiss was her undoing. All her bravado crumbled under the power in that kiss.

Tears trickled from her closed eyes, and she fought for some fleeting bit of control.

He pulled back and looked at her, the anger draining from his face, too. He looked at her eyes, then searched her face. "What's this, Scottish? Tears?"

She took a deep breath, and her misty gaze met his. She tried very hard not to choke on the words. "She must have hurt you very badly."

"Who are you talking about?"

"Lady Juliet."

He swore, closed his eyes for a telling instant, then opened them. He reached out to touch her shoulder. Thinking the gesture one of pity, she turned away.

"Just what did you hear?"

"That you were to marry her, but she married someone else. And that it happened only the day before you married me."

"That's true."

"Do you love her so very much?"

"No."

"Please don't lie to me."

"I'm not lying. I did not love Juliet." He forced her chin around so she had to face him. "Why does this concern you? I'm not married to Juliet. I'm married to you."

"You are married to me, but you don't love me either."

"I never said I did."

The truth of his words made her ask harshly, "Why did you marry me, then?"

He tensed and straightened. "It matters not. We are married now."

"It matters to me."

"Why should it? You have a home, wealth, the protection of the Belmore title—things that are important. What more do you want?"

"I want love."

"Love doesn't enter into this. This is a marriage, not a play. I never made any promises of love nor will I." He turned his back to her as if looking at her was too difficult.

"I wanted part of your heart," she admitted so quietly she wasn't sure he heard.

"Is that all you foolish women think of—love?" He spoke

the word as if he were swearing. "Women speak of half marriages, pieces of the heart. Is this where you get those ideas?" He grabbed her book from the table and held it up in front of her. "From these damned books?" He shook it in her face and when she didn't answer he turned suddenly and flung it into the fire.

Joy gasped, stunned. The flames burst upward, devouring the book. The fire crackled. Then there was nothing in the room but tense silence. She watched the blue and yellow flames, feeling nothing.

He looked at his hands as if he couldn't believe what he'd done. Then he looked at the fire. "God Almighty." He ran his hands through his hair, his expression bewildered and frustrated. "Am I mad or are you?"

"Am I mad?" She looked at him through narrowed eyes, then slowly raised her chin. "Yes, I am mad, good and mad." She threw a hand up in the air. "Alec, up!"

He shot upward toward the ceiling shouting, "Bloody hell!"

She stopped moving her hand, and he jerked to a halt and hovered just shy of the gilded molding.

His face registered shock, grew pale with it.

"See?" she said, giving him a taste of a witch's anger. "I used my magic on you, and I'll wager you know it."

He looked at her as if he couldn't believe this was happening. Very slowly his color changed—pink to red to purple. "Get me down!"

"No."

"I said get me down!"

She crossed her arms and shook her head.

"I'm your husband. You will obey me. Now."

Tired of his arrogant orders, she waved her hand and he flew sideways.

"Bloody hell!"

She lowered him a few feet and heard him mutter, "I need a drink."

She gave him a wicked smile and, with her other hand, sent the brandy glass up to the ceiling to hover a few inches from his hand.

"Your drink," she said innocently.

He looked suspiciously at the glass.

"Help yourself," she told him and watched as he slowly reached for the glass. She twiddled it just out of his reach.

"I do not find this amusing, wife. Get me down."

"I thought you wanted a drink."

"I'm warning you . . ."

"Who—me the wife, or me the witch?"

His eyes narrowed.

"This is the wife . . ." She slowly sent the glass toward his face and then up, up and up, until it was right above his head. "And this . . ." She flipped her index finger. The glass emptied on his head. "Is the . . ."

"Witch!" he said in a hiss, brandy dripping from his hair and down his red cheeks.

"Yes, I am, and now you have your brandy." She flexed the fingers on her right hand. "Would you prefer to spit toads or grow a few warts?"

He pinned her with a damp look that said "you wouldn't dare."

She gave him her sweetest smile. "Tell me why you married me."

"I wish the hell I knew!"

"I think you know exactly why you married me and that hardheaded English pride of yours won't let you admit it."

"Get me down."

She shook her head.

"Now, wife."

"Say it, Alec. Just say it!"

"Get me down."

She'd asked for the truth, but had wanted him to say he cared. She could feel the tears burning her eyes. She could feel that empty hollow feeling begin to swallow her whole. Sighing defeatedly, she slowly lowered her arm until Alec stood on the floor just a few feet away.

"Damn you, woman! I'm the duke of Belmore—"

"Oh, and don't I know it. No one who knows you would ever doubt exactly who or what you are."

"Just what the hell is that supposed to mean?"

"You work so hard at it, Alec. Believe me, everyone knows you're the duke of Belmore."

He turned to walk away.

"Coward," she whispered.

He ground to a halt and slowly turned around. His face was a red mask of anger. "You want to know why I married you? All right. I'll tell you. Because Juliet cried off, dammit! She made a fool of me! I refused to be made the fool by anyone." He strode toward the door. He turned and looked right through her. "I married you because I needed a wife. You were there, willing and convenient."

It took her a moment to find her voice. "Alec!"

He paused in the doorway and turned, his face as stony as his heart.

"You refuse to be made a fool of, and yet you made a fool of me. You knowingly used me, didn't you?"

Guilt flashed darkly in his eyes just before he closed the door. She had her answer.

# Chapter 24

Atop the roof of Belmore Park, a random little breeze whipped at Joy's skirts, and the squat heels of her shoes tapped a slow beat on the iron as she walked to the south corner. The silent days and lonely hours seemed to have melded one into the other. The play had been barely a week ago, yet it had seemed like a month. The morning after the play had dawned without cold, rain, or fog, but instead a rare bit of February sunshine. Polly had awakened Joy from a mindless escape into sleep with a breakfast tray, a headache powder, and the news that His Grace had ordered her to read the morning paper. Glaringly circled was an article on the wondrous mechanical stage effects created for last night's performance of *Macbeth*. No one, it seemed, would take responsibility for the production's unexpected success until the prince announced his pleasure and his desire to reward the innovator. At last count fifteen people had come forth to claim the reward.

She had closed the paper, drunk the headache powder, and listlessly allowed Polly help her into a traveling costume. Little more than an hour later they had left London—Joy, Polly, and Beezle in the carriage and the duke conveniently choosing to ride a spectacular stallion newly purchased from Lord Addersley. Again the fourgon plodded behind filled with baggage and two additional servants. Prior to the ball, Alec had agreed to Joy's suggestion that they take Forbes and Hungan John to Belmore Park, where duties were plentiful and where Forbes could be given a position in which he would be less disruptive.

However, Joy might have welcomed a disruption to break the cold rigidity of her husband. He spoke only when necessary—usually to issue an order that needed no answer —nor did he await one. Once they arrived home, there was almost no interaction between them other than a silent dinner at opposite ends of the sixty-foot table. He left two days after their arrival to join Richard and Neil at his hunting lodge, leaving Joy with nothing to do but think and wander and seek solace in the gardens and on the roof.

She leaned against the balustrade and looked down, remembering how Mrs. Watley had received her unorthodox servants. One could hardly have said she welcomed them, but then, she didn't welcome Joy to Belmore Park either. Once Alec had made it clear that Hungan John and Forbes were to be given positions, the housekeeper had wisely kept her dislike of them somewhat tempered. The same could not be said about her scorn for Joy.

The sound of Hungan John's deep voice drifted upward from the gravel path behind the kitchens. He stood amid a group of servants, on a small grade where the path widened and led down to the massive Belmore stables; he was directing the enlargement and replanting of a vegetable garden. She caught sight of Forbes's ancient white head and had to smile. A kitchen maid was helping him turn his coat right side out.

Her gaze shifted to the other servants, who worked to the rhythm of a quirky Caribbee tune. Two of the kitchen maids held up their aproned skirts and danced a jig down a row of freshly worked soil while the others hoed in time to the song. The kitchen door slammed with a curse and a bang and Joy caught a flash of white. Beezle scuttled across the yard, heading straight for his most recent prey—a long black braid. Hungan John must have sensed or seen him because he ended the song with a loud comment about weasel stew. Beezle whipped a quick turn and went after one of the stable cats instead, leaving everyone laughing.

Listening to Hungan John's voice as he began a new song,

she glanced longingly at the goings-on below. She stood far above them, watching them dig in the dirt and talk and laugh and enjoy a bright day that hinted at the coming spring. She had never felt more alone. Her hands tightened on the balustrade and she watched the laughter, the joy, with the hungry eyes of one who's been excluded, like a poor child being forced to watch Christmas from outside a locked window.

Odd, and sad, that she felt more companionship from her servants than from her husband. She rested her arms on the railing and sighed, wondering how long it would take her to fall out of love with that man. Obviously it was going to take longer than it had to fall in love. For sanity's sake she had decided that her only option was to conquer her own foolish heart, since she couldn't conquer Alec's.

She wished her puny magic could cure a broken heart. 'Twould be so nice to snap her fingers and no longer care. Yesterday she'd even tried a spell, although in retrospect she didn't know why. She knew her powers weren't strong enough to even begin to master a love spell, let alone trying to reverse a heart that hadn't been controlled by witchcraft. The result of yesterday's spellcasting had been a huge crack in the music room's marble statue of Cupid. She blanched. She hadn't found a way to fix that yet, but on the positive side she had managed to get rid of all the bright red broken hearts—hundreds of them—that had floated around the room.

So today, like the other days, she had taken refuge on the roof. Hiding. Isolated. She'd repeatedly heard that the Belmores answered to few, because of their title. Yet she, the duchess of Belmore, cowered out of the way, hiding in a place that was supposedly in her home. Something was wrong, very wrong.

Sighing, she rested her chin on a fist and stood there for a very long time. Soon the fanciful sound of Hungan John's deep voice had her head swaying and her fingers tapping. The warmth of the sunshine and the refreshing sound of the servants' laughter had her thinking about her situation, and she came to a decision. From that moment on she would no longer try to be the duchess of Belmore. She did not like what she was becoming. She would be what she was, just Joyous.

She glanced down at the laughter below and took a fortifying breath of fresh air. With a new determination, she descended the stairs and ten minutes later she was on her knees and up to her elbows in freshly hoed dirt, planting parsnips and truly laughing for the first time in days.

Two hours and much dirt and refreshing laughter later, she stood, planted her hands on her hips, and surveyed the garden. Staked off in neat dark rows was a large fertile area that would soon provide carrots and rutabagas, turnips, lettuce and the like. She smiled. There was something kindred about the workings of nature that touched a witch in the most personal way. Nature, too, was magic—the loamy scent of peat-blended soil that was so strong one could almost taste it and the invigorating warmth of the sunshine that floated down and bathed everything below it. It felt good to work hard, she thought, pushing a straggly strand of damp hair from her sweaty cheek. Soon their labors would result in the plumpest vegetables ever seen at Belmore. And if they didn't, she would sprinkle a little starry magic on the garden when no one was looking, just to make sure they flourished.

Dusting her hands off on her filthy, wrinkled gown, she rounded a corner humming and bobbing her head, her steps in time to the song, but she slowed when the squeak and rattle of a rickety wagon caught her attention. Pulled by two mangy oxen, the wagon rolled up the drive and the driver, a crusty old man in a fisherman's garb—a woolen cap, naval coat, and high oiled boots—stopped near her.

"Be this Belmore Park?"

She nodded, again pushing the hair from her face with a dirt-smudged hand.

"I got something fer the duke of Belmore." He thumbed toward the back of the wagon.

"I believe deliveries are usually received at the back door," she explained with a smile.

"Not this 'un. This 'un's fer himself."

"The duke isn't here, but I'm the duchess."

He drew his head back and squinted at her, then said in a belligerent tone, "And I be His Majesty, King George."

Joy looked down at her dirt-caked dress, the muddy hem and shoes, the tangled strands of peat-flecked brown hair that hung over her shoulders, and realized the man had good reason to doubt her claim.

She laughed. "I never said I looked like one. Come. I've been working in the garden. Follow me, please." She marched up the front steps, the driver skeptically following behind her. The front doors opened, Henson holding them, and he gave her a quick bow. "Your Grace."

She heard the old man snort in surprise, then mumble about the oddities of the gentry as he followed her into the drawing room, his cap suddenly and respectfully clutched in his gnarled hands. She quickly wiped her hands on her gown and sat down. "Now what have you brought my husband?"

He stood and gaped at the opulent room for a stunned second. His gaze went from a gold vase to the huge diamond-paned windows to the majestic portrait above the chimneypiece, then up to the painted ceiling. His mouth hung open. So she wasn't the only one. She cleared her throat and he regained his composure only to fumble through his coat pockets for a crinkled envelope, which he handed to her and rocked on his heels as she opened it.

She unfolded the letter and read it, a little stunned herself. She looked up at him. "This states that my husband is to be guardian for someone named Stephen, at the request of Mr. Rodney Kentham upon his death."

"That be the case, and his death were just two days ago."

Concerned and unsure, she sat there for a minute, then explained. "My husband is gone for a few days, but I can send word to him to come home quickly. Who's taking care of Stephen now?"

The man pointed to himself. "He be in the wagon."

Joy jumped up, horrified to realize that a poor child had been left sitting in a wagon full of old broken furniture and other oddments. "We left a child out there alone?" she said over one shoulder as she rushed from the room. Skirts in hand, she ran down the front steps and around the wagon.

Relief washed through her when she saw for the first time the fisherman's helper, a big humpbacked man who appeared to be in his middle twenties. He wore a wide-brimmed oilskin hat and apron and smelled of the sea. He sat hunched on a crooked willow chair in the wagon bed next to a couple of chests with a splintered rocker strapped across the top. His presence meant the child hadn't been left alone. She stood on her toes and peered around the rubble in the wagon, thinking the wee laddie must have been frightened witless. "Where's Stephen?"

The helper didn't answer, so she looked at him. He cocked his large head and watched her from beneath the brim of his hat with the childlike eyes of one of those poor souls whose minds were thwarted from birth. And those shadowed eyes held fear when they met hers. She smiled and tried again more slowly and more calmly. "Where's Stephen?"

He didn't speak.

"The laddie?" she tried, looking into his eyes. "The boy?"

"Yer Grace." The fisherman took a step forward and held out a hand toward the helper. "That be Stephen."

Alec rode the stallion down a grade, wondering for the hundredth time what might be the urgent problem at Belmore. He kicked the animal into a lope. His wife had sent the message and that was reason enough to quicken the pace, but he wondered if he should be riding hell-bent homeward or hell-bent out of the country. His mind played havoc with his nerves, imagining all the possible disasters awaiting him—dancing statues, floating objects, broken clocks that fix themselves, riding crops and tambourines. Bloody hell, what if she had sneezed up something truly unspeakable? What if she had actually made someone spit frogs? Sweat broke out on his forehead and he rode even harder.

He cursed the foolish weakness that had sent him to seek refuge hunting in the Somerset hills. One didn't run away from responsibility. It hadn't taken him long to realize that he couldn't escape the fate that had darkened his existence of late: the fact that he'd married a witch—a witch who could control him with her magic—and he had no weapon with which to defend himself. She could become angry at any time as she had on their last night in London, and with a stroke of her hand send him flying around the bloody room. He, the duke of Belmore, had lost control. Completely.

He wanted to wring her neck. Literally. He wanted to go back in time and change everything. He wanted to order her to be what she should be instead of what she was.

What she was . . .

He thought about that for a pensive moment. She was a Scottish witch, hardly something one could change. Yes, she might not change, but he could teach her control. He knew all about control. Where would he be if he had not learned control.

Happy . . . a tiny voice said, but he willed it away. Perhaps he was asking the impossible, expecting her to change and be what he demanded. He wasn't even sure what it was he wanted her to be. She could no more change what she was than he could change the way he felt about her—and that was what really disturbed him. He—a man who had trained himself not to feel anything and who prided himself on his lack of emotions—felt something for her, something strong and potent.

An image flashed in his mind—Joy looking up at him through worshipful green eyes as if he had just given her all the stars in the sky. For a brief insane instant he heard her husky voice calling him Alec, her Alec. Something deep within him tightened, as if she had just touched his heart—the one he didn't have. Until now. Bloody hell.

"I'm scared." Stephen sat next to Joy on the stone bench in the garden.

She looked at his bent head and asked, "Of what?"

He worried his large work-callused hands and didn't look up. "This place. I want to go home."

"This is your home now."

He shook his head vigorously. "No. No. It's not home. I don't live here. I live by the sea, with Roddy."

"But Roddy can't take care of you any longer."

"I knowed. He died. I had a dog once. He was my friend. He licked my face. He didn't think I was ugly. He died too."

"What was his name?"

"Dog."

She smiled, then told him, "I have a weasel."

He looked at her. "You do?"

She nodded. "His name is Beelzebub."

Stephen laughed. "That's a dumb name."

"I call him Beezle."

"That's kinda dumb too. Why didn't you call him Weasel?"

"I don't know. I suppose I never thought of it."

"I did." He was quiet for a minute then asked hopefully, "Does that make me smart? I want to be smart, so people will like me."

She leaned over and peered under the large hat Stephen insisted on wearing whenever he was outside. "You must be smart, then, because I like you."

He stopped worrying his hands and rubbed his palms on his trousers. "I like you too. You don't turn away or say mean things or shout." He looked up but stared straight ahead with a distant look. "Some people look at me, then turn away because I'm ugly and dumb. Roddy never turned away."

"I won't turn away."

Very slowly he raised his shame-filled face and looked at her. She steeled herself against showing any emotion, not wanting to make Stephen uneasy or let him know the turmoil inside her. She wondered what Alec would say when he saw Stephen. She didn't know which man she wanted to protect more, poor, simple Stephen who had suffered so much hurt or her husband who was about to.

Stephen cocked his head and watched her. She gave him another smile of reassurance.

"Do you think I'm ugly?" he asked quietly.

"No. Do you think I'm ugly?"

He laughed. "You're not ugly. You're very pretty. And nice too. You don't turn away or look scared or anything. And you don't shout at me."

"Has someone here shouted at you?"

He stared at his hands and began to wring them again, but before she could say anything else she saw a footman leading Alec's stallion along the path to the stables. *Oh, God.* She took a deep breath and stood up. "My husband, Alec, is home. I want to go speak with him before you meet him. Will you stay here?"

He nodded. "I like it here. It's quiet and no one shouts at me. Do you think Alec will shout at me?"

"Everything will be fine." She patted his hand and smiled, not knowing what was going to happen, but knowing she had to prepare her husband, and if he so much as raised his voice to this poor soul she'd do to him what she had done to that Brummel fellow.

She crossed the garden, looking back over her shoulder once and giving Stephen a wave, feeling calmer when he waved back. She passed Henson and said, "Go get Beezle and show him to Stephen. I'm going to speak to His Grace first. And, Henson?"

"Yes, Your Grace?"

"Stephen is frightened and feels out of place."

"I understand."

"Thank you." She turned and headed for the library. She entered the room and stopped, her throat tightening the second she saw her husband standing in front of the west windows.

As if he could sense her presence he turned. The dark blue eyes that returned her look were filled with suspicion. In a hard voice he said, "Now what have you done?"

She closed her eyes briefly, searching for patience and a calm reply. "I have done nothing."

"Then what was so urgent that you needed to send for me?"

Joy took the envelope from her skirt pocket and closed the distance between them. "Here."

He looked at the envelope, then took it and opened the

custody letter. He read it and sank into a chair. "A child? I've never heard of this Rodney Kentham."

"The ward is not a child."

"What do you mean, he's not a child? The letter says the duke of Belmore is to be contacted and is to assume responsibility for Stephen should anything happen to this Kentham fellow. I can't be responsible for an adult."

She crossed the room and stood near the east garden doors where Stephen was plainly visible, hunched over the bench. "Come see. He's outside. There."

Alec stood and joined her, looking out the window. "My God . . ."

"He's frightened and confused. He needs your understanding."

"Understanding? I don't even know who he is."

"Could he be a cousin?"

"My father was an only child, as was his father. My mother came from a small family too, and they're all dead."

"Perhaps you should meet Stephen and then decide what to do." She opened the doors, and Alec followed her down the stone steps and over to the bench.

Stephen still sat there, the hump in his back making him look awkward and defeated. But he was dangling something shiny above Beezle, who was sitting up on his fat haunches and slapping the object with his black-tipped paws. Henson looked up. Alec nodded toward the door and the footman gave a quick bow and left, unnoticed by Stephen.

"Stephen?" He looked up at the sound of her voice. His drooping eyes widened with fear when he saw Alec, and she heard her husband's intake of breath and rushed on, "This is my husband, Alec, the duke of Belmore."

The tension-filled moment seemed to creep by, Stephen and Alec both stunned and silent—one with fear and possibly recognition and the other with an angry realization that she knew must have created a sea of turmoil within him.

With animal instinct, Beezle reacted to the tension and scrambled up onto Stephen's shoulder, knocking the wide-brimmed hat from his head.

Stephen's hair was gray.

Alec stiffened, then swore quietly, his face revealing conflicting emotions that Joy could only imagine, for her husband was staring into a misshapen version of his own face, his own dark yet drooping sad eyes, a tragically twisted double whose family tie no one could possibly deny. Stephen was a Castlemaine.

# The Truth

**And all our yesterdays have lighted fools.**

*Macbeth*, William Shakespeare

# Chapter 25

"Aye, I know who Stephen be. He's yer brother. Yer father had me drive the carriage th' took him away," Old Jem admitted, looking Alec straight in the eye.

"When?" Alec's voice was devoid of emotion—surprising considering he was so close to the edge.

The coachman appeared to think about that for a few seconds. "Ye were over three. Yer father already had ye riding yer first pony. The youngling were but a few months old, I'd say. Yer mother couldn't even look at him. Yer father sent him to live in one of the crofters' cottages till he could send him away. In quiet."

Alec tapped the letter opener silently against the embossed leather edge of the desk pad. "All these years and I never knew. Why hasn't anyone mentioned him?"

"'Twere done in the middle of the night. Most believed what yer father told 'em—that the youngling died."

Alec stared at a portrait of his father on the opposite wall. The fourteenth duke of Belmore—his father—stood among his hounds, his pride evident in the arrogance of the pose, so in control he could send his own son away. The dukes of Belmore—an old myth shattered. He closed his eyes and took a deep breath that helped little. "That'll be all, Jem. Saddle the new stallion for me and have him brought around."

Jem grunted a response and rose slowly, turning to walk toward the door, his shoulders slumped, head bowed. Alec saw every one of the man's years in his bearing. Today's revelation had made Alec feel just as old, just as tired, as if he'd lived for some fifty-odd hard years.

"Jem?"

The old man's leathery hand paused on the doorknob handle and he turned back.

"Why didn't you tell me?"

Their eyes met, questioned and challenged. After a second of silence Jem answered, "Yer the duke of Belmore, have been fer many years. Even if I hadn't given yer father me word, I wouldn't've told ye. 'Tweren't me place."

Those last three words said it all, brought the situation into sharp focus. Yawning before him was the chasm of English social class—the very system he was taught to respect. He felt the burden of his title more at that moment than at any other. And he suddenly saw the ludicrousness of the notion that one human being was better than another, of the belief that a title—an ancient trophy granted at the whim of a king—and a subsequent accident of birth made one man more deserving respect than another. There was insanity in that concept and in the fact that it was so readily accepted by an immoral world.

And the ultimate irony, that his father, the esteemed duke of Belmore, a man who had been cold and hard and calculating—a man so in control he was devoid of compassion, a liar who hid one son away while he demanded the other son serve their revered family name to the exclusion of everything else. Everything human. Alec thought of his brother. Everything humane.

The door clicked closed and he turned, his mind a crush of dishonor, frustration, and anger. He crossed the room and looked outside. His wife and his brother stood together. The woman no one knew was a witch. The man everyone regarded as an ogre.

His fists shook in angry reaction to the knowledge that he'd been living a sham. Nothing was as it seemed. His blood ran hot, his muscles tightened; he felt a desperate need to strike out, to hit something, shattering it into a thousand pieces, because that's the way he felt. Shattered.

A flash of black caught his attention. The restless stallion was saddled, but it reared and balked at being made to stand and wait. Alec wrenched open the door, feeling little satisfaction at the sound of it crashing against the wall. He strode down the steps, and a minute later there was no sound but the thunder of the beast's hooves beating the ground. A damp snort of equine breath blew into the air as they sailed over a hawthorn hedge, splattered through a trickling brook, spraying up water, then dust. Across the grass, past the lake, up a hill they flew, horse and rider moving as one, drinking the wind and beating to death a worthless lifetime.

Stephen sat in the old splintered rocker. "This is my chair." He stood up quickly and pointed to a pile of old broken furniture. "My things. My special things."

Joy smiled, seeing the pleasure and pride he took in the pitiful belongings he insisted be brought to his room. She scanned the interior, which was as opulent and richly decorated as the rest of Belmore Park. Everything was rich deep blue accented by gilt, marble, and crystal, but Stephen couldn't have cared less. The gleam of excitement in his eyes came not from the large bed atop a dais, not from the crystal prisms dangling from the bedside lamps, not from the thick carpet or the bas-relief that circled the ceiling, but from a lopsided old table so weathered the wood was gray, from a creaky splintered rocker, and from a jumble of shabby old possessions that only he in his simple pride could have treasured.

He set each piece in a special place, then stood back to admire it, and Joy had to hold the gasp in her throat, for his face held a look of pride that she knew too well. It was the look that Alec had worn—until yesterday.

"This is my book." Stephen held up a ragged Bible. "It has a title. Like Alec. He is the duke. This is . . ." He pointed to the letters and, with effort, he slowly sounded them out. "The bi . . . bull."

"You can read," Joy said, trying to keep surprise from her voice.

That Belmore pride lit his face again, and he nodded

vigorously. "I want to be smart. I worked hard to learn my letters. People that read are smart. Roddy was smart. He taught me." His eyes suddenly looked lost, as if mentioning the name of the man who had raised him brought forth his simple expression of grief. Tears.

Joy said nothing but waited. His sadness passed with childish speed. He leaned over and picked up an old willow broom. "This is my broom." He held it up so she could see it, turning the crooked, knobbed handle this way, then that. "I do my job good. Roddy told me I do my job good. Sometimes the other men at the docks asked me to go with them after work. I think it was only when I did a special good job, because they'd say, 'Bring yer broom, Stephen.' They would like me then. I could tell. They would take me to the Empty Net with them, like I was a friend. All the fishermen went to the Empty Net after work. They would say, 'Show everyone how you sweep off the dock, Stephen.' And I would take my broom and sweep the tavern floor. Everyone would laugh and slap their knees and say that Stephen is a real Joe Miller, he is."

Her heart was somewhere near her throat because she knew that a Joe Miller was a jest, a fool's joke.

"I didn't know who Joe Miller was but I think he must've been a good worker. So I like being a Joe Miller. I told them that, and they all laughed again. I laughed too, because I was proud that I did good work. And if I always do good work, people will like me. Then they won't leave me out."

Joy couldn't speak through a throat clogged with suppressed tears. A choked sound of anger, barely audible, came from the doorway and she turned.

Alec stood there, one white-knuckled hand gripping the doorjamb, his haunted eyes locked on the broom in Stephen's large hands. From his hard expression she could tell he'd heard Stephen's story. She prayed for both the brothers' sake that he wouldn't vent the rage she saw trembling in him. She watched him take long deep breaths, saw the hand at his side tighten into a fist of fury, and finally watched with relief as the hand loosened. Their eyes met. She glanced at Stephen, who was now burrowing through a trunk. She started to speak, but Alec shook his head. He gave his brother one last unreadable look and quietly left.

After that, she spent a large part of each day with Stephen, helping him adjust to his new home, feeling desolate because she couldn't help his brother. And Alec . . . it seemed as if he did little but try to ride the legs off every horse in the Belmore stables. She'd heard the servants' comments about the duke, had seen him taking the stallion out only to return later, exchange the lathered horse for a fresh one, and ride off again. At other moments she'd caught sight of her husband watching as she and Stephen talked or walked in the garden or sat together in the music room where she would pluck out a Scottish ditty on the pianoforte and then teach her brother-in-law to do the same.

Alec never showed up for meals, never came into their sitting room or to her bed. She'd stayed up two nights listening for him, but she'd never heard him and both times had finally fallen asleep as the sun began to rise. She wondered where he had slept, where he had hidden. She told Henson she needed to speak with him, but Henson would return and shake his head sadly. Alec had locked her, and everyone else, out of his life.

He stood in utter silence atop a hill that offered a panoramic view of the endless spread of his ducal lands. Alec dropped the horse's reins and let the animal graze and drink from a small brook that dissected the hillside.

He walked over to an outcropping where he sat on a flat rock. The sun was full and beat down on the hilltop, but he felt nothing beyond confusion. He'd asked himself over and over how one could set aside everything he knew and believed in. He was the duke of Belmore. But what was that? Little more than a part in life. His duty. His whole life had boiled down to that one thing—his duty. His role in life.

Odd that he'd always looked at life in terms of roles. Much was becoming clear now. He'd been taught to value above all else his pride in being a duke, his role in society—dictated by an immoral ton, by hundreds of years of ritual without reason, and by his father's rigidly skewed perception—a blight he had passed on to his son. One of his sons. The one he claimed.

Alec had also been taught to value and protect the Belmore name above all else. He laughed, a sarcastic sound that was caught by the wind and carried into the crowns of the nearby trees in all its caustic glory.

God . . . What pride was there in a name that placed a reputation before a human life, pride before ties of blood? His mind went back in time, to memories of a childhood alone, to the hours that had seemed like days to a young boy of four or five who was so isolated that he talked to the walls, the chairs, pretending they could listen—until his father caught him and flew into a rage so violent that Alec never again spoke in his presence unless prodded to. He might as well have been deaf and dumb, for that was how he had lived. In silent fear.

Eton had come as a welcome escape. There even the stiffness that hid his fear of the other students, even his aloofness and silence, hadn't discouraged the two lads who still stood by him today despite his pompous behavior.

What had Scottish called him? A hypocritical prig. Quite perceptive, and right. He was his father's son. And he'd allowed his rigidity to spill over into his personal life. He'd constantly reminded Scottish that she was the duchess of Belmore, his wife, and that she should conduct herself as such.

There were the roles again. Scottish wasn't a role to him any longer. She wasn't his duchess, his wife, a witch, a monster. She was a living, breathing woman who could make him forget a lifetime of sadness with a pair of innocent eyes that bespoke her love.

God, but he needed that now. And he needed her.

He rested his elbows on his knees and stared down the hill, seeing little but the memories of the last few days. He'd watched her with his brother and realized that the two seemed to delight in each other's company. He'd seen them walk outside, watched her point at some silly thing like a bird or a flower, and heard their laughter. He wondered if it was easier for Stephen to see fairies, and diamonds in snow and crystal.

Alec had felt foolish even talking about such things. He had boasted over and over that he refused to be made a fool of, yet his father had made him the biggest fool. And still he knew that having his pride pricked was nothing compared to what Stephen must have gone through in his twenty-five or so years. He would have given anything to get his hands on those fishermen. Their cruelty made him ashamed to be part of the human race.

He could feel the angry tension swell in him again. His stomach tightened with it. He took deep calming breaths to fight away the image of his brother, a huge man who was forced by nature to go through life with his head and shoulders bent as if in shame. A man with the features of a Castlemaine—twisted and yet the same. But instead of cruelty or coldness or anger, those sadly drooping eyes reflected need and shame.

Alec raised his head and looked upward, wanting to fight with the God who had made both him and Stephen, the God who had made their father. Yet he knew it was a useless fight. The damage was done, some twenty-odd years' worth. But no more. If there was one thing he had gained out of all this confusion it was a determination that never, as long as he lived, would he allow anyone to make a fool of Stephen again.

# Chapter 26

"Look what you've done, you clumsy fool! Look!" Mrs. Watley's harsh voice echoed up the wide stairwell in the front hall.

Stephen backed away, his head bowed in shame, his shoes crunching on broken pieces of porcelain. "I'm sorry. I didn't mean to break it."

"That vase was over two hundred years old and worth a fortune. Bah!" she spat in disgust. "Idiots don't know the worth of anything."

Stephen stared in horror at the fragments of the vase scattered on the marble floor, then hunkered down and began to pick up the broken pieces. "Here," he said, stammering as he worked his mouth to get the words out. "I—I'll try to—to paste it back to-together."

"You stupid fool! You can't fix it!"

"But see." He held up two pieces together like a puzzle and moved on his knees toward her. "They fit."

"Get away!" Stepping back, Mrs. Watley held up her hands as if to ward off a monster, not seeing the group of servants who stood back watching in horror and blocking Joy from getting through. "You're nothing but an animal! A beast! You should be in an asylum! Look at you! You don't belong here!"

Stephen began to sob, the porcelain pieces clenched in his hands. "I didn't mean to . . . I didn't mean to . . . I'll fix it."

Furious, Joy raised her hands to zap Mrs. Watley clear to the devil.

"I believe it's you, Mrs. Watley, who doesn't belong here." Alec's seething voice stopped Joy midspell and made the angry housekeeper turn her head.

Her face still held its revulsion, her arrogance, but her sharp eyes showed fear when she met his dead, cold stare. "Your Grace."

"Get out." He stood in front of the open front doors, slapping his riding glove against a hand, his predatory stance that of a man who would let nothing stop his need to avenge. "You have one hour. If you are not gone, I will bloody well throw you out myself. And count yourself lucky that's all I'm doing."

The woman turned her hate-filled eyes toward Stephen and gave him a look of pure disgust. "Gladly." She raised her head and marched up the stairs, ignoring the mutterings of the huge crowd of servants that thinned enough for Joy to get through.

She rushed to Stephen's side and knelt with him, her arm around his hunched and shaking shoulders calming his silent shaking. "Stephen. It's all right. Come, stand up. You and I will go outside. I have something special to show you."

He stood awkwardly and shuffled with her into the salon and toward the terrace. She had just opened the doors when she heard her husband speak to the servants.

"The same goes for any of you. He is my brother and will be treated with respect by everyone I employ. Is that understood?"

She took a deep breath of relief and led Stephen outside, where they walked in silence. A few minutes later they sat on the bench in front of that old elm tree. She saw his hand still clutched into a fist around the fragments of porcelain. "Stephen?"

He appeared lost in thought, so she patted his leg to get his attention.

"What?" he asked without looking at her.

She touched his fist. "Here, give me those."

He looked down and opened his hand. His face said everything—shame, embarrassment, frustration. "I would have fixed it."

She took the pieces. "Mrs. Watley has shouted at you before, hasn't she?"

He nodded, his eyes locked on the stones that flagged the garden. "Whenever she saw me she said I was stupid. She was right. I am stupid. I broke that vase."

"I've broken things, too. That doesn't mean I'm stupid. The vase doesn't matter, Stephen."

"It does to me."

She sat there, searching for something to say to make him feel better. Unable to find the right words, she just began to talk about anything, everything, about things she knew, about feeling hurt inside and how to help the hurt go away. Five minutes later they stood on either side of the old elm, gazing up at its crown.

"It's so big." Stephen frowned.

"That's because it's old." Joy smiled at him. "But that's good, because the older the tree, the stronger the magic. Now press your head against the bark and hold on tight. Then close your eyes and take slow, deep breaths."

"There's ants on my side."

"Oh, sorry. Come over on this side." She waved him over and adjusted his arms around the tree, then she went to the other side and studied the trail of ants traveling up the tree bark. She peeked at Stephen. "Are your eyes closed yet?"

"Uh-huh. Very tight."

"Good." She glanced around, scanning the area, and a wicked grin lit her face. She flicked her hand and zapped the ants straight into Mrs. Watley's bags, which were being loaded onto a wagon near the carriage house. She looked back at the tree. The ants were gone. A smile of satisfaction curved her lips, and she brushed her hands together.

"Joy?"

"I'm right here." She reached around her side of the tree. "Wrap your arms tightly around the trunk. Then just relax and let the tree make you feel better."

A few moments later the click of bootheels on the flagstones broke her concentration. She opened her eyes. Alec stood there, a look of absolute bewilderment on his face. "What are you two doing?"

"Hugging a tree," they answered in unison.

"I see." He was quiet for a moment and when no explanation followed, he said, "May I ask why?"

Joy peeked around the giant tree trunk. Her gaze met Stephen's. "Shall I tell him or do you want to?"

Stephen appeared to think about that for a few minutes, then shrugged. "I don't think I can pronounce it."

"Then I guess I'll have—"

*"Somebody* tell me, please."

"Rejuvenescence."

"What in the devil is that?"

Joy sighed and stepped back from the tree. Dusting the bark from her hands, she walked over to Alec and looked up at him, then mouthed the word "witches" and said aloud, "They believe that the wonder of life flows through nature, especially trees. I told Stephen it was nature's magic. It's very strong in old trees like this one. If you feel sad, you hug a tree and its magic will flow into you and make you feel better." She saw her husband's skeptical look and asked his brother, "Do you feel better yet, Stephen?"

He opened his eyes and stood back, taking his time to answer. Then he grinned and nodded vigorously.

Alec was silent while he studied his brother; then his pleased look met hers. They stood there, neither speaking. Finally she averted her eyes. He reached out and tilted her chin up. "Thank you, Scottish."

She took a deep breath and smiled.

Stephen pointed at the tree and tapped his brother's arm. "You try."

Alec broke into a choked cough.

"Oh, Stephen, that's a wonderful idea. What a shame we do not have a eucalyptus tree. Those are particularly good for coughs."

Alec scowled at her and cleared his throat. "I do not need to hug a tree."

Stephen moved closer and searched Alec's face. "His face is twisted up, not forever ugly like mine, but he feels bad, see? He needs a tree. Come. Try my side."

Joy watched the play of emotions on Alec's face. Then he

looked at Stephen for a long moment and the hardness in his face melted away. He gave Joy a wry look but turned to his brother and said kindly, "What do I have to do?"

"Come here." Stephen waved him over and helped him place his arms around the tree just as she had helped him. "Are your eyes closed yet?" He was repeating her exact words. "Wrap your arms tightly around the trunk. Then just relax and let the tree make you feel better."

She couldn't hold back her giggle.

Stephen looked at her, his face suddenly worried. "Aren't I doing it right?"

"You're doing a fine job. Just perfect."

Stephen beamed and Alec opened one eye, pinning her with it. She hadn't known a person could scowl with only one eye. That made her laugh harder.

"Your eyes aren't closed," Stephen told him, and Alec closed his eye. Stephen shuffled over to the stone bench and sat down next to Joy. "I wish I'd known about tree magic before."

"Why?"

"Because there was lots of times when I was little that I felt bad. Just like when Mrs. Watley yelled at me. Like when I asked the other children if I could play hide-and-go-seek with them. Sometimes they said yes, but they always made me 'it.' I could never find them. Sometimes I'd look and look but they weren't there." He looked up, staring at nothing in particular but his face showing every bit of puzzlement and every bit of shame he had felt.

"Finally when it was cold and dark outside I'd go home. The next day they said I was dumb. Sometimes they'd look at me and yell 'Stephen, Stephen, God got even.' I felt bad because I didn't know why God was angry that I couldn't find them. I didn't know God got angry about games. Roddy told me I didn't do nothing wrong, but I still worried about it."

Joy looked past Stephen's head, bent in abjection, to where Alec stood against the tree. She knew Stephen was hurt, but Alec's face told her that he took the blame for that hurt. She wished her magic could take away all the hurt and pain and disillusionment suffered by both these men.

All three were quiet, lost in their own thoughts. After a few more minutes Stephen said, "I didn't want to make God mad. I read about what happens when God gets angry. He sends lots of rain and floods and balls of fire and plagues and pes . . . pestal ants."

Stephen turned to Joy, his expression suddenly speculative. "Those ants on the tree—were they pestal ants?"

"What ants?" Alec stiffened and quickly stepped away from the tree, frowning and brushing off his sleeves.

"Those ants." Stephen stood up and pointed. Then he looked closer, almost pressing his nose to the tree trunk. "What happened to the ants?"

Joy locked her gaze on the toes of her shoes and resisted the urge to hum innocently.

"There were lots and lots of ants on this side of the tree, weren't there, Joy?"

"Hmm?"

"Joy, where are the ants?"

"Yes, tell us where the ants are." Alec moved to stand right next to her.

Stephen scratched his head and walked slowly around the tree. When he was on the opposite side Alec leaned toward her, and she knew before he even spoke that she was caught. "I know that look, Scottish. What did you do to the ants?"

She raised her chin proudly and admitted in a hurried whisper, "I zapped them into Mrs. Watley's baggage, and a few on her back. Along with spiders and beetles and gnats. All black."

His gaze shifted to the baggage wagon, which just began to roll along the drive. She followed his stare and they both silently watched until the wagon, the horrid Mrs. Watley—who was swiping at her back—and her infested baggage had disappeared over the crest in the hill.

Alec turned and laughed.

Stephen's face grew bright with pleased surprise. "Seals!" He looked left then right, searching the area. "I heard seals."

Joy hid her smile behind a hand, but when she looked at Alec, who had suddenly clamped his mouth shut, she could tell she hadn't hidden her amusement very well. "I think you heard Alec laugh. 'Tis a sound rarer than seals in the Cotswolds."

The brothers stared at each other. Alec kept his mouth firmly closed and his face masked with indignation to cover what looked to be embarrassment, but Stephen picked that moment to lean forward almost nose to nose and study Alec as if looking for hidden seals.

One look at Stephen's face and Alec laughed again.

"It was you!" Stephen's eyes widened and he looked from Alec to Joy and back to Alec.

She patted Stephen's arm. "You'll have to forgive him. He's a little rusty, but he'll improve with practice."

Alec drew himself up—all imperious duke. "And just what is wrong with the way I laugh?"

Joy and Stephen exchanged looks, Stephen rolling his eyes. She bit back a grin, chewed her lips and said innocently, "Nothing."

"Alec, your face is all twisted up again. You need the tree. C'mere." Stephen waved Alec toward the tree.

Joy laughed. "His face is almost always like that."

Alec stiffened. "What is that supposed to mean?"

"Just that you're always scowling and you never smile."

"That's ridiculous."

"No, it's true."

Alec appeared ready to say something, but she interrupted. "You wouldn't smile when we were at the snowbound inn. You said I was foolish."

He gave Stephen an odd look. A minute later he bared his teeth and muttered through them, "There. Are you happy?"

"Happy about what?"

"I'm smiling."

"You are?" Joy stepped back and looked. "Really?"

"Yes," he answered tightly.

Joy walked over until she was only a few inches from his face. She looked up and studied him. Nowhere on his face was there any delight. That was not a smile. He looked like a Highland wolf with lockjaw. Slowly she reached up and placed a finger on either side of his mouth and tilted it up.

"What are you doing?" he asked through his teeth.

"Experimenting." She cocked her head and looked this way and then that. Alec looked stunned, which was probably the only reason he went along with her, until a curious Stephen lumbered over, eyeing the two of them.

Unable to resist, she tilted the corners of Alec's mouth downward. Stephen shook his head. She bit back the urge to smile and tilted Alec's mouth back up.

"What do you think?" She ignored the retributive narrowing of her husband's eyes.

Stephen moved his face close to Alec's and squinted thoughtfully. There was a long pause. Then he said, "My face isn't nice like his, but I think I am the brother with the good smile." Stephen grinned and a second later his gentle chuckle mixed with a wee Scottish giggle and a raspy, long-neglected bark.

Laughter had come to Belmore Park.

"Alec!" Joy tripped and felt herself falling.

Her husband's strong arm captured her waist. "I have you."

She took a deep breath of relief, then took advantage of their position and slowly slid her hands up his chest and over his shoulders. "If you want me to wear this blindfold, then you'd best slow down or carry me."

"In that case . . ."

She could hear the laughter in his voice, and an instant later she was in his arms. As always, she sighed and leaned her head into his warm neck, filling her senses with his scent. "Oh, my goodness, you do that so very well."

"So I've been told."

"Where are we going?"

"'Tis a surprise."

"I know. You told me that already."

"Then stop pestering me."

"I wouldn't want you to be bored."

"Believe me, Scottish. I've not been bored since the day we met."

"You did it again."

"What?"

"Managed to change the subject."

He was silent.

"I'm still curious."

"So was Pandora."

"I'm not sure I care for that comparison." She tried to add an indignant tone to her voice but even she could hear her pleasure. She, like Alec, enjoyed their banter. It was a new side to their relationship, a form of verbal foreplay in which they both seemed to revel. After a silent minute she smiled to herself. "I could cast a spell to make you tell me."

"I could drop you down these stairs."

"Ah, but you wouldn't."

"Are you so certain?"

Yes, she thought, I'm certain. Her hope was back, full force, and she was sure that she had garnered a wee corner of his heart. He had all of hers.

"If you did drop me I'd could zap myself to safety," she said smugly.

"Please don't use that word."

"What word?"

"'Zap.'"

"Why not?"

"My feet get cold."

"Alec! You made a joke!"

He grunted something. After a moment he went on, "Speaking of your magic, if you ever levitate me again—"

"Oh, didn't I ever apologize for that last night in London?"

He stopped and shifted her slightly, then stepped backward through a doorway. "No, you didn't, but then neither did I . . ."

She felt the cool night air brush her skin.

". . . Until now," he finished, then set her on her feet and loosened the cravat he'd used to cover her eyes.

The blindfold fell away, and her breath caught in her throat. "Oh, my goodness!"

# Chapter 27

Glittering light from hundreds of stanchioned candelabra gleamed like a spill of gold dust across the dark iron roof of Belmore Park. Near the statues, torches guttered and cast a wavering amber glow on the angel, the unicorn, and the gallant knight who stood along the skyline like golden guardians. Waist-high urns filled with countless hothouse flowers bordered a path to the domed dining room whose double doors stood wide open in welcome. Up above, in the dark depths of the heavens, the moon hung high and full and shone pearl-bright. No daydream, no wish, no fantasy, could compete with the sight before her.

"Oh, Alec . . ." Her voice trailed off in awe. She swallowed around the thickness in her throat and wondered if she had choked on tears of happiness or on the wealth of her love for this man. She closed her eyes for a second just to make sure the sight before her was real. Then she looked up at him.

He watched her intently, which surprised her. He seemed anxious, as if he was unsure how she would react. She touched his hand and he drew himself up tall, all proud duke. That made her smile. "Thank you."

He exhaled so subtly that if she hadn't been looking for it she'd never have noticed. He held out his hand. "Come."

She smiled, sliding her hand into his, and they walked toward the domed room, bathed in the warm touch of candlelight and surrounded by the sweet perfume of stock, hyacinth, and hollyhock. She glanced once at his dark hand so casually yet possessively holding hers, and could feel that something had truly changed between them, something deeper than his need or her love, some mystery greater and more timeless than the mere joining of a man and a woman. The intensity of it frightened her, but her need for happiness, her hope, the promise of his touch, overcame that fear, made it seem almost forgettable and small compared to the elation that awaited her in his arms.

Amid a dream more wonderful than the starshine and winter magic, she walked by his side, nearing the lighted room. Her gaze followed the candle glow upward to the top of the dome. It was glass, as clear as fine crystal. Alec's hand slid to her lower back, and he guided her inside. She still looked upward, and the silver face of the moon, the twinkling of a few bright stars winked back at her from the night sky.

She said his name in an awe-filled whisper, and his answer was to lightly grip her shoulders and turn her so she faced a table for two, little more than three feet across and set with diamond-bright Belmore crystal and gold-etched bone china and gleaming silver around a bud vase with pink roses.

The aching memory of that scene—the private dinner that never took place, the pain of the unfulfilled hope she had pinned on that night weeks ago—melted like ice in the sunshine, replaced by a love so strong she couldn't speak.

She turned to him and slid her arms around his neck, leaning her head against that special place on his shoulder, and the words came. "This is the most beautiful gift I've ever received."

She felt his chest swell a smidgen and gave a smile as misty as her eyes. His hand slid under her chin, and he turned her face toward his. "This cannot compare to what you've given Stephen. And me. Thank you, Scottish." He lowered his head till his mouth covered hers. He made a deep sound of male pleasure that did delightful things to her insides, and he slowly dug his hands through her hair. His tongue stroked her lips, and when she opened them, it sank deep into her mouth, filling and stroking and reminding her that her world was in his arms.

Stepping between his spread legs, she moved her chest lightly against his, and his hands left her head and gripped her bottom, pulling her against him, hip to hip. She moaned with a need so strong it made everything around her fade into nothing but a thin golden light behind her closed eyelids.

His mouth moved to her ear, and in that deep bewitching voice he growled her name, half plea, half prayer, and seemed to revel in the feel of her as she reveled in his taste, the chilling plunge of his tongue and the soft molding of his hands and body against hers.

With a groan he pulled back. When his mouth didn't touch her neck or shoulder or ear, her eyes drifted open and she looked into the face she loved.

He nodded toward a wall where stood a square table laden with silver warmers and serving dishes. "Dinner will grow cool."

Her fingers fumbled with the studs on his shirt and she removed one, then another, until she held them all. "Not now," she said, dropping the studs on the floor and turning her face toward his. "Kiss me, Alec. Please. I don't want anything else." She slid her hands up his chest, but he grabbed her wrists.

"Wait." He released her and stepped back, pulling closed the doors, sliding the bolt in place. He closed the distance between them in two strides and slid one hand around her neck and commanded, "Turn around."

He caressed her neck as she turned, his hand spanning it, rubbing in a soothing lover's caress of tendon and flesh and bone, then he undid the closures on her gown, pausing to kiss her back, brush his mouth across her skin until the white silk of her shift blocked his damp lips. With a tenderness that made her ache, he moved his mouth to her neck, ran his lips along the feminine line of her neck, then down to her collarbone. A flick of his hands and her gown fell away and pooled at her feet.

Holding her bare shoulders he turned her around, then knelt before her, his hands skimming the stockings down her legs, his lips and tongue caressing her thighs through the silk of her shift and teaching her what the sense of touch was all about. She stared at his bent head and gripped it, gasping when his mouth grazed her cleft. At the sound, he looked up, and she met his heated gaze. She knew that all her want and need were reflected on her face, but she didn't care. This desire was stronger than either pride or fear.

Wordlessly he rose and slowly pulled the pins from her hair. It tumbled down to her thighs, and she heard his breath stop. He stood stone still, as if he needed to just take in the sight of her.

He had stoked a pride in her femininity that she had never before experienced. A woman's power she hadn't known she possessed. Restless for his touch she slid the straps of her shift off her shoulders, sending the slick silk garment sliding down her body like a caress of his hand.

She stood before him, naked, waiting, wanting. "Please," she whispered, and he reacted to her husky voice by tearing off his shirt and tossing it away. Then she was in his arms and he carried her across the room, laying her atop a down-soft daybed. At the sound of his boots hitting the floor she opened her eyes, her vision caught for an instant by the moon and sky above, but a second later his mouth traced the inside of her calf, upward where his tongue grazed her inner thigh. His hands slid beneath her knees, continuing to warmly slide upward, spreading her legs over his wide shoulders until his hands cupped her bottom.

His breath whispered a caress against her dampness just before his mouth kissed her mind away. She cried out his name and her hands twisted the fabric beneath her. With each stroke she moaned, moved her head, unable to do anything but feel the flaming touch and lick of his swirling tongue. It sent her higher and higher, to a place known only by lovers.

He paused. So did her breath.

"Come, Scottish, against my mouth. I want to feel the pleasure I give you. Taste it."

Tears of passion blinded her, but she cared not, lived only for this instant and this need, the intimate feel of his mouth, knowing she'd die if he paused again. The moment his tongue slid inside her she pulsed with ecstasy so strong her legs shook. Roses rained down in bursts that matched Alec's throaty sound of male pleasure, until the petals littered his head and back, her breasts and belly. The scent of satisfaction mixed with that of rose oil and wrapped itself around her till the throbbing slowed, faded. His mouth still kissed her, but it was slower, only the slightest brushing movement of his lips. He lowered her hips, gave her one brief kiss, then gently slid her legs from his shoulders.

She opened her eyes and watched him lower his head again and move up her body, blowing the petals from her belly and ribs, then moving his tongue across them until her breast was in his warm mouth and there was nothing but dark passion in his eyes. The rough hair on his chest rasped against her belly and she arched upward, threading her hands through his thick silver hair and pulling his mouth to hers. He pulled back, rose petals in his hands, and rubbed them over her lips, then over his own.

His mouth touched hers. She tasted musk and roses, then felt the probe of his hardness and drew her knees up in open welcome. He sank inside her, and she gave a small gasp. He pulled back, then thrust again, drawing another small gasp.

"God, what that sound does to me." He stilled, savoring the moment, then lightly brushed her mouth with his. "Tell me what you feel."

She took a breath and whispered against his damp lips, "Only you. My Alec." Her words seemed to catch him off guard and light some hunger within him. As if driven to do so, he gripped her hard against him and turned them both over, sliding his hands through her hair and down to her bottom. He pulled her knees against his hips, opening her, and stroked her from behind, trailing his finger over the tender private flesh between. One hand continued the touch, but the other moved to the back of her head and held her firmly against the power of his mouth and tongue. Then he rolled his hips and his hard shaft touched the very heart of her, once, twice, then slowly rocked and rocked making her aware of his size and length and strength as his body bonded in splendid ecstasy with hers.

Seconds drifted into minutes, eternal minutes of long, slow loving, their hearts moving closer in time and unison. Soon he moved in long thrusts till the mating of their bodies matched heartbeat for heartbeat. Moisture beaded between them and dewed slickly inside her and she felt the rise, the sparkle of bliss, felt the waves of fulfillment coming faster and faster, the same tempo of his hips. She cried out for him; he called her name again and again, never once missing the perfect beat of his possession—the taking of her body, the giving of his.

His lips moved to her ear and he rasped, "So good, Scottish."

Her breath halted in pleasure. But the rush came faster, flooded her.

He gripped her head and groaned, "So good." Her body clutched him in hard spasm. The first of the new petals fell. He drove deeply, matching her throb for throb. She cried out his name, in one last weak plea for consciousness before the little death swept her over the dark edge of passion.

"I'm hungry again."

Alec watched his wife slide from the bed and cross to the serving table through an ankle-deep carpet of pink rose petals. His shirt covered her. Her petal-sprinkled hair covered his shirt and hung to the backs of her thighs. She wore nothing else. He rested his hands behind his head and watched that loose hair of hers sway while she hummed, popped pinches of gingerbread into her mouth and appeared to fill a plate with one of everything, for the second time that night.

She turned back around and, heaping plate in hands, walked toward him. His shirt hung to her knees, but covered little since she could only find one of his studs amidst all the petals. With each step she took, the shirt split to reveal the thighs that had tightened on his hips, his waist and shoulders, had cradled him and ridden him through most of the night.

But the image that seared itself into his memory and fed his pride was her face, the delight, the pure joy and still innocent love that sparkled from her eyes. She scrambled back on the bed, plucked a chicken leg off the plate and bit off a mouthful, chewing with relish and comically widening her eyes as if roasted chicken were the food of the gods. He shook his head at her antics, but couldn't for the life of him take his eyes off her mouth, the mouth that could set him afire, could issue little gasps that made him pleased he was a man; yet it was the smile on that mouth that taught him the power of happiness.

"Here." She shoved the chicken leg in his face. "Take a bite."

He gave her chest a pointed look. "I prefer the breast."

She gave a delighted gasp and set the plate aside. "Oh, Alec, you do have a sense of humor after all." But before he could respond, she glanced down at the open shirt and tried to pull it closed with one hand. "I can't imagine where those studs are." She glanced over the edge of the bed. He took in the rear view and smiled.

"Seems odd that I could only find one. How many were there?"

"Eight." He sat up and moved toward her while she frowned at the petals on the floor. He slid an arm around her small waist, then pulled her on top of him and closed his mouth over the tip of a breast.

"Hmm," he said. "Not cold at all."

She gasped, half outrage, half laugh.

"So you do remember," he said, moving to test the other breast for temperature.

"Aye." She slid her hands to his shoulders as he moved over her. "And I remember thinking when Jem said that you wanted to say something."

He looked down at her, a million thoughts flying through his mind, but he said nothing, instead just kissed her.

A minute later she pulled back. "You did want to say something, didn't you?"

He trailed his mouth downward again. "Not half as badly as I wanted to test the theory."

In response, both her laughter and her arms surrounded him. A few seconds later his hand drifted over the edge of the bed. He opened his fist, and seven shirt studs fell to the floor.

In almost no time the estate came alive, as if it had been awakened after a cold, dark spell by the warm magic and light of laughter within. There was always a song—a Caribbee tune or a Scottish ditty—to set the servants' toes to tapping, their heads to swaying, and skirts to swirling. Forbes, who'd been appointed silver steward, would hum completely off key as he supervised the polishing and care of seven hundred years' worth of Belmore silver. Beezle's fur was fast reddening into his spring and summer coat. Henson's hair had grown back. Hungan John's braid had shrunk. Three of the stable cats were bald.

But the true sign of change was something that startled every Belmore servant. His Grace was seen whistling as he strolled down the hallway one morning. He even stopped on occasion to ask a servant's name, nod, then appeared to mentally catalog it before going on. Such uncharacteristic behavior from their previously cold and rigid employer caused a gabble of talk for a few days. Some speculated that he'd fallen and knocked his knob when he spent that one week riding hell-bent over every blade and brook of Belmore Park.

And even more queer and unexplainable were the pink rose petals that trailed from his boots and sometimes littered even the most peculiar and secluded places. The general consensus was that all that blue blood made the aristocracy a smidgen looby.

Alec rode into the stable yard after his morning ride. He dismounted, gave the stallion a word of praise and a quick stroke, then tossed the reins to a stableboy and moved toward the gardens. He stopped after two long strides and turned, eyeing the lad. "What is your name?"

The poor lad stiffened. He turned a worried freckled face toward Alec.

"Not to worry, boy. You've done nothing wrong."

The lad gulped with relief and answered, "Ned Hoskins, Your Grace."

"Ned," Alec said to himself. "That will be simple to remember. I haven't encountered a Ned yet." He frowned and muttered thoughtfully, "'Tis all those Marys that have me befuddled. If I ever had a daughter I shall not name her Mary." Remembering himself, he glanced up at the boy again. "That's all. Run along now." He turned and strode up the path, mentally adding Ned Hoskins to his rapidly growing list of servants' names.

He slowed at the stone steps that led to the maze outside the topiary garden, remembering yesterday morning when he had stood in this same spot, listening to Scottish and Stephen talk. They had been standing near the maze entrance waiting for him to join them. Both he and Scottish had spent time playing hide-and-go-seek with his brother in the intricate mazes, making sure he found them when he was "it." The changes in Stephen had become evident very quickly. He had readily adapted to the knowledge of who he was, as if he had been starving for a family. Like Alec.

His wife had charmed them both despite their early uneasiness and fear. The awkward questions from Stephen had made Alec shake with anger at the cruelty and stupidity of his parents. Yet through kindness, patience, and love, Scottish had given his brother confidence and comfort, and had given Alec a family, a life he'd never have known had it not been for her.

Had he ever doubted her place in his life, that doubt would have fled yesterday when she and his hunchbacked brother stood in front of a topiary camel, a thick volume from his library open in her small hands while she read to him about the wonders, strength, stamina, value, and dignity of the animal to whom God had given a hump.

He shook his head at the memory. Only Scottish.

Kneeling beside Stephen, Joy looked up from the herb bed. "Oh, Alec! There you are! Come see." She watched him walk toward them, his long legs encased in riding breeches and tall black boots. The sight of him made her breath catch, just as it had the first time she ever saw him. The duke was still there, with his pride, the tinge of arrogance that came naturally to him, and the aura of command, but now his face revealed his pleasure and when he stood above her, she saw all that she had first seen in him, including the side that needed others but would never admit it. Gone was the aloofness and coldness he had once used to ward people off. This was Alec, her Alec.

She smiled up at him, not knowing her eyes held her heart and her delight. "Stephen was trying to guess what this is. Do you know?"

"I've never given much thought to gardens."

"But it's your garden. Don't you know anything about the plants here?"

Alec slowly scanned the garden. "They're green."

Stephen laughed at that, and Joy saw Alec's lips twitch.

"Here." She shoved a sprig in his face. "Smell this."

He took a whiff.

"Well," she said impatiently. "Does it smell familiar?"

"Reminds me of roast lamb."

She started laughing. "It is indeed used to spice lamb. It's rosemary. Rosemary stands for remembrance."

Stephen had a look on his face she had come to recognize. "Who is it named after, Rose or Mary?"

"Neither," she answered, ignoring some comment Alec muttered about remembering another Mary. She gave Stephen an understanding smile. "It's the same as butterflies."

The day before, Stephen had commented when they saw a butterfly that he'd never understood why they were called butterflies when everyone knew that butter wasn't black and orange and didn't fly.

"Oh, my goodness, look there! I hadn't noticed those."

Both men followed her pointing finger to where a small patch of blue and white flowers had just begun to bloom.

"Periwinkles!" she said, delighted, then oohed and aahed over the first flowers in the gardens. "Come see." She held up a small blue flower. "Periwinkles stand for early friendship."

Stephen picked a small bouquet and handed some to her and the rest to Alec and said, "My friends."

Joy gave him a quick kiss on his rough cheek.

He hung his head and muttered, "Mush."

She bent down and plucked a few white flowers. Handing them to Stephen she said, "White periwinkles stand for the pleasures of memory."

Stephen accepted the flowers, and she handed some to Alec.

He took them and pinned her with a very private look. Then he whispered in her ear, "The only flowers that bring me pleasurable memories are pink roses."

She flushed bright red.

Stephen's worried voice broke their private moment. "Joy, are you hot?"

Before she could gather her wits and respond Alec did. "You know, I believe she is." Alec slid an arm around her small shoulders. "She's been very hot ever since last night. Haven't you, Scottish?"

She jabbed her elbow into his ribs. Her husband did have a sense of humor, but all his jests were bawdy.

His confident expression said he had her right where he wanted her. "As I recall, the first time she was hot, she plastered her lips against the carriage window."

She gasped, felt her face flush even redder, and gaped up at him. He was staring at her mouth.

"I have something more refreshing than cool glass, Scottish." He leaned down and covered her mouth with his.

Not two seconds later a familiar voice mumbled in disgust, "Mush!"

# Chapter 28

The music of a fife band rippled in the bright spring air above the village green. Little girls, their long hair woven with primroses, and laddies garbed in bright paper hats laughed and giggled and rode high on their parents' shoulders to see the festival procession. Costumed as maidens and robbers, horses and dragons, villagers danced to the tune of the kettledrum, fiddle, and fife in front of the eight garlanded oxen that pulled the Maypole. Made from the straightest and tallest of birch trees, the pole had been stripped of its branches and whitewashed and now moved toward the center of the green.

"I say, 'tis a tall one," Neil said, raising a quizzing glass that hung around his neck on the same chain as did his ague charm and a feathered voodoo fetish given him by Hungan John.

Richard mumbled something caustic and leaned back against the folded leather bonnet of the Belmore landau. Neil turned to him and grinned. "Wish to use my quizzer, Downe? Must be difficult to see with only one good eye."

Richard glared at him through both his eyes, the good one and the blackened one.

"Tell Joy and Alec how the hellion managed to rainbow your eye."

"About the same way I intend to rainbow yours, only I assure you it won't be an accident." Richard sat there quietly assuming an uncomfortable posture of anger and embarrassment.

"Rumor was the chit nailed you with a cricket ball."

The earl's fine jaw tightened, and Joy was sure he had just ground his teeth down a good bit. Part of her felt sorry for him. Like Alec, he was a proud man, but instead of hiding from the world behind an icy exterior, the earl of Downe shielded himself with anger and cynicism. Since Alec had told her how Richard and Neil had championed him at Eton, even when he hadn't wanted to be championed, she had been more tolerant of the earl, had even begun to like him, especially since he, like Neil, had immediately accepted Stephen and been kind to him, no questions asked. In her eyes, they proved their friendship.

She bit back her smile and her husband said nothing, but Stephen knew no such tact. "The earl looks like a badger."

"I say there, Stephen, I do believe you're right." Neil chuckled, then turned his quizzer on his friend and appeared to take great pleasure in eyeing him thoroughly.

Richard leveled Neil with a threatening look. "You're going to need all those charms of yours in about two seconds, Seymour."

"Oh, look!" Joy pointed toward the green. "They've put up the pole."

The Belmore party, still sitting in the landau, turned their heads just as the music started again. Within a few minutes red, blue, green, and yellow streamers rippled downward from the top of the high pole, where a colorful bouquet of pink and blue rhododendrons formed a wide floral crown. From each streamer hung a silver ball and several golden stars; twined around the pole itself were garlands of deep green English ivy, fragrant white and green honeysuckle, sweet violets, and yellow primroses.

"The races will start soon. We'd better go." Alec stepped down from the carriage, then helped Joy down.

She threaded her arm through his, and they strolled along the village path. "This is almost as festive a Maying as we have at home. I missed the bonfires, though."

Very quietly Alec said, "I believe we burned enough fires last night."

She jabbed him in the ribs. Another bawdy jest.

"What fires?" Stephen asked, turning to walk backwards as he watched Joy, intently awaiting the answer.

"There was a problem with the fire in our sitting room, Stephen, 'Twas nothing," she lied and out of the corner of her eye she saw her husband's lips twitch. She changed the subject quickly. "Those wreaths above the doorways are lovely."

Alec laughed then, drawing a few strange stares before Stephen politely began to explain that there weren't any seals around even though people might have thought they heard one.

"Tell Scottish what the wreaths are for, Seymour."

"They keep the witches away," Neil shot back over a shoulder.

She stared at him.

Alec leaned closer. "Perhaps I should have worn a wreath that night on the North Road."

"Which would you prefer—toads or warts?"

He laughed and slid his arm around her shoulders. "Neither. I'd prefer to go a-Maying with you in the woods."

She stuck her nose in the air. "I've already been in the woods today, thank you."

"Ah, yes. I almost forgot about the miraculous dew."

"I say, did someone mention the dew?" Neil asked. "My mum and grandmum always washed their faces with May morning dew. 'Twas what kept them young."

"See?" she said. "I'm not daft. Washing your face with May dew does keep a woman beautiful. Besides, I was not the only woman out there. Almost every woman under the age of fifty was doing the same thing."

He stopped and slid his hand in slow inches up from her shoulder to caress the line of her jaw before it tilted her head so she looked up at him. "Nothing could possibly make you more beautiful, Scottish." He ran a finger over her lips. "I don't think I've ever seen anything as beautiful as you."

She stopped breathing and almost started crying. Unable to say anything, she placed her hand on his heart and smiled. The loud roll of a drum broke the spell, and she turned toward the sound.

"The race is starting. I need to judge the winner," Alec told her.

"I know. We'll be fine. You go on." She watched his tall frame disappear into the crowd. When she could no longer see him, she scanned the hundreds of villagers, old and young alike, who filled the crowded green. Many of the Belmore servants were among the holiday celebrants who stopped at booths to buy anything from medicinal remedies and May dolls to willow brooms.

She stood with Stephen on the rim of the crowd, watching the children skip and weave around the Maypole, and when the adults started in, they joined the dancers for one round. Stephen lumbered through the skipping steps, but his face revealed his delight every time he passed her. They stood watching the other dancers and drinking lemonade for a while, and then Stephen went to watch the horse races with Neil and Richard, leaving Joy to wander at her leisure through the village.

Everywhere she looked, the flowers of spring reigned. Cowslips and oxslips and coronets of roses and columbine crowned the young girls' heads. Nature's sweet perfume provided a heady scent that mixed with that of the fragrant thyme bushes that lined the edge of the green. A colorful booth displayed May dolls bedecked with trailing ribbons and tiny violets. They were hugged tightly to the chests of the little girls who won them. The roofs of the whitewashed cottages were havens for bluebirds, sparrows, and doves that roosted in the thatch. And the music, both man-made and natural, blended with the peals of laughter and gaiety that welcomed May with the true sense of magic.

Half an hour or so later, while Joy was munching on a pear tart, Alec joined her, slipping his arm around her waist. With her mouth full and speechless, she lifted the tart for him to taste. To her dismay he ate the whole thing, which started a whole conversation about appetite, most of it bawdy enough to make her blush.

"Where's Stephen?" Alec asked after she refused to rise to his bait.

"He's with Neil and Richard. They went to watch the races."

Alec scanned the crowd. "The horse races are over, and the wagon races will start in a few minutes. Let's find them."

They worked their way through the crowd of villagers, who were dressed for a spring festival. Some wore costumes —Robin Hood and his merry band were moving through the crowd picking pockets for fun; later that day they would sell the plunder back to their victims for mere pennies in a mock auction. The village women wore coronets of columbine and primroses, some with bright ribbons that floated behind them like the streamers on the Maypole. Men wore ivy wreaths and collars or tall satin hats, and on all of the cottage windows and doors were garlands of hawthorn branches with pink and white blossoms, ivy and violets, to welcome the spring. In the arbored May House a small group of musicians struck up a merry tune. Joy hummed and moved her head in rhythm as she searched the crowd for Stephen's green jacket and wide-brimmed hat.

The sharp sound of laughter came from a group of men standing around a hogshead of ale. Joy followed Alec and stood on tiptoe, trying to see the spectacle. She felt Alec stiffen and looked up to see his face wore the same expression it had when he confronted Mrs. Watley.

"I do my job good. I'm a real Joe Miller."

Stomach near her knees, Joy wedged her way into the laughing crowd. Stephen stood in the middle of the group, willow broom in hand, proudly sweeping the flagstones.

Slowly the laughter faded, as each man looked not at Stephen but at the duke of Belmore, standing among them with a look on his face that left no one to doubt the extent of his anger. He looked to be carved out of ice.

Richard placed a hand on his arm. "We tried to stop him, Belmore, but he kept saying he wanted them to be his friends. He wouldn't let me take the broom away. I tried."

Alec said nothing, just stood there while the crowd slowly thinned.

Joy went into the center and touched Stephen's arm. "Come along. We need to leave."

"But they're my friends. I was showing them what a good job I do."

"I know, but it's time to leave."

Head bowed in disappointment, Stephen allowed her to lead him down near the town road where they stood quietly with a crowd to await the wagon race. She didn't know what to say. Her gaze strayed back to Alec. He stood stiff and angry, listening to something Richard was saying.

She turned back to Stephen. "Are you hungry?"

He shook his head and hunkered down to pet and play with a small brown dog.

Her gaze went back to Alec. He turned and walked toward her, his face a stone mask she knew well but hadn't seen for a long time. It seemed to take forever for him to join her. She placed her hand on his arm and instantly his muscles tensed. "Alec."

"Where's Stephen?"

"Behind me." She turned, but the spot was empty. "He was playing with a dog."

"He's not there now," Alec said coldly. They searched the crowd, weaving in and out, looking for Stephen's green coat and wide-brimmed hat.

In the distance a gun went off, signaling that the wagon race had begun. The ground rumbled beneath them from the pounding of hooves. There was a shout. They scanned the area. The crowd keened and roared.

Alec and Joy turned with them. A wee little girl of perhaps four had wandered onto the road. She bent down to pick up a bright blue ribbon with a shining silver ball. There was another shout. The rumble of thundering horses. The rattle of wagon wheels. The crowd across the road parted. Stephen stood among them. He looked at the road.

A woman screamed, a terrified, bloodcurdling sound, as if someone had ripped out her heart. The sound froze everyone in place. She screamed a child's name.

The little girl looked up. A wagon came at her. There was a flash of green. Another scream. A child's cry. A groan and the gutting sound of the wagon and team trampling human flesh.

Then came the sound of crying—fearful child's tears. The little girl lay sprawled on the burn of the road, unhurt but sobbing, a wide-brimmed hat clutched in her small fists. Dust still curled shroudlike in the wake of the runaway wagon, drifting down and down until it settled atop the crumpled form of Stephen Castlemaine.

"Is there anything we can do for you?" Richard asked Joy.

She shook her head. "No. Stephen passed out again just as the physician arrived." She looked at the earl, whose face said what he didn't—that from the looks of Stephen's injuries unconsciousness was probably a blessing. "Thank you for bringing the doctor so quickly."

He nodded, looking as helpless as she felt. She crossed the study and stared out a window, seeing nothing but a blur. She could hear Neil and Richard speaking softly behind her, but soon their voices faded and her head was flooded with the memory of Stephen's frightened whimpers of pain, then the sound of his raspy voice asking if the little girl was safe. He had seemed to relax somewhat when he learned she was fine.

A loud male cry pierced the air. She spun around, her hands to her mouth to silence her whisper of Stephen's name. The shout had come from the floor above the study. She stared upward. Neil and Richard shot to their feet, looking up at the ceiling too. Stephen cried out again, an agonizing wail, and tears pooled in Joy's eyes and clogged her throat, until the burning was so strong they spilled over. She wiped them away and took deep cleansing breaths.

She turned back to the window and said, "I need some air."

Richard nodded and Neil looked at her through worried eyes. "Wait." He crossed the room, taking her hand in his. He pressed his charms, all of them, into her hand. She stared at them, then looked up at him. The man who always had something to say said nothing. He nodded, then turned back around and joined the earl.

Joy stepped out through the French doors and walked down the steps through the closing darkness. A few minutes later she was hugging the old elm, holding it as tightly as she held Neil's good luck pieces. She took long, deep breaths, then opened her eyes and found herself staring up at Belmore Park. A tall silhouette stood at a dimly lit window, looking down. For an instant it didn't move. Then the figure jerked the drapes closed.

She hugged the tree tighter, until she had little sensation left in her arms. Slowly she stepped away, feeling numb, feeling nothing. She walked back toward the study doors and stepped inside, turning and quietly closing the doors. She looked at the earl and viscount, who were still sitting in silence.

"Any word yet?" she asked.

"None," Richard answered, just as a door closed upstairs. All three of them looked up. The sound of voices drifted down. The front door closed. Footsteps clicked closer. Alec came into the room, his face drained of any color or feeling. He just stood there, not speaking, not looking at anyone.

"Stephen?" She took a step toward him.

"He's alive."

Relief swept through the room, and she took a deep breath.

"But nothing can be done for him. The doctor thinks he'll probably be dead by morning."

The tall clock ticked away silent seconds. Finally Richard stepped forward. "Is there anything you need?"

Alec shook his head, then turned toward Joy and said, "Come with me."

Without hesitation she followed him out and up the stairs, neither speaking. Alec opened the door to Stephen's room and she walked inside. The drapes had been closed and the room was dark and dank with only a few candles giving light. For the first time in her life she could taste, smell, and feel death. Her skin chilled with the eeriness of it.

A maid sat by the bed, and Alec turned to her. "Leave us."

The girl was gone in a breath.

He walked over to the bed and looked down, his face haunted. "I was embarrassed."

She gave him a puzzled look.

"At the May fair. I saw him with that broom sweeping and saying he was a real Joe Miller, and I was ashamed." He looked at her. "Now look at him. God . . ."

Stephen's breathing was uneven and labored. His face was purple with bruises, and he had bloody gashes on his forehead and cheeks. His lips were swollen, blue, and cut, and one ear had been stitched. He turned and moaned, his breath rattling.

She couldn't say anything, do anything. She felt helpless, angry, adrift, guilty. Yet she could only imagine what Alec must have felt. His face was tense. She reached out to him.

"Make him well," he said.

"What?"

"Make him well. Use your magic."

"I can't."

"You have to."

"I wish I could."

"Do something." There was desperation in his voice.

"I told you before. My magic can't—"

"For God's sake, he's dying!"

Stephen moaned and turned, then moaned again. He began to toss and kick. Both of them reached for him, trying with soothing voices to quiet him. He finally settled, but cried and cried and cried, mumbling his pain. She looked up at Alec. His face wore the look of a man betrayed.

"It hurts," Stephen moaned, "so bad. . . . Help me." He lost consciousness.

Her hands shook, and tears streamed down her cheeks. Alec dropped into a chair and ran his hands over his face. He pulled them away to show a face twisted with torment and grief. His hands gripped the arms of the chair so tightly his knuckles were white. "Then put him out of his misery."

She froze, her face crumpling in reaction to the compassionate horror of what he had asked. Very quietly she whispered, "I cannot do that, either."

He stared at his brother, his hands suddenly falling from the chair arms. He gave a cold bark of laughter that had nothing to do with humor. "I was foolish enough to believe in that magic of yours. What good is it?"

She took a step toward him and placed her hand on his shoulder.

He closed his eyes. "Leave."

"Alec—"

"I said, leave."

"Please let me be with you."

"Get out." He fell silent and stared at the bed.

She stood there searching for something to say to break through that icy wall of his.

He turned and gave her a look so angry she could almost feel the heat of it. "Damnation, you foolish woman! Can't you see I want to be alone? Just . . . get . . . out. Leave us alone. I don't need you."

A cold black void closed around her, tightly, so tightly she felt as if it squeezed the very breath out of her. She backed away slowly until she was pressed against the door. She took one look at her husband, his profile as hard as that of a marble statue, then spun around and pulled the door open.

Without even realizing it she was running, running as fast as she could, down the stairs, through a hallway. Someone called her name, but it was far away and she couldn't stop running any more than she could stop her tears. Her shoulder hit something hard. There was a shattering crash. She didn't care. She flung the front door open. At the same instant the skies opened up and rain cried down.

She ran on and on, faster, faster, across the sodden grass, over hills, down the graveled drive. Lightning cracked through the black sky and the gates blew open with an echoing crash. She ran through them and onto the road. The wind swirled harder, the rain pounded down, soaking her, while the cruel wind whipped at her skirts and blew the pins from her hair. It flowed out in wet skeins behind her. The weight of it almost pulled her to a stop. The mud sucked at her feet. But she ran on emotions so powerful nothing could stop her.

She thought she heard her name again and looked back

once, then stumbled in the mud and fell down, sinking. She lay there, her head in her arms, sobbing as the wind and rain beat down on her back. A loud wheeze sounded in her ear. She looked up at Beezle, soaking wet and staring at her through wise and sympathetic brown eyes.

"Oh, Beezle." She hugged him to her and he buried his wet nose against her neck. She clung to him and sat in the muddy road, broken and alone. As if drawn to do so she looked back toward the house. "I can't help Stephen. . . . Alec was right. What good is my magic if it can't help them?" She looked up at the dark skies and cried, "Why? Why can't I help them?" She hugged Beezle even tighter. "Please . . . please, I'd give anything. . . . Please . . ."

The rain ceased. The wind stopped. A golden cloud zigzagged downward from high in the black sky and hovered above her for a second, then lit barely three feet away.

"The MacLean," she whispered, wiping her eyes with the back of a hand.

With an aura of sparkling gold, her aunt materialized, standing tall and regal in all her golden beauty. She looked at Joy, and her kind and knowing eyes softened with sympathy. An instant later she knelt down, her arms outstretched. "Joyous."

Joy fell into her aunt's arms, sobbing. "I cannot help Stephen."

"I know, little one." The MacLean watched her from wise gray eyes.

"I thought Alec needed me."

"He did. If ever a man needed some magic it was Alec Castlemaine."

"But what good is it? My magic can't save Stephen. It can't." She buried her head against her aunt's shoulder. "I failed again."

Her aunt's hand stroked her damp back. "You didn't fail, Joyous. Alec failed you."

Joy looked up at the MacLean. "He doesn't understand, but he was starting to. He just needs more time."

Her aunt shook her head.

"But Stephen is the one who's suffering," Joy said. "He's suffered more than any man should have to. And I cannot help him."

"I can save Stephen."

Joy's face glowed with elation, and she hugged the MacLean. "Oh, thank you! Thank you!"

"But you have to leave, Joyous."

She pulled back and frowned. "What?"

"You must leave."

"No . . ." She looked back over her shoulder. "I can't leave." She turned back and held her aunt's shoulders. "No. Please don't—"

"You cannot stay with them."

"But I love him . . . both of them."

The MacLean said nothing.

"Why?" Joy turned her face up and looked at her aunt. "Why must I leave?"

"Because Alec doesn't understand. He hasn't learned the value of love."

"Please . . . Not now, when he's hurting. It's so cruel. I love him. Please."

"He does not understand love," the MacLean said, looking at Belmore Park. She shook her head. "I cannot give you to him."

Joy tried to take a breath, but could only take in shuddering gasps.

"You must choose, Joyous."

Still clinging to Beezle, she turned once again to look back at Belmore Park. The lightning flashed. For one brief macabre instant the storm's light limned the beasts along the roof. Candles flickered from a few of the windows. They looked like stars and seemed just as distant and as untouchable.

In her mind's eye she saw Stephen—sweet, simple Stephen—innocent and dying. She saw Alec—hard, unyielding, becoming little more than a marble statue, a shell of a man; what little life he had found for a brief time was gone.

Gone. She knelt in the mud, hugging her familiar while

tears poured in rivers down her cheeks. She closed her eyes and felt them burn. Biting her lip, she took a one last shuddering breath. She opened her eyes and stared at the estate, then said to her aunt, "Save Stephen."

The house was cast in darkness, only a black silhouette in the distance. The wind picked up. The rain splattered down even harder than before, pocking the muddy road.

"Alec," she said in a hoarse whisper. "My Alec."

And in a puff of golden smoke, Joy disappeared.

tears poured in rivers down her cheeks. She closed her eyes and felt them burn. Biting her lip, she took one last shuddering breath. She opened her eyes and stared at the [illegible], then said to her aunt, "Save [illegible]."

The house was cast in darkness, only a black [illegible] in the distance. The wind picked up. The [illegible] down even harder than before, [illegible] the muddy road.

"Alec," she said in a hoarse whisper. "My Alec."

[illegible] disappeared.

The
Magic

Poor human nature,
so richly endowed with nerves of
anguish,
so splendidly made for pain and
sorrow,
is but slenderly equipped for joy.

George Du Maurier

# Chapter 29

A distant pounding broke the silence in Stephen's room. Alec ignored it. It sounded again. He glanced up, not really seeing anything.

"Belmore! Open the door!" came a muffled shout, followed by more pounding.

He stood up and wrenched the door open, saying nothing. Downe stood there, his hair windblown and his clothing damp.

"Your wife's run out in the storm. I tried to follow, but I lost her. What the hell happened?"

Alec shook his head and looked back at the bed where Stephen lay quietly. He was struck by a surge of guilt so strong it sapped his mind of thought.

"Goddammit, Belmore! Do you want to lose them both?"

Alec couldn't move.

Downe grabbed ahold of his coat and jerked him around. "Belmore!"

Alec heard him, felt him, but nothing registered.

Downe shook him.

Nothing.

"Ah, hell . . ." Downe's fist hit Alec's jaw.

The pain was instant. It shot through his teeth, down his neck. He staggered back, hand to his jaw, then shook his head and looked up at the earl, stunned but cognizant.

"You stupid bloody fool! Your wife is gone!"

"Gone?"

"Yes, gone."

"Damn." He took two steps and jerked the bellpull. A few seconds later Henson entered. "Send someone to saddle three horses. Then stay with my brother." Henson left.

"You can be a hard-headed ass sometimes." Downe gave him a look that told Alec he knew what he'd done. "You tried to drive her away."

He didn't respond, but knew in his grief and guilt that that was exactly what he had done. Henson returned a second later and saved him from having to answer. Then they were running down the stairs, through the hall across the scattered pieces of a broken vase, and out the front doors, where Seymour joined them. The rain poured down in blinding sheets. Alec stood on the steps, disoriented, until he saw the horses. A second later he mounted his stallion, pausing for a moment to glance up at the dark skies.

Whenever Scottish cried, it rained. He took one deep breath and pressed his heels into the horse's sides, gravel spitting in his wake. The wind howled. The three men rode, following Downe's lead. He slowed his horse and turned back, shouting, "I lost sight of her over that rise." He pointed at the hill ahead of them. They split up and rode through the rain in different directions, each one searching an area.

Alec cupped his hands around his mouth and called, "Scottish!" He waited for an answer. All he got was the cry of the wind. He swiped the water from his eyes and brow and searched, threading his horse among the trees along the side of the road, calling her name again and again.

"Over here!" Seymour shouted. Alec kicked the horse into a lope and spotted the two men at the top of the next rise. He reined in and dismounted, sloshing through the mud to where Seymour was crouched down. He shoved past him.

No Scottish. There was nothing there. He spun around. Seymour held out his hand. A rabbit's foot, an ivory tooth, and a feather charm lay wilted and muddy in his palm.

"You called me over because of those bloody charms?" Alec reached for Seymour.

Downe gripped his shoulders and stopped him. "He gave them to Joy before she left."

Alec stared at the charms for a long minute before he looked up. "Then she has to be here somewhere."

He cupped his mouth and shouted again. "Scottish!"

There was nothing but the wind.

"Scottish!"

Nothing but the rain.

"Scottish!"

Nothing.

The clock chimed four in the morning, and Alec broke his vigil. Stephen hadn't cried or awakened for the past three hours, and he needed a few moments away. He tugged on the bellpull, and Henson came in. "I'll be in my chamber, then in the study. Come and get me if there's any change. When Downe returns, I'm going back out."

He went to his chamber, closing the door behind him with a click that sounded as loud as a gunshot in the silence of the empty room. He looked around. Everything was the same, but somehow distant, as if he were on the outside looking in and not seeing what he sought. He crossed to the window and stared out. The hills were dotted with flecks of light, the lanterns of the search parties looking for Scottish. His stomach tightened. He'd spent hours looking for her, then had come back to see about Stephen, splitting his time between them, at Downe and Seymour's insistence.

With a heavy feeling of despair, he watched the lights move over the hills and through the valleys. The search was fruitless. He knew somehow that Joy wasn't there. He took a deep breath and gave in to the question he'd avoided asking for the last few hours: where was his wife?

She could have tried to zap herself somewhere using her magic, but God only knew where. He remembered London's dark alleys, drifts of deadly snow, icy rivers. God, she could be anywhere, anywhere at all, and he couldn't tell anyone the truth about his concern. He rubbed his forehead. A foolish gesture since it wouldn't ease the worry. The regret. He closed his eyes. What the hell had he done?

"Scottish," he whispered, staring at nothing. He swallowed hard and felt the thickness in his throat. "I'm sorry."

"Please, Aunt, just let me see them for a few minutes. Please."

The MacLean stood across the room, her arms crossed stubbornly, Gabriel sitting at her feet and watching her through bright blue eyes.

"Please," Joy whispered, stroking Beezle's head once more before setting him down.

"Just this once, Joyous." The MacLean raised her arms, and Gabriel hissed and arched his back. A flash of gold light burst from the window.

Joy watched the light glow and widen, forming the image of Stephen's chamber.

The physician stood by Stephen's bed, shaking his head. "I've never seen anything like this. I could have sworn his lungs were punctured." He leaned back over Stephen and said, "Just relax please."

"That always means it's gonna hurt," Stephen said, frowning and pulling back.

Joy smiled at that. She watched with pride and pleasure the gentle way Alec reassured him.

The physician stepped back a minute or so later and said, "Except for those cuts and bruises, he appears to be fine."

"I told you so," Stephen grumbled. Then he looked around the room. "Why are all these people here?"

"They were worried about you," Alec told him.

"Where's Joy?"

The words gripped her, and her breath stopped. She looked past the faces of Richard, Neil, and Henson to Alec.

He didn't stiffen. He didn't scowl. He didn't evade the question. He just said truthfully, "I don't know."

"I like Joy. She thinks I'm smart." He paused thoughtfully, then asked quietly, "Wasn't she worried about me too?"

Her body tightened with a wave of threatening sickness and she had to grip the back of an old chair.

"She was very worried," Alec told him. "She didn't want

to leave your side but I was angry. I said some cruel things to her."

"That was dumb."

He looked Stephen straight in the eye. "It was. But I'll find her. I promise I'll find her."

*He'll never find me.* The ache was so great that Joy fell to her knees, covered her face with her hands, and sobbed. When she pulled her hands away the image had faded. A plea on her face and anguish in her voice she turned to her aunt. "I love him. Please. He needs me."

The MacLean watched her, then glanced at the blank window. A moment later she shook her head, turned, and left the room.

And so it was that the days dragged by, empty, silent, and devoid of magic. Stephen recovered and spent most of his time in the garden, caring for the flowers and plants that Joy had taught him about. He would say with simple unshakable confidence that she would come back soon. Alec had promised.

But Alec's confidence had waned.

He had ridden over every acre of Belmore Park. He'd sat slumped in a chair in his chamber for hours on end. In a kind of deliberate self-punishment, he surrounded himself with reminders of her. The only food he would eat was roasted chicken legs, turnips, and gingerbread. On every table and every mantel in the rooms he frequented stood vase after vase of pink roses.

One day a wagon had come from London filled with heavy crates. It had taken three footmen to carry the stacks of Gothic romances into the duchess' room. They were stacked along a wall seeming to await her return.

He memorized the names of his servants, then confused the wits out of them when he ordered all the clocks set for different times. He went through the gardens looking for small birds and first blooms. He walked on the roof at night looking at the stars, and wondered if he'd ever look down and see them in her eyes again. He prayed for snow. He picked a sprig of rosemary and remembered. And every so often, when he was alone at night, he cried.

Alec stared off in the distance, remembering. Like the ribbons on a Maypole she had twisted and twined her way into his life. He laughed to himself. What life? He'd had no life before Scottish. He'd had his pride and his name, neither of which mattered to him anymore.

That cold shell of a life seemed to have existed long, long ago. Now he had a brother he loved, but still the house was empty, lonely, cold. Without Joy he could find no peace. He felt wounded, and he knew with surety that he would never heal without her.

He craved her magic. But it wasn't her witchcraft—weak and feeble and often disastrous—that he needed as surely as he needed breath. It was Scottish. The strongest magic she had was herself.

The clouds above the garden broke a bit. Rain sprinkled the flagstone walks. Alec wondered if she was crying. He closed his eyes briefly, then let go of the elm tree.

Alec watched the door of his study close in the wake of the royal messenger. He turned back to stare down at the royal invitation to the fete in honor of His Grace, the duke of Wellington. He tossed it across the desk. "I don't give a bloody damn who the prince is honoring, I'm not going to London. I won't leave until I find her."

"I take it there's been no word." Downe sat across the room, twirling a cane.

Alec shook his head. "Nothing. Not a thing for two months. I received the report from Surrey last week. She's not there. The Lockleys knew nothing. I've got every man I could hire turning all of England upside down. All reports are the same. She's disappeared. The only reports I've yet to receive are from James and Fitzwater. They're combing the isle of Mull."

Seymour fumbled with the growing collection of charms that weighted the chain on his waistcoat, then looked up. "Thought I spotted her myself a week ago in London. I scared the wits out of Billingham's wife. He almost called me out. From the back she looked exactly like Joy."

"You'd think there would be some clue. Something," Downe said, frowning.

Alec sagged back in his chair and shook his head in defeat. "She's gone. I don't think I'm ever going to find her." He looked at his friends. "Where else can I look? There's got to be some clue, something I've missed."

"Did those two servants ever come back?" Downe asked. "What were their names again?"

"Hungan John and Forbes."

He nodded, then looked uncomfortably at Alec. "Do you suppose they had anything to do with her disappearance?"

Alec shook his head. He suspected that Joy had had something to do with their disappearance, but he couldn't explain that to Downe, so he lied and said they had been checked out. There was nothing else he could do but wait and hope. He clasped his hands behind his head and stared at the ceiling. Where the hell would a witch go?

As he mentally cataloged the possibilities for the thousandth time, the room became silent, too silent. It drew his gaze from the ceiling to his two friends.

Downe seemed caught off his guard, and Seymour's mouth gaped open. The viscount closed his mouth and drew himself up straighter. "Seems a tad out of line to call Joy a witch, Belmore." Seymour's tone was defensive.

He had spoken aloud. He was going out of his mind. Insane.

Seymour harped on, "Joy's no witch. Everyone knows witches look like that old hag that told us about her in the first place."

Alec blinked once, then slowly looked up. The clock ticked away the seconds. Alec slammed his hands on the desk with a bang and shot to his feet. "Bloody hell! That's it! The old woman. I'd forgotten about her. But that's it!" He crossed the room, his long legs eating up the distance in three strides.

His hand on the doorknob, he turned back to his friends,

who were scrambling to follow. "I'm going to search every street corner in town until I find her." He ripped open the doors and shouted, "Henson! Pack my things. We're leaving for London."

His deep voice echoed down the marble halls, and three maids looked up in fright at the duke running toward them, shouting. He stopped in front of one of them and pointed at her. "Mary White."

The maid nodded, clutching her feather duster to her white apron.

He looked at the next maid and said, "Mary Jones."

She nodded and remembered to curtsy.

He turned to the third maid, whose head was already bent almost to her knees. "Mary Brown."

She slowly looked up and nodded.

The duke of Belmore smiled. "Well, Marys, don't stand there. Run and tell Stephen, we're going to London."

# Chapter 30

One month later, the London season was at its peak. Balls and soirees ate up the idle time of the quality, and provided gossip and scandal—daily sustenance of a starving ton. Just last week news had arrived from the Continent that a certain countess was seen in Paris on the arm of the brother of her husband's current mistress. This latest *on-dit* set aside the rampant speculation about the strange behavior of the duke of Belmore. It was whispered between deals at snug little card parties and teas that he'd gone batty with grief at the disappearance of his duchess. Rumor had it that he'd been accosting the flower sellers on the street corners. The duke of Belmore!

But this week the gossips had new fodder: the prince's fete—the largest single event of this flamboyant season—was to take place tonight. From early in the morning, ladies had begun to flutter and flit, donning jewels and silks, feathers and fans, preparing to flaunt their wealth and taste before those who *mattered.* Before their mirrors, gentlemen practiced the brooding stares that would gain them the mystique of a dark poet. They perfected that smooth pinch of snuff and the turning of a fine masculine leg.

The royal musicians tuned up their violins, cellos, and flutes and the finest florists in London delivered the hundreds of imported potted lemon trees, which had become the Rage. As was done before, the trees would line the ballroom at Carlton House, a sight that was rumored to have cost in the thousands of pounds. The Regent, however, refused to be bothered by ha'pennies, for tonight the ton would welcome home England's newest peer and hero, the duke of Wellington.

The Belmore carriage was one of the hundreds that lined the route to Carlton House. Packed three deep from Pall Mall to the top of St. James's Street, the conveyences stood waiting to deposit their occupants at the corner where Horse Guards framed the entrance line to the gates. So here was the whole of the ton, sitting in their carriages in the light of the new gas lamps, dressed up in all their finery, and waiting to pay tribute to their hero and their prince.

"Blast it all! What a crush!" Seymour opened the carriage window and stuck his coppery head outside.

"Watch out for my leg, Seymour." The earl of Downe rapped the viscount with his cane.

Seymour poked his head back inside and glanced at Downe's leg. "Oh, sorry 'bout that. Forgot all about your foot."

"Damned female," the earl muttered and adjusted his foot so it was well out of the way of his eager friend.

"What damned female?" Stephen asked in innocent curiosity. Alec turned and glared at Downe.

The earl stammered through some kind of explanation that Seymour said was a "lame excuse" and then explained his pun to Stephen, who laughed after a few minutes of thought. The regent had come across Alec and his brother in the park early one morning and had taken a particular liking to Stephen Castlemaine. The lad had shown such an extensive knowledge of plants and flowers—a subject dear to the regent's heart, since he was midway through the design of his personal gardens—that Prinny had requested another audience with the duke's brother.

When the Archbishop of Canterbury quietly commented that the younger Castlemaine was a bit slow, the prince had angrily replied, "So was Moses," which silenced the royal contingent. Within a day, Stephen Castlemaine had become a royal favorite. Alec still chose to protect his brother, preferring to keep him away from fickle society, but tonight he'd agreed to let Stephen accompany them.

"I say, there. It could take us another hour just to reach the line to the gates," Seymour said. He scowled when Downe removed a silver brandy flask from his coat.

"It's not for me," Downe said, handing it to Alec. "Here, Belmore."

Alec gazed out the window, his mind back on the roof of Belmore Park, his senses filled with the scent of roses.

"Belmore?"

Stephen leaned over and with one finger poked him in the arm. "Alec!"

He shook his head and looked up. "What?"

Stephen pointed at the earl, who held out the flask and said, "You look as if you could use this."

Alec shook his head, then turned back just in time to catch a glimpse of a faded red hat bobbing through the crowd. "Bloody hell!" He threw open the carriage door and stood, gripping the open window to keep his balance. "It's the flower seller! It's her!" He jumped onto the street and threaded his way through the crush of carriages, moving onto the walk and running as best he could through the crowd. He lost sight of the red hat and shoved his way through. Women screeched and men swore, but he didn't give a damn. He would not lose her. He leapt onto the top of Harbinger's gig and searched the crowd. A few hundred feet ahead he could see the old woman's hat.

"Stop her!" he shouted, pointing. "Stop that old woman!" But the hat bobbed onward, the crowd looking at him as if he was as insane as he felt.

"Belmore!"

Alec ignored the murmurs and turned. Seymour, Stephen, and Henson ran toward him, and Downe, with his cane, hobbled along behind swearing the air blue.

"Over here!" he shouted and waved them forward. Then he took off again, seeing an opening between the carriages. He ran, ran as fast as he could around mincing teams and rolling wheels. It was her. He knew it was her. She was his only hope, his last chance. His breath came in pants. He ran faster, weaving his way through the crowd and yelling at the woman to stop, not caring who or what was in his way.

A carriage shifted, blocking his way. The team started to balk and the carriage rocked. He couldn't get through. Like thunder, panic beat through him. And desperation. Overwhelming desperation. This was his only hope. His last chance.

"Damn!" He shifted left, then right, then dashed through a small opening between teams. He was in the crowd again, but he'd lost sight of her. He stretched upward to try to spot her. Then, frustrated as hell, he shoved his way to the iron fence that circled the royal residence. He grabbed it and pulled himself up, hanging on to the fence with one hand.

"The duke of Belmore has a thousand pounds for anyone who can hold that old flower woman in the red straw hat!"

A loud murmur traveled wavelike through the crowd. He yelled it again, and then, ignoring the stares, forged his way through. There was another shout.

"There she is!"

Alec ran in that direction, pushing and shoving his way past the gates. He spotted her. About thirty young bloods, most of them known for their lack of funds, blocked his path in their rush to reach her.

Like the waters of the Red Sea the men parted. He ran at her, just as she held up a posy, her back to him.

"A lovely posy fer yer lady!"

He grasped her small shoulders and spun her around. "Where is she? Where is my wife?"

A pair of sharp and familiar gray eyes stared up at him. "Who?"

Panting, he rasped, "You know who! My wife!"

"Who be ye?"

"You damn well know who I am. I'm the duke of Belmore!"

The old woman eyed him for a long time, silently, then dismissed him and said, "Don't know what yer talkin' 'bout." She turned around to the crowd and held up her flowers. "Lovely posy fer yer lady!"

His breath still coming in staggered spurts, Alec stood there, frustrated and helpless. A hand touched his shoulder and he turned to face Downe, Seymour, and Stephen. "She won't tell me anything." He ran a hand through his hair, helpless.

Downe reached into his pocket and took out a money pouch. He limped to the old woman and shoved the money in her basket. "Tell him where she is."

The old woman turned very slowly. She looked from the earl to Alec, then at the pouch. "Ye wish to buy me whole basket o' posies, yer lordship?"

"Tell Belmore where his wife is. You told his fortune. Said he would meet her. Months ago . . . On the steps of White's. Where is she now, old woman?"

"I just sell posies, yer lordship."

"Those months ago you sold more than that."

Seymour and the others stood beside him. The viscount dropped his purse into her basket, then took off every charm, fob, and amulet on his person and dropped them in her flower basket. "Bring her back."

Stephen looked at the hag and stated simply, "Alec needs Joy. Look at him."

She remained silent.

"Damnation, woman!" Alec shouted. "Tell me where she is. What do I have to do? I've torn London apart looking for an old flower woman in a red hat. I finally find you and you won't tell me anything. What do I have to do?"

She remained silent, but watched him closely.

"I've hugged every tree from Wiltshire to London." He turned around and spotted a maple a few feet away. He strode over and wrapped his arms around it. "Where's the magic, woman? Where?"

The crowd began to titter. He ignored them. "I eat gingerbread. Hell, I don't even like gingerbread! I look for fairies. I wish on stars. I sleep with roses. Pink roses. I wake up calling her name at night. What do I have to do? Tell me! Please . . ." His voice tapered off, and he was quiet for a moment before he said, "I love her."

There was absolute silence. Those wise gray eyes pinned him for the longest time, then she slowly turned and walked away. "A lovely posy fer yer lady! A lovely posy fer yer lady!"

He watched her walk away. His hope went with her. He sagged back against the tree and stared at the ground. The crowd stood frozen, thinking God only knew what. He could feel their stares. He didn't give a damn.

After a few minutes the crowd began to murmur, then move and Downe limped over to Alec. "Come on inside, Belmore."

Alec took a deep breath and pushed away from the tree. Wordlessly he followed them inside, purposely sidestepping the reception line. He didn't want to talk to anyone now. He made his way across the ballroom, but something touched his arm. He turned in hope.

Lady Agnes Voorhees, flanked by her gossips, stood there looking as if she could burp feathers.

He just looked at them, feeling nothing.

"Why, Your Grace! I've never seen anything like that! You poor man. Well, I said to my Henry, isn't that just like a Scot to run out. Can't face anything. Weak blood. Which reminds me . . . I just met Stephen. Over there with His Royal Highness? Why, your brother is as sweet as can be for someone who"—she leaned closer and whispered—"who isn't all there. But that's still no excuse for that girl to leave you."

He looked at London society's version of the witches from *Macbeth* and said, "I should have let her do it."

"Do what, Your Grace?"

His eyes narrowed. "Both warts and frogs." He spun around and walked away, not seeing the little bump that had just popped onto Lady Agnes's beak of a nose. Two days later, a nice black hair would grow from it, and from the other wart on her chin . . . forever.

Like a cipher, Alec moved toward the terrace doors. He needed air. He needed space. He needed isolation. A few seconds later he sat on a stone bench under a tree in a dark corner of the garden, his head leaning against the trunk as he stared upward. Through the dark crown of the tree, he looked up at the sky, at the stars Scottish saw such wonder in, wished upon and believed in.

Without her, he had nothing to believe in anymore. He had nothing.

The orchestra struck up a waltz. It was that same waltz. He smiled a bittersweet smile. He bowed his head and sat there, elbows on his knees, the heels of his hands pressed against his eyes and relived the memory.

What had she said that time? Something about having to make memories. Memories were all he had.

"I love her," he said to the ground, needing to hear himself say it again.

He thought he heard something and looked up. The garden was empty.

He exhaled. "My Scottish."

The trees rustled slightly, a breath of a breeze whispering, "Alec."

He looked upward at nothing. But he could have sworn 'twas her voice.

"Alec."

Frowning, he looked before him, some small amount of hope still flickering inside him. There was nothing. An empty garden.

"Alec."

God . . . He was insane. He'd go through life hearing her voice.

"My Alec."

At that he straightened, and turned around.

She stood there. Scottish stood there, a smile on her face, that wonderful face. Three mindless steps and she was in his arms. Real. Alive. He gripped her so tightly she gasped.

"I love you." He buried his face in her sweet neck and said, "God, Scottish. . . . How I love you."

Her hands held his head. "My Alec," she whispered, then their mouths touched and he knew this was real, for he tasted all he loved, his world, his life, his wife. Eternity.

Long moments later, he pulled back, looking at her, touching her, holding her, afraid for an instant to let go lest she disappear again. As if reading his mind, she smiled and whispered, "'Tis forever this time."

The notes of the waltz drifted on the air. He pushed back, looked at the golden light of the ballroom, then back at her face. That face.

A second later he pulled her with him. "Alec! Where are we going?"

He said nothing, just ripped open the terrace doors and stormed inside until they stood in the middle of the dance floor. The dancers slowed, then stopped.

Surrounded by the ton, he gripped her head in his hands and finished kissing her.

A gasp ran through the room, the ton suddenly witness to a new scandal. The music ceased. Voices twittered. Fans flew up to shield ladies' faces, yet their curious eyes peered over, watching. Some ladies fainted. Some ladies smiled. Most ladies envied. He didn't notice. He didn't care.

There was the feeble sound of applause, and at that, Alec broke the kiss, looking a few feet away where three people stood—the only people in the room beside Scottish whose opinion mattered. Stephen hung his head and muttered "mush." Seymour grinned and held up his crossed fingers. Downe leaned on his cane, but it was he who was awkwardly clapping.

Alec felt Scottish shift, then turn slowly, following his gaze. He saw her look at the earl's cane, then she turned back to him. There was a pause, a flash of laughter in her eyes. They both spoke at the same instant: "Letitia Hornsby."

He caught her laughter with another kiss, held her close and ignored the mumble of outraged sensibilities. He swept her into his arms and she pulled back, smiling up at him as he carried her through the stunned crowd.

"Alec?" Sighing, she leaned her head against his shoulder.

"Hmm?"

She placed her hand on his heart. "You do that so very well."

# And They Lived Happily Ever After . . .

**Should all men pile their
joys up on a single spot,
mine would surpass them all.**

*Juventius*

# Epilogue

How happily? Well . . .

All Hallows Eve was a very special holiday at Belmore Park. If one looked down from the fanciful roofline, through the leaded glass windows that sparkled like starlight, and into the great room—the busiest and most lived-in room inside the ducal home—one would see that there was magic in the air. It floated through the room along with a table, a book or two, and a few chairs, including the one occupied by His Grace, the duke of Belmore.

"Marianna."

"Yes, Papa?"

"Put the chair down, please."

A floating book sailed past his head. "Marianna."

"Sorry, Papa," she said, then he heard her mutter, "I need to concentrate."

Alec stifled a groan and leaned over the arm of the chair to look down at his eight-year-old daughter. Standing about eight feet below him, she was dressed for the holiday celebration in green silk taffeta and lace, and her black hair was held back from her innocent face with bright green ribbons that matched her eyes, those gamine green eyes. She stared up at him as he hovered above her, bit her lip, then gave him a small wave. "Hallo, Papa."

He smiled down at her. "Having a problem?"

She nodded.

"You can do it, sweet. I know you can." He gave her a nod of confidence he was far from feeling.

She smiled up at him as if he had just given her all the stars in the sky. She raised her chin a notch, closed her eyes so tight that her small face twisted with her effort, raised her hands high, then slowly lowered them.

The chair slammed to the floor. He shook the ringing from his ears and loosened his tight grip on the chair arms. He'd had plenty of practice landing over the years.

His daughter opened her eyes, as if she expected to have failed again. But one tentative look and delight shone from her face. She ran into his arms. "Oh Papa! I did it! I did it!"

He held her tightly. "Yes, sweet, you did it." He raised his eyes to the doorway where his wife stood smiling, her love for him showing in her face. That face. She still looked as young and bright as she had that day in the forest, despite the fact she was the mother of six. She hardly changed, but she'd changed him, had shown him what it was to live, and over the past thirteen years they'd made plenty of memories.

She mouthed a thank-you, then cleared her throat. "Everyone's waiting."

Nodding, he stood and stooped down so his daughter could climb onto his shoulders. Her giggle bubbled through the room and she turned to her mother as he ducked under the doorway, her small hand patting his head. "Papa does this so well."

Hours later, after the songs, the bonfires, the dancing and games, the whole family returned to the great room where a tall clock chimed eleven, the ormulu clock on the mantel chimed four, and the walnut century clock chimed midnight. The duke of Belmore checked his pocket watch. It was nine o'clock.

Shaking his head, he leaned back in a chair, a grounded chair, and watched his children—a mixture of mortals and witches who were loved and cherished by their parents. They were his life, his blood, his pride, and he made sure they knew it. Jonathan, the eldest son and heir, now age ten, glanced up at the mantel and with a casual wave of his warlock's hand fixed every clock in the room. It was said his magic was even stronger and more flawless than that of his great aunt, the MacLean—Mary MacLean—whom all their daughters were named after and who sat across the room examining Gabriel's newest bald spot. Over the years Alec had come to know the woman who'd given him Scottish. He'd learned to ignore her and her familiar's penchant for taking other forms—haggard old flower women, inn-keeping giants and dwarfs, Caribbee servants, and deaf butlers.

His warm gaze drifted to a quiet corner. Marian's corner. She was the eldest child at twelve and the tradition breaker —the only female firstborn in the Castlemaine line in seven hundred years. One finger idly twisted her mink brown hair while she read about knights and ladies and dragons, occasionally glancing up with a dreamy look in her midnight blue eyes. Marianna was now playing draughts with her seven-year-old brother, James. He was the only mortal in the Castlemaine lot, but he was sharp and quick and could usually outmaneuver his siblings' magic—with the help of an ermine weasel named Beezle.

Six-year-old Marietta sat in her uncle Stephen's lap while he slowly read to her about meanings and symbols of all the flowers and plants in the gardens. Her eyes began to drift closed, and Alec smiled, watching his brother read on while she fell fast asleep. Just that afternoon she'd proudly announced that she'd zapped the warts off every toad in the lake.

Alec stood up, dusted the gingerbread crumbs off his coat, and walked across the room just as four-year-old Rosemary galloped in on a willow broom. She blew him a kiss as she trotted by. Shaking his head, he mounted the stairs and heard the MacLean clear her throat and chide, "Subtlety, Rosemary. A witch must learn subtlety."

He laughed to himself and greeted by name each of the servants he chanced to pass as he continued up the flights and down the hallways. He opened the roof door and stepped outside where his Scottish was waiting.

For it was there, among the fanciful beasts, under all the glimmering stars in the clear night sky, and amidst a sprinkling of pink rose petals that the duke and duchess of Belmore made magic.

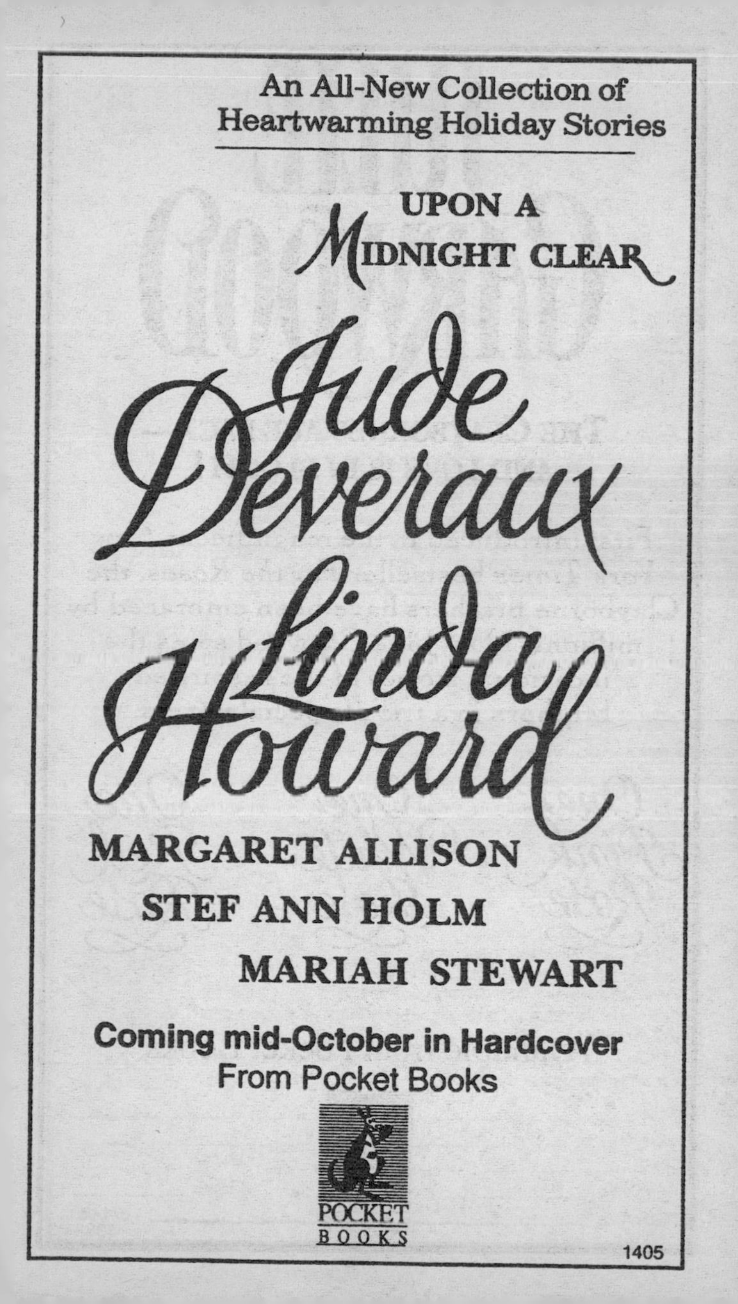
An All-New Collection of
Heartwarming Holiday Stories
UPON A
MIDNIGHT CLEAR
Jude Deveraux
Linda Howard
MARGARET ALLISON
STEF ANN HOLM
MARIAH STEWART
Coming mid-October in Hardcover
From Pocket Books
POCKET
BOOKS
1405